Sir Tony Robinson is one of Britain's foremost faces of popular history through presenting twenty seasons of Channel 4's archaeology series *Time Team* and as the creator of the worldwide icon Baldrick in *Blackadder*. In a varied and international career, he has won two RTS awards, a BAFTA and the International Prix Jeunesse. He is the author of over thirty children's books and several adult non-fiction books, including his autobiography, *No Cunning Plan*. An ambassador for the Alzheimer's Society since 2008, Sir Tony received a knighthood in the Queen's Birthday Honours 2013. *The House of Wolf* is his first adult novel.

THE HOUSE OF WOLF

TONY ROBINSON

SPHERE

SPHERE

First published in Great Britain in 2025 by Sphere

1 3 5 7 9 10 8 6 4 2

Maps by David Andrassy

A CIP catalogue record for this book is available from the British Library.

Hardback ISBN 978-1-4087-3153-6
Trade paperback 978-1-4087-3154-3

Typeset in Garamond 3 by M Rules
Printed and bound in Great Britain by
Clays Ltd, Elcograf S.p.A.

Quote on p 540 taken from *Shadowplay*
by Joseph O'Connor (London: Harvill Secker, 2019)

Papers used by Sphere are from well-managed forests and other responsible sources.

MIX
Paper | Supporting responsible forestry
FSC® C104740

Sphere
An imprint of
Little, Brown Book Group
Carmelite House
50 Victoria Embankment
London EC4Y 0DZ

The authorised representative
in the EEA is
Hachette Ireland
8 Castlecourt Centre
Dublin 15, D15 XTP3, Ireland
(email: info@hbgi.ie)

An Hachette UK Company
www.hachette.co.uk

www.littlebrown.co.uk

This book is dedicated to my wife, Louise, who has been my constant support throughout the writing of it, and is in memory of my dear friend Professor Mick Aston who taught me to love the mark made by the Anglo-Saxons on the English landscape.

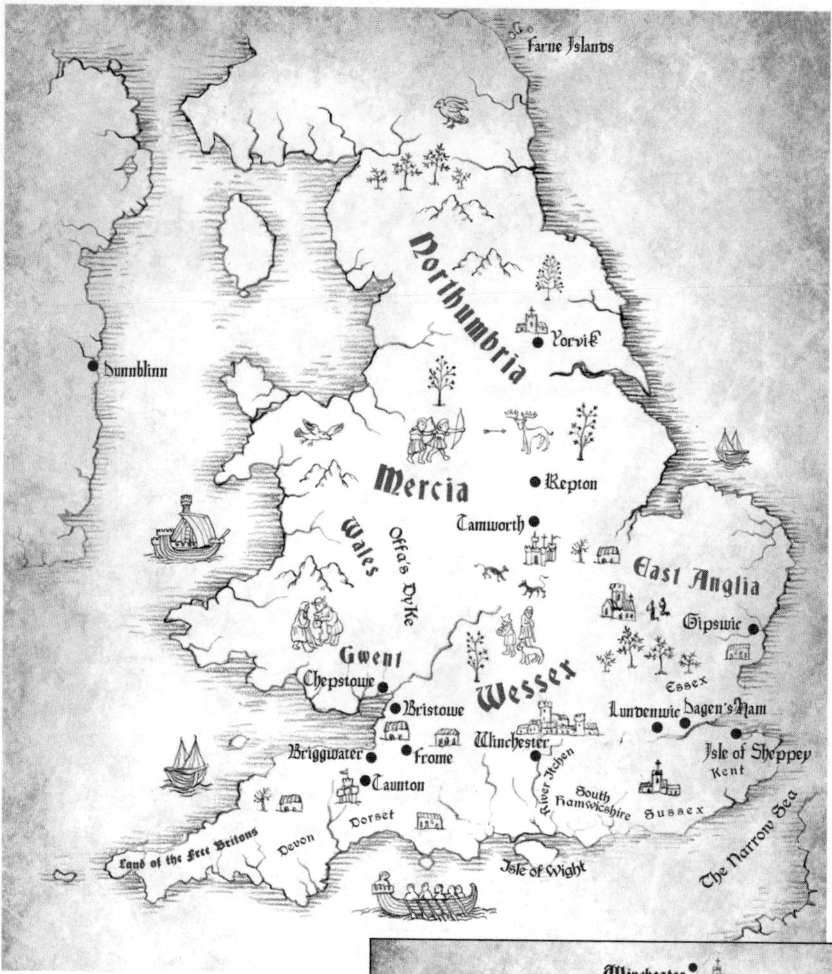

Wolf's Wessex and the Surrounding Kingdoms

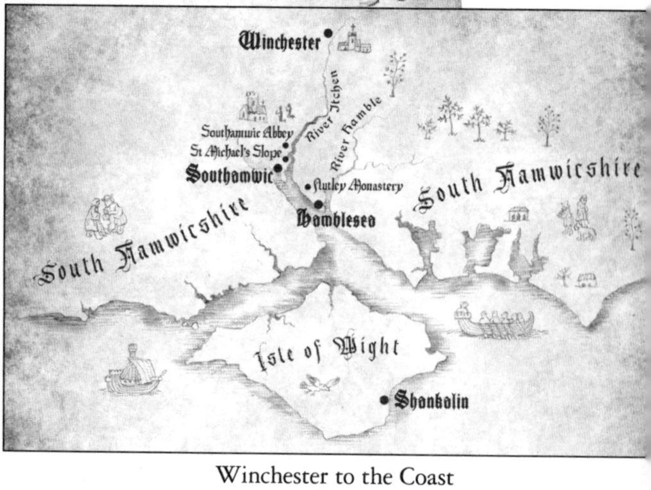

Winchester to the Coast

Wolf's Pilgrimage to Rome

Cast of Characters

NUTLEY MONASTERY

Brother Jude

Abbot Cuthbert

HOLY ROMAN EMPIRE

Charles the Bald, Emperor

Prince Louis, eldest son of Charles

Judith, daughter of Charles

Seneschal François, Charles's chamberlain

ROME

Pope Benedict of Padua

Cardinal Stephen Balotelli

Father Asser, priest of Balotelli's faction

Father Plegmond, priest of Balotelli's faction

Father Kennet, priest of Balotelli's faction

Father Philip, priest of Balotelli's faction

Doctore Guido, aide to Balotelli

Abbess Clothilde, of St Catherine's Abbey, supporter of Balotelli

Enzo Gilotti, head of the Notarii

Fabio Gilotti, brother of Enzo

Claudia Gilotti, sister of Enzo

Father Vincente Ponti, undersecretary to the Notarii

Cardinal Barberini, member of the Notarii

Cardinal Zuppi, member of the Notarii

Halfnose, papal dungeon master

Thadeus, an Antonil heretic

Ruth, a heretic

Petr of Macedon, an Antonil heretic

Rollo and Mountjoy, twin brothers, sometime bodyguards of Father Asser

Elswith, pickpocket, novice nun and Alfred's school assistant

Abdulalah, an alchemist

Clovis, Abdulalah's assistant

Mirandolina, a puppeteer and spy for Asser

Master Spinoza, head of the Emmaus seminarium

John of Old Saxony, caretaker at the Saxon school

Cuddie, a school boy

Carlo, a wealthy saddler and supporter of Balotelli

Trug, slave and gardener at the Emmaus

WESSEX

Aethelwolf, High Aethel of Wessex

Agnes (deceased), Wolf's first wife (mother of Bear, Hawk and Swift)

Osburgh, Wolf's second wife (mother of Red and Alfred)

Aethelbear, Wolf's firstborn

Aethelhawk, Wolf's second son

Moira, Hawk's wife

Swift, Wolf's daughter

Aethelred, Wolf's third son

Winifred, Red's sweetheart

Aethelfraed (Alfred)
Wolf's estranged son

Bishop Humbert
of Winchester

Harold Godwin,
chief alderman

Wendolyn, Harold's wife

Ham, a flagman

Wigan, Swift's bodyguard

Agneta, Swift's
childhood nurse

Rhiannon, a slave girl

Simon Eadwig, alderman
of Hamblesea

Goodwife Bredbaker,
a peasant woman

Stub, Wolf's sergeant-at-arms

Brocc, a sea captain

Cyril of Clacton, an alderman

Kretch, Hawk's
sergeant-at-arms

Leof, a stonemason

MERCIA

Prince Burgred,
Swift's cousin

Burrt, King of Mercia

Frith, son of King Burrt

Gareth, King Burtt's
chancellor

Wigmund (deceased)
former King of Mercia

Wynstan, son of Wigmund

High Bishop of Mercia

Fria, a free Briton

Rhys, King of Gwent

Ithael and Maurig, sons
of Rhys, King of Gwent

Brother Hercules,
Swift's bodyguard

Captain Derwin, one
of Burgred's officers

THE NORLANDERS

Guthrum, a fighter

Erik Longshanks, clan chief of the Farne Islands

Dagmar Longshanks, son of Erik, a fighter

Sigurd, cousin of Guthrum, a fighter

Haakun Haakunson, clan leader of the Shieldsmen

Astrid Haakunson, Haakun's wife

Ivar the Boneless, Norland leader who controls Dunnblinn (Dublin)

Prologue

Nutley Monastery, Wessex, AD 857

The letter T. A vertical column supporting a bold crosspiece, adorned with devilish heads and tongues of fire, the whole terrifying image barely the size of a woman's hand, a signpost illuminating God's word.

How honoured Brother Jude was, only twenty years of age, the son of a humble ploughman, to have been tasked with caring for this fearsome letter, and for all the other letters, words, verses and chapters that shone forth from the ancient leather-bound book of Christ's Gospels. He pursed his lips and scrutinised the vellum for traces of the minute worms that loved to burrow in its folds, then took a small fox-hair brush from his wallet and swept the page with tiny, methodical strokes. *There shall be a great tribulation such as has not been seen since the beginning of the world.*

Outside, the bell tolled loudly and insistently. Once every month or so it signalled that the brothers of Nutley Monastery should leave their labours and gather on the top field, an exercise in preparation for some violent act of God or man. It was a sensible precaution but an irksome one. No serious problems had arisen in Nutley for over a year, apart from the usual winter food riots, the hangings, and the furious badger that had lodged itself under the altar last Easter morning and taken unkindly to all attempts to remove it.

Jude blew the tiny fragments of dust from his brush. *There will be famines, pestilence and earthquakes. Nation shall rise against nation, and kingdom against kingdom.* No one would chide him if he completed the twenty-fourth chapter of St Matthew before he left to join the others. The next page gave him intense pleasure; no illuminated letters, but in the right-hand margin a tiny drawing of a guttered candle with a spider hanging from it, a jest passed down through the centuries by the solitary scribe who'd first copied out the words.

He sniffed the air. Could he smell burning? No doubt the brothers were clearing the stubble from the bottom field. A gull gave a harsh call, and for a moment it sounded like a man crying out in pain.

He rose and opened the shutters. The window was little more than a slit, but he could see smoke coming from the buildings down by the river, and four or five monks running across the grass with buckets of water. His stomach lurched. A fire in the outhouses, how on earth had that happened? He made out more brothers among the trees, waving their arms and shouting, but they were too far away for him to hear what they were saying.

He snuffed out the lantern and crossed to the doorway. Two monks were half-walking, half-running across the quadrangle, and behind them, Abbot Cuthbert, a fierce old man who had trouble with his legs.

'Help me!' snapped the abbot. 'Hurry! Hurry!'

Jude hastened to him and took his weight, and together they stumbled through the main archway and out into the monastery grounds. The cowsheds and buttery were burning now;

the smoke was thick and his eyes were watering. He could see panicked figures moving among the billows.

'Raiders!' called a monk. 'Flee!'

Jude wondered if he'd misheard. What kind of raiders? A gang of thieves from Surrey, or villagers bearing some grudge? Surely not Norlanders; they hadn't been seen this far round the coast for twenty years. He shuddered with apprehension. He'd been too young to remember the last raids, but he'd heard the stories. Who hadn't? Every instinct was telling him to obey the shouting monk and run as far and as fast as he could.

But the book of Gospels. His sacred duty was to protect the book.

He propped the abbot against the stone footing of the big monastery wall, apologising profusely as he did so, and ran back to the scriptorium. He closed the book, heaved it off its lectern and lugged it across the empty quadrangle and out through the archway. The abbot had slid down the wall and was crying out in indignation. Jude ignored him; the book was far too heavy for him to stop and put it down. He ran across the grass. Half a dozen monks were ahead of him, clutching their habits and heading for the trees. Jude shouted out to them to come back and help the abbot, but they didn't even turn their heads. By the time he reached the upper field, they had vanished. He was alone, and his arms ached unbearably.

If he could reach the trees, he could bury the Gospels in the bushes. But all the buildings save the monastery itself were on fire now – the stables, the kitchens, the privies, the travellers' rooms – and the smoke was so dense he no longer knew which way to go.

With a crack, his head collided with something rough and solid, and he staggered backwards, dazed by eye-watering pain. He felt the ground behind him disappear, and before he could stop himself, he was tumbling backwards into a ditch. The

Gospels slipped from his grasp, and with a twist of agony his ankle gave way. For a moment he lay there, confused and exhausted, his head and foot throbbing. Then the smell of smoke and the terrible sounds from the monastery brought him back to his senses.

He pulled himself back up onto the grass, picked up the book and surveyed his surroundings. He could see the low-hanging branch that he'd smacked his head against, and beyond it, something else. A figure curled up on the ground among the buttercups. Brother Anselm. Was he asleep? Jude shook him, but he didn't wake. He sat down by his friend's side and tried to pray, but he could think of nothing but the devils' heads on the letter T, and the tiny dangling spider.

What was happening? Was Wessex about to plunge back into the nightmare from which it had emerged twenty years ago?

Behind him, through the smoke, the whole monastery was burning, and someone was screaming. Yet even above that, he could hear his heart thudding impossibly loudly.

There was a gust of wind and the smoke cleared for a moment. Jude wondered whether the figure that loomed in front of him, with long blond hair and a scarlet shirt open to the waist, might not be a man at all, but some giant from the old tales. He knew he should run, but it was as though roots had sprung from his feet, securing him to the spot.

He could only stare as the stranger snatched the precious book from him and dropped it on the ground in front of him as though it meant nothing. Now he was whirling his war axe around his head like a giant sycamore seed caught in an autumn eddy.

'A great tribulation,' whispered Jude. 'The prophecy has been fulfilled. The earth and all its works will burn for eternity.'

PART ONE

ONE

Sleek Birds

The messenger sat at a rough wooden table on his tiny plot, breaking his fast with peppered goat's brains and watered wine. Occasionally he glanced at the cloudless sky. He felt content with his life here in Aix-la-Chapelle. The dean had been giving him three copper coins a week for tending the birds, money that put brains on the table and curds in the baby's mouth.

He looked up again. A tiny black spot was heading towards him from the horizon. He knew what it was from the path of its flight. He took out his knife, spread the buttery remnants of his repast on a piece of bread, washed it down with a mouthful of wine and walked across to his cages.

He had four and twenty pigeons, sleek birds, and took a lot of time and trouble over them. He cut a long piece of twine and put it between his teeth, then gently opened a cage door and pulled out a bird. He tied one end of the twine to its leg, wound the other round his wrist, and, cupping the bird in one hand and picking up the cage in the other, walked to the middle of his plot. It didn't take him long to find the black dot again, closer now. He stood very still and waited. When he knew the pigeon in flight could see him, he let go of the bird in his hand, which attempted to fly but was restrained by the twine and could only flap about. He jerked the string and the bird's movements became wilder. The pigeon in the sky altered its course and flew towards him, fascinated by the commotion. When it was sufficiently close, he unwound the twine from his wrist, put his bird back in its cage, took a handful of seed from the bag slung across his chest and scattered it on the ground.

'Come, my beauty! Come, my lover!' he called. The descending bird landed at his feet. He dropped to his knees, and as it pecked the grain, he carefully unwound the little cartouche that was strapped to its leg.

Dean Balotelli was basking in the pleasure of his thick coverlet when the messenger knocked. Back in Rome, he'd have overseen his first morning service by now, conducted one or two meetings with senior churchmen whose feathers he wanted to unruffle and given a lecture to a few eager dissident priests on the uncomfortable fact that two of the Gospels failed to mention Christ's miraculous birth. But as an émigré here in Aix, the first city of the Holy Roman Empire, he was reliant on the hospitality of the emperor and had nothing to do all day but write letters and scratch his balls, and he could perform either or both of these activities lying in his bed, at least until his bladder dictated otherwise, which, given his advancing years, wouldn't be long now.

He pulled on his gown and answered the door. The messenger gave him the cartouche, and he extracted a small piece of parchment. The use of birds for such communication had fallen into disuse since days of yore. But before his expulsion from Rome, Balotelli had discovered in a dusty corner of the papal library an essay on the art of secret messaging written seven hundred years previously, in the reign of Emperor Marcus Aurelius. It estimated that if six birds flew thirty leagues with the same piece of coded information, at least one would reach its destination. So supported by the emperor's bottomless purse, he'd ordered the creation of a rudimentary line of birds and messengers between Aix and Rome. It took a long while to establish, and was crude and unpredictable, but the journey on horseback took three weeks, while his birds could bring him the information he needed in ten days.

He unrolled the tiny parchment and smiled. This message alone would justify the cost.

No building in Western Christendom had been able to match the exquisite architecture of ancient Rome, until fifty-seven years ago, when the Emperor Charlemagne had appeared like a blazing comet from among the ruins of Frankia. He had created a new Holy Roman Empire, an explosion of wealth and ideas, the centrepiece of which was the palace at Aix, a glorious conglomeration of thatch, stone, wattle and brick.

Charlemagne was long dead, and his grandson, also Charles, now reigned supreme. Beset by potential invaders on all sides, he was canny and ruthless, paid little attention to his dress and was as bald as a babby. Balotelli had once known the leader of a gang of horse thieves who had gained control of Napoli. The emperor was a little like him. If ever a man was born to live in this magnificent but vulgar palace, it was Charles the Bald.

He was sitting at his ornate silver table, browsing through a pile of documents while eating a honeyed pear, when Balotelli arrived.

'Pope Leo is dead,' Balotelli announced.

The emperor continued reading. 'Send his family my condolences,' he said. He turned the page he was reading, and on discovering there was nothing written on the other side, he screwed it up and dropped it in the silver receptacle beside him. 'Leo was a shit Pope,' he added.

'Not the finest,' agreed Balotelli. 'He had no fight in him.'

'An accident?' enquired Charles.

'How perceptive you are! He fell from a window.'

'And this is the first you've heard of it?'

'The birds worked their magic. He will be missed, of course, but . . .' Balotelli left the sentence hanging in the air.

For the first time, Charles looked up. 'But his passing may be of some advantage to us?'

Balotelli took two steps closer to the emperor's desk. 'The whole world is awry,' he said. 'Lowlanders press you in the west, the Poles in the east, and everywhere is infested by the stink of Norlanders. Europe is under a threat it has not faced since the days of the Goths and the Visigoths.'

He paused for a moment. The incompetent Pope Leo had frustrated each and every proposal for radical change, but now, if Charles was prepared to listen, a new future might well beckon.

'Continue,' said Charles, and pushed his documents to one side.

'The right Pope might ease your problems, your Majesty,' said Balotelli carefully.

Charles scowled. 'Popes are a pain in the arse.'

'They have been,' agreed Balotelli. 'They have persistently inhibited the growth of your empire since the days of your grandfather. But imagine for a moment an alliance between you and the Pope that summoned up a mighty army of the righteous, the largest army since the days of the ancients, to fight against the Norlanders. You would provide most of the fighting men, the papal blessing would give it Christ's authority, and he would summon all Christian nations to play their part, thus freeing you to deploy the rest of your forces elsewhere.'

Charles stared at him. 'The Empire and the Church working in concord?'

'For the first time in a century.'

The emperor gave a grunt of acknowledgement. 'The righteousness of such an army holds little attraction for me.' He paused, and Balotelli held his breath. 'But its size and unity might be of interest.'

'I have a list of potential papal candidates, your Majesty,' the dean said.

'Of course you do.' Charles accepted the proffered parchment and scanned it. 'There's only one name on it!'

'I didn't want to waste your valuable time, Majesty.'

'Benedict of Padua,' the emperor read. 'Would this Benedict be able to deliver such an army? Rome is crawling with schemers, and your enemies in the Notarii are highly resistant to any expenditure that doesn't immediately fill their pockets. Will he have the measure of them?'

'He will,' replied Balotelli. 'If he has the right man at his shoulder to give him guidance,' and he gave Charles a smile as reassuring as one bestowed by a lover in the moonlight.

TWO

Asser and the Antonil

Could a man grow bored of pain? Sometimes Asser thought he might – just as he had grown bored of cold, hunger and the discomfort of being hung by his arms from a damp stone wall. But whenever the guards yanked on his chains, when he screamed amidst their laughter, it was as if he had discovered true agony for the first time.

He'd become something of an expert on pain during the thirteen months he'd been incarcerated in Rome's papal dungeon. He'd write a meditation on the subject when he got out. If he got out.

He wouldn't get out. No one ever did. If the Pope designated you a threat to Christendom, you were executed. There were stories of a man who'd been reprieved long ago, but that was probably all they were . . . stories.

A key rattled in the rusty metal door, and the din of the prisoners, the complaints, threats and tedious protestations of innocence, fell silent. Halfnose, the dungeon master, stood in the doorway holding a parchment with an elaborate seal attached. Alongside him was the chief inquisitor, dressed in his tawdry red and gold gown and his red felt hat, holding his ceremonial wand.

The inquisitor stepped down into the big open dungeon and peered slowly around with a puzzled look on his face, as if he'd forgotten what he was looking for. It wasn't a well-executed performance, but he had his captive audience in his thrall. Who would his wand alight on? Would today's victim rage and howl? Would he shit himself?

Asser closed his eyes, the calm broken only by the sound of the inquisitor's footsteps and occasional whispers among the prisoners. The wand finally touched his shoulder and rested there. Halfnose caressed his cheek with the document and the inquisitor croaked: 'Your death is decreed for the morrow.'

A psalm entered Asser's head, and he tried to calm himself with its words.

Levavi oculos meos in montes, unde veniet auxilium mihi.

He felt achingly sad that his life had been wasted.

But at least there'd be no more floggings, no more ripping-out of fingernails or being woken in the night for the pleasure of the bored guards. He told himself it was a relief, and tried to believe it.

The psalm continued to reverberate in his head.

My help is from the Lord who made heaven and earth.

Halfnose, whose features had been eaten away by the pox, unchained him and dragged him to a holding cell. It had an open horizontal window near the ceiling, which let in a slanting band of light. For the first time in over a year, he could see clouds, the tops of cedar trees, the occasional pigeon. He could smell the familiar odours of the city again: horse dung, fish guts and the sweetness of rotten fruit.

Two condemned apostates were already there. Asser knew them both. Thaddeus the Antonil, a harmless white-haired old man; and Ruth the Mad, who looked like a ghost in a fairy tale.

Asser had always had a soft spot for heretics like them. They didn't drink the blood of virgins; they merely considered the crucial issues of life and death and wove fantasies around them. Was their belief that Mary Magdalene married Jesus more shocking than his own suspicion that some of Christ's disciples had been women, whose memory had been expunged from Holy Scripture by St Paul and his woman-hating acolytes?

'I have nothing to fear,' Ruth crowed. 'I am Jesus Christ. I will rise again from the dead.'

'You probably will,' agreed Asser.

He and Thaddeus exchanged a sad glance. He'd grown fond of the old man. Thaddeus and his fellow Antonils venerated a long-dead priest called Antoni the Bulgar, who they believed had been the son of God reborn. Asser had teased him about it and asked him if Antoni's innumerable children had been sons of God too, and if the curing of lepers had run in his family, and Thaddeus had laughed and said no, but caring for the needy did – which was a good answer.

The three of them sat all day on the bench. Ruth would rave occasionally about the ten thousand souls whose sins she had forgiven, then her head would drop and she'd snore like an old dog. Thaddeus cried, and Asser put an arm around him. Towards evening, they were given a bowl of greasy water, which they sipped and passed round as though they were receiving the Host. Asser asked for some bread for Ruth, but none came.

The night was long. They dozed and occasionally sang a hymn together. Eventually a solitary blackbird announced the dawn. Not long after, Asser heard footsteps and chattering in the courtyard, then a chanting vendor selling liver titbits and cooked snails, and a commanding voice instructing people where to stand and where to sit.

At sunrise, the door swung open. Halfnose yanked a hessian hood over Ruth's head, and she was led away, still passionately proclaiming her divinity. Thaddeus and Asser sat in silence, listening to the ceremony outside in the courtyard. The inquisitor gave an address that echoed unintelligibly around the yard, then there was a long pause, punctuated by Ruth's cries of agony, and a triumphant roar from the crowd.

Next they came for Thaddeus. As he listened to the old man's screams, Asser tried not to speculate about the nature of his own demise. There were no rules. It could be hanging, burning, being torn apart by teams of oxen, or anything else the torturers devised.

He remembered the sublime confidence he'd felt that day a year previously when he'd organised thirty priests and laity to assemble outside the Emmaus seminarium, then march into the city and preach the renewal of Christ's vision in the streets, just as the Apostles had done eight hundred years previously. They'd waved gaily coloured pennants and banners, sung rousing psalms and clapped their hands in a staccato rhythm.

Their message was unsullied by the cant and hypocrisy of Mother Church. The rich were to be brought low, the humble and meek restored to their rightful place. Word would sweep through Rome like a summer hurricane, and their friends and sympathisers in the myriad churches dotted around the city would occupy the pulpits and proclaim the news. Within days the Pope would fall, and a people's church would rise.

Asser was to be the first speaker. But as he'd climbed onto a vegetable cart and drawn breath, Sister Clothilde had walked past, her head bowed. He recalled the feeling of unease that had crept over him: why was she there? She should have been watching from nearby. She was only supposed to come into the market square if they were under threat. 'Go!' she whispered. 'Run!'

He looked around. All seemed well. Then city guards burst out of every door and from around every corner, and it had been far too late for Asser to escape.

Had it all been for nothing? he reflected. Some would doubtless say so, but Asser had seen the sickness and poverty in the back streets of Lazio; the children dying from lack of nourishment only a few paces from the halls of the great families. Few would remember the preachers who'd called for a return to Christ that day, but perhaps God would.

Halfnose returned. He led Asser outside, hooded and shuffling. The hood was thick and smelt of stale sweat. Asser could hear the deep-throated growl of the crowd, feel the sting of a stone against his cheek. His arms were yanked behind his back and he was bound tightly to a stake. Halfnose giggled in his ear. 'Asser, you little ferret-faced turd. We're very excited. You're going to be crushed slowly. We haven't done that in years. I hope we remember how to do it.'

The inquisitor began to recite the list of sins Asser had committed. He had plotted against his Holiness the Pope and attempted to set Beelzebub on the papal throne in his stead. He and his army of demons had devised plans for the Church's treasures to be melted down and given to drunkards and wastrels as a reward for their lust and sinfulness. Naked prostitutes were to preach from the pulpit and cardinals would be forced to lie with lepers . . .

All around him, people chattered and laughed. How many Roman citizens had gathered to watch his final agonies? There must be hundreds. He could smell cooked sausage and onions. Holy Mother of Christ, they'd brought their breakfast! How long did they think his torture was going to last?

'. . . and you brazenly called for the adoption of all these foul things in the streets of Rome, while exposing your manhood to nuns and children,' intoned the inquisitor.

'Crush him! Crush him!' the crowd chanted. Asser could hear the clatter of heavy instruments. A drum rolled and a trumpet rang out. Something cold and unyielding was clamped to his left leg. There was a grunt of effort as it was tightened, and a searing pain shot through him. He called out desperately to the Lord for help, but his plea was greeted with cackles of laughter and obscene heckling. He'd denounce his friends, he'd denounce *their* friends, he'd denounce his mother as a whore of Satan, he'd say anything to make them stop hurting him.

There was the sound of running feet. A command was barked and a heated argument broke out somewhere nearby. Hands grabbed him and he flinched in terror. The bag was whipped from his head and his face was flooded with light. Weeping Jesus! Were they going for his eyes next?

His bonds were untied. 'Please don't! Please don't!' he begged, but the words sounded slurred, his voice distant.

'It's over, Father,' a voice said.

What was over? Who was he talking to?

'An order has been received for your reprieve.'

A guard unscrewed the iron jaws from around his leg. His head swam, his body was shivering uncontrollably. Darkness beckoned, but it was no longer the darkness of death.

THREE

Wolf in Winchester

Winchester: three thousand inhabitants crammed into a space too small for five hundred, surrounded by the crumbling remnants of a wall built by giants, still stained by the fires the Norlanders had lit when they tried to burn the town down twenty years previously. Through it ran the River Itchen, dark brown and stinking of the town's waste. Towering over it was Winchester Minster, a vast old church of wood and thatch.

On a gentle slope a little way out from the town's hurly-burly was the moot house, where the Wessex aldermen deliberated on the great issues of the day. Beside it was the royal compound, dominated by a great hall, above which were the royal quarters of the High Aethel of Wessex, alongside several smaller halls, kitchens, servants' huts, slave pens, gardens, livestock, and a tower from which a profusion of pennants was fluttering.

It was early morning. High Aethelwolf, a hulking man who swathed himself in fur even in midsummer, stomped down the steps of his hall, and stared up at the thirty-nine flags of

Wessex: Devon, Oxford, Bodmin Moor, Exeter, Kent, Southern Down, Essex, Sussex and the rest. The mightiest banner, the great blue Wessex dragon, rose into place and flew proudly above the others.

Ham the flagman ran down the tower steps as quickly as his old legs would allow. 'All done, High Aethel!' he said.

'Oxford is frayed,' said Wolf. 'Attend to it.'

'Yes, High Aethel,' replied Ham, and began the long climb back to the top.

'Have you seen Harold Godwin?' boomed Wolf.

'No, High Aethel,' came Ham's echoing voice.

Wolf should have been feeling happy. This was Landing Day, the greatest day in the Westsaxon year, and the banners proclaimed that Wolf had assembled more ports, towns, villages and shires, more rivers, lakes and forests under the Wessex flag than any high aethel had ever done before. This was a blessed day – or it should have been, except that Harold Godwin had gone missing. All morning Harold's wife Wendolyn had been berating Wolf for ordering the kidnapping of her husband. But why in the name of the crucified Christ did she believe he would do such a thing? Did she think he would want his chief alderman and ally dead? To kidnap him would be madness; the other aldermen wouldn't tolerate it. They'd sweep Wolf off the throne like rat shit off an altar.

Perhaps the Mercians had taken him. They constantly tried to drive a wedge into Wolf's northern flank. Or the East Anglians. Or some wandering group of thugs and assassins. His eyes rested on a building a little distance ahead, and it dawned on him. Not the Mercians, and not the East Anglians. He knew very well who had taken Harold.

He crossed the royal compound, ignoring the kitchen slaves gutting fish and slicing sausages for the feast, and the local women hanging brightly coloured garlands from the walls.

He strode up the slope towards the smaller hall belonging to Aethelbear, his firstborn, who used it as somewhere to wrestle with his friends and tether his horse when he was too drunk to take it back to the stable. The paint was peeling, the window slats were loose, and in front of it was a battered skull on a pole with broken arrows buried in it.

'I know you're in there, Bear, you piece of shit!' he bellowed. 'Stop fucking around with Harold Godwin!'

The door slowly opened and his son appeared, blinking in the light. Bear was a strong man, almost as powerful as his father, but twenty years younger and unmarried, with a ruddy face and dishevelled curly hair. He was wearing a grubby nightshirt, and Wolf caught a waft of rancid cheese.

'Return him immediately,' he snarled.

'I don't—'

Wolf headbutted him in the face. His son tottered backwards into the hall and landed on a rickety wooden chair, which collapsed under his weight.

'I don't have to take this,' Bear mumbled, and wiped the blood from his nose.

'What? Speak up!' demanded Wolf.

'I don't have to—'

'I can't hear you!'

The goading worked, as it always did. Bear jumped to his feet and drew his sword. 'I'll run you through, you stupid old bastard!'

Wolf roared with laughter and drew his. 'Run me through? You jest!'

They stared furiously at each other for some time. Eventually Bear sighed and said, 'You're confused again, Father, as you were last week when you thought I'd loosened your saddle so you'd fall off and break your neck.' Slowly he put his sword back in its sheath.

Coward! thought Wolf, and did the same. 'I know you tried to kill me. That's why you kidnapped Harold Godwin, isn't it? Because you thought it would make the other aldermen rise up and oust me.'

'Father, I'm your heir and you're an old man. I don't need to oust you.'

'We don't have heirs in Wessex, boy,' Wolf said. 'No one succeeds me till they receive the endorsement of the aldermen, and you've chewed up your chances and shat them down the Itchen with this little plot, haven't you! You're expelled from the council of aldermen and stripped of your rank as captain of the royal guard.'

Bear's left eye was red and watering from the blow. 'Calm yourself, Father. I'm the finest fighting man you have.' He grabbed a carved ivory box from a table and flipped back the lid, revealing several scrolls. 'I have something for you!' he said. 'The dice were good to me last night. These are the deeds to the seven islands of Somerset.'

Wolf looked at them disdainfully. 'You had a brawl,' he said. 'There's blood on the parchment.'

Bear fanned them out. 'Take one. It was going to be my Landing Day gift to you.'

Wolf didn't move.

'I'll choose one for you, then. Look! Stern Isle! Seventy paces by fifty, a healthy crop of samphire, and home to several hundred guillemots.'

'I gob on your gift! It means nothing to me,' said Wolf. 'I'll cut your left leg off at the knee and banish you to your pathetic little islands, and you'll spend the rest of your days pissing samphire!'

He pocketed the scroll and staggered off. Bear's voice called after him. 'I couldn't have taken Harold, Father. I'm freshly returned from Briggwater. I've a dozen witnesses.'

As he was halfway down the slope, a twinge of doubt struck Wolf, and he suddenly felt tired. Why had he been so sure it was Bear? This had been happening more and more recently: ideas flashed into his mind, overwhelming him, then moments later he'd realise they were baseless, almost as though they'd been somebody else's ideas that had taken occupation in his head. He closed his eyes and blew out his cheeks. He needed a cure for his shitting mind. Something to help him think rationally, stop him jumping to . . . A thought came to him, and anger roiled in his gut. This time, he *knew* who had taken Harold.

There were four small halls in the compound, one for each of his children, all the same size to avoid feuds. The hall of his second son, Aethelhawk, was at the top of a hill and was tidy, cold and miserable, like the nursery of a barren queen in a children's tale. When Wolf slammed the door open, a little breathless from the climb, Hawk's wife, Moira, was lying on their bed, staring at the wall. She turned to look at him with resentful eyes.

'It was your husband, wasn't it?' Wolf raged. 'It won't work, you know. The aldermen won't let him take the throne. He's petty and loathsome.'

Moira said nothing. She seldom spoke.

'What's he doing now?' Wolf persisted. 'Forging his name on some dead farmer's will? Slashing the back legs of his neighbour's cattle? Tell him I need Godwin back at my high table by the time the feasting begins.'

She gave a crooked smile, then rolled back towards the wall.

Horrible woman! Wolf felt a twinge of guilt about forcing his son to marry her. A part of him could understand if Hawk still felt resentful, but he couldn't be allowed to prance about kidnapping senior aldermen. Although . . . the doubt returned again, like a wave knocking him off balance. Hawk wouldn't dare challenge his father's authority like this, would he? He'd never been as brazenly defiant as Bear. In fact, he was terrified of him.

It must have been one or other of his hapless children. Wendolyn Godwin had said the abductors were members of the royal guard, and they only took orders from Wolf and his immediate family. So perhaps it was Swift. She'd always been a plotter. He headed back down the hill. His daughter wasn't in her hall. She'd be parading around down south again. He'd given her the title of Warden of South Hamwicshire and the Sussex Coast, but it meant nothing. It was all part of Wessex, just as Kent and Essex were. But she lusted for power, and it suited him to keep her quiet for a while. Yet as demanding as Swift was, Wolf had to admit that it would have been difficult for her to orchestrate the kidnap from so far away. There was only one other option.

Aethelred, Wolf's youngest son, was sitting on his front step, broad-shouldered, bare-chested and as innocent as a virgin saint. Wolf sat himself down gently next to the lad. 'Do you know who ordered the guards to abduct Godwin, my son?' he said.

'No,' replied Red. 'Look at my fleet, Father. Aren't they fine?'

His son had fashioned half a dozen little ships out of leaves, sticks and nutshells, and arranged them on a tree stump.

Wolf was overwhelmed with sadness. When he was younger, Red had been a magnificent boy, as capable as Achilles. But then he'd had his accident, which hadn't been Wolf's fault despite what anyone might say, and all he wanted to do nowadays was ride horses, make toy ships and play with his sweetheart, Winifred. What a waste of a potentially great fighter.

'This one's beautiful, lad,' he said picking up an elaborately painted acorn. 'You should call her *Winifred*.'

'I will,' said Red, 'and I'll rig a sail for her.'

Their reverie was broken by crashing, banging and shouting in the courtyard.

A butcher's cart bringing sides of meat for the celebrations had come lumbering through the gate. It hit a deep rut and a wheel sheared off. A large wooden box toppled off the cart and smashed onto the ground, sending pigs' heads rolling across the compound. Servants ran about trying to catch them.

Chaos! That was what Wolf must avoid at all costs. The aetheldom was never secure. Before he'd taken the throne from his father, it had been nothing but a fiefdom of squabbling gangs and greedy foreign mercenaries. It was he who had pacified it, and he who had driven the vile Norlanders from its shores for ever. If he fell, the old enmities would bubble back to the surface, the Norlanders would return and the Mercians and East Anglians would come flooding over the borders in their thousands.

'One day you'll have a ship of your own, lad,' he said.

'And I'll be the captain of the fleet, won't I?' Red replied.

'You're an aethel. You can do anything you set your mind to,' his father replied.

He stood up. It was time to . . . what? What should he do next? He was no closer to uncovering the whereabouts of Harold Godwin. He was so overcome by exhaustion he could barely walk back to the great hall. It was mid morning already; his guests would soon be arriving, and he hadn't eaten yet. He prayed no one would notice he was trembling.

FOUR

The Devil's Dean

Asser came back to consciousness drenched by a bucket of icy water. Halfnose, a look of disappointed contempt on his face, threw him a clean cassock, while the guards bandaged his leg. He was half carried, half dragged up the Vatica Hill to a small, elegant palace with a jaunty rectangular tower set in the shadow of the great Basilica of St Peter.

The guards manhandled him through a discreet side entrance, where they were met by a sleek official.

'Where am I?' Asser mumbled.

'At the new cardinal's palazzo,' came the terse reply. 'Don't speak unless requested.'

He was dragged into a room full of busts of dead Popes on pedestals. A gold-painted statue of Christ crucified hung on the wall. Two priests wielding quills sat on one side of the room. On the other, behind a vast marble desk, was a well-manicured middle-aged man of ample build, dressed in the black robes of a cardinal. He was reading a document with a large seal attached, which obscured his face. 'Put the priest down!' he said, without looking up.

Asser was deposited on a straight-backed chair. He tried to sit upright, but it was all he could do not to topple onto the floor.

'Wine?' enquired the cardinal, still poring over the parchment.

'Thank you, your Eminence.'

The official handed Asser a goblet. He took two polite sips, then thirst overwhelmed him and he dispatched the rest in one gulp.

'Have you eaten?' came the cardinal's voice. The man had still not looked up from his page.

'Not recently, your Eminence.'

A biscuit was proffered on a Chinese plate. Asser snapped it in two and pushed both halves into his mouth, then licked his finger, dabbed at the crumbs and swallowed them. The wine had made him dizzy. He wanted to curl up and go to sleep for ever.

Silence reigned save for the scratch of quills upon parchment. Finally, the cardinal finished reading and raised his head. Asser's mind reeled.

'You may leave us,' the cardinal said to the attending men.

The priests scuttled from the room, followed by the guards. The official bowed and closed the door behind him with a click.

'Father Asser!' The cardinal smiled.

'Balo-fucking-telli!' replied Asser faintly.

He would not grovel at Balotelli's feet after all he'd been through, even if he was a cardinal now. The Devil's Dean, they used to call him. Asser had listened to dozens of his sermons over the years, and had thought him the most inspiring man he'd ever heard, until that day in the market square.

Balotelli picked up the parchment again. 'Fornicating with cattle?' he read. 'Drinking from the devil's teats? They say you were one of my supporters. The crimes they accuse you of are a little more energetic than the modest reforms I was advocating. Although I think we should seriously consider naked prostitutes in the pulpit. They'd guarantee larger congregations.' He sighed. 'Never forget how base our opponents are, Asser,' he said. 'They are like children shouting obscenities in the street, and their spite has no end . . . as you have already experienced.'

He picked up a second document. 'So, you are eight and twenty years old and came to Rome from Wessex as a child. You were trained for high office at the Emmaus seminarium, a deeply unpleasant institution in my opinion, and while you were there, you developed what they refer to here as troubling signs of heterodoxy, so they expelled you and you eventually became senior advocate at the Tribunal of Reconciliation. In other words, you are a troublemaker who wasted ten years of his life in the most minor and underfunded of all the Church's offices, pacifying outraged parishioners and resolving disputes between country churches. How jolly for you!'

'It was unremittingly tedious. But there were moments of satisfaction . . . and I was good at it.'

Balotelli stared long and hard at the young priest. 'I know you were,' he said at last. He continued reading. 'And during this time you were also a leading member of the secret band of hotheads who'd been affected by my modest works, and the instigator of the noisy events in the market square after which all our travails began.'

There was a time when Asser would have blushed to think that Dean Balotelli knew so much about him, that he could distinguish him from his countless other young followers. Now, though, he felt anger rising. Only Balotelli had known what they were planning. Only he could have informed on them.

'Our travails? It was you who betrayed us!'

'Don't be foolish. When the purge began, I was punished too.'

'Not tortured, I suspect.'

'I fled to Aix-la-Chapelle.'

Asser let out a wheezy, bitter laugh, then doubled up in pain. 'What a martyr you were!' He was beginning to doubt himself. For a year he'd been convinced that Balotelli had betrayed them, but had he been deceiving himself?

The cardinal crossed to a large cupboard. 'More wine?' He returned with a green glazed jug and a handful of fruit-encrusted griddle cakes. 'I didn't suffer your indignities, that's true, but I hadn't been as foolish as you. So perhaps it's me who should be angry.'

Asser looked at the cakes with a show of disinterest, then took two.

'My time in Aix wasn't wasted,' continued Balotelli. 'I won us the support of the Holy Roman Emperor.'

'Bravo,' Asser said. 'And he had you made a cardinal?'

'Not until three weeks ago. After the old Pope died.'

'Leo is dead? He was hardly an old man. Was he assassinated?'

Balotelli ignored the question and refilled Asser's glass.

'I have a job for you,' he said.

Asser snorted. 'Why would I work for you?'

Balotelli smiled. 'I'm not sure you have a choice. You're looking peaky. It's turned midday, would you care for a little dinner?'

FIVE

The Green Man

Lady Swift, Warden of South Hamwicshire and the Sussex Coast, wandered through Hamblesea, her heart fluttering like a bird in a net. If all went well, today would be the fulfilment of months of planning and the beginning of her ascension to power.

Since the Norland raids twenty years ago, Hamblesea had been little more than a hamlet. A few clusters of huts, a battered church, mounds of rubbish piled high like warts on the face of a giant, a handful of desultory market stalls, and a pebbled bay dotted with rotting reed coracles, torn nets and strands of barnacled rope. When she was young, she'd believed it was on this beach that the hero Hengist had landed when he arrived here with his comrades from the Saxon forests at the dawn of time. She liked to spend Landing Day in South Hamwicshire with her people; it was far more pleasant than the frenzy of Winchester. But there was another reason she was here today: no spies would be watching her.

The women were setting up a little Landing Day feast in the

middle of the marketplace. She'd helped them take the doors off the church and put trestles underneath them, and now they could lay the food out and arrange it in a comely fashion.

She smiled at the stallholders, their squashed Southsaxon faces like the dogs her father kept for badger baiting. Not that she considered herself a beauty. She was too tall and thin, her nose too sharp, and her long black hair bore streaks of grey. But men still looked at her with interest, which was irritating but useful, and the common people respected her because of her fierce passion for the south coast. She often walked down the hill from her estate to visit them, kept their wells clean and removed the beggars from their muddy byways. Now she toyed with the bone combs dangling from strings and gave them her approval, admired the scented soaps even though they smelt of dead horse, and feigned a passionate interest in their crudely made wooden tools.

Wigan, her bodyguard, limped along behind her, his eyes darting to and fro. Many years ago he'd been one of her father's men, but he'd been given to her on her twelfth birthday after he'd rescued her from an attack by Anglian bandits who would have done Christ knew what to her. He had let her pull the rope on them herself, and they'd dangled and swayed outside her hall for months until her mother had made her cut them down because they were too depressing. Wigan was older now, and stiff after years of fighting, but he was still canny, and she'd hold him to her for a while, at least until he could keep her safe no longer. As long as her brothers Bear and Hawk were alive, she'd need someone to watch her back.

A dog barked, distracting the villagers. Swift crossed discreetly to the nut stall and ran her fingers through the piles of cobs and hazels.

'He's in the byre,' whispered the old woman behind the stall. It was Agneta, who'd nursed her as a child, whom she trusted with her life, who'd brought her here to Hamblesea each summer when her mother and father had been away on royal procession. It had been an exciting place for a young girl: fairs with jugglers and performing bears, horse racing, cock fighting, and pilgrims flocking in their hundreds to the Church of St Ignatius the Martyr. But the Norlanders had laid the south coast to waste. They'd razed the town to the ground, smashed the saint's coffin and thrown his bones to the foxes.

Agneta's arms and legs had never grown properly; she was short and stocky, standing only as high as Swift's waist. She wore a constant look of disapproval, and coarse black hairs sprouted from her upper lip. What she lacked in height she made up for in fierceness, but she was kind of heart although few knew it.

She raised her voice so the villagers would hear her and enquired, 'The privy pit you want, is it, Lady Swift? Over there. Take these rags.'

Swift would rather have died than surrender to the embrace of the stinking pit to which Agneta was pointing, but she strode towards it purposefully with Wigan in tow. Once out of sight, she threw the rags on a pile of rubbish and headed away from the privy and towards an old byre.

Wigan pushed the door. It creaked open and she went in. She'd be safe here from prying eyes. There were no cows, no goats or chickens, just a few rotting stooks of hay, a pile of dung and a collapsed manger; the only sound the buzzing of flies and the scuttling of an occasional mouse.

'Lady Swift?' A figure stepped out of the darkness. 'It is I, Seneschal François, chamberlain to the Holy Roman Emperor.'

She was expecting to meet a handsome soldier with clear hazel eyes and a small duelling scar above his left eye, the man to whom she was secretly betrothed. This jackanapes was portly, with a small pointed beard in the continental style, and was wearing a long green jacket and a little hat adorned with a brown feather. She recognised him from her stays in Frankia when she was a young girl. He had been the little boy who slammed doors and played his pipe constantly and tunelessly. My, how high he'd risen!

'Where is Prince Louis?' she demanded.

'He cannot come,' said the seneschal. He spoke in an over-enunciated way, like a child's tutor, which irritated her beyond measure.

'You have travelled a hundred leagues to tell me he has broken his promise? Do you know what is at stake here? You are a foreign envoy, and I am conducting a clandestine meeting with you. If my brothers hear of it, they'll have me hanged for treachery.'

'Lady Swift, I am here because the prince is deeply distressed that he broke his word to you. He is under siege in Cologne. He cannot leave until it is raised.'

'And that is true? Not some tale concocted by his father the emperor to extricate him from our agreement?'

Seneschal François shook his head vigorously. 'No, I assure you.'

'So the emperor is happy with the arrangement?'

'All emperors are happy, Lady Swift, until they are not.' There were cries of alarm outside, and the sound of running feet. 'Please be patient,' said the seneschal. 'The prince will come soon.'

'So you say,' she replied.

He looked at her earnestly. 'You do know that the Norlanders are on their way?'

Swift's whole body tautened. It was not unexpected news – she'd been warning her father of the threat for months – but to have it confirmed was terrifying. Nevertheless, amidst her dread was something else: a small flicker of excitement. This was her chance to prove what she could do.

'Are you sure?'

'I am,' he replied.

'I thought they'd come. I've been building beacons along the coast.'

'Too little, too tardy, I suspect, m'lady,' he said.

'My father is ignoring the danger the Norlanders pose. He's in Winchester, consumed by plots and counter-plots.'

'After what happened to his kingdom the last time they came, his insouciance is a luxury he can ill afford.'

The noise outside was growing louder.

'Go now,' she said. 'Tell Louis I'll always hold him in the highest esteem and—'

The door burst open.

'Norlanders!' shouted Wigan. 'They're coming this way.'

Swift hurried outside and followed her bodyguard's gaze. The peasants had disappeared, the stalls left unattended. The only sign of life was the sound of a slave girl locked in a shed a little way off, chattering away to herself. But the hill beyond the village was swarming with people. At its summit was the unlit beacon she'd ordered to be erected a few days earlier. She headed up the slope after the crowds.

She smelt burning before she saw it. Five miles away on Hay Tor, a beacon was blazing. Five miles beyond it was another, and on the horizon she could make out a third. Holy Jesu!

When she reached the top and pushed her way through the crowd, she saw Simon Eadwig, the local alderman, clutching a blazing brand.

'Light it, quickly!' she ordered.

He stood frozen to the spot, overwhelmed by fear and confusion. She snatched the brand from his grasp.

Wigan breasted the rise, breathing hard. Swift, legs astride, the blazing branch above her head, called out to him. 'Ride to Winchester and warn my father.'

'I cannot leave you unattended,' he shouted over the din, and put his hand on the shoulder of one of the old men. 'Alfrick, take my horse and ride to Winchester.'

'Find my father and tell him the Norlanders have returned,' said Swift. 'We'll hold them at bay as long as we can.'

She turned back to the beacon and plunged the torch deep into its heart.

SIX

A Jug of Hare

Asser and Balotelli gazed at one another across a table set a little apart from the hundred or so other priests and monks in the papal refectory. The cardinal sat on a leather-backed throne; Asser slumped in one of the high padded chairs given to the old monks whose limbs were failing. It was very comfortable, but his leg throbbed intolerably. He needed to keep his wits about him.

The refectory was a voluminous brick building constructed by the Emperor Nero half a millennium previously, with a ceiling the height of a church tower. The day's lesson was being read by a portly, florid monk well versed in the declamatory arts. It was taken from the Epistle of St Paul to the Thessalonians, and would have been well received had it not been for the thundering echo of a hundred spoons scraping a hundred platters.

Balotelli was dicing a small apple. Asser was attacking a jug of hare and onions with a long spoon.

'What happened to you in Aix?' demanded Asser between

mouthfuls. 'Did the broiled frogs addle your head? For years I listened while you preached that the Church's cardinals were thieves and hypocrites. Now you're one of them!'

'The new Pope requires wise counsel,' Balotelli said calmly.

'From you, Stephen Balotelli, the people's dean?'

'From me, Stephen Balotelli, the new Pope's chief adviser.'

Asser guffawed. The monks at the next table turned to look at him, but were met by the cardinal's glare and swiftly turned away again.

'You secured the election for him.'

'That isn't possible,' Balotelli replied. 'The cardinals and our great families choose the new Pope.'

'And the only man rich enough to buy their votes is the Holy Roman Emperor.'

'Softly, please!' Balotelli smiled.

'Who *is* the new pontiff?'

'Benedict of Padua.'

'Your old tutor? You rescued him from obscurity?'

'He is a brilliant man.'

'Ten years ago he was a firebrand. I remember him proclaiming that Christ had championed the common man, so anyone who didn't do likewise was no Christian. But his latter years have been spent buried in the obscure writings of the early saints. He has no experience of church politicking.'

'I have.'

'You delivered a Pope who'd be amenable to Emperor Charles the Bald, and who you could control. You sly bastard!'

For a moment Asser wondered if he'd gone too far. He often did. But Balotelli merely observed him with a slight smile.

'As a young man, you were renowned for being outspoken.'

'As were you.'

'Asser,' he said, ignoring yet another jibe, 'you wish us to return to Christ's teaching, don't you? You wish the mighty to be put down from their seat and the humble and meek lifted up, am I correct?'

It was a question barely worth the asking.

'So how do we begin?' Balotelli continued.

'We tax the rich and feed the poor as Benedict has proclaimed all his life. It must be our very first priority.'

'And what else?'

'We teach the clergy to read so they can disseminate Christ's vision to rich and commoners alike.'

The cardinal slammed the table so hard the dishes moved. 'And what else?' he demanded.

Asser looked blank.

'Do you know how much gold we give the Norlanders each year to stop them invading Rome?' Balotelli hissed. 'Of course you don't. The Church is far too embarrassed to share that information. One hundred thousand gold pieces! And Charles the Bald gives them something similar, even though he rules the largest empire the world has seen since the days of imperial Rome. Our coffers are empty and will remain so until we rid ourselves of the heathen invaders. There are a myriad profound changes we wish to make for the betterment of Christ's people, but we will achieve none of them,' he banged the table again, 'none of them until we have resolved the Norland problem.' He took a scroll from his sleeve. 'Read this,' he said. 'Keep it flat on the table, peruse it discreetly and return it directly to me.'

Asser's eyes scanned the scroll.

Cardinal Balotelli, forgive our presumption. We are military men unschooled in the complexities of government, but we write to you out of love for Christ and because Christendom is on the verge of destruction. All Europe from the Danube to Hadrian's Wall has been encircled by the Norlanders.

> They currently comprise only of discreet fighting bands, and consequently have been underestimated by our superiors, who buy them off rather than engage them in battle. Once they are united, as they will be soon, they will swallow us whole, and Thor and Odin will hold sway where once Christ ruled. Only a mighty Christian army can drive this pestilence from the face of the earth, and as lovers of Christ's word, we believe this army should be more than a mere harbinger of death. It must carry with it ten thousand good priests and witnesses for Christ who will transform the churches of the countries it occupies, feed the poor and hasten the Second Coming.

He passed it back and shook his head. 'Ten thousand good priests?' he said. 'We'd struggle to find fifty.'

Balotelli leant towards him so closely Asser could smell the bittersweet scent of his breath. 'Does the letter contain a little too much hyperbole? Of course it does. Its writers are young fighting men stationed in Illyria, putting their careers in jeopardy by expressing such views. But they are right. Sometimes God creates a tiny fracture in the edifice of the world that it is our duty as Christians to exploit. The Holy Roman Emperor supports such a proposal. With a great army at our disposal like the one the soldiers describe, we could make tangible the vision we've dreamt of for so long.'

'A tiny fracture? Like the death of Pope Leo? How did he die?'

'He fell from a window.'

'Why am I not surprised?'

'The new Pope has agreed that I should form a discreet group of clear-sighted clerics who will assist us in bringing all this about.'

A seminarian wearing a canvas apron offered them more

wine. Asser's mind was spinning like a child's whirling stick. He tried to speak calmly. 'A secret brotherhood?'

Balotelli shook his head vigorously. 'No, no! You'll simply be part of my administration – a few additional advisers and assistants. But you'll also be working surreptitiously to advance our shared vision.'

'Surreptitiously? Why?'

'Because otherwise our lives will be in danger from those in the Church who oppose us.'

Asser was feeling cold now. He thought of the poverty of his childhood, his visceral hatred of the Norlanders, of the day long ago when they came to his village. Of his sister, Anna.

'I am a lowly priest,' he said. 'Why would you seek me out to be one of your number?

'You come recommended as wayward but sometimes brilliant, you risked your life for us, you have exercised authority, albeit in a paltry fashion, you—'

A shadow fell across their table.

'Good morning, Stephen.'

The man who had interrupted them bore the hallmarks of Rome's great families. He was slim and well spoken, his gown was long, black and elegant with a modest golden trim, his cheekbones were defined, his skin smooth, and he wore a look of disdain tempered by a glimmer of wit.

Asser had seen him once or twice many years ago, but only from afar. He was Enzo Gilotti, the Church's primicerius, the head of the Notarii, which oversaw the Church's financial dealings. If Balotelli was the gatekeeper of Pope Benedict's wishes, Gilotti was similarly employed with the Pope's money.

'You look well after your time away from us in Aix, my friend,' he said, as smoothly as fresh cream. 'Now you have a fine new position, which I'm sure you'll execute creditably. However, you'll not be offended if my committee performs the tedious task of scrutinising your potential expenditure, will you?'

'Rest assured I will act only on the instructions of his Holiness, Enzo,' replied Balotelli. 'If you have concerns, I'm sure he'll be prepared to listen to them.'

'Of course,' replied the primicerius. 'But you have responsibilities to the wider Church too, you know that. We've all made lavish promises during papal elections in order to affect their outcome, there's nothing wrong with that. Yours, though, were particularly . . . cornucopaic. How will we pay for them, Stephen? More taxes? I think not. Be prudent. Please. For everyone's sake.'

Gilotti smiled again, before his attention was drawn by an abbot who had entered the refectory and was about to sit down and dine a little way off. 'Francis!' he called. 'So glad to see you . . .' and he walked languidly towards him.

Balotelli picked up his paring knife and continued eating his apple. 'Cornucopaic?' he said. 'What a tomfool that man is.'

'His point is well made, though, Cardinal,' said Asser. 'The changes you plan to introduce, let alone your Norland adventure, will be colossal. They'll come at great cost.'

'One step at a time, Asser, that is how we'll manage it. Not so long ago you brought together a little band of insurrectionists and they appeared happy to accept your leadership. Now I want you to do the same for me.'

Asser's mind was moving back and forth like a moorhen attending her chicks.

'I'd need assistance . . . and a purse.'

'You would. I believe you know Doctore Guido?'

'Of course. A man of great kindness and understanding. He tutored me at the seminarium.'

'He teaches no longer. Now he is my aide and confidant. He's the shrewdest of us all. He worked for the previous Pope and was able to orchestrate my return to Rome. He's also ensuring that opposition to our plans is kept to a minimum. He will supply you with all you'll need. But let me warn you, the cardinals tolerated my advancement because the Doctore offered them blandishments. Now that they understand the enormity of the changes I intend to make, they'll stop at nothing to scupper our plans. Take care. Wear a thick leather jerkin under your habit. It will be a cold winter.'

SEVEN

Wolf's Children

Exhausted by his search for Harold Godwin in the halls of his children, Wolf sat on the step of his great hall with a jug of sweet ale and a bowl of porridge. It was a large and impressive hall, the finest in Wessex, with two floors, like the houses of the great men in ancient Roman times, only when the weather turned, half of it was penned off for the animals to shelter in and constantly smelt of goat. The choir was practising the Magnificat in preparation for the Landing Day feast, repeating the same phrase over and over. The sound of the young boys' piping voices was balm to his soul. He felt less agitated now, though his head was still banging like an Irish drummer.

Why had the Lord punished him with such difficult children? He'd wanted to be proud of them, to be excited by their promise. Instead they were dolts or conspirators or both. Why couldn't they be like him when he was their age? He'd battled the Norlanders and driven them back to the furthest islands of the northern sea. He'd rid Wessex of pagans and cut down their sacred groves. He'd paid for missionaries to cross the land preaching the name of Christ, and whenever his own people rose up against him, he'd hanged the troublemakers and burnt down their cottages. Yet still the Lord was heaping the sufferings of Job upon his head. If the other aldermen came to the conclusion that he'd imprisoned Harold Godwin – or even worse, killed him – they'd rise up faster than a yeasted loaf in a cottage oven.

He heard wheezing and groaning, then Bishop Humbert was standing in the doorway, his massive bulk almost blocking out the light. His size constantly surprised Wolf. He'd not been a big man when he was young and had been appointed to the see of Winchester like his father before him. He'd certainly possessed a dominating presence, but he had been waspish, energetic and totally dedicated to Wolf and the royal house. He was still shrewd, some would say conniving, but his consumption of sweetmeats and strong drink had given him a girth of remarkable proportions. It amazed Wolf that he could still move from one place to the next without the aid of a stick or a cart, but his energy was undiminished, even though he dripped with sweat and announced his arrival with heavy breathing.

'I've interviewed your guards,' Humbert said. 'They were nowhere near the Godwins' house. They'd received an order sending them to quell a disturbance in Havant.'

'I gave no such order!' Wolf frowned.

'Of course you didn't. There was no disturbance. It was a forgery. But they couldn't have taken part in Godwin's abduction, they were leagues away.'

'Wendolyn Godwin said she saw them.'

'She was overcome by hysteria, as women often are in moments of crisis. It was all in her imagination.'

'Are you sure?' Wolf demanded. 'Those men would betray me in the blink of an eyelid. Shall we show them the hand-screws?'

'It would be imprudent to threaten your own guards, High

Aethel,' the bishop replied. 'Never fear. We'll find Alderman Godwin soon. I'm sure he's not dead.' He bowed his head and wandered off lugubriously towards the kitchens.

Wolf watched him go. He trusted the bishop more than anyone else in Wessex, but that wasn't saying much.

He turned back to the courtyard, where his wife, Osburgh, was supervising the beating of the tapestries.

'Harder!' she snapped, and slapped a young slave boy round the head.

A second wife was the dream of all red-blooded men, he thought, a pretty little thing with a lithe young body, devoted to her husband like a daughter to her father. But it rarely worked out like that. His first wife, Agnes, had been his companion; she'd ridden with him, tended his cuts and bruises, and given birth to Bear, Hawk and Swift without complaint. But Osburgh was a misery, and their son, Red, had become a halfwit. His three older children called her 'the Shrew', which was apposite, but they must stop. It irked her, then she became peevish with him.

The dust rose; he sneezed and sneezed again, and Osburgh spotted him as she always did.

'Have you found Godwin?' she snapped.

'Not yet.'

'Suppose he's been killed?'

'Then the full weight of my wrath will come crashing down on the murderer,' he said.

'Not if it's one of your children,' Osburgh replied. 'You'll forgive them. You always do.'

'Nonsense. None of my children are trustworthy. I'll hang all four if I have to.'

'You have five,' Osburgh said, snatching the carpet beater from the slave and hitting the tapestry so hard it made him wince.

'Don't start that again,' he growled. The dust was assaulting him, getting in his eyes and up his nose.

'You have five children!'

'I'm going to lie down.'

'Our glorious boy Fraed would never have plotted against you,' Osburgh said. 'You know he wouldn't. If he were still here, none of this would be happening.'

Wolf gave her a glare that would have silenced Babel. 'Aethelfraed's gone!' he said. 'He's dead to me.'

EIGHT

The Ragged People

The early-afternoon repast over, Asser was led back to the cardinal's palazzo by Father Plegmond, a skinny priest with spiky hair and buck teeth. Every stone in the path drove through him like the nails through Christ's hands, the jugged hare had given him crippling indigestion, and he was exhausted by the events of the morning. He knew he should feel grateful for his freedom, but he was deeply suspicious of what might lie ahead of him.

Finally they arrived back at the elegant palazzo the guards had dragged him into only a few hours earlier. It was illuminated by the summer sun. Even in his pain, he could admire the freshly tiled roof, the crisp daub, the neatly planted garden, and the fountains in the shape of dolphins. At the far end of the building was a small wing with white walls and a terracotta roof. Plegmond supported Asser up a long set of stone steps, through a pair of black double doors bearing a golden knob in the shape of a lion's head, and along a shiny corridor. 'Welcome to your new home,' he announced, and, like an excited courtier welcoming him to a dancing party, pushed open a polished wood door with a flourish.

The room was covered in drapes and carpets, soft chairs and a lacquered desk, and there was a large gold and mahogany cross on the wall that would have paid for the feeding of the five thousand. Plegmond helped Asser into a goose-feathered bed and laid a coverlet of beaver fur over him. Asser caught sight of himself in the burnished bronze of the big cross: short, thin, with the face of some curious forest animal, his eyes exhausted but implacable.

'Would coddled eggs and ham suffice in the morning?' enquired Plegmond.

Asser could think of no adequate response.

'And these documents,' Plegmond continued, pointing to a pile on the desk. 'I've sorted them out for you in advance of . . . whatever it is the cardinal wants you to do.'

'Give me whichever you consider the most important,' said Asser.

'You wouldn't rather sleep, after all your travails?' said Plegmond solicitously. 'I think you should.'

Asser pushed aside the coverlet and held out his hand. 'It's the middle of the day,' he said.

Plegmond browsed through the documents thoughtfully and gave him one. 'This is an assessment of the Norlanders' strength. And of ours,' he added.

Asser began reading.

'Shall I go now?' Plegmond said, but Asser was too immersed in the document to reply.

A short while later, there was a knock at the door. Terror seized him and he started violently. Was Halfnose about to drag him back to the papal dungeon?

The door opened and he almost cried with joy. Two figures stood there with broad smiles on their faces.

'How are you, old friend?' enquired Father Kennet, rosy-cheeked and with the belly of a toper. When they were young, and the other boys at the seminarium had been slaving over the tedious books of Leviticus and Numbers, Kennet had taught him riddles about cocks and arses and introduced him to the minds of new theologians like Alcuin of York and Johannes of Scotia.

'I will mend,' replied Asser.

'You're looking older,' said Kennet.

'St Catherine on her wheel!' exclaimed Asser. '*I'm* looking older? A year ago you had hair the colour of a black cat.'

'Time hasn't been easy on any of us,' said Father Philip, who'd been the strongest and bravest of their gang of boys. He'd once climbed the outside of the seminarium tower and set a stuffed dummy of Master Spinoza on the very top. Now he'd grown in bulk and looked more like a butcher than a man of God.

Kennet, Philip and Asser, boyhood rebels and brothers in arms. They'd feared nothing and no one, they'd drunk purloined communion wine late into the night and written sagas so bawdy they'd have made the devil blush. They were arrogant and witty and argued their mentors into the ground.

'I suppose I have you two to thank for my liberation,' Asser said.

'No, we thought you were dead. Plegmond's your saviour. He sifted through countless lists of miscreants and finally found you in the Pope's dungeon,' Philip replied.

'And Balotelli had you freed,' added Kennet.

'Balotelli would have struggled to remember my name had it not been written on the parchment in front of him,' replied Asser.

Philip and Kennet sat on his bed and they talked for a long time. Father Philip had escaped to Macedonia after the events in the market square; he'd fought in a bloody war against the

Church in Constantinople and returned home to find his mistress and children dead from the measles. Kennet had spent months hiding in the old catacombs under the city, eating rats and other filth. Asser's heart bled for them, but he couldn't fight the fog of fatigue that was creeping over him.

'Our vision. Everything we dreamt of,' he said, his eyes heavy with sleep. 'We will bring it about, my friends.'

'If we live long enough to do so,' replied Kennet.

'We'll leave you now,' said Philip softly, and they tiptoed out of the room.

A face looms over him, gaunt and sad, two faces, ten, a hundred. He's walking through Wessex, past shacks and shanties. Ragged figures are crying out in despair, children are being eaten by rats, rats are being eaten by the starving, the starving are prostituting themselves with brute-faced soldiers.

Now he is standing on a beach, a child looking for worms holding a swill bucket and a big wooden spoon. Men appear from nowhere, six or seven of them. The one at the front is calling out to him. He has curly ginger hair down to his waist, a long coat with moons and stars on it, and tiny blue jewels under his eyes. He scoops Asser up, twirls him round in the air and sets him on his shoulders.

He is at the compound. His da is coming out of their hut with a dreadful expression on his face. He points at the men. 'Norlanders!' he screams.

An axe flies through the air and buries itself in his da's forehead, another in his chest. Asser screams, but the man with the curly hair holds his legs fast. He leans forward and bites the man's ear as hard as he can, and tastes the metallic tang of blood. The man cries out. Asser heaves himself from his grip and runs.

His da is lying completely still, the axes still protruding from his head and chest. Two of the men are lying on top of his ma. They cut her from her neck to her secret parts.

They are dragging his sister away. 'Asser!' she is calling.

Now the ragged figures are returning and are calling to him too. 'Asser! Asser!'

'Asser!'

He opened his eyes. A face was looming over him. He felt strange, soft sheets beneath his fingers. Where was he?

'You've been dreaming, and you've bitten your lip; here, let me wipe it for you.'

Confusion overwhelmed him, and he tried to pull away from the person standing over him, but then recognised the voice as that of the one he loved best: Doctore Guido, his teacher from the seminarium, kind, gentle, full of understanding.

'I don't . . .' he began.

'Good afternoon, my friend. You're at Balotelli's palazzo. My rooms are down the corridor and I heard you shouting.'

For a moment Asser was overcome with happiness, then his dream came back to him, as vivid as before.

He clutched the Doctore's hand. 'We must not forget them,' he said.

'Forget who?'

'The poor, the hungry. We are planning to embark on a terrible war, but it will count as nothing unless we free our people from their misery!'

'I know that, Asser,' replied the Doctore. 'We all do. It's why we have put our trust in you. You will twist and dodge and lie for us. You will put your soul in mortal peril. But you are Christ's soldier, as are we all.'

'Balotelli's to be trusted?'

'He is the most brilliant man I know, and I thank God for him,' said Guido. 'He wishes to heal the Church and rid it of corruption, and in that he has my absolute support. But he is at his happiest when he's immersed in schemes and stratagems.

Perhaps one day he will overreach himself. And if that day comes, I pray we will be able to set his plans aright. Now go back to sleep,' he said softly, and he stroked Asser's head as he had twenty years previously, when Asser was a young, frightened boy far away from home and had lost his family to the Norlanders.

NINE

The Landing Day Feast

The carpet beating had been completed, the guests had arrived, but Wolf was buried away in his wine cellar. He carefully lifted down a cask the size of an African egg from the furthest recesses of its highest shelf. He blew off the cobwebs, cracked it open and poured the syrupy contents into two large goblets. 'From the vineyards of Bedminster,' he announced. 'The most potent of my honeyed wines.'

Bishop Humbert buried his nose in the goblet and basked in its rich odours. 'Glorious!' he proclaimed in a tone of hushed reverence.

'You are the truest of friends and the most loyal of servants,' Wolf said.

'Godwin wasn't difficult to track down,' replied the bishop modestly. 'I doubted he'd been abducted. The whorehouses seemed the best place to start looking.'

'But Kingsworthy!' Wolf laughed dismissively. 'It's barely two leagues from here. Hardly very discreet. '

'Dead drunk, and face-down on the floor.'

'So was his wife lying about the abduction, or did she not know where he'd been either?'

The bishop tapped his tongue against his lips and rocked his head from side to side. 'I can taste cherries, I think. And a hint of old leather.'

'Well?' Wolf demanded.

'Forget the Godwins, High Aethel. Today is your special day.'

Wolf shook his head. He didn't believe the whorehouse story. Harold Godwin had never been a frequenter of brothels; he was far too concerned with keeping his cock clean. He'd been dumped there because someone wanted to discredit him. But at least the immediate problem had been resolved. 'I could have lost my throne. I could have been slaughtered by vengeful aldermen.'

'Thankfully that was not the case, High Aethel.'

'One of my family did this. Godwin will never forgive us.'

'He already has. I gave him eighty silver coins, which I deducted from your children's stipends. I doubt they'll notice.'

'My own blood trying to undermine me!' Wolf exclaimed. 'How shameful is that? Bear is waiting for me to die, Hawk thinks he's cleverer than me, Swift wants to punish me because I won't let her become high aethel of the south coast, and Red's so gullible he'd kill me if the others told him to.'

'Children, eh,' mused the bishop. 'Didn't you try to kill your father once?'

'That was different,' Wolf said. 'He was pounding my mistress against a dairy wall. I think I might have strangled him if my men hadn't pulled me away,' he added thoughtfully.

'So perhaps you shouldn't be too hard on your own offspring. At least until they lay their hands on the hilts of their daggers.'

Wolf silenced him with a glare. 'It's gone noon. We'll go to the party and make merry, but we'll watch every smile and every flicker of every eye.'

*

There weren't many days of the year when common folk were allowed to dance with the aethels, but the Landing Day feast was special. Three hundred and thirty years previously, the hero Hengist and a few boatloads of Wolf's ancestors from the far-off forests of Saxony had dropped anchor on the southern coast of Britain. They'd subjugated the local savages, fought among themselves, and after a few bloody battles, the kingdoms of Essex, Sussex and Wessex had been born. And now Wolf had swallowed up Essex and Sussex, and God's glorious garden of Wessex reigned supreme. Today was a celebration of his triumph. Every one of his servants, gardeners, kitchen maids, chambermaids and the like, his forty-strong royal guard, the aldermen and all the minor functionaries, the farmers and the traders would spend the day carousing at his expense. Even the slaves in their hovels and the homeless in their ditches would receive something: a few ribs, some apples, whatever the kitchen could spare.

Wolf snatched a skin of ale from a passing house slave, and smacked her rump so hard she stumbled into a wall. 'Happy Landing Day,' he roared. 'The day we took your land, eh?'

The woman dabbed her grazed face with her sleeve and muttered something in the old tongue.

'What did you say?' Wolf demanded. 'I was jesting.' He felt Osburgh glance at him contemptuously. She had no sense of fun or frivolity. How unlike his first wife she was.

The musicians were playing 'Fork the Hay', and aethels and commoners alike jigged along shouting, 'Hay! Hay! Hay!' at the appropriate moment.

Wolf lumbered round the great hall with one wench after another, hugging them, stroking their cheeks, occasionally shifting his glance to the top table, watching for signs of disloyalty. Harold Godwin, once as handsome as King David, now obsequious and chubby at the neck, gave him a honeyed smile, as though nothing of any import had occurred, but his wife, Wendolyn, pointedly ignored Wolf, even though her wealth had been significantly increased in the last few hours.

As for his children, Bear was leaping up and down with three farmers' daughters from Swine Down, while Hawk, tall and round-shouldered, with a long nose like a heron fishing on a bank, had his hands on his wife's shoulders, but the two of them were barely dancing, merely shifting their weight from one foot to the other. Again Wolf felt that tinge of regret. But alliances needed to be brokered regardless of what dreadful woman your child had to marry. At least Moira had stopped trying to flee home to Northumbria.

The door swung open and sunshine illuminated the hall. An old man tottered in breathless and exhausted. His lips were moving, but the dancers' din was deafening. 'Hush!' Wolf bellowed.

The music stopped save for the discordant drone of the musicians' pipe bags. Wolf felt a terrible sense of foreboding. The look on the man's face, the way he'd blundered into the great hall without explanation or apology reminded him of the story of the peasant who'd run ten leagues to tell the Greeks that the Persians were about to arrive and had then dropped dead.

'What is it?' he demanded.

'I've come from the coast,' gasped the old man. 'The Norlanders are back. They're heading towards Hamblesea.'

There were sobs and cries of terror. 'Not again!' someone shouted.

Wolf closed his eyes. There'd been rumours of warships raiding coastal villages, but stories like that cropped up every year, the gossip of fearful peasants mistaking a school of porpoises for a fleet of raiders. Calm yourself! Think! If it was true, his guards could chase them off. It would be easy.

They'd be mounted; the invaders would be on foot with their backs to the sea. Slowly his fear turned to exhilaration. He was a fighting man; he had been all his life. He knew how to fend off a couple of boatloads of raiders. He drew a deep breath, put his thumb and first finger to his lips and blew the call to arms he'd learnt from his father, who'd learnt it from *his* father, a piercing upturned sound like a peewit in flight. Three times he blew, and his guards leapt to the ready. They swept the food from the tables, and helmets, breastplates, swords and axes were torn from the walls and thrown down in their stead.

Wolf strode out of the hall and into the courtyard, followed by his men. The horses were already being saddled, and the pumps laboured as slave women filled sheepskin flasks with water from the well. 'Bear!' he ordered. 'Take the left flank!'

'I'm not your captain,' retorted Bear. 'You demoted me this morning.'

'I'm reinstating you. Take ten men. You can have five of mine if you—'

'You called me a traitor!'

'Don't piss me off, boy. This is war!'

Hawk and Harold Godwin were in deep discussion. 'Are you two plotting?' Wolf demanded.

'We can't deploy all our men to the south coast,' said Hawk. 'We're short on numbers.'

'We'll do as I fucking say,' Wolf replied.

'But respectfully, High Aethel, you remember what happened twenty years ago,' Godwin said. 'They lured us to the coast, we left Winchester unattended, and they burnt down the town walls and took the gold plate.'

Wolf was struggling with his shoulder guards. 'So you two wish to stay here, do you? Why does that make me uneasy?'

'I'll do whatever you require,' Godwin said.

'You stay, Harold. Fortify the walls with the old men. Hawk, come with me and marshal our right flank.'

Osburgh was lashing water bottles to his saddle. 'Watch your back,' she hissed, 'or one of your sons will run you through in the heat of battle.'

The brothers were pulling their aethels' headdresses over their helmets, one fashioned like a brown bear's head, the other feathered like a bird of prey and sporting a carved beak.

Bishop Humbert moved among the fighting men murmuring prayers, placing his hand on their hearts and swords. 'The devils have returned. May God keep you safe and your arm strong. May your enemies scatter and their boats be broken.'

Wolf watched him keenly as he leant close to each man as he blessed them. Was he whispering to them? Could Humbert be working against him? He shook his head. Now was not the time for distrustful thoughts. He would wipe all thought of Godwin's abduction from his mind. The answer to the conundrum was bound to reveal itself eventually, but not today.

His men were ready, their horses frisky and kicking. Osburgh had forbidden Red from fighting. He and his plump young sweetheart Winifred sat watching the men and taking bites out of an overripe plum.

'Red!' bawled Wolf. 'Grab your helmet and sword! You're coming with us.'

'My liege!' Red sprang to his feet, throwing the plum into the air. 'You won't regret this, Father.'

'Ride behind me and watch my back. Put your life on the line if you have to. Today we'll make you a man. I don't want you ending up a milksop like—'

'Like who?' Osburgh demanded. 'Like the finest of your sons? The one you sent away? The only one who could save this benighted land?'

Wolf ignored her.

'Like your son Fraed,' she shouted.

'Let's go!' Wolf yelled.

A roar broke from the throats of his army, his horse reared and pawed the air, and they rode off, scattering chickens and dust as they went.

TEN

The Serpent's Kiss

Swift and Agneta gathered the villagers on the patch of mud and seashells that passed as Hamblesea marketplace. They were good souls, but old and weathered; the younger ones had left long ago looking for labouring work or a husband with a field. There were a few men, most with the shaking sickness or old man's stiffness. The women were strong, beady-eyed, their bodies bent by years of remorseless toil. Swift had no doubt more than a few would be lost today.

'How will we stop them?' demanded Goodwife Bredbaker, an old maid with hands like a man. She wouldn't tolerate nonsense, but now there was fear in her voice. 'Could we cast a spell?'

They all looked at Agneta, who knew how to coax wondrous effects from herbs and wood bark. Folk went to her when they were sick or wished to lose an unborn child. She gazed up to the sky as though trying to draw down divine inspiration. 'The serpent's kiss,' she said eventually. 'That'll do the trick.'

'What?' asked Goodwife Bredbaker suspiciously.

'It's a spell that eats a man's senses. They say the serpent gave it to Eve to ward off the Philistines.'

'And you can summon it?' asked Swift incredulously.

'Not me,' replied Agneta, and shrugged her shoulders. 'The kiss is old magic and I'm a good Christian woman. But there's one of Beelzebub's sisters locked in the shed. She'll know what to do.'

Set back from the privy among the discarded bones and piles of stinking limpet shells was the damp and mildewed shed where the mad boy had been kept till he ate his own tongue and choked to death.

Agneta knocked out the wooden pegs that held the door in place. A young slave girl with the white, pasty face of a Briton staggered out, blinded by the sunlight. She was barely fourteen years of age, with a brand on her cheek and a sneer on her face. 'Holy Jesus,' Agneta exclaimed. 'What a slattern you are!'

Slaves didn't interest Swift. They were necessary – how could the fields be tended without them? – but they were part of the landscape, like rats and birds. She stared closely at this one, though, as Agneta told her the story of the girl's acquisition. She'd been found half drowned in the hold of a wrecked Irish slaving ship, chained up with a dead pirate who'd had his face nibbled away. She'd been locked in an old oyster hut, but had burrowed her way out through the shingle, pulled up Goodwife Bredbaker's turnips, cooked them in a bucket with a skinned cat, wolfed down the whole mess and fallen asleep in the church porch. The villagers had whipped her, thrown her in the shed, and given her water and scraps when they remembered. If she fattened up, she'd be taken to Winchester and exchanged for a few cheeses or a blunted ploughshare.

Agneta grabbed the girl by the throat and pulled her close. 'You will teach me the serpent's kiss,' she said fiercely. 'In return, I'll let you out of this shithole, give you a place to lie down in Simon Eadwig's barn, maybe someday even set you free. But if you play me false, I will shave your face off with a blunt scraper.'

The girl stared at them for a while, then shrugged her shoulders.

Swift and Agneta made their way to the Church of St Ignatius. It had been built in the days when the south coast was wealthy and folk could afford to make their places of worship out of stone. Now it was surrounded by blight and poverty, but it still had its cross and other fine things, because whenever raiders came calling – Irish pirates, drunken East Anglian fishermen and the like – the priest hid in a tiny cellar under the flagstones clutching them to his bosom and shitting himself.

A few of the old people were taking communion. The priest held up the chalice and its gold rim caught the candlelight. The two women burst through the open doorway, strutted confidently down the aisle and headed for the small sacred table. The priest ceased his plainchant and stared at them disapprovingly.

Swift yanked the big cross from its holder. 'Our need is greater than yours,' she said.

'These good people could be dead tonight,' said the priest.

'They will be if you don't give us that chalice,' she retorted.

Wigan and a few of the old men were in the briar bushes at the edge of the village, clearing out trenches dug by the villagers years ago in case of attack. The women climbed in and were covered with willow mats and armfuls of leaves. Swift and Agneta trudged up the slope to another trench, and Wigan covered them too. From inside their hidey-hole, they could make out the village, the sea, and Wigan heading off towards the church.

Time passed. Swift was hot and damp. She was being bitten by countless tiny creatures, and the earth pressed in tight on her. But she'd wait as long as it took.

ELEVEN

God Has Abandoned Us

Wolf's riders galloped through Twyford, Otterbourne and Colden Common, jumping fences and ditches, startling cows, trampling meagre vegetable plots. They were acting like boys, swearing, laughing, catcalling, boasting, but he joined in their foolish banter as he always did, his heart racing, his breath pumping, even though he was haunted by memories of returning from battles of old – a friend dangling lifeless across a saddle, a young warrior screaming like a child because he'd lost a leg; or worse still, those who didn't return and suffered who knew what horrors at the hands of the barbarians.

The local people stared at these mounted figures – half men, half monsters – whooping and yelling, led by a wolf, now overtaken by a bear, then by a hunting hawk. Red lifted his fox headdress, waved at them cheerily, and they waved back. It wouldn't be long before they grew surly and would have to be put down forcibly again, thought Wolf, but today they were cheering. 'Sweet Jesus bless you, Master Red,' they shouted, the women curtsying and the young girls blowing him kisses.

Wolf called his riders to a halt. How unlike his fighting force of yesteryear they were! Now they bore swords that shattered, shields that split in twain, and half the men so old they were as breathless as the horses. It was only their shouts and the thudding hooves that kept Wessex safe.

He spied wisps of smoke between the trees. Ahead was Nutley, his monastery. He knew every inch of it. He took absolution there and played knocker ball with the younger monks. But the church bell was ringing in an odd, irregular way and his stomach twisted.

He called his men to walk on. When they rounded a bend in the road, they saw two monks striding towards them. He shouted a greeting, but they stared beyond him as though there was something terrible on the horizon.

A little monk was propped against a tree, his neck sliced through by an axe, his head tilted quizzically to one side. More monks were walking back towards the monastery, shocked and shaking. Others peered cautiously from the trees.

'God has abandoned us!' one cried. 'The world has ended and there'll be no Second Coming.'

The soldiers drew their swords, but Wolf suspected that the men who'd launched this attack were long gone; there were no cries for help, and the blood on the ground was dark and congealed.

He pressed on ahead, through the archway. Ahead of him was the bell tower.

'Holy St Michael and all his angels,' he breathed.

Abbot Cuthbert's body was dangling from the clapper of the bell, swaying slowly. Wolf looked away, and then back again. Cuthbert. His old friend! Sweet Saviour, he would make this a day of terrible retribution.

'Stub!' he shouted. His sergeant-at-arms cantered over to him; a long-faced man whose wife and children had been slaughtered by raiders twenty years previously and who hadn't smiled since. Wolf nodded to the bell tower and watched as Stub's serious face grew pale. 'Cut the body down,' he ordered. 'Treat it with care. The man was a saint. Find out what they've taken.'

Stub dismounted and called to two of his men. Wolf sat on the edge of a low wall, staring at the monastery. His first wife, Agnes, had been the benefactress of this place, and when she'd died he'd taken over her duties. He'd paid for festivals of music, and boy choristers had acted out the story of David and Goliath for the local people. He'd brought in carpenters to replace the rotting windows, and sent for an artist from Cluny, the biggest monastery in the world, to paint a fresco of Lazarus rising across the chancel. And when Abbot Cuthbert had told him that the church at Pevensey was on the verge of ruin and was prepared to sell its illuminated Gospels, they'd ridden there together, he'd paid for the book in gold pieces, and they'd got so drunk they'd had to be taken home in a cart. He was proud of that book. The pictures were wonderful to behold. He wished Agnes could have seen them. He hadn't been a good husband – he'd drunk too much and had taken pleasure with her handmaids – but after she'd died, he'd done his best to keep her memory alive.

Stub was back. 'It's all gone!' he said.

'Even the Gospels?'

'Them too.'

He watched Hawk crouching among the broken glass, attempting to fix the pieces back together like a children's puzzle. Hawk loved this place too. Agnes had paid for a family chapel to be built here, where they could worship together without being stared at, and where the young Hawk could pray for repentance after one of his terrible tantrums. God! He'd been a difficult child. And a difficult adult too. Who knew what he was capable of?

A monk was passing round skins of monastery wine, which he'd retrieved from some hiding place among the trees. 'Don't give my father any of that,' Hawk snapped. Wolf took a skin anyway.

'The fresco's in a bad state,' said Stub. 'They drew on it . . . filth.' Wolf's father had used that same word when they'd ridden into battle against the first Norland raiders. Filth, that was what they were, he'd said, like the soulless fiends in the old stories. Every one of them should be killed, young and old, women and children, and the killing shouldn't stop till there was not a single one left this side of Northumbria. And it had been done; they'd been wiped from the face of southern Britain . . . only now they had returned. And it was Wolf's fault. He'd been warned, but he'd been deaf to the intelligence, too obsessed with petty family plots and squabbles. What was the matter with him? Guilt coursed through him like the Severn bore.

'Let's go . . . now!' he yelled.

His men lumbered to their feet. Some began lashing wineskins to their saddles, others relieved themselves behind the grave markers.

'Come, lads!' Wolf shouted. 'We'll destroy Satan's army. Every severed limb will be a prayer to Christ the Redeemer.'

TWELVE

They Walked Like Heroes

Guthrum the Norlander guided his boat silently to shore. Thirty men slipped over the side and onto the pebbles, checked, turned, then moved on again as delicately as bridesmaids dancing at a country wedding. Skule Bawdson, Martin Hennig, Ragnar Ironside and the rest. They were his pride. They'd fought with him since they were boys; now they walked like heroes, their boat so full of loot that the sharp edges of the golden crosses chafed their ankles as they rowed.

A few paces ahead, already disembarked, were Dagmar Longshanks and his crew of thirty more. They let out a few mumbled curses and made the occasional crunch on the pebbles. Dagmar was trying to reach the top of the stone rise before Guthrum's crew. It was a game – a stupid game, because rushing meant noise, and noise meant alarms raised, but Dagmar had always been a fool.

They'd been raiding along this coast since first light, their treasure was slowing them down, they hadn't eaten for days, and the blazing beacons told him the village had been warned of an attack. If Guthrum had been battle chief, they wouldn't have stopped here. The sun was high in the sky; it would be prudent to begin the voyage home while the good weather lasted. But this wasn't his command. Before they'd left the Farnes, he'd called a thyng, a meeting of the elders. He told them they were simple-minded to send out only two longships and no support vessel, and their answer had been to set up Dagmar in his place. Dagmar was an old hand and a good fighter. His teeth were sharpened to points; there were studs embedded down the length of his nose. He looked fierce, but he was no leader.

All sixty raiders were hidden out of sight below the top of the ridge. The scouts disappeared over the crest and the rest waited for their return, swords and axes in hand. Dagmar was softly whistling 'Ingrid of the Isles' through his pointed teeth. It was irritating. Dagmar was always irritating, but he seemed proud of himself and Guthrum could understand why. Nine sorties he had carried out, nine monasteries and settlements burnt to the ground; enough loot for each of them to buy a farm, not that they'd want one. They revelled in theft, not husbandry. Dagmar would soon be a hero, but he'd had the luck of Loki. The Saxons had been unprepared and unarmed, unlike in the old days when they'd fought for every goblet and candlestick.

Stig Hammerson was back first.

'Clear?' demanded Dagmar.

'Clear!' replied Stig.

Snorre Magnussen came next.

'Clear?'

'Aye!' He grinned broadly. 'They've put on a fine spread for us. Come and see!'

Below the ridge was a ramshackle cluster of huts and market

stalls, and in front of them a feast had been laid out on a long carved wooden door. Ham, apples, preserves, fruit, bowls of curds and soft cheese, boiled pike sprinkled with dried herbs, dishes of pickled herring and piles of loaves. At each end of the door a gold candlestick had been set, and a large golden cross had been plunged into a pile of stones in front of it. By the side of the cross stood a ragged slave with a brand on her cheek and garlands in her hair, her head twitching, her eyes flashing.

Guthrum had seen food, slaves and gold laid out like this before, bribes offered by terrified Saxons desperate for the Norlanders to sail off and leave them unharmed. Sometimes it worked, sometimes they killed the villagers anyway.

Dagmar's men slithered down the stony bank towards the feast, their weapons drawn and grins on their faces as though they'd found a baby dolphin in a rock pool.

'Wait!' barked Guthrum. They stopped. He was no longer their commander, but he was a giant of a man, and in his five years as battle chief he'd not lost a single fighter.

'Ignore him. He's an old woman,' said Dagmar. 'What is it, Guthrum? Do you fear the spread is blighted? Could a handful of Saxon peasants cook up enough poison to kill the crew of two Norland fighting ships? Even the apothecaries of Constantinople couldn't perform that miracle.'

'But what if we become sick? We've a long journey home,' said Martin Hennig, who was always cautious.

'It's their Landing Day feast,' said Stig Hammerson, whose mother had been half Saxon.

'They've run away and left their food for us, along with bright shiny gifts and a slave girl to fuck,' said Dagmar. 'What cowards those Saxons are.'

Guthrum was as hungry as the rest of them; their provisions had run out long ago. He strode to the table, drew his knife, sliced off a hunk of ham and stuffed it in the slave girl's mouth.

She gulped it down. He tore off some bread and she devoured that too. He walked round the altar taking pickles, cheeses and pieces of fish and shoving them in her bulging cheeks. With a mighty effort she swallowed it all in one mouthful, and the men whooped and applauded. He thrust a bright, shiny goblet into her hands; she drank so deep the liquid cascaded down the sides of her mouth and onto the ground.

'Now watch and wait,' he said.

He walked round the girl, pulled her eyes wide open, lifted her arms and felt her hands and forehead. Time passed; the men grew restless.

'She's fine. Eat, lads,' shouted Dagmar, and shoved the empty goblet at the girl. 'You, slave, bring more wine.'

The girl shuffled off towards the huts while the men fell on the food like gannets, plunging their faces into the bowls of curds, ripping up the cheese and rubbing it in each other's faces. Arne the Joker lay on his back with his mouth open, pretending to pleasure a herring that was dangling from his fingers.

They ate and drank for a long time and sang the songs of the frozen north. They grew listless. Arne danced on the laden door but stumbled and rolled off. Yorre Anderson recited a poem but forgot the words. Lars Hansenn was dabbing his forehead with his shirtsleeve, Skule Bawdson was slapping the side of his face, Ragnar Ironside was biting his own arm.

Guthrum looked from one to another in horror. Great god Odin, what was happening? He was sweating too. He was shouting, but the voice wasn't his own. He had seldom felt fear, but now, staring at the slave girl handing out food as though nothing was untoward, he was filled with terror. She was transforming before his eyes. She'd grown fangs and claws and a tail; her brand was a snarling cat's head and she had adders in her hair. He lurched over to her, grabbed the snakes in his hand and threw her kicking and screaming into a pile of broken lobster pots. He picked her up again like a moth-eaten carpet, slammed her down on the ground and kicked her between the legs. He would not be overwhelmed. He would make the bitch pay for her terrible enchantments.

THIRTEEN

Wolf! Wolf! Wolf!

As the serpent worked its magic and sent the Norlanders into a world of madness, Swift struggled out of her bug-infested hole and shook the filth from her hair. It was time. She gave an ululating battle cry, and the villagers burst out from under their leaf-strewn mats like ghouls in a nightmare.

She grabbed the black-winged headdress from her belt, threw her head back and gave another cry. The nearest Norlander was on his knees, eyes rolling. She slashed his stomach with her sword, he toppled over and she kept on running. It wasn't her first kill; her father had let her go on sorties with his men for many years. She'd slain one of the Cornish Britons who'd tried to set fire to Plymouth, and when a Frankian freebooter had been caught on Chesil Beach, she'd driven the final thrust through his guts. But this was the first time she'd fought un-aided. Exhilaration coursed through her. Behind her she could hear the villagers stamping on the man she'd brought down. Ahead of her a raider was banging the side of his head with his fist and rocking from side to side. The women clubbed him with stones and farm tools, and thrust a meat knife between his ribs. Simon Eadwig, the last surviving fighter from the Norland wars of old, crept up on a raider who was staring at the horizon and hit him with a kettle hammer. Twenty years of rage were in that blow. The man fell forward, and Simon hit him again and again till he stopped moving.

Swift sliced through the hand of a man trying to steady himself against the old church door still covered in the remains of the feast, and he fell to the ground writhing in agony. She leapt up on the door and looked about her. The raiders were staggering around on the beach, some fighting the air, others crying or talking to invisible apparitions, while the Hamblesea women cut through them like sticks through lard. A few of them were still blundering around up at the huts. Her fighters grabbed them and dragged them across the stones, their clothes torn and bloody. Small groups of women ripped the jewellery from their ears. Goodwife Bredbaker hacked off a nose with a line of studs running down it and tucked it away in her pocket.

Soon there were only a dozen or so Norlanders left alive, stumbling about in the shallows like children seeing waves for the first time. The shouting and cries of pain had stopped, the silence so eerie Swift felt as though her ears had been stuffed with beeswax.

Until . . . Was she imagining that faint chant from somewhere among the trees? No, it was growing louder. 'Wolf! Wolf! Wolf!' Of course. She felt a sourness in her stomach as though she'd eaten a bad apple. She should have known her father would appear in her moment of triumph.

Within minutes, there they were. Wolf's soldiers burst out of the trees, into the village, and swept down to the beach.

'Out of the way!' they bawled.

The villagers stared about them, panting for breath. When they realised who the riders were, they dropped their weapons and joined in the chant, pointing out the few Norlanders attempting to run away or lying twitching among the piles of dead bodies. They were blissfully happy that the battle was won and their heroes had arrived. Some tore off the Norlanders' bloodied garb, pulled it over their heads and danced in the sand; others pissed and spat on the corpses, all the while still shouting, 'Wolf! Wolf! Wolf!'

Hawk on the right flank cantered across the beach gesturing at fleeing raiders and ordering their execution. Bear on the left yelled and screamed as he brought his horse to a skidding halt. Leaping off, he pulled a corpse to its feet, rained blows down on it and kicked it repeatedly before racing off and doing the same to another lifeless body.

The wings of the Saxon line cantered out into the water and swung round ahead of the Norlanders. The circle of fighters and horses tightened. The Saxons hacked and chopped, stabbed and strangled till the water was red and the raiders were nothing but a mess of sodden, misshapen carcasses.

Swift's father drew level with her, leant out of his saddle like a young buck and embraced her. 'My daughter!' he cried. 'Have no fear. I have saved you, as I always will!' He kissed her warrior's headdress and, before she could reply, rode off again bellowing orders.

Swift was consumed with rage. He would claim victory, as he always did. Every rat she'd caught as a young girl, every boy she'd fought, every fox she'd cornered, every interloper she'd driven off, always he or her bullying brothers had taken the credit and basked in the praise. But this latest humiliation would be the final peg in the coffin. She would bring him down, and the rest of her family too, and one day – and it would be soon – she would rule over all Wessex as the new Boudicca, and she would be feared and glorious.

FOURTEEN

A Pinch of Mandrake

Night fell on Hamblesea beach. Word had spread and folk appeared from as far afield as Hamble Green. Children dodged among the bodies of the raiders pretending to be Wolf's warriors, the older girls flirted with the fighters, a few lads played victory songs and the old women danced the Saxon dances.

Swift, Agneta and Wigan roasted turnips on a fire. Wigan pulled one out with a pointed stick, slathered it in butter and gave it to his mistress.

'Where were you?' Swift demanded.

'When?' he replied.

'When we were killing Norlanders.'

'Under the church slab with the priest. Once I'd covered up all the villagers, there was nowhere else for me to hide. I wanted to join the fighting, but the priest was a coward and smashed the wooden ladder so I couldn't reach the slab to lift it. He refused to give me a leg-up till I threatened to kill him. He's still down there. I'll let him stew for the night.'

Swift laughed, but she wasn't happy with him. He was getting old. He'd refused to ride to Winchester, and he hadn't watched her back when she needed him.

Agneta held up a battered earthenware pot. 'Want this on your turnips?' she asked. 'The serpent's kiss. What the little slattern mixed up for you: snails, henbane, foxglove, tiny-tit mushrooms and a pinch of mandrake. It won't kill you, but a few mouthfuls and you'll think the world's full of goblins and dancing jellyfish.'

'So why didn't the slave bitch go mad?' asked Wigan. 'She wolfed the stuff down.'

'Aye. But the first chance she got, she swallowed a skin of my green mutton brew behind the huts. It's what makes folk throw up their badness.'

The girl was squatting beside the giant's body, hacking at his hand with an axe and throwing the bloodied stumps of his fingers over her shoulder.

'You did well today,' said Swift. The girl had leapt on him like a rat on a pigeon, smashed his face with the church candlestick, then sworn at him in the old tongue and crooned a song of triumph. 'What's your name?' she asked her. The slave didn't answer. 'Your name?' Swift repeated.

The girl shrugged. 'I have no name,' she replied.

'Even dogs have names. What did your last owner call you? Grimalkin? Little Whore?'

The girl sprang to her feet. 'I am Rhiannon!' she shouted, and her voice had a bubble and ring like fast-flowing water crossing stones. 'I am Rhiannon, daughter of Rhiannon! Rhiannon of the Twin Valleys! Rhiannon, Slayer of Men!' She sat back down on the giant's body and stared defiantly at Swift and Agneta.

'Her squawking is vexing me. Take her home with you, Swift,' the old woman said. 'If Wigan trains her to keep her mouth shut and stab like a man, you'll never need to watch your back again.'

Swift took off her headdress and scratched her scalp. 'What do you think, Wigan?' she said.

'She's a killer already, but I'll make her a fighter,' he said.

Rhiannon tugged her hand hard, and held up one of the giant's amputated fingers as if she'd pulled off one of her own. 'Magic!' she crowed. Even Wigan laughed.

'You're a clever little kiss-cunt,' said Agneta. She stepped over the giant's body, oblivious of the blood still seeping from his hand, and she and Swift walked down to the beach arm in arm to join the celebrations.

FIFTEEN

The Norland Boy

Dawn. Wolf sat on the sand, warming himself by the glowing embers of the fire, Bear beside him. The pair watched two fighters heave the body of a Norlander down to the water's edge. One took the arms, the other the legs, and they swung the corpse back and forth like a baby in a cradle before flinging it onto a Norland boat. The Southsaxon folk cheered as it thumped onto the deck. Hawk sat a little way off, sorting through the rescued loot, ignoring the fun.

Wolf took a ferocious swig from his ale skin and wrapped his fur-covered arm round Bear's neck, pulling him close. 'Why do you want to usurp me, my son?' he whispered. 'I'll be dead in a few years.'

'Sometimes we squabble,' said Bear, his voice muffled by the fur, 'sometimes we disagree about how many fighting men we should muster, but I don't want to steal your crown.'

'We don't need some grand permanent army. Think of the cost of feeding, training, barracking,' his father replied firmly. 'We won a glorious victory today with my forty guards.'

'Forty old men,' Bear said, gesturing to the fighters lying dozing on the beach, 'most of whom you've known for at least two-score years. If we need more, we're forced to knock at farmers' doors and thrust a helmet in their hands.'

Wolf heaved his son up and dusted the sand from his jacket. 'Listen, clodpole,' he said. 'If I had a standing army, five years hence my head would be rolling across the floor and its general would be sitting on the throne.'

The tide was coming in. Wolf's men were getting to their feet. It would soon be time to go back to Winchester.

'If the Norlanders return and we haven't got a standing army, they'll fuck us in three places at once like they used to in the old days,' persisted Bear.

Hawk stood up. Evidently their conversation had snagged his interest. 'I beg your leave, brother,' he said, 'but I have to go to the rainbow's end to find the gold to pay for your imaginary army.'

Wolf opened another skin of ale. 'At least he wants to fight, Hawk,' he said. 'What do *you* want, a warm bed?'

'A little parlaying perhaps,' replied Hawk. 'It's cheaper than fields full of dead sons.'

'Father's parlaying brought you your lovely wife, Moira, who graces Wessex every day with her sunny disposition!' said Bear, and snorted with laughter.

'When she bears me a son, the smile will disappear from your face,' replied Hawk icily.

'Terror!' said Wolf suddenly. 'It's the only answer. It's served me well for forty years. It costs nothing and is never forgotten.' He looked towards the water's edge, where four men were struggling with the corpse of a huge Norlander. Eventually they managed to swing it up, and the body crashed onto the boat, sending it rocking and swaying.

Stub, his taciturn sergeant-at-arms, was wiping his hands and walking back up the beach.

'Is that the last of them?' Wolf called.

'Almost,' Stub replied.

A little way off, a bedraggled Norland boy with his hands tied was squatting on the sand surrounded by a circle of Wolf's fighters, who were drinking and throwing the occasional handful of sand at him.

Wolf pulled himself to his feet and lumbered over to the lad. 'Stand up,' he said softly, and gestured with his sword.

The boy had blue eyes and a dark shadow round his chin. One day he'd have the beard of a fighter, but for now it was as soft as the fur on a rabbit's belly. Wolf had sired sons like him, but they'd all turned to shit sooner or later.

He ran his finger along the lad's jaw. 'Ask who sent him,' he called to Brocc, a bow-legged sea captain, who as a boy had worked in East Anglia with Norland shipwrights and knew a little of their language.

Brocc spoke gently; the boy looked at the ground.

'If you don't tell me, you know what they'll do to you, don't you?' said Wolf.

Brocc spoke to him again, and the boy shrugged.

'They'll cut your bollocks off. We wouldn't want that, would we?'

When Brocc repeated his words, a tear ran down the boy's cheek and he mumbled a name.

'Erik Longshanks of the Farne Islands,' Brocc said.

'You've come a long way, lad. Will you send him a message for me?'

The boy nodded.

He looked so innocent, beautiful even. Wolf almost wanted to kiss him on the lips. But in a few years this same child would be slitting open Saxon men and raping Saxon women. He thrust his sword deep into the lad's stomach, and twisted and yanked it from side to side. The boy dropped like an anchor stone.

Stub pulled the sword from the body, wiped it on his shirt-sleeve and handed it back to Wolf, then picked up the corpse, carried it down to the boat and threw it in. No one cheered, but it didn't matter. Next time some bastard Norlander violated one of their daughters, they'd remember this moment.

Wolf turned to Brocc.

'Want one of their ships?' he said.

Brocc, who several years earlier had lost his own vessel to the Norlanders off Pewsey Sound, looked at the corpse-filled boat with respect. The Norlanders might have been the scum of the earth, but they made fine craft: sharp prows, low in the water, room for thirty oarsmen and a sail for extra speed. 'I'll take both if they're on offer, High Aethel. I thank you very much,' he laughed, his voice permanently hoarse from thirty years of calling into the wind.

'I'm not jesting, I mean what I say. I always do. But you'll need to go on a little jaunt for me first, in and out of the Farne Islands . . . like a ghost.'

'I've no crew,' Brocc replied. He looked like he hardly dared believe the high aethel's offer.

Red, who had been lying on the sand gazing at the Norland ships, clambered to his feet and piped up. 'I'll go!'

Wolf nodded; yes, the time was right.

Red hugged him. 'You are the finest father in the world,' he said.

If Red drowned, it would be hard telling the Shrew, but every father had to offer his son to the Fates at some time.

Swift was marshalling the villagers as they raked the beach and chased off the gulls with gobbets of flesh in their beaks. She had a face like a thunderstorm this morning. What was wrong with her? thought Wolf. Was she on her bloods? How many rulers' daughters had been given a kingdom as their plaything?

He could have taken the south coast for himself when Agnes died, but he didn't. He'd given Swift wardenship of it to do with as she liked, as long as she acknowledged it was still part of Wessex. He'd spoilt her, but she barely noticed. She always wanted more land, more power. If she understood the price she'd have to pay, the loneliness and despair, she'd hurry back to her weaving, but she wouldn't listen to him.

Hawk was loading donkey carts with loot from the boats: statues of martyrs, countless crosses, and the illuminated book of the Gospels, which Wolf had hugged like a baby when they'd found it. There'd be no galloping home; the carts would dictate the pace. Wolf was relieved. He'd drunk more than he should. A few bouts of vomiting had helped, but his guts still weren't as steady as he'd have liked. He shouted for his men to mount up, and threw Alderman Eadwig a gold piece. It was an overgenerous gesture, but he needed all the support he could get in these dangerous times, and it worked on Eadwig, who clutched Wolf's leg and told him he was Christ the Saviour returned.

They wended their way up the hill overlooking the village. At the top, they could see the two Norland boats heading out to sea, one towing the other, which was piled high with dead bodies.

He looked for Red but couldn't see the lad on either ship; his sight was blurred and they were too far away. Aethelfraed was gone, now Red was Osburgh's only child, and she doted on him like a three-legged puppy. He must become a man. He spent all his time with Winifred, a buxom young maid, an only child, who had inherited the land rights to the Isle of Wight. Were they to marry, the island would become Red's, and he'd need to shoulder that responsibility. A storm-tossed voyage would surely shake some sense into him.

The two ships were almost out of sight. Wolf had won a

great victory, or at least everyone thought he had. He waved his arms and shouted into the wind, 'This is my message to the heathens of the Farnes. As Samson smote the Philistines, I, Aethelwolf of Wessex, have smitten your brothers and sons. Now I return them to you. But if you fuckers ever come back again, ever, the temple roof will come crashing down on your fucking heads and every last one of you will be crushed to a bloody, fucking . . .' He wanted to say more, but the words seemed to slip from his grasp. He was exhausted; his mind was drifting, as it did so often these days. He should probably go home.

When Wolf arrived back in Winchester, the town erupted with excitement. A mighty crowd sang 'The Song of Brave Wessex', and branches of pine and yew were hoisted high above his head, as though he was Christ entering Jerusalem. He smiled so hard it made the back of his neck ache, but his mind was jangling like a tuneless harp. All he could think of was the dead Norlander boy.

He felt even giddier now, so drunk he could hardly see. But as he walked into his hall, he could just make out those who loved him best: his aldermen, his servants, his beautiful wife. They must be so proud of him. Frankia had Charlemagne, Mercia had Offa and his fucking dyke; now Wessex possessed its own hero, High Aethelwolf.

'Drink, everybody!' he roared, and collided with a table covered in small delicacies hastily prepared for the celebrations. The noise made him agitated again. 'With this fist I smashed them,' he roared, and sent a pile of platters flying.

'Stop now,' whispered his wife.

He pulled her to him and whispered in her ear. 'Agnes, I missed you so much.' He kissed her passionately, his tongue seeking out every delicious part of her soft, enticing mouth.

But when he opened his eyes, it wasn't Agnes. Jesus Christ! It was the other one, the Shrew.

He shoved her away in horror, his heart racing. He was more confused than ever. When they were riding home, he'd joked about a slave girl someone had brought, and he'd said she was sulky and smelt of sour milk and should be strangled and dumped in a ditch. And Agnes had got angry and said the girl was hers, only it wasn't Agnes, she was dead, it was their daughter, Swift, and he'd started blubbering. He was still a lion among men, he could throw a war axe seventy paces, but his mind was . . . What was the word?

He was stumbling now, grabbing at tapestries, ripping them off the wall. 'I tore the hair from their heads, I threw their bodies back into their own boats.' He picked up a chair, hurled it across the room, then yelped in pain because he'd strained his ribs when he'd brought his sword down, down and down again. All those dead men looking up at him from among the pebbles, and the boy, the innocent boy . . . He shut his eyes, but the child wouldn't stop staring at him. He dropped to his knees and shook his head. The boy was still there, as he had been all day. 'Leave me alone,' Wolf pleaded. 'Leave me alone I beg you.'

Bishop Humbert pulled him into an anteroom, breathing heavily from the exertion.

'Aethelwolf. My dear lord,' he said softly.

'Humbert, I have done . . . terrible things.' He thought his head would split asunder.

'You defeated a mighty Norland army, my lord,' the bishop was saying. 'And as has happened so many times, the price you have paid has been these terrible visions.'

'A boy died! I killed him.' He had wanted to show how ruthless he was, more heartless even than the Norland berserkers. But had he intended to kill the child? He didn't think so; he wasn't sure he even remembered doing it.

'You are Christ's instrument,' said Humbert.

He was, but it was a lonely burden. 'Those Norlanders were nothing,' he whispered into Humbert's ear. 'They were sick or mad or drunk. They weren't true Norlanders. They were shaking and some of them were crying.'

'Listen to me,' Humbert said, his breath still labouring. 'They were not infirm. They were not insane. No one wants to know that. You are a mighty king and you saved your people from slaughter. Anything else is a lie. You understand?'

Wolf groaned.

'You destroyed a mighty heathen enemy!' insisted Humbert. 'Everyone shall know this. I will write to his Holiness the Pope and tell him.'

The Pope, yes! He would understand. Wolf's mind was sick, stale and confused. He'd talk to the Pope and receive his forgiveness for all the dreadful things that haunted him. His father had done the same years ago. He'd disappeared, and returned a year later a mighty ruler once more.

He closed his eyes. The Norland boy's face melted away. In its place, the Holy Father stood in front of him, arms outstretched, dressed in pure white, wearing an expression of such deep sympathy that it brought tears to his eyes. He was kissing Wolf's cheek, whispering in his ear, 'Come to me! I will lift the despair from your mind, my son, I will give you the strength to be great again.'

Wolf looked up at the concerned faces surrounding him. 'I will go to Rome,' he said. 'I will make a pilgrimage. The Pope will help me.'

SIXTEEN

The Undercroft

By Asser's tenth day in the palazzo, he was growing restless. He called for Plegmond who cut his long straggly hair into a neat crown, and shaved the top of his head into a tonsure.

When the Doctore arrived, he was in his room, bending and stretching. 'Are you truly well?' Guido demanded.

'I am,' replied Asser. 'No bone was broken, the gashes in my leg have healed. I'm ready to work.'

'Then come with me.' The Doctore gestured towards the door.

He was a handsome man, slim and grey-haired – Christian, of course, but with a Moorish face and a hint of the Atlas Mountains about him in his high-collared tunic and baggy trousers. When Asser had first arrived at the Emmaus, the Doctore had calmed his mind with tales of Al-Haddin and Sinbad the Seafarer. He had loved his new master with a child-like adoration and now, after all his suffering, the pair were reunited.

Asser held up the hem of his cassock and danced a jig along the corridor. 'Like Lazarus, I've risen,' he said. He readjusted his attire and they walked up the hill towards St Peter's.

'Don't be too skittish,' said the Doctore. 'We are all in danger.'

'I've spent thirteen months being brutalised,' replied Asser. 'I am immune to the threats of our enemies.'

When Asser was seventeen, Master Spinoza, the dean in charge of training the boys and young men for holy office, had expelled him from the seminarium. 'You had the talent to become a senior churchman,' he'd said. 'You could have tended the souls of a thousand Christians. But arrogance and insubordination have made you intolerable.'

Asser didn't care. He'd go his own way and champion the poor and needy. The Doctore, however, was heartbroken by Asser's expulsion, and paid a friendly bishop to ordain him a priest, which meant he could obtain lowly employment at the Tribunal of Reconciliation, a run-down office of the Church situated in a litter-strewn alley in the leather-making quarter. It had been set up to appease those who'd complained about church corruption, but the air stank, he had no support from the papal office, and the leaky roof constantly dripped on the few miserable clergymen working alongside him, who like him had been passed over for high office.

Strangely, Asser enjoyed his job. It allowed him time to read, think and drink, all of which he did copiously, and he won occasional small victories on behalf of beleaguered villages and impoverished congregations. He quickly became good at what he was asked to do, and was eventually appointed senior advocate and given charge of the whole tribunal. But he hadn't lost his sense of outrage, and in the evenings, along with a few like-minded young priests from the Emmaus, he plotted to bring down the entire church hierarchy. Eventually two dozen of them decided it was time to express their outrage publicly. It had been foolish and untimely and had cost him imprisonment and torture, but now he was back stronger than ever, striding up the Vatica Hill whistling 'Jump the Tumbril'.

In the shadow of St Peter's was an old chapel that centuries previously had been part of the mighty basilica and was now an ecclesiastical dumping ground surrounded by broken masonry.

The Doctore entered, opened a small door on the right and disappeared down a curved flight of crumbling steps. At the bottom was a thick curtain so old and moth-eaten it was no longer possible to discern its pattern.

'From behind here, we will change the world,' he said. 'Ours will be the most radical papacy in two hundred years. Welcome to Balotelli's Undercroft.' He pulled the curtain aside dramatically. 'I have some business to attend to; I will come back for you later.' And he turned and climbed the steps again.

Asser was confronted by the smell of dirt and neglect. Shafts of light revealed a huge vault piled high with rotting wooden misericords, broken statues bearing the faces of long-forgotten saints, and the remnants of arches, pillars and stone windows. But amid this clutter a space had been cleared, and standing in it holding mops and brooms was a band of tonsured priests, their long, woollen cassocks tucked into their rope belts, exposing their hairy knees. They were his friends and comrades from that dreaded day in the market square, bright, energetic, earnest men whose lives were totally committed to the cardinal's vision. He seldom cried, but he did so now, and couldn't stop. He waved a hand as if to indicate that this foolishness would soon be over, and finally the tears abated. 'What are you idiots doing in this shithole?' he said.

There was a wave of laughter.

'This is the office of Balotelli's new advisers,' said Father

Kennet. 'Until we have access to some funds, he has rewarded us with this glorious pigsty. It's part of the old basilica, but has been long forgotten. What could be more discreet? We will work on Balotelli's plans far from prying eyes. Our opponents won't be apprised of what we're devising till each order has been countersigned by the Pope, by which time they'll be powerless to subvert it. Once this place is clean, it will serve us very well.'

'But you're the cardinal's men; you should be dripping with wealth,' said Asser.

'Enzo Gilotti's Notarii are making our lives as difficult as they can,' said Father Philip. 'They delay payment to us at every turn. Balotelli has quartered you and the Doctore in his palazzo, as befits your new rank, but we have rooms on the top floor of an ancient, crumbling barracks in the city.'

Asser took hold of a mop, Father Kennet opened a flask of mead, and they scrubbed, brushed, drank and talked about their youth, their running battles with the church authorities, services they'd disrupted because the priest had been a scoundrel, the theologian from Turin they'd invited to address them who'd been chased out of town by the Pope's guard . . .

Noon came and went, and the Doctore returned. 'You're exhausted,' he said, and Asser gratefully took his leave, weary but almost content.

On their way back to the palazzo, he and the Doctore stopped at St Peter's.

'It's been ten years since the Moors sailed up the Tiber and torched our great basilica,' the Doctore said. 'And still the Notarii refuse to bear the cost of its renovation. But Balotelli is determined it should become the heart of Christendom again.'

'You said we have no money.'

'He's sold the crown of the blessed St Helena.'

Asser roared with laughter. 'That old charlatan?' he said.

'The Emperor Constantine's mother? The one who alleged she'd rediscovered the pieces of Christ's cross?'

'The very same,' said the Doctore.

'The perfect use for her riches,' said Asser.

'I agree. But it's a challenging project, and the sale of the crown won't provide us with all we need. I pray we are able to finish it.'

Scaffolding had been erected all around the nave, and teams of masons were climbing around the balcony restoring the battered statues of the twelve disciples, who stared blankly down on the worshippers below – St Matthew the tax collector holding his abacus, St Andrew clutching his net full of fish, all of them with their various holy accoutrements.

Asser saw a flicker of movement directly above him and the shadowy figures of two men among the scaffolds. He caught the flash of a yellow tunic, and St Andrew rocking precariously on the edge of the balcony. Instinct possessed him. He threw himself at the Doctore, and as they skidded across the floor, there was an almighty crash that reverberated around the entire church.

The two of them lay in a tangled heap, surrounded by broken pieces of the saint and his fish.

'Are you hurt?' asked Asser.

The Doctore shook his head and got to his feet.

'Mother of Christ!' said Asser. 'Some fool of a builder failed to lash those saints securely! We must quiz every man working here and ensure such an accident never occurs again.'

But the Doctore was staring thoughtfully up at the scaffold, his brow furrowed in concern. 'It wasn't an accident,' he said after a moment.

'You mean . . . ?'

'The message is clear. The war we are fighting is not simply one of words. Our enemies intend to take our lives.'

*

Many hours later, back in his room, Asser sat at the table reading intelligence about the fresh waves of Norlanders settling on the Irish coast. There was a knock at the door, and without waiting for admission, Balotelli entered and placed a small flagon of sweet wine in front of him.

'Goblets?' he enquired.

Asser took a pair from an alcove above his table.

'I'm deeply sorry about today's incident,' Balotelli said. 'It must have been a great shock.'

'The Doctore was nearly killed,' replied Asser.

'I'm told it was the work of a vengeful verger who'd been overlooked for advancement,' said Balotelli.

'It wasn't. Everyone has been interrogated; no such verger exists.'

'For the moment, we'll say it was,' said Balotelli. 'It'll prevent unhelpful speculation.' He sat down in Asser's most comfortable chair and gave a small groan. 'Let me tease your brain a little,' he said. 'Our army of the righteous – where would we wish them to engage the Norlanders in battle?'

'As far from Rome as possible,' replied Asser.

'In Britain, perhaps?'

'But where in Britain?' Asser held out his goblet for replenishment. 'Not in the lands of the Picts or the Scots, they're too mountainous. Northumbria and East Anglia are already full of Norlanders, so Mercia perhaps?'

Balotelli poured himself more wine. 'Tell me about Wessex, about High Aethelwolf,' he said.

Asser considered.

'The day after his father died, he murdered his rivals. His kingdom is racked with internal strife, but he's held it together for thirty-five years.'

'Would he fight with us? Is he capable of being at the head of our holy army if we deployed it to Wessex?'

'Perhaps. If he survives. But Plegmond's documents say his mind is failing, and his children are a hapless bunch.'

'Even Aethelfraed?'

'Jesus wept, Cardinal, you know about Aethelfraed?'

Balotelli gave a small nod of acknowledgement. 'I know he's intelligent and devout, and when he was sixteen, his father banished him. We thought he'd been crushed to death by an avalanche, but it appears he's in Rome.'

Most of Asser's life had been drear, monotonous and sometimes painful. But occasionally he was presented with a potential opportunity so intriguing it was as though the sun had appeared from behind the clouds. 'Perhaps we should try to find him,' he said.

'Perhaps,' replied Balotelli, and took a long, thoughtful swig of his wine. 'Perhaps we should indeed.'

SEVENTEEN

A Beetle in the Tassels of a Rug

A few days later Asser and the cardinal leant over the rail of Hadrian's Bridge, watching the boats come and go. Next to them some skinny Libyan boys fished in the Tiber with pieces of bread on string. They pushed their way between the two clergymen and tried to drop their hooks onto a shoal of tiny fish below. Balotelli ruffled the hair of the smallest fisherman and gazed thoughtfully across the water. 'You're happy taking on the leadership of the Undercroft?' he asked.

'I suppose so,' replied Asser. 'We are constantly thwarted by our lack of money and the duplicitousness of the Notarii, and frankly we could do more were it not for the Pope's vacillation, but soup is being distributed at night, shelters for the homeless are being created in some parts of the city, and talks are taking place about the exact composition of the army of the righteous. Sometimes I want to scream with frustration from the roof of St Peter's, but . . .'

'We're moving in the right direction?'

'We are.'

The boys had caught a few little fish and put them in a chipped pot. Now they waved them in the men's faces, jumping up and down like puppies at feeding time. Balotelli delved in his pocket and gave them a coin.

'Father Philip has questioned all those who were working at St Peter's on the day the statue was dislodged,' said the cardinal.

'And . . . ?'

'Philip can be very persuasive. Sometimes too persuasive. But even so, no one will say anything, though they're being pressed hard.'

'I fear whoever was behind the attack will remain unpunished,' said Asser.

'Nonsense. We'll find them next week, next month, whenever,' said Balotelli.

'And then?'

The cardinal grimaced. 'We will squash them like maggots under a swill bucket. But until that moment arrives, we will conduct ourselves as we always do, quietly and efficiently.'

A boat was pulling towards the bank, an impressive sight: a barque painted black and gold, with liveried oarsmen, guards in white uniforms, and seven cardinals waiting demurely to disembark.

'The Notarii are here,' murmured Balotelli, 'about to attend their weekly meeting. Doubtless they'll attempt to shave a little more off my expenditure. What will they steal from me this time, I wonder? My money for tending the mad, my support for the infirm elderly? It's strange. I've known most of them my entire life, yet now . . .'

'Was it one of them, do you think, who ordered the attack on the Doctore?'

Balotelli shrugged.

'I used to yearn to be like them,' Asser said wistfully. 'All that power they hold in their manicured hands to change the world . . .'

'We have that power now,' replied the cardinal. 'The challenge is to keep hold of it.'

They reached the end of the bridge. The barque had moored. Enzo Gilotti, the primicerius, was the first to disembark.

'Stephen,' he exclaimed. 'What a pleasant surprise. We're about to enjoy a little luncheon.'

'Will you join us?' added Cardinal Zuppi, a small, round man with a kerchief continually at his nose. 'We'll be addressing church costs, a subject in which I know you are interested.'

'Sadly I can't,' replied Balotelli. 'I have to attend the lepers in Trastevere. Unless of course you'd like to take my place.'

Zuppi smiled politely. He and the other cardinals began climbing the hill towards their discreet place of dining.

One final figure emerged from the barque, a fussy man about thirty years of age, weighed down by piles of documents.

'Cardinal!' he said, and gave the slightest of bows.

'Ponti! My day is incomplete without the blessing of your presence . . . Asser, this is Father Vincente Ponti. He was a clerk in the Office of Christian Orthodoxy for some years, until Pope Benedict decided he was a little overenthusiastic with his interrogations.'

'That wasn't universally agreed,' interrupted Ponti testily.

'Perhaps, but the Pope thought it so and that's all that matters. He suggested you work in the church cleanliness department, I believe. A worthy calling, though a little unfragrant.'

'I have been summoned back,' replied Ponti. 'The Notarii have called me to become their undersecretary.'

'Their undersecretary!' exclaimed Balotelli. 'How grand.

Your Second Coming. I congratulate you. Now please excuse me. I have some fish to fry.' He nodded cursorily, then turned and walked away, admiring the contents of his little chipped pot.

Asser found himself alone with a man he knew only too well: the cold eyes, the bubbles of spittle he constantly wiped from the corners of his mouth.

'I recognise you, Father,' said Ponti. 'Remind me, did I visit you last year in the Holy Father's place of incarceration?'

Loathing coursed through Asser's veins. On some spurious excuse, Ponti had given Halfnose a few coins and had spent several hours experimenting with the torturer's equipment, pulling out Asser's toenails and beating the undersides of his feet. Asser had cried and begged for mercy while the man laughed. Now he stared into Ponti's unpleasant little white face and swore he would never cry like that again.

'How ever did you get out?' Ponti asked.

'With God's blessing, Undersecretary,' Asser said steadily.

'I hope your period of correction has taught you righteousness and humility. Father Asser, isn't it? I never forget a name.'

'I beg your leave,' replied Asser. 'I have Cardinal Balotelli's work to attend to.'

'Of course you do. But a word of advice. You're embarking on a new life. You must use it to the good. Don't become entangled in Balotelli's little schemes. It is impossible to satisfy the needs of the poor; Christ himself could only feed five thousand. And as for the cardinal's latest fancy of a righteous army to exterminate the Norlanders, it would require the wealth of Croesus. You are not a foolish man. You know in your heart that what I'm saying is true. People are beginning to grow angry; they are saying Balotelli's men only want a war because it would weaken the Church and they could assume the cardinalships. Sometimes such outrage can't be controlled; violence breaks out and innocents like you lose their lives. If you are ever concerned about your safety, please call on me.'

And with that, Ponti turned, and scuttled away into the crowd beyond the bridge like a beetle into the tassels of a rug.

EIGHTEEN

A Kingdom Divided

Swift entered her father's retiring room and pulled off her gloves. 'Time to wake, Father,' she called. 'A little pottage?'

Wolf was lying in his bed, his eyes shut tight, his lips cracked and parched. Osburgh, Bishop Humbert and Swift's brothers were gathered round him.

'What a caring daughter!' muttered Hawk. Swift ignored him.

Above Wolf's head, the wall was littered with antlers, like the stark trunks of a winter forest. 'Pottage would kill me,' he murmured.

Swift looked at him dispassionately. Her fury with her father hadn't left her, but now was not the time to reveal it.

'I'll clean your face,' she said. 'You smell like a tavern privy.'

Taking a hyssop-scented compress from the bed table, she wiped his cheeks and softened the crust on his eyelids. Slowly he opened his eyes. 'Water!' he croaked. She offered him a large jug from the bedside, which he grabbed eagerly, taking several noisy gulps.

'Good morrow, Father,' said Bear. He and his brother took Wolf's hands.

'Let go of me,' Wolf growled.

'We've been watching you all night,' said Hawk.

'Well you can fuck off now!'

Wolf heaved himself into a sitting position, shook his head vigorously and looked around the room. 'Right, Rome!' he said. He flung off his covers, rolled out of bed and stood barefoot on the floor, his arms outstretched, wearing only his shift.

'I'm coming too,' said Osburgh.

'Where?' replied Wolf.

'To Rome,' she said.

'No you're not. You're a woman. The road is long and ill-made. There will be brigands and cutpurses and nowhere for you to attend to your private needs. It would be . . . I forbid it.'

'I'm coming,' Osburgh repeated, and there was a steely determination in her tone.

Wolf muttered something unintelligible, then bawled, 'Dress me!' His slaves and servants came running. 'And you three,' he added, turning to his children. 'Unless you want to take a look up your father's hairy arse, get out.'

The three siblings walked down the little flight of stairs into the great hall.

'He didn't tell Humbert to leave,' said Hawk. 'That's unnerving.'

None of them trusted the bishop, though they all relied on him, thought Swift.

'They're doubtless cooking up plans for what will happen here once Father's gone,' said Swift. 'Bear, what are you doing?'

'I'm sitting down,' Bear replied.

'On Father's throne?'

'It's fortunate he's going to Rome,' said Bear, pushing himself up on its arms and swinging his legs back and forth. 'We're threatened with invasion on all sides. Once he's out of the way, I'll raise an army to defend our borders.'

'Your heroics can wait,' said Hawk, who'd taken out his hunting knife and was slicing an apple into pieces. 'Stop prancing around like Achilles. Before we fight any more battles, we need to pay back the money we spent during the last five years' fighting. We're on the brink of penury.'

'Cease your squabbling, both of you,' Swift said to her brothers. 'Far more important than your nonsense is who the Shrew will meet in Rome.'

'Meet?' repeated Bear, who was fiddling with one of the throne's loose armrests.

'Don't be obtuse,' said Swift. 'You know who I mean. Fraed! He's alive. He's been seen there.'

'He has,' said Hawk, 'and if the Shrew finds him and brings him home . . .'

'Does Father know where he is?' asked Bear.

'Father knows nothing. Fraed can't even be mentioned in his presence,' replied Swift. How sad it all was, she thought. Fraed had been such a bright boy. But it was not her concern.

'We can't let him come back!' said Bear indignantly.

'We can't,' agreed Hawk. He speared a piece of apple with his knife, popped it in his mouth and buried the point firmly into the tabletop. 'You'd be in particular trouble, Bear. Fraed will never forget your bullying.'

'*I'd* be in trouble? He'd put *you* in your place in an instant. He could dance rings round your book-learning even when he was a child and you were one and twenty.'

The hall doors swung open. Half a dozen slaves burst in carrying trestles and tabletops, and proceeded to set them up around the perimeter of the hall.

'For the love of Christ, stop that banging,' yelled Bear,

swinging himself off the throne. 'I can't hear myself think in here.'

'There's nothing in your head to hear,' muttered Hawk, and he too got up from his seat.

The pair left the hall still bickering. Swift watched them go. Would her father really leave Wessex in the hands of one of those two dolts? Such an idea was intolerable. She glanced at the table and saw her brother had left something behind. She picked up Hawk's knife and slipped it into the goatskin pouch hanging from her girdle.

She found her father in the garden with Bishop Humbert. He was conversing with the slaves, talking to them like children while they laughed dutifully at the puns and riddles he'd told them a hundred times before. She smiled. In truth, however repugnant his behaviour might be, she retained a modicum of affection for him, particularly when he was among the common folk. He must be removed from the throne of course, and she must take what was rightfully hers, but only when the time was right. Perhaps the rigours of his forthcoming journey would hasten that day. She felt both sadness and satisfaction at the idea.

'Take time on your pilgrimage, Father,' she said. 'You must stop on the way and visit the emperor at Aix-la-Chapelle, as I did on my journey around Europe. He and his family were kind to me. To build a strong union with him would be a fine achievement. But be courteous!'

'When am I not?'

'Often,' replied Swift.

'Don't distress yourself. I'll pour honeyed words in the emperor's ear. I know what I'm doing.'

A slave was harvesting rhubarb, hacking off the colossal leaves and trimming the stalks. He presented one to her. It looked like a huge fan, and she curtsied low as though he'd given her an exotic gift. He was a Westsaxon who'd lost his family, his house and his crops and had sold himself into slavery. She couldn't remember his name.

'So,' she said, turning back to her father, 'who's it going to be?'

'Who's what going to be?' Wolf replied.

'High Aethel, while you're away.'

Wolf shrugged.

They walked along the garden path for a while, father and daughter, and the bishop behind them, his presence marked only by the grumblings of his dyspepsia.

'Harold Godwin could act as your regent,' Humbert finally suggested.

'I think not!' scoffed Wolf. 'This is a family matter.'

'I should do it,' Swift said.

Wolf bent down and poked around in a vegetable patch.

'I won the battle for you,' she added. 'You know I did. I govern South Hamwicshire; our yields are high.'

'Do you want an onion?' Wolf said. 'I love an onion.'

'My people are happy.'

'Daughter, South Hamwicshire is the size of a pancake. Wessex is a monster. It requires a monster to rule it.'

'So it's Bear, is it?' Swift persisted.

'That lummox! He's a danger to us all. He has no idea when to fight and when to stay his hand,' replied Wolf. 'And he's an arsehole.'

Yes, he is, thought Swift. An arsehole who has shat away his advantage as your firstborn son.

'Hawk?'

Wolf laughed contemptuously. 'Want a bite?' he said.

So not Hawk either. Of course not. He was mean and small-minded and had less character than a pickled plum.

'Perhaps . . .' mused the bishop, 'perhaps the problem is a little more complex.'

Wolf nodded. 'It is. Whichever of my wretched sons I leave in charge, the other will try to kill him.'

'All must be in balance for your return,' said Humbert. 'That is the only thing that matters.'

In balance? What did he mean? thought Swift. She eyed the bishop suspiciously. What were his plans to keep Wessex stable while the old man was away? Would they involve her, or was her territory about to be swallowed up by one of her brothers? She prayed that Louis, her betrothed, would arrive from Frankia soon with the fighting men she needed.

'In balance!' said Wolf thoughtfully. 'Absolutely. Only till I get back, mind you.'

That evening, the division of spoils took place. Forty Saxon warriors strode into the great hall dressed in their finest cloaks, some trimmed with fur, others with woven Flemish collars.

A harpist sang 'The Victory at Hamblesea', which he'd written that morning and was almost identical to the song he'd written the previous year about the battle against the Irish pirates. Toasts were drunk in the fighters' honour, garlands were hung around their necks.

Bear approached Swift, swaying, his speech slurred from the drink. 'What schemes are running through your head, sister? Do you think that when Father returns and finally drinks himself to death, the aldermen will choose you to replace him?'

'I'm a woman,' replied Swift, sweetly. 'I have no such aspiration.'

Bear glowered at her and began to speak, but at that moment Harold Godwin tapped his staff on the ground. Wolf pulled himself to his feet and his guests formed a polite semicircle around him.

'While I'm away, Wessex must remain secure,' he announced.

Hawk, who'd been conferring with his henchmen, stepped forward. 'Yes, Father, and I have prepared some documents to—'

'Give them to Bishop Humbert,' interrupted Wolf, 'I'm sure they'll be helpful. I will be away for some time, meeting the crowned heads of Europe. I've pondered hard on the question of who should take my place until I return, haven't I, Humbert?' The bishop nodded sagely. 'Wessex is a mighty nation. It flourishes because I am strong and I know the meaning of . . .' He paused and gestured, as though trying to pluck the words out of his forehead.

'Good governance,' said Humbert helpfully.

'Good governance,' repeated Wolf. There was a smattering of applause. 'Westsaxon unity must endure. My father had a similar problem. He needed to lead his army into East Anglia but had fractious children who would inevitably try to seize his throne while he was gone. I think you understand what I'm saying. So he did what I am about to do.'

Humbert gestured to Stub, who pulled back a curtain at the far end of the hall, revealing a crude painting.

'This is a map of Wessex.' Wolf stared at it for some time. 'Explain its significance, would you, Humbert?'

'I will indeed, High Aethel,' said the bishop. 'Your father divided his kingdom into three parts and gave each child governance of one part. When he returned, he was able to judge their capabilities by the way they'd conducted themselves in his absence. You have decided to do the same. Bear will take responsibility for everything to the west of this line from the River Ox to the sea – in other words, our heartlands of Wessex, Dorset, the Summerlands, Wiltshire and Devon. Hawk will take Essex, Kent and Surrey; and Swift will continue to be Warden of South Hamwicshire and the Sussex Coast.'

'All this until I return, and only till I return,' added Wolf.

'And should there be any dispute between you, I have given Bishop Humbert the keys to my treasury, to be used to raise an army to enforce my will.' He looked at his children steadily. 'That's neat, isn't it?'

They made no reply, but stared fixedly at the map, their eyes narrow, their jaws taut.

PART TWO

NINETEEN

Filth

Wolf's royal barque, *Pegasus*, was a stately vessel that overawed the Saxons of Dover and Deal but pitched and rolled even in the calmest waters. By the time they were off the coast of Frankia, Wolf was desperate to get off.

He lay curled up like a baby with his head in Osburgh's lap. When she was young, she had been exquisitely beautiful. He'd rescued her from slaughter when he was fighting the Norlanders in the Summerlands, and she'd flung her arms round his neck, kissed his face a thousand times and told him he was the most handsome man she'd ever met. With so many bodies still unburied, it would not have been prudent to bed her straight away, so he'd taken her back to Winchester. For some reason he couldn't remember, he'd married her, and had been moderately happy till she'd turned sour. Why couldn't she have remained as amiable as she'd been when he first met her? He could have had a good life. But now everything was wrong and would never be righted. A terrible pain welled up inside him.

'I've shat myself,' he mumbled.

'I'll fetch you clean clothes,' she said.

At the Frankish port of Oostende, the gangplank was lowered. Two-score Saxon soldiers clattered past him in their fighting gear and animal headdresses, with their horses on a tight rein. Behind them processed a few courtiers and lady's maids, and Lady Osburgh wearing a small jewelled cap and a finely cut Saxon robe. She stopped beside him.

'Are you too unwell to make an appearance?' she asked. 'May I tell them you wish to rest a while?'

'No!' he replied fiercely. 'Go!'

She didn't move, so he pushed her in the back.

'Go!' he repeated, and she stumbled down the gangplank.

He waited for the crowd to settle before he followed her.

He was a little unsteady on his feet, but he knew he looked magnificent in his black tunic secured with iron studs, and black boots of fine Northampton leather. His cloak was made from the skin of a giant Pictish wolf, and on his head was his wolf headdress. He was a great king bursting out of the body of a wild animal.

The quayside was littered with barrels, carts and piles of old fishing nets, hastily pushed aside to make way for the Westsaxon royal party. Twenty or so local dignitaries and their lackeys dropped to their knees, and the town garrison and a handful of bystanders shouted *Hourra!*

Shakily Wolf mounted a white horse at the front of the column of imperial guards who were to accompany him on his long journey, first across Frankia to the emperor's palace, then south to Modena and finally to Rome, nigh on three hundred and fifty leagues in all. But though his temples were pounding and he felt bilious from hours of pitching and rolling, he was determined to complete the journey without mishap and in a dignified fashion.

*

For the next ten days the autumn sun stayed bright and clear, finches flocked in abundance, and Wolf felt in finer fettle than he had for many a month. He was free from the strife and strain of Wessex, from his children's conniving, even from his wife, who had been deep in conversation for days with the emperor's seneschal, a garrulous young man who dressed in green and looked like a gooseberry.

A few leagues from Aix, they encountered the mighty River Meuse. It flowed slowly and gracefully, its banks draped with willows, patrolled by speeding kingfishers more numerous than he'd ever seen. They travelled a little way south to reach the ferry crossing. All was as it should have been until they rounded a bend, and he was engulfed by the smell of smoked fish and latrines. Moored to the bank was a fleet of twenty longships, and behind them a host of torn tents, shanties and hundreds of grubby-looking folk washing clothes, carving wood, mending nets, grinding corn and performing all the usual activities of country life. It would have been a pleasing scene, but the cut of their tunics and the sly, hostile looks on their faces told him they were Norlanders, and his sense of bliss plummeted like a stone down a well.

'Filth!' he exclaimed. He hated everything about them, even the shape of their noses. He felt violently sick. They were an offence to God; it was his duty to wipe them from the face of the earth.

He glanced at his men, saw contempt on their faces too, and hate in their eyes. He nodded. They donned their helmets and brought their horses into line behind him. He rose in his saddle, raised an arm and heard the familiar susurration of forty swords being drawn from their scabbards.

Instantly the little green seneschal barked a command and the emperor's soldiers circled round in front of him.

'Such a course of action would not be wise, High Aethel,' said the man.

'Not wise? Massacring a plague of Norlanders? In what possible way would it not be wise?' retorted Wolf.

'They are under our protection. Do you not see?' The seneschal pointed to the hill beyond. The emperor's soldiers were patrolling along the top and his banner was flying.

'Why do you keep such wretches here?' said Wolf. 'Is this some camp where you pen them before their slaughter?'

'I would it were,' replied the seneschal. 'But no, there are a thousand times this number of Norlanders milling across the border who would dearly love to burn Aix to the ground. They don't do so because villages like this exist and the inhabitants won't let them pass.'

'Why not? They're all related, aren't they?'

'Because we pay them.'

The words sent Wolf into a paroxysm of outrage. 'Pay them?'

'What else would you have us do?'

'Raise a mighty army and drive them out,' said Wolf, his hands trembling with rage.

'Wise words,' agreed the seneschal. 'That is what we must do. But we cannot do it on our own, you understand? We need help. We need allies. We need you!'

Wolf feared that the dreadful episode at the Norland camp would plunge him into an intense gloom, but once they'd crossed the river and were back among honest Christian Franks, he heard a little church bell ringing in the distance, then another. Gradually more bells joined in, a concatenation of tones and rhythms. 'Very melodious!' he said, and his pleasure redoubled as quaint villages came into view and happy Frankish peasants ran out of their freshly garlanded huts waving and chanting his name.

'What wonderful people!' said Wolf. 'Am I so well known in these parts?'

'Of course,' said the seneschal. 'You are a great among men. The whole empire knows of your victory at Hamblesea.'

'Bless you!' Wolf called out to the villagers. 'And bless your sweet children.' He knew their cheers were paid for; he wasn't stupid. But what did it matter? Ahead of him was the largest, most wondrous building he'd ever set eyes on, a giant palace, bigger, finer and far cleaner than the great cathedral back home in Canterbury, with its doors open wide in welcome. Flowers were thrown, trumpets were playing. This would be a night to remember.

TWENTY

The Wide-Eyed Girl

The market at the bottom of Vatica Hill was the finest in Rome. Other markets had an air of desperation about them, but here the customers were wealthy, the products fresh and the stallholders courteous.

Asser approached a stall to purchase one of its excellent moist ginger cakes for his friends at the Undercroft, or perhaps two. He leant over an array of strawberry funnel buns in order to examine the luscious cakes, but as he did so, he felt something brushing his hip, and on putting his hand to his purse, he discovered his money had gone. He spun round and shouted out, but there was no one in front of him other than a wide-eyed girl wearing a look of youthful seriousness.

'Have you been robbed, Father?' she enquired.

'I believe I have,' replied Asser.

'There were two young men behind you only a moment ago. I recognised one of them. He's from North Afrique, and I believe his name is Abrahen. The other was small, with a twisted leg. They went towards Hadrian's Bridge.'

'I thank you for your help,' said Asser, and ran hastily in the direction in which she was pointing. He scoured the little streets and alleys, but to no avail. Eventually he returned to the market and sat down on a step close to the cake stall, hoping the thieves would return.

He was annoyed by his negligence but knew he shouldn't be too distressed. He was well fed, with good friends, and his work was challenging. He had a certain authority, and his fellow priests seemed happy to defer to him. He would rather have been lying on the grass watching the gulls or riding one of the cardinal's horses in the hills, but his new responsibilities gave him great satisfaction. Most importantly, he'd written a document for the Pope on the subject of why Wessex was the most suitable location from which the army of the righteous should attack. It was concise, well argued, the most finely crafted document he'd written for years, and word had come back that it was to papal liking.

'Good morrow, Father!'

'Are you going to buy us a drink, Father?'

Rollo and Mountjoy were standing in front of him, twin brothers as alike as podded peas.

They had been brought before Asser's tribunal many years previously for selling nails from the cross of Jesus by the bucket-load. But they were so charming and their misdemeanour so absurd that he'd been won over by them and had ordered them to pay for the care of orphaned children rather than sentencing them to be hanged, which was the usual punishment for the crime of simony. They were fascinating men, travellers who'd been tradesmen, builders, mercenaries and gamblers, and for some time the three of them had often caroused together, but he'd not seen them for some years till he'd bumped into them a few days previously in the Grand Bazaar and they'd renewed their friendship.

'You'll have to treat *me* to a drink, I'm afraid. I've been robbed,' Asser said. 'Have you seen a rascally Moor named Abrahen and his companion with a twisted leg?'

'I don't know such men,' replied Rollo, 'but by your description they shouldn't be difficult to find. How old are they, would you say?'

'I didn't see them myself,' replied Asser. 'A young woman described them to me.'

His friends looked at each other quizzically.

'What young woman would that have been?' asked Mountjoy.

'She had a comely face, a dimple on her left cheek, I think. She was well-spoken and her accent was familiar. She may be Westsaxon.'

The twins guffawed and ruffled Asser's hair.

'You've been gulled, Father,' said Rollo. 'You've been worked a treat.'

'What do you mean?'

'Stay here,' said Mountjoy. 'Don't go away.'

They hurried off, returning a few minutes later with the young woman tucked under Rollo's arm like a carpet.

'Behold your thief,' he said, and sat her down firmly on the step. 'Give the man his money back, Elswith,' he demanded.

'I haven't got it,' said the girl.

'Give it back or I'll tip you upside down and shake it out of you,' said Mountjoy.

The girl sighed. 'Turn your heads away,' she said.

The three men did so, Rollo still gripping one of her arms firmly. When they looked back, she'd retrieved the coins from wherever she'd hidden them and put them on the table.

'You're nothing but a common pick-a-pocket,' said Asser, outraged that her feigned innocence disguised such cunning.

'I'm a young girl brought low by circumstance. I have no

money to feed myself, and I'm faint from hunger. Will you not exercise your priestly charity and give me some bread and dripping?'

'Stop your cadging, Elswith, you wicked child,' said Rollo, but despite the reprimand, he took one of Asser's coins and went off to buy them victuals.

'You speak so finely,' said Asser. 'I cannot believe you were born into poverty.'

'I was not,' she replied. 'I'm of good Yeovil stock and my mother and aunts taught me well. I wished to pursue my studies in a house of God, and after my father died, my mother's new husband, a sea captain, brought me to Rome so I could join one of the fine nunneries here. But I overheard him bragging to his crew that he was going to sell me to a Damascan slave trader for five silver pieces, so I ran away and was left penniless and alone.'

As the girl spoke, a bitter vision roiled round Asser's mind, and a gaping fear and sense of loss engulfed him. It was the memory of his sister, Anna, the one person he'd truly loved, being dragged away from him after the murder of their parents. He wondered for the ten thousandth time if she was still alive. Would she have a story like this to tell? Wouldn't he want someone to help her if she did?

'Do you still wish to become a nun?' he said.

In the early days, it had been hard for a young woman to be taken seriously among the group of bumptious, over-energised men who followed Balotelli, but Sister Clothilde, though quiet and thoughtful, had a mind as sharp as Toledo steel. She only spoke when it was necessary, but under the tutelage of her sympathetic parents, she had learnt to paint, compose music and argue gently but persuasively on the subject of the place of women in Christ's church.

She was one of Balotelli's favourites, and on becoming chief papal adviser he'd given her charge of St Catherine's Abbey, the finest in Rome, where nuns had practised scribing and copying for centuries. The new abbess was barely two years older than Asser, and the Notarii were shocked by her appointment. But although conversations between priests and nuns were actively discouraged, Asser considered her a friend. Christ himself had treated women with respect and affection, so why shouldn't he?

When Asser and Elswith arrived at St Catherine's, Clothilde greeted him warmly and took them to a large room where twenty or so black-veiled sisters were working at tables copying and drawing. Asser explained that his new charge wished to take holy orders and began to recount her story. But Elswith stopped him and insisted on telling the tale herself.

When it came to an end, she asked if she might examine the nuns' work, and wandered off to the tables, while Clothilde talked at length about her plans for the abbey's future.

'I would welcome more nuns,' she said. 'The cardinal gives us the challenging task of copying his work and promulgating his vision, but we are hard pressed to do as he requires.'

They were called to a table by one of the sisters, who was trying to hide her amusement. Elswith was sitting with a pen in one hand, another between her teeth and a look of deep concentration on her face.

'Show me,' said Clothilde.

Elswith held up her drawing. It was a portrait of the abbess, her well-proportioned oval face sad and dignified, but with a hint of kindness in her eyes.

Clothilde took it from her, laughing. 'I will not be beguiled by this image,' she said. 'You make me look as woebegone as the women at the foot of Christ's cross. But you show great artistry. God has given you a rare talent. You may stay awhile, and if you're so suited, perhaps you will become a novice.'

'I thank you for your generosity,' said Elswith.

'But if you steal from my purse,' added the abbess, 'I will brick you up in the abbey wall and we'll feed you through a hatch for the rest of your life.'

TWENTY-ONE

Guthrum in Hell

At first Guthrum thought he was dead, along with the rest of his comrades. There was only the faintest glimmer of light, but he could make out Martin Hennig above him, and Arne the Joker's nose was pressing into his cheek. Other bodies crowded in on him too. They smelt like Norlanders – the tar, the sweat, the ambergris – and their clothes were ripped and torn, revealing taut, muscular bodies. He had no doubt they were his companions, even though their faces were slashed and twisted and their jaws akilter. He manoeuvred his hand just enough to touch the body next to him. Arne's cheeks were cold and his eyes wide open. He felt his own face. It was warm, and when he put his hand to his mouth, he could feel his breath. He was not dead; the gods had decreed otherwise.

Why should this be? Why should he still be breathing when all his comrades had left him? Had the shades of death swept him up in the aftermath of battle and brought him here, unaware he was still mortal?

Guthrum tried to recall what had taken place in those

moments before he woke in this death heap. He and his crew had been overcome by madness. A snake girl had attacked him. He had flown through the air, and darkness had rushed to meet him. Nothing more.

He was hungry. There was a slab of dried venison in the pocket of his undershirt, but the press of the dead made it almost impossible to move, and when he forced his left hand inside his shirt to grasp the meat, it throbbed with an agonising intensity. He gently lifted it out again, the pain growing more fierce as every moment passed. Why did it hurt so much? He felt it with the other hand.

Frig of the High Mountain, where were his fingers?

All that remained were stumps like moist and broken mushrooms. Who had done this? He forced himself to breathe slowly. Every Norland fighter had at some time been struck down by a terrible injury and had persevered regardless of the pain. He would weep for his hand another time. Now he must clean and bandage it, but that meant finding water.

He tried to move the bodies of his comrades off him, but they were as heavy as sacks of grain. Every time he pushed a corpse out of the way, it rolled back on top of him and made his task even more difficult.

He was dripping sweat, and the enclosed space in which he was trapped was bucking and creaking. It was a boat! He was sailing across the River of Death. He must find the Valkyrie rowers, gain their attention and beg to be set free. He eased the last few bodies away and struggled to the surface.

He felt a breeze on his face. He could see the immortal warriors sitting on planks between the dead, pulling their oars. He drew breath to call out to them, but they were not Valkyries; they were men, mortal men, speaking in syrupy Saxon tones. He ducked down again among the bodies of his friends, and the enormity of what he had seen engulfed him. He shook his damaged hand furiously to drive the pain away, then broke out once more from between the corpses and looked about him, his gaze landing on the carving of a crane on the prow. *The Flying Crane* – this was his ship!

Where were these bastard Saxons taking her? And how were they able to row so fast? She must surely be attached to the tow rope of another vessel; the bodies were far too heavy for the rowers to pull them so far unassisted.

His hand felt as though he'd cast it into a furnace. He knew where to find water; two skinfuls were stored in the aft hatches. He crawled carefully across the bodies, then burrowed downwards till he came to a hatch door. He swallowed half the contents of the water skin in one long gulp and poured the rest on his broken hand. Now his thirst had been sated, he could assess his situation more clearly. His companions had been slaughtered, his hand had been damaged beyond repair. He alone had been saved. He had been chosen. He felt strangely elated.

He thought of his mother and wondered whether she was still alive; he thought of his dog, Scout, and of what a fool he'd been not to ask Arne's sister Greta to keep his bed warm while he was off raiding. But most of all he thought of that last dreadful day, and a memory that even now returned to him – waves of Saxons riding out of the forest with their swords held high, chanting 'Wolf! Wolf! Wolf!' He would not forget that name.

Time passed. The sun rose and fell, the moon waned, the venison was now only a faint memory. The corpses grew soft, pliable, and began to stink. He could bear the pungent odour no longer. He waited till it was dark and he was sure the Saxons were asleep, then eased his way to the surface. His eyes closed, his head still, he breathed the fresh air for a while.

*

For days he lay concealed among the rotting corpses of his men, escaping only at night. One day, in the faint glimmer of morning, he sensed from the cry of the birds, the tang of the seaweed and the call of the young seals that he was approaching the Farnes. Soon the never-ending chatter of nesting terns told him they were close by New Moen Island, half a day short of his home. He waited, scarcely noticing the stench of the bodies as he counted down the time.

Eventually the boat pulled into a bay and the rowers began heaving out decaying bodies. He lay motionless, barely breathing. Would they discover him and torture him to death barely a league from his own hut? He could not believe that was his destiny. He was his people's messenger. Odin had chosen him for a great task.

There was the sound of hammering and sawing. Men were calling for rope, slippery bodies were toppling and being pushed upright again, there were gales of crude laughter. Shortly before dawn, the strength of the breeze and the motion of the waves beneath him told Guthrum they had set off again. But all was strangely quiet, and he risked heaving himself up. He was alone. The rowers had rejoined the lead boat; *The Flying Crane* was crewless and they were being towed along.

He lay back down. They'd soon be passing the outer islands. *The Flying Crane* lurched violently and swung round a little. The ever-fainter *dip dip* of oars told him the tow boat had set her free and was disappearing. He felt the pull of the current, and could hear land birds, larks and pipits. He was drifting towards Lind, the largest of the islands and his home. For days he'd been waiting to escape this stinking mass of bodies, but now he felt weak with exhaustion.

Eventually he forced himself onto his side so he could look out from under the death heap. His settlement was coming into view, the brightly coloured poles dotted between the huts bearing the faces of Thor and Odin. Above him, like a giant whale-shark stripped of its blubber, were the ruins of Lindisfarne Abbey.

The Flying Crane drifted into the shallows. The villagers stepped out of their huts and watched impassively as it ground to a halt piled high with their fathers and sons, naked and dead.

The sight of his fellow islanders gave Guthrum the strength he needed. He forced his way out of the pile one final time. But as he clambered to his feet, he saw around him a terrible sight: corpses holding out their hands in greeting, others dangling from the yardarm, three nailed to upside-down crosses, several engaged in acts of unspeakable wickedness. It had not been sufficient for the Saxons to kill his people; they'd humiliated them even in death.

He staggered to the top of the heap, dazed and covered in dried blood. Some of the islanders pointed and cried out, others watched in silent horror as he appeared, a tortured soul returning from hell. But Guthrum was calm, his mind focused on the mission ahead. The task the gods had given him was clear. He would take their lands and wipe the Westsaxons from the face of the earth.

TWENTY-TWO

The Grand Bazaar

Asser lay under a rough-hewn tavern table, staring at the grease and congealed food that had oozed between its planks. The matins bell was tolling; he should have been at the Undercroft hours ago. He'd spent the evening with Rollo and Mountjoy. It was a long time since he'd drunk so much. He clambered to his feet and begged a mug of water from the tavernkeeper's wife. He was shaking, and his head was throbbing. He needed to talk to Abdulalah the Alchemist. He walked wearily to the Grand Bazaar, as sick as a slaughterhouse donkey.

Half a millennium previously, the bazaar had been the Emperor Diocletian's pleasure garden, a vast construction of imperial hubris that had required the demolition of several hundred shops and dwellings. But the elegant gardens and lakes in which Diocletian and his mistresses had romped had long since been filled in, and now rows of tents jostled with shacks and tumbledown shelters for the visitors' attention, half-demolished towers, shrines and grottos transformed into food stalls, dog-fighting rings and fortune-telling booths. All the detritus of Rome was for sale here: worn carpets from Ephesus, one-eyed dogs from the Bulgar mountains, runaway slaves from Afrique, stuffed ostriches, Egyptian corpse powder and the severed remains of the world's most exotic creatures.

He approached a familiar wooden shack covered in magic symbols. A coloured pole, red, blue and white, protruded from above the door, and around it were the neatly painted words *ABDULALAH'S HOUSE OF ILLUSION.*

'Are you low, Cuckoo?' its owner asked solicitously as Asser staggered unsteadily in. 'Have you torn the nails from your hands and clambered down off the cross?'

'I can't speak,' mumbled Asser. 'I need . . .'

'A medicinal miracle? Of course you do.'

Abdulalah was perhaps fifty years old, but it was hard to tell. His hair straggled down to his knees and he sported a beard almost equally long, waxed and twisted like that of a Chinese khan. His silk gown was tattered and torn, and his dirty hands clenched and unclenched when he talked, as though he was trying to capture the air, bottle it and sell it. He led Asser to a room, windowless, filled with strong-smelling pots of powder and potions, lit only by a few greasy candles casting feeble multicoloured shadows through a row of tall glass jars full of gaudy liquids.

'Father Asser! Father Asser!'

Asser heard his name being called from one of the adjacent alleys. Was it Father Plegmond, the earnest young man with hair like a hedgehog, who had adopted the role of his assistant recently, albeit an unofficial and irritating one? Asser certainly didn't want to talk to him now.

The old man used a pair of tweezers to pick a length of dried orange root from a metal vessel, and tapped it with a little hammer till it crumbled to dust. On the table was a pot of dried flowers. He took one out, cut off a piece of its hollow stem the length of his hand and inserted one end into Asser's nose. The young priest inhaled vigorously. The dust hit his throat like a shower of needles.

'Good?' enquired Abdulalah.

Good? It was as though he'd been baptised in a river of ice. 'Perfect,' he replied. 'Perfect as a mother's love for her newborn child. Perfect as the first spring day after a bleak midwinter. Perfect—'

Father Plegmond burst into the room. 'Father Asser!' he exclaimed. 'Thank our sweet Saviour I found you. I've been searching since dawn. Eventually I woke Father Kennet and he suggested I try here.'

'I've been busy,' said Asser.

'His Holiness has summoned you to the palace.'

'Who?' retorted Asser, unsure whether he'd heard correctly or if his mind had become deluded by Abdulalah's elixir.

'Pope Benedict! You must come immediately.'

'Bugger me with the staff of St James,' exclaimed Asser. The Pope was asking for him? Was it because of his paper on the Norlanders? Shit, he hadn't done something horribly wrong in the night of which he had no memory, had he?

'Shall I wrap the rest for you?' enquired Abdulalah.

Asser tilted his head from side to side as though considering the pros and contras of the proposition. 'Please do,' he replied, and drummed on the marble worktop with his fingers. 'But one more small inhalation before I go, if you please.'

As he strode out of the bazaar, Plegmond, struggling to keep pace with him, was trying to offer him advice about what he might say to the Pope. Asser was flying like Icarus. The medicine was as efficacious as always.

'Have you found Aethelfraed yet?' he demanded.

Plegmond shook his head. 'It could take months. Two

Westsaxon intelligencers claim to have seen him. It was in a letter from Bishop Humbert of Winchester to the Holy Father's office. I've written back requesting more information.'

'Wouldn't it be quicker to look for him?' said Asser tartly.

'Of course, Father,' said Plegmond. 'But we don't know what he looks like, and I suspect he's in hiding.'

'Try the Saxon quarter.'

'We have,' replied an increasingly breathless Plegmond, 'but to no avail. I'm sorry. I'm doing my best.'

Asser entered the Pope's palace. He was led through countless marble-clad rooms, all unoccupied save for one or two in which high-ranking churchmen were wagging their fingers at each other while furiously debating affairs of state.

Eventually they came to the Pope's attiring room. Seamsters were cutting and sewing fine church apparel, others were steaming mitred caps and brushing tiny specks of dust from sashes and stoles. Balotelli stood waiting for him. 'Christ's resurrection!' he exclaimed. 'You stink of liquor and you've vomited down your cassock. Change it immediately.'

Asser splashed his hands and face in a proffered bowl of water, slipped on a clean habit and followed the cardinal into the Pope's receiving room.

At one end was a golden throne, and in it sat a tiny man – or perhaps the throne was very large and the man merely appeared to be small. No, he was little. And old! A little old pope! Asser smiled. He was feeling much more confident than might have been expected when confronted by the holiest man in the world.

Balotelli knelt respectfully on a step in front of the great, tiny man, and Asser did likewise.

'Father Asser!' said Pope Benedict. His voice was as high-pitched as that of a precocious child. 'We have read your document and find your proposal compelling. The notion that our righteous army should be deployed in Wessex has become extremely pertinent. We have learnt that High Aethelwolf of Wessex is to visit us on pilgrimage. He is even now passing through the Holy Roman Empire en route to Rome and will stay for a while in Modena before completing his journey. The emperor wishes for closer military ties with him. This would be in our interest too, but as you know, we have a far more ambitious proposal and wish to be party to any discussions they may have.'

Asser glanced round the room. He had never seen such a proliferation of gold. Benedict of Padua had been Balotelli's inspiration, a difficult man but with an original and radical mind. He'd spent twenty years in Europe's dungeons for accusing the cardinals of theft and pimpery, and from his prison cell had written tracts that were smuggled out and into the hearts of priests and monks throughout Christendom. He was highly courageous. Asser had said anything Halfnose wanted him to as soon as the irons were pulled from his fire, but stubborn Benedict never recanted.

'If we are to build this righteous army, it must carry Christ at its heart, it must work miracles, it must feed the poor and house the homeless,' the Pope continued. 'You will join the negotiations on our behalf and persuade the high aethel to sign a concord so profound it will transform Wessex and become a shining example for the rest of Christendom.'

'I will, your Holiness,' Asser said, barely able to comprehend the magnitude of what he was being asked to do.

'If you are unable to make a satisfactory agreement, we will not support the creation of this army and it will never see the light of day. So you must keep your mission secret till we can announce its successful conclusion in Rome in front of the crowned heads of Europe.'

'I understand,' said Asser. Was it the powder that was making him feel so confident?

'You will need a mark of my authority, so I am appointing you my legate to Wessex. Give me your hand.'

Pope Benedict produced a large golden ring bearing his seal and slipped it on Asser's finger. He could scarcely believe what was happening to him. A few weeks previously he had been lying in his own shit in the old Pope's dungeon; now the new Pope was putting the future of Christendom in his hands.

He wanted to dance round the papal chamber like a sailor returning to his lover. Instead he kept his eyes down, his face respectful, and moments later he was back in the attiring room with an amused Balotelli standing over him.

'I would my mother had been here,' said Asser wistfully. She had ardently believed he'd make a mark on the world, even though they hadn't had a pot to put a pickle in.

'We all do at such moments,' said Balotelli. 'But mothers seldom live long enough to see their sons achieve high office.'

High office, thought Asser. He was entering the world of kings and princes. 'This is why you set me free, isn't it?' he said. 'You wanted Wessex to be our bulwark against the Norlanders from the start, and you needed a Wessex man to make that happen.'

'It appears you are adept at negotiating, at offering few concessions while gaining many, at making your opponent feel like your best friend even while you're picking his purse. Word has reached me of your talents from several quarters.'

'You have fifty churchmen at your disposal far more experienced at such negotiations than I.'

'I do,' replied Balotelli, 'but they are not you. They do not share our vision. You will keep your mission secret, they would not.'

Asser stared at the ring on his finger.

'It's heavy,' he said.

'You will learn to bear the weight,' said the cardinal. 'We all will.'

TWENTY-THREE

Toledo Steel

The emperor's dining chamber in Aix was four times the size of Winchester Great Hall, and as tall as twenty men standing on each other's shoulders, with two dozen arched windows high up in the walls flooding it with light. Its floor was covered in Baghdad carpets and it was plastered from top to toe with rose-coloured swirls, soft and delicate as though sculpted by angels. And as for the food! Trays of pies in the shape of mountain ranges, sweetmeats tumbling like waterfalls, an edible castle made from the flesh of countless birds and animals with a moat filled with fine red wine.

Charles the Bald was sitting on his throne at the head of his table of honoured guests but was paying them virtually no attention. He was truly hairless, as bald as a baby's arse. He looked like a grasshopper, with a long, thin body, bulging eyes and a small, round head.

When Wolf had first arrived, the emperor had treated him like a long-lost brother, putting his arm round his shoulders, kissing his cheeks, telling his courtiers about the Battle of

Hamblesea and how courageous Wolf had been. 'You are the kind of man I wish to see riding by my side into battle,' he said. 'Next year I will draw together twenty kings like you, we will cut a swathe through the Norlanders and you will be—' But the emperor had been interrupted by a messenger whispering in his ear, and Charles had stamped out of the room, returning a few moments later with a pile of documents. 'Work! Work! Work!' he'd growled, and there'd been no further conversation. Charles sat engrossed in his papers, signing them or tearing them to shreds, and shouting orders to harassed messengers. Rulers were supposed to enjoy feasts and bask in the pleasures of the flesh – God's reward for shouldering the weight of kingship. But Charles worked like a nest of ants that had been hit by a stick. Little wonder he was so thin and bald; he was in a permanent state of furious agitation.

'You are such a hero, High Aethel,' exclaimed a woman with a tower of rose-coloured hair decorated with silk lilies.

Despite the emperor's inattention, Wolf was enjoying himself. Osburgh had retired, of course, but the remaining ladies laughed at his jests in the sweetest fashion.

'You have a fine sword, but such a b-brave champion deserves the very b-best,' said the emperor's eldest son, Louis the Stammerer. He was about five and thirty years of age and was a military officer. His impediment was both charming and strangely sophisticated.

'Kentish iron has served me well,' said Wolf. 'It's good and strong, though it does tend to shatter.'

'P-perhaps you should try our new Spanish blades. T-Toledo steel. They're very light and flexible.'

'I'd like to see one.'

'B-better than that, I'll give you one. It would be my p-pleasure,' said Louis.

'You deserve the finest equipment,' added Seneschal François. 'It would be our honour to help you obtain it.'

Were they trying to sell him arms or donate them to him? Wolf wasn't sure. His mind had become distracted by a small hand that had appeared from under the tablecloth and was moving here and there as though searching for food. It found an orange, seized it and disappeared. A second hand snatched an apple, a third an entire bowl of raspberry curds.

'Go to bed,' growled Charles, somehow aware of the thievery despite not looking up from his documents. Four handsome young children appeared from under the table and clambered over him, pushing aside his parchments, stroking his shiny head and kissing his face. 'Go now! I'm eating!' insisted Charles. But they took no notice.

'Children! To your rooms!' A girl about twelve years of age was standing in the doorway. They ran to her. 'Kiss me good-night. Hurry, I'll be up soon,' she said firmly. They disappeared, and she crossed to Wolf's table. 'I apologise, High Aethelwolf,' she said. 'My younger brothers can be a little troublesome. You are welcome to our house. We will make your stay as pleasant as we can.'

Wolf had never heard a child speak like this before. 'Prettily put, young lady,' he said. 'This is your daughter, Charles?'

The emperor nodded.

'She is a credit to you,' said Wolf.

'Sometimes,' replied Charles.

There was a roll of drums, and the girl clapped her hands in pleasure. 'Our troupe has arranged a show for you, High Aethel,' she cried.

'Call me Uncle Wolf!'

'Certainly, Uncle Wolf,' replied the girl, 'and I am Judith.'

The drumming reached a frenzied climax, and two fur-covered monsters burst into the room. They chased each other round the tables, leapt onto the stage, and performed a lewd dance. Four monkeys followed, carrying a large, sparkling black cloth, which they held in front of the cavorting creatures. There was a flash of green light and the cloth dropped to the floor. The monsters had miraculously metamorphosed into gigantic, bulbous whores with bright red lips, huge blue eyes and pendulous breasts swinging wildly from side to side.

Wolf turned to Judith. 'Should you be watching this, my dear?' he said.

'Should *you*, Uncle Wolf?' she replied, and held his gaze for longer than was necessary.

What a strange girl she is, thought Wolf. Very disconcerting.

The following morning, Wolf stood eating honeyed hazels in a room set aside for the emperor's family. Outside he could see messengers coming and going on immaculately plumed and groomed horses, and squads of brightly uniformed soldiers marching in squares, observed by courtly ladies who waved at the officers and blew them kisses. The emperor strode up to a guard and punched him, though it was not clear why.

Osburgh was eating jellied raspberries, and the emperor's children were rolling around on the floor, egged on by their much older brother, Louis the Stammerer, who was gentle and courteous and seemed entirely unafraid of his violent father.

'You and Charles are k-kindred spirits. You should work together,' Louis said.

'We should,' replied Wolf, although he had no idea what the prince meant. Some kind of treaty, perhaps? He wouldn't be happy with that. He had no desire to be dragged round Europe in the emperor's wake. 'Come here, little Lothair,' he growled, picking up one of the children and sitting him on his lap.

The woman with the rose-coloured hair laughed. 'What a fine father you must have been,' she cried.

'So powerful, yet so gentle with the children,' agreed another woman, older but still quite comely.

Wolf laughed merrily. He knew they were trying to make him feel part of the family. That was fine; he was happy to bask in their admiration as long as they didn't try to dupe him. The temptress Flattery never arrived without an agenda.

Lothair was grizzling. Louis lifted him off Wolf's lap and sat him back on the floor. 'You're s-so like Charles,' he said. 'I'm b-beginning to think I have a new father.'

'I certainly have a new uncle,' added Judith, clapping her hands.

Sadness engulfed Wolf. Charles's children were so full of sweetness, while his own were bitter as gall.

'You are such a f-fine man,' said Louis. 'You'll join us for the campaign next summer, won't you?'

Wolf's face grew serious. 'We are an island people,' he replied. 'We don't feel the need for anyone else.'

'Talk to my father,' Louis continued, as though Wolf hadn't spoken. 'I'm off to B-Burgundy to do battle, but he will join you on your travels. He is keen to see the new P-Pope. It will be jolly. Judith and my little brothers will come p-part of the way in order to visit their mother in P-Pisa.'

Wolf's heart sank when he thought of the long ride ahead. He'd felt so confident about the journey at the start, but there was another three hundred leagues to go and already he was weary to the bone. Could he ride much further without gloom and confusion descending?

He thought of the Frankish villagers cheering his name, and what a hero he was to them. What were a few more miles of highway? He was High Aethelwolf of Wessex, slayer of a thousand Norlanders. He could do anything he set his mind to.

TWENTY-FOUR

Man of Straw

Swift sipped a larkspur infusion. She could hear the clank of an iron chain outside, the squeal of an old wooden gate, the outraged clucking of chickens. Wigan was letting Rhiannon out of the henhouse. She seemed happy enough being kept in there. There were feathers to keep her warm at night, water in the trough, raw eggs if she was hungry.

Swift ducked through the door of her hall into the courtyard. She was looking forward to putting Rhiannon through her paces. Her brothers' lust for power would be unleashed now their father had gone. She needed someone who would lie next to her at night and draw a knife at the creak of a floorboard. The girl offered an interesting challenge. If she could be taught to obey, she would give Swift the security she needed.

They travelled a mile or so out to the downs, Wigan on a donkey cart, the girl behind chewing stalks of grass, Swift bringing up the rear riding like a man.

They pulled up at a flat, grassy terrace, Rhiannon sullen and contemptuous. 'You are mine,' Swift said. 'You will scrub my floors, wash my clothes and defend me from my enemies. You have a talent for violence, which is why I bought you, but Wigan will teach you to kill silently and well. If you do as I say, after five years I will give you a pig, a hut and a husband and set you free.'

The girl looked at her suspiciously.

'But if you ever draw a knife on her,' added Wigan, 'or steal from her, or try to run away, I will hunt you down, skin you and leave you hanging from a gibbet.'

Swift seldom stayed long in Winchester, but today she had someone to meet. She took a wicker hamper from the cart, spread out a chequered cloth and sat under the shade of a sweet chestnut tree watching and waiting. She took in the view, the sparkling meanders of the River Itchen, the stone circles left by giants, the crumbling chapels and tiny villages, the ragged slaves cutting the meagre harvest of wheat and barley, the unmanaged copses and clogged ditches – so much beauty, so much poverty. Once she was in possession of the south coast, she would build an army two thousand strong and take this land too.

Wigan showed the slave girl how to run at speed without tiring herself, how to walk softly, how to duck and crouch and dive and spring. She executed each movement listlessly even when he shouted at her. Eventually he stopped, took a straw figure the size of a man out of the cart and set it in the earth. He gave her a blunt wooden sword and demonstrated how to thrust deeply and accurately.

'My mistress has ordered me to teach you,' he said, 'but you are a foolish slut. She offers you freedom and you laugh behind her back; I offer you fighting skills and you act like a petulant child. Learn how to kill this man of straw by the day's end or you'll be sent back to live among the common slaves.'

Swift had decided to keep Wigan for a while. His pace had

slowed but his loyalty to her was undimmed, even in the way he admonished the slave girl.

A rider approached. Swift unwrapped bread, cheese, meat and smoked fish from the hamper, arranged it on prettily painted platters, took Hawk's knife from a neatly bound sack and set it beside the assembled fare.

'Good of you to come, Harold,' she said as the horseman came to a halt.

Harold Godwin had once been a fine-looking man, but now he was running to fat and his conversation was dull. He had boundless confidence and a flirtatious look in his eye. Swift thought him a handsome-faced turnip, but this had been a rare opinion among the doting ladies of the court, at least until he'd been found in the brothel.

He swung off his mount and bowed low. 'When the beautiful Lady Swift orders me to attend on her, it is my pleasure to do so.'

'I wanted you to see us train my new slave. I thought it might amuse you.'

They ate for a while. 'Did you bake this bread?' he enquired. 'It's very good.'

She looked at him askance. She'd not dipped her hands in a mixing bowl since childhood. She was a princess, not a goodwife, but men like Harold were removed from the lives of women – even royal ones. He shared some court chatter with her and she feigned interest. His knee pressed gently on her thigh, but she ignored it. She cut more bread and fish and passed it to him. 'I'm so sorry you were abducted, and discovered in such unfortunate circumstances.' She snapped a stick of celery in two and bit a severed end.

'I was drugged, I think. I remember very little.'

'Every woman in court was concerned about you, Harold,' she said. He tilted his head gallantly. 'Until this dreadful event occurred, they all sought your favour. Even my father's wife was under your spell.'

Harold's eyes widened with something that might be panic. 'Absolutely not. She's an honourable woman.'

Swift had to prevent herself from rolling her eyes. Did he think she was unaware of the Shrew's litany of conquests? 'I must be mistaken,' she replied. 'I apologise.'

Rhiannon was squatting on the grass. Swift threw a handful of discarded food in her direction. She gave Harold another cut of meat, and his fingertips touched her hand. Dear Mother of Christ, did he expect her to lie on her back with her legs in the air while she fed him her ham!

'Nevertheless,' she continued, 'your reputation has suffered irreparable damage. I was not alone in seeing a bond between you and the Lady Osburgh, innocent though it may have been, and someone wished to put a stop to it. They abducted you and you were shamed; my stepmother was angry and will no longer continue her alliance with you.'

Harold shook his head. 'Your words are a maze, Lady Swift. My mind is a tumble of confusion.'

'Is it? Suppose what I am saying is true. Suppose you are a fallen man, friendless and discredited. Suppose you need a new ally, someone who will set you back atop the pinnacle on which you so richly deserve to be.'

'For Jesu's sake, move yourself, girl!' bawled Wigan.

Rhiannon gave a high-pitched scream, broke into a run and hit the figure with the full force of her body. It slumped backwards and she grabbed it, shook it, yanked it back and forth and wrenched it out of the ground. She threw it down hard, leapt on it, buried her teeth in its face and throat, stabbed it again and again, and finally pulled its head off.

'At last,' Wigan said. 'Good, but a little slapdash.'

'A vicious young animal!' remarked Harold.

'Indeed,' replied Swift. 'How ruthless females can be.' He laughed a little too heartily. 'Even my brothers underestimate me,' she continued. 'Their enmity will become ever more apparent now. They loathe me because I am cleverer than they are and I govern the south.' She speared a small lump of cheese and gave it to him on the end of the knife. 'You have been observing this weapon?' she asked.

'Yes, a fine piece of work.' He took it from her and examined it. 'The bird of prey carved on its hilt is particularly elegant. It belongs to Aethelhawk?'

'Indeed it does. Be careful, the blade is sharp and could do a great deal of mischief. Perhaps you'll return it to him . . . or perhaps not. It is in my interests that my brothers should turn against each other. Perhaps you could use this weapon in some way to help bring this about. It would be of great assistance to me, and you'd be well rewarded.'

Harold said nothing, but he kept the knife.

His loyalties had always vacillated from one day to the next. Would he serve her? This would be a good test. He certainly wouldn't betray her; his position was too tenuous, and he wanted her body, that was clear. She had no particular interest in offering it to him, but she was intrigued to see how events would pan out.

'A portion of curds?' she enquired.

TWENTY-FIVE

The Names of the Dead

'You are a cripple and a coward,' said clan chief Erik Longshanks. He was at the head of the thyng table, around which the island's laws were made. The elders sat along each side of it, Guthrum was standing a little way off. It had been a long, hard road to recovery, but he could now walk the length and breadth of the island five times in a day, raise his body twenty times with his strong hand, and ten with the broken one.

'When your comrades were attacked, you left your post,' Erik continued. 'When they were dead, you hid among their butchered bodies. You have the blood of fifty-nine men on your withered stump of a hand. You have shamed us all.'

Guthrum stared straight ahead. These were the tired rantings of an old man, a foolish one who'd sent his own son to his death. He waited patiently while the clan chief intoned the names of the dead. 'Dagmar Longshanks, Snorre Forkbeard, Bjorn Radisson, Ivar Radisson . . .'

Finally the old man came to a halt. It was Guthrum's turn to speak. 'Elders, Erik Longshanks speaks true,' he began. 'Fifty-nine of us did die ... But why? Because we were hungry, and hunger made us reckless. We were hungry because we had no food, we had no food because we had been supplied with no support vessel. If we'd had such a ship, its crew would have kept watch when we went ashore.' Slowly he walked round the table behind the backs of the elders – good men mostly, who yearned for better leadership than Erik gave them but were too set in their ways to rectify the matter. 'Not enough ships, not enough food, not enough men, no support ... And did I plan this sorry venture? No! I spoke long and hard against it. It was one man's responsibility, his plan, which caused the death of his son ...' he looked at each elder in turn, 'and of your sons too. Erik Longshanks, you are no longer fit to be chief of Clan Farne.' He wrapped his arm round the chief, drew his knife and sliced, all in one action.

Erik clutched his throat, blood pumping between his fingers. He tried to speak, but nothing came from his mouth but bubbles. The elders sat motionless. The issue had been resolved the Norland way. Not one man protested. Erik's head crashed onto the table and he lay in a pool of ever-darkening red.

'Fellow Norlanders, send word to our cousins on the mainland,' said Guthrum. 'We will return to Wessex next fighting season, but with five times as many ships and five times as many men. And I, Guthrum Stumphand, will lead them.'

TWENTY-SIX

Storm Clouds Gathering

Wolf, the emperor and their party were slowly heading for Modena, where they would take rest before the final eighty leagues to Rome. Everything seemed sharp to Wolf, the colours too bright, the sounds too loud; lambswool felt like the stroke of a carpenter's fingers. Nothing was true or real, only his despair. It wasn't the sadness he'd felt at the death of Agnes or the pain he'd experienced the first time he'd noticed the look of contempt on his children's faces. There was no reason for this misery other than his exhaustion from the weeks of travel, but it bubbled inside him all the while, like burning pitch. No one noticed his distress; at least they made no sign of having done so. If anyone called to him, he replied with a *hulloo*; he was the first to rise every morning and the last to bed at night.

'If we don't reach Modena by the first day of the festival, we'll miss the hunt,' grumbled the emperor, who seemed far less companionable than he had when they first met.

'We shan't miss it,' said Wolf, and he galloped to the front of the line and cajoled them all to ride faster. The carriages bumped along at a furious pace. He was constantly badgering everyone to keep up the pace; it was the only way he could drive the misery from his head.

When they finally arrived at the Modenese palace, a gaggle of elderly servants gave them a dreary welcome and served them an uninspiring repast with aching slowness. Eventually a band of boyish local huntsmen arrived, brimming with excitement. Wolf heaved himself onto a fresh mount and they set off.

He returned covered in blood and threw three sets of antlers at the feet of the waiting ladies. He should have enjoyed his triumph – no other hunter had slain more than one animal – but he was indifferent to the flattery showered upon him. He was still engulfed in despair and confusion.

Fifty years previously, Modena had sparkled with wealth and sophistication, but now the palace was barely occupied, the paint had peeled. The servants had grown decrepit and barely noticed the crumbling plaster and rotting drapery.

Wolf retired to bed and lay staring at the damp patches on the ceiling. He thought of the emperor's children, Judith in particular. There was no malice in her chatter; she was artless and direct. He remembered his own children when they were young, lying on the grass at the end of the day talking of horses and battles and childish foolishness. He grew heavy with sleep. His eyes closed and he dreamt of Aethelfraed barely twelve summers old, mounted on a white horse, leaping hedges, waving his sword, crying, 'Wolf! Wolf! Wolf!' His eyes sprang open. Why had that little cocksucker invaded his dreams again?

He glanced around the room. He had no idea where he was till he doused his face with water and the pain subsided. It was morning. He had no appetite, but he forced down a bowl of porridge. His hunting companions came chattering into the hall to break their fast, and when they saw Wolf they howled with laughter. He was still dressed in the previous day's blood-stained attire, clots had congealed around his fingernails and in the calluses of his hands.

'High Aethel,' a young hunter said, a look of feigned horror on his face. 'Have you fallen from a church tower?'

The emperor stood, observing their jinks for a moment, then slapped the hunter so hard his head hit the table and he spat out two teeth.

'Fucking idiot,' he said. 'Come! Put a smile on your face.'

Wolf assumed he was referring to the hunter, and was grateful for the intervention, but he was growing weary of the emperor's brutality. He'd punched almost every one of their party during their long journey, including Osburgh's maid, whose nose was broken and whose eyes were still blackened a week later. Wolf dealt out the occasional thrashing to his household staff, and to his children – it was his right and duty to do so – but the emperor's blows were remorseless.

The festival of St Hubert, the saint of hunting and animal husbandry, was held on one of Charles's farms half a league out of the city. By the time the royal party arrived, the fields were crowded with both rich and poor, dressed as best they could in coloured chausses and little round hats. The emperor dragged Wolf from stall to stall piled high with dead partridges, rabbits and songbirds. There was a row of hares pinned up on a hemp rope by their ears, and a pen of yapping baby foxes being thrown chicks and ratlings by a dirty boy.

Judith ran out from among the common people and tugged him by the hand. 'Let's see the badgers, Uncle Wolf,' she shouted, and pulled him through the crowd, who were patting him on the back and shouting, 'Long live the Norland slayer!' A tall mound of earth with tunnels dug through it was surrounded by growling dogs, long-bodied, with short legs and sharp claws. Farm labourers with glee in their eyes were wagering their few precious coins on which dog would be first to draw a badger out of the mound.

The dogs were unleashed and dived in. There was muffled barking and yelping as they attempted to pull the brocks out, but the beasts inside were fighters, and it was a long while before a dog reappeared, to much cheering, with a badger's muzzle between its teeth. If Wolf had seen such a thing in Wessex, he would have found it an amusing diversion, something for his children to watch, but today he barely noticed the raucous cries, the money changing hands and the dogs licking their wounds. It was as though he was trapped in a nightmare in which the killing never stopped.

The emperor strode towards him surrounded by his sniggering men. 'Look at you, Wolf, how miserable you've become. Your face grows longer by the day. And it's about to grow even longer. My son Louis is short of men, I've been called to Burgundy to help him and I'm sending the children to Pisa.'

Panic rose in Wolf. The children had been his rock. The only time he felt clear-headed was when he was surrounded by them.

'Could they stay with me?' he asked. 'They're such excellent company.'

'Their mother needs them. She hasn't seen them for a year.'

'I don't—'

'You can keep Judith,' the emperor said. 'She's never been her mother's favourite. They're too alike.'

'If she wishes to stay, it would be my pleasure,' said Wolf.

'Do you hear that, Judith?'

'Of course I'll stay with him,' replied the girl. 'I want to show him more animals. Look over here, Uncle Wolf.'

She led him to two concentric circles of stakes that had been set in the ground close together. A tethered lamb had been placed in the central ring; a wild wolf had been lured into the outer one and the gate shut tight. The angry animal was trapped, and paced backwards and forwards, its fur bristling, its eyes malevolent, occasionally attempting to scale the stakes to seize the lamb.

'They'll let it out tomorrow,' said Judith. 'May we join the hunt, Uncle? May we?'

The crowd had gathered round him and were begging him to bless their foreheads with his bloodied fingers. Osburgh and her ladies were playing with a pair of sparrowhawks, feeding them mice and pieces of chicken. Emperor Charles was riding off with his men. It was growing dark. Storm clouds were gathering.

The wolf trotted back and forth, back and forth, back and forth.

TWENTY-SEVEN

The Battle of the Moot House

Hawk had little interest in the lands assigned to him, other than the revenue they yielded. He sent out his stewards to collect the taxes from Rochester and Colchester, but had no wish to travel to Essex or Kent himself and since his father had left six weeks previously had spent most of his time in Winchester.

One morning he was lying late in bed, staring at the ceiling and mulling over the amount of wealth he'd be accruing, while his wife, Moira, snored in fits and starts. Suddenly Bear burst through the door and seized him by the collar of his nightshirt. 'You shit,' he roared. 'You odious shit,' and he lifted Hawk from his bed and slammed his head against the wall.

'What?' gasped Hawk, his head ringing from the blow. 'I've done nothing.'

Bear grabbed him by the heels and dragged him towards the door.

'Hush!' murmured Moira, her eyes still closed.

'You stabbed my sweet girl,' Bear said.

'What sweet girl?' He was mad, Hawk thought, completely mad.

'Rosa! My horse! My pride and joy! She's lying in my hall dripping with knife wounds.'

'It wasn't me!'

'What's this?' cried Bear, waving a bloodstained hunting knife in Hawk's face. 'A fucking toothpick? It's yours and it was buried in her back!'

Hawk stared at the knife in his brother's hand. It was his, sure enough, but he had no idea who'd used it to slay Bear's horse. 'I had nothing to do with it. I mislaid that knife weeks ago.'

Bear grabbed Hawk's nose and shook it vigorously. 'As soon as Father left for Rome, you began your spiteful attacks on me. You sent your men to my monastery at St Albans and they stole the rents from my churches and my farms.'

'That money is mine, brother,' replied Hawk plaintively, attempting to crawl away. 'St Albans is in Essex.'

'It's in my half of Wessex,' replied Bear, dragging him back again. 'The deeds clearly state . . .'

'. . . that it's in Essex,' said Hawk, desperately trying to wriggle out of his brother's grasp.

'No it isn't!'

'Why did you go to Basildon and steal the gold plate?' said Hawk.

'Why do you assume it was me?'

'You thrashed the bailiff and hanged the shire reeve!'

What could Bear say? The man had been insolent. 'Leave my land immediately and bury yourself in Essex. But make no mistake, I will make life difficult for you. I will harry you and fret you, and make your people so miserable they'll assassinate you within weeks. And in recompense for Rosa, I'm confiscating the Church of Redemption on Gants Hill from you.'

*

Aside from the fuss with his brother, life became better for Hawk once he'd left Winchester. He hadn't wanted to go, it was humiliating, but for the first time in his life he was the undisputed leader of his own realm of Essex, Kent and Surrey, at least until Wolf returned. He could make what decisions he liked when he liked, and could feed off the fat of his new land and people.

He took possession of a suitable hall and a swathe of common land around Dagen's Ham, a delightful Eastsaxon village hard by the River Thames. He didn't like Essex people; they were loud and ignorant and spoke a harsh, almost unintelligible tongue. Nevertheless, life was sweet. Moira stayed quiet, and Hawk made the occasional raid into his brother's lands to demonstrate that he wasn't going to be intimidated. Under his management, wealth soon began to roll in.

One morning a few weeks after his brother's irrational outburst, a delegation of Essex aldermen stormed into his hall, led by Cyril of Clacton, who had distinguished himself in battle many years previously and now, in the autumn of his years, was dedicating himself to his church and people.

'Your brother is conducting a vendetta against you and we are the innocent victims,' he boomed. 'His men are erecting fences along our borders, preventing us from reaching our fields. There are new road tolls, villages have been split in two . . .'

'I'll send someone to look into it,' replied Hawk, barely raising his eyes from the money he was tallying.

Cyril would not be deterred. 'Do you think you're immune to such incursions?' he shouted, banging his fist on the table and sending piles of coins cascading onto the floor. 'You want to organise a new tax system, don't you?'

'I do,' replied Hawk, bending down to retrieve them.

'How will we be able to pay your taxes if we can't go to market? How will you purchase the arms you'll need to drive off this summer's Norlanders? Because they will come back, they surely will. Essex is vulnerable, as are Kent and Surrey. Our markets are grinding to a halt, and you're sitting at home counting your wealth!'

'I'll speak to my brother.'

'It's not only us who are outraged,' Cyril insisted. 'Thousands of men in Bedford and Cambridge have had their trade put in jeopardy by your brother's attacks. They'll help us redress our grievance. The house of Wolf rules only by the consent of its aldermen. We'll go to the Winchester moot house and tell them how unjustly we've been treated. We'll persuade them to agree to pay us hefty reparations and give gold to our churches by way of apology.'

Cyril had Hawk's full attention now. Might these angry men in Bedford and Cambridge turn to him for leadership if he obtained redress for them? If so, he could double the size of his territory. His heart was beating fast. Bear would regret trying to push him around. By the time their father returned, he could be ruling more than half of Wessex, and with power like that, Wolf would be forced to nominate him as his successor. But first he had to win the debate at the moot house.

Fifty horsemen rode into Winchester behind Aethelhawk, each one with a sprig of Epping Forest oak leaves pinned to his breast.

The aldermen among them entered the moot house behind him, the commoners waiting in the courtyard, occasionally glancing at the small huddles of local men, who stared at them suspiciously.

Hawk sat down on a large chair mounted on a dais at the far side of the room and waited listlessly. He was fond of the moot house, a round, sensible building close to the gates of the royal compound where important issues of the day were settled, its walls lined with shields and lances, symbols of ancient battles won and heroes fallen.

The door swung open and Swift entered. She stared at Hawk disdainfully and nodded to her slave girl, who picked up a chair from the back of the room and put it down alongside him on the dais. His sister sat silently in her newly acquired place with her hands in her lap and her slave at her feet.

Time went by and a horrible realisation dawned on Hawk. Bear's benches were still empty. No one else was coming. There'd be no lots cast, no reparations made. The silence made his brother's absence doubly palpable.

'Where is he?' said Cyril loudly. 'I've travelled forty leagues to be here. Bear has to walk a mere forty paces.'

'Be patient, my friends,' said Hawk a little nervously. 'I'll go and attend on him.'

Outside, a crowd of Winchester men with clubs in their belts were surrounding his horsemen. A local reeve made a vulgar comment, which he chose to ignore. He made his way towards the great hall. From inside it he could hear his brother shouting. 'Hawk's brought an army with him. If he thinks I'll be intimidated into going to the moot house, he's very much mistaken.'

Harold Godwin came out looking deeply embarrassed. 'All these men you have with you. It's very provocative!' he said.

'No it isn't,' replied Hawk. 'They are fellow Saxons who've been treated badly and wish to be heard.'

'Bear says you want to ignore your father's wishes and snatch more of Wessex for yourself.'

'That's nonsense.'

'Everyone believes it to be true,' replied Godwin.

'I wouldn't do such a thing,' said Hawk. 'Why would I?'

They began to walk back towards the moot house.

'Get back to Essex!' shouted one of the locals.

'Wessex for the Westsaxons!' yelled someone else.

Their fists were clenched and some were holding stones.

'Where's Bishop Humbert?' said Hawk. 'He's supposed to keep the peace.'

'He's been taken sick,' said Godwin. 'He's left me in charge. I'll send your people home.'

'You'll do no such thing. Remember what happened when you played fast and loose with my stepmother?'

The look on Godwin's face vividly demonstrated how humiliated he'd felt the morning he'd woken up on the brothel floor.

'Please!' he said. 'I'm in a difficult situation.'

'Talk to my aldermen,' Hawk said. 'Tell them.'

'Tell them what?'

'The truth. That Bear refuses to come.'

'Holy Christ!' murmured Godwin, but one glance from Hawk was enough to convince him. 'Very well,' he added.

Hawk opened the door of the moot house, but Godwin did not follow him inside. Instead he stood in the doorway as though planning a hasty retreat. 'Fellow aldermen!' he called. 'Aethelbear is concerned about the ramifications of this meeting.'

'We're not leaving,' shouted Cyril of Clacton.

'He doesn't want to waste your—'

'He can come in here and tell us what his concerns are. Then we can determine whether the meeting should continue.'

'It's not his meeting,' added Pelham of Walton. 'It's a meeting of the aldermen of Wessex, to which he is obliged to come. If he doesn't wish to do so, we'll carry on without him and call a vote.'

'He says now is not the time for votes, tempers are too high,' Godwin replied.

Cyril of Clacton pushed him out the door and slammed it in his face. 'We are free Saxons!' he roared. 'Not puppets dancing to the tune of some overbearing warlord. We are staying!' He heaved the massive bolts into place, then picked up a bench, tipped it on its end and rammed it against the door.

Hawk turned to Swift. 'I know this is a little disturbing,' he said, 'but I trust I have your support?'

She shook her head. 'This is your doing. It has nothing to do with me.'

He was feeling sick. Stones were thudding against the walls of the moot house. He turned to his aldermen. 'The men outside are your brothers,' he said. 'We don't wish to harm anyone. Perhaps we should do as Aethelbear suggests and—'

'No!' A roar rolled through the air like thunder. More aldermen grabbed benches. They were old men well versed in the art of warfare; they knew how to build a stout barricade.

Swift stood on her chair, peering out of a tiny window slit.

'What are they doing?' Hawk asked nervously.

'The crowd's bigger,' she replied. 'They're attacking your horsemen.'

'Let me see,' he snapped, and climbed onto the chair beside her. Bear's supporters were trying to unseat Hawk's riders, pulling at their legs, snatching at their reins and yanking them from side to side. One of them tried to grab a saddle, but his hand became entangled in the strap and he was dragged along twenty or more paces before he could free himself.

'My men are riding off,' said Hawk. 'They're leaving me unprotected. There's no way out of here.'

'Well! . . .' Swift began to laugh.

'Well what?' he demanded. 'What?'

'I'm not getting involved,' she said.

The stones were like a hailstorm now. Bear was striding to and fro giving orders.

'Brother!' shouted Hawk through the window. 'It is the inalienable right of the aldermen of Wessex to meet in this moot house whenever they deem it necessary.'

'Brother!' retorted Bear. 'You are on my land! You must leave!'

'I have thirty enraged aldermen in here who wish to discuss the tolls and fences you've erected.'

'And I have a hundred out here who have no intention of discussing them. Fuck off!'

Outside, Bear was yelling like a drunken farmer. Inside, Hawk's men had torn down the armour from the walls and were standing ready to attack behind their barricade of tables and benches.

'We will stay here for forty days if we must,' yelled Cyril of Clacton defiantly. 'But we will not be denied our meeting.'

'Yes you will, you old fool,' shouted Bear from outside, and raised his arm.

Six of his men charged at the door with what appeared to be an ancient battering ram. Where had they found the cursed thing? Hawk thought, paling. He braced himself for the blow. When it came, dust fell and the building shook, but the door stayed firmly shut. The ram hit the door a second time. It rocked a little, but still remained intact. At the third blow, the head of the ram burst through the door, which crashed to the floor, and the entire frame collapsed. There were creaks and groans like the dead rising, and the roof above the shattered doorway tumbled down in a cloud of wattle, daub and plaster.

A roar of triumph erupted outside, but when the dust cleared, it revealed that the aldermen's barricade was now reinforced by a mass of fallen debris.

Bear will drag me out and kill me, and he'll tell our father he did so to prevent an insurrection, thought Hawk.

Swift was standing with her arms folded.

'They're upon us. How can I get out, sister?' he pleaded. 'Help me!'

'Why in the name of the risen Christ would I do that?' Swift replied.

'I'll give you land,' he said, 'good land.'

'Sheppey,' she said.

'What?'

'Give me Sheppey.'

Hawk considered. He had no idea why she wanted such an isolated, muddy little island. It was practically infertile, but it was a paltry price to pay for his life.

'Are you sure?'

'I want Sheppey.'

The rest of the ceiling was cracking like an icy river. A chunk of plaster crashed down on the floor between them.

'All right, Sheppey,' agreed Hawk. Swift might think she was being her usual clever self, but she'd soon wish she hadn't asked for it. 'Now show me what to do!'

The whole ceiling was groaning like oxen at milking time. Then half of it collapsed. A pall of dust engulfed the room. Old men crawled about dazed and confused. A breach appeared in the barricade. Pelham of Walton was run through the thigh; a brick was thrown and Cyril of Clacton fell to the ground.

In one corner of the moot house there was a privy behind a small door. Below it was a tiny stream into which the piss and shit dropped. Swift grabbed Hawk's hand and bundled him and the girl in.

'Rhiannon!' she whispered. 'Take him to the shrine of St Kilda, then find his horse.'

'I cannot crawl through that fetid stink-hole,' Hawk said.

Swift shrugged. 'Do so or die,' she replied, and left the privy, closing the door behind her. For a moment Hawk wondered at her daring. But then, he reminded himself, she was a woman, and Lady Swift of South Hamwicshire no less. She'd return home unscathed.

He clambered out through the shitty tunnel behind the slave girl. He stopped to be violently sick, then staggered after her up to St Kilda's shrine a hundred paces away. Stinking and terrified, he hid behind the old wall on which the saint was carved, while Rhiannon scampered away in search of his horse. He kept his head down and prayed to St Kilda that the girl would return soon.

Eventually she came back with an old nag. His horse had been taken, she said, this was the only mount she could find. Gradually the noise subsided, and by nightfall all was quiet. Hawk peered out from behind the wall. It seemed safe enough now.

He rode with his head bowed and covered by his cloak into the centre of the town. At Bishop Humbert's house, a distressed priest led him to the bishop's bedroom. Humbert, wearing only his undergarments, was propped up in a gilded chair surrounded by monks and nuns, one half of his face twisted and frozen, one arm dangling uselessly by his side.

'What in the name of Christ has happened to him?' Hawk gasped.

A nursing sister was mopping up the slobber that was dribbling down his chin. 'He's been touched by the stroke of an angel's wing, sire,' she replied.

'Will he live?'

'If God wills it, sire,' replied the nun. 'But I doubt he'll fully recover.'

'Will his face mend? It looks dreadful.'

The sister shook her head.

The bishop attempted to speak, but only grunts came from his mouth. The man Wolf had charged with keeping Wessex lawful was now powerless.

Hawk smiled. It appeared he could take revenge on his brother and seize all the land he wanted, and there'd be no one to say nay to him.

TWENTY-EIGHT

Little Creatures

'It grows tall, sticks up in a bed, it's hairy underneath and it makes the housemaids cry. What is it? . . . It's an onion!'

Asser had never been accompanied by armed guards before. If ever he'd travelled long distances, he'd taken a friend, a big stick and nothing more. But legates were occasionally attacked or kidnapped, so as he had been given a bulging papal purse, it had seemed a sensible precaution to hire men for the journey to Modena. The Pope had guards, the cardinals did too, and the wealthy merchants and landowners. The city had a couple of hundred whom anyone could rent when they weren't being used elsewhere. Asser borrowed two from Balotelli, three from the papal palace and paid for seven more, including the twins, Rollo and Mountjoy. Father Kennet would be his second in command and was bound to keep the journey cheerful.

They rode for eight days, regaling each other with songs and riddles.

'My lord pokes his head inside me and pushes it up till it fits tightly. What am I? . . . A hat!'

When they arrived at the Modenese palace, Father Kennet and the guards were fed in the kitchens and Asser requested to be taken to see High Aethelwolf. A tight-lipped courtier in a crumpled coat accompanied him down an endless maze of gloomy corridors till they eventually came to a pair of ornate, antiquated doors, from behind which they could hear the sound of piping voices. The courtier tentatively pushed a door open, revealing a music room, decorated with colourful friezes of the god Pan playing his pipes and comely peasant women cavorting round him with their ample breasts in plain view. There was a small stage at one end on which two portly young boys were singing a simple song about a chirruping bird in a tree, accompanied by a man with a bagpipe. An audience of elderly courtiers watched them impassively.

A figure sat in a voluminous padded chair to one side of the stage, wrapped in a long black coat despite the heat, a look of profound sadness on his face. The song came to an end, the audience applauded politely and the miserable man dropped his head into his hands. The music began again; the man looked up. High Aethelwolf, once the mightiest of kings, whose word was law, who put terror into the hearts of all who opposed him, was staring blankly into the distance.

'What in the name of the holy carpenter is wrong with Wolf?' demanded Asser. He had been whisked into one of the kitchens, where the others were already guzzling a selection of jellied pies. On the far side of the table a little round man dressed in green was hovering. He introduced himself as the emperor's companion, Seneschal François.

'It is very sad,' he said. 'For a little while after we left Aix, the high aethel was hale and hearty. He and Emperor Charles played drinking games, danced, visited a local wrestling contest, everything you'd expect from warrior-kings. But Wolf's memory began to wander, and he was seized by the darkest of moods. It became impossible to talk to him about military matters, or indeed about anything at all. Eventually the emperor tired of him, announced he'd been called away to Burgundy and left me to escort Wolf to Rome. He still wants me to try to tease some kind of military commitment out of the old man, but I doubt he'll even reach the Holy City, let alone come to an agreement.'

'He's not dead yet, my friend,' said Asser, and patted the seneschal on the back. 'Like him, I'm a Westsaxon. Perhaps he will respond to the voice of a fellow countryman.'

They finished their pies and a bowl of eel and apple porridge, and after a brief sleep, Asser was led to Wolf's private quarters. The old man sat naked and shivering in a stone bath of freezing water surrounded by agitated physicians. One was attempting to affix leeches to his cheeks and forehead, but the little creatures were unable to sink their tiny teeth into his skin and kept tumbling into the water. Another was bleeding him through a tube that had been inserted into his neck, while a third was forcing large spoonfuls of a dung-coloured liquor between his lips.

Asser was outraged. Wolf was a great king; this kind of brutal treatment was unforgivable. He showed his papal ring and demanded the physicians remove the high aethel from the bath. They dried, powdered and dressed him in warm clothing. Asser ordered them out of the room and squatted in front of the blank-faced Wolf.

'Look at me, High Aethel,' he said. There was no response. He placed his hands gently on the troubled man's cheeks. 'Listen!' he said gently. 'I have been charged by the Holy Father to attend your needs. Like you, I am a Westsaxon. When I was five years old, you came to my village. You showered me and the other children with copper coins and sweetmeats. You told us we should be proud to be Wessex men, then you rode off to battle and killed six Norlanders single-handed. I have never forgotten that day.' Asser painted such a vivid picture he almost believed it to be true. 'What I am as a Saxon I owe to your example. I will do everything in my power to return your mind to its full strength. I swear it!'

He carefully opened a small parcel and placed a generous pinch of its contents on the palm of his hand. Then he produced a short dried stem and looked steadily into Wolf's eyes. 'I will insert this into your left nostril, and when I instruct you, you must inhale the powder. Do you understand?'

Wolf stared back dolorously.

'What are you doing?' a woman's voice enquired imperiously. 'Are you trying to poison my husband? Leave him be.'

Asser turned to see a woman standing in the doorway. She was some two-score years of age, but in her face there were still echoes of the great beauty she had famously possessed twenty years previously. But there was an iciness about her too, and a steely resolve. It was not unattractive, but it made him feel a little uneasy.

'I am the Pope's legate, Lady Osburgh,' he said, and proffered his ring. 'I wish to make your husband well, but I am a man of God, not a physician. I cannot conjure back his memory, though I believe I can dispel his demons. This powder is designed to reinvigorate the wounded soul.'

The woman's face was inscrutable, but after a moment she gave the smallest of nods.

'High Aethelwolf,' Asser said, turning back to him and gently placing his cupped palm and a pinch of powder under the stem dangling from the man's nostril, 'Inhale now!'

Wolf stared at him, then blew hard through his nose. Mucus and moist orange powder dribbled through Asser's fingers.

'We'll try again,' said Asser, wiping away the mess. He placed another large pinch on the palm of his hand. 'On my command . . . inhale.'

Once more, Wolf stared blankly. 'Sniff!' ordered Lady Osburgh, the sound of her voice so piercing the doves nestling in the rafters fluttered round the room in alarm. Half the powder vanished inside Wolf's nose.

'Thank you,' said Asser, and inserted the stem into Wolf's other nostril. 'Once again, please.'

'Sniff!' repeated Lady Osburgh.

The high aethel inhaled, then nodded, nodded again, and nodded a third time. 'Yeesss!' he said, and the word was deep and sonorous. The powder was acting at the speed of a galloping horse. He stood up, paced briskly round the room and sat down again. 'Yes! Yes!' he repeated. 'You're a good young man. Very good. Why are you here?'

'To make you well, High Aethel, to escort you to the Pope, and to help you make Wessex a strong Christian nation again, greater even than Offa's Mercia in times of yore.'

'Yes!' said Wolf. 'I like that. We should do it. Definitely.'

Did he realise what he was committing himself to? It certainly seemed so. Perhaps, Asser thought, this was a man he could work with after all.

Osburgh looked at Asser and gave a vigorous little sniff, and they both smiled. Aethelwolf's health had been restored, at least for the moment.

TWENTY-NINE

A Mermaid Blowing Kisses

Asser was seldom proud – he was too tainted by the guilt and shame he imposed upon himself to indulge in that particular sin – but two days after his encounter with Wolf he felt a tinge of pride permeate his soul. Abdulalah's powder had worked its miracle, the high aethel had come back to life, and an agreement had been reached between Asser, Wolf and the seneschal. Now they could cease their parlaying for a while and take a walk in the countryside with an excitable young palace greyhound called Fire. The old man threw sticks for it, but it didn't retrieve a single one.

'Are you sure you're happy to host a mighty Christian army? It will be a colossal undertaking,' Asser said.

'Anything to get the Norlanders off my land,' Wolf replied.

'And in return the emperor will give you fresh arms, and his surveyors and engineers will build roads and ports for you.'

'Excellent. My people will be very happy.'

'And our priests will reform your Church and teach your children.'

'Yes, yes, yes,' said Wolf as Fire rolled onto his back with his paws in the air and the high aethel vigorously rubbed his stomach.

'Good boy,' he said. 'Very good boy.'

'And you'll sign a concord to that effect in Rome?'

'I don't think so. I'd rather shake hands. That's the Saxon way,' said Wolf, and he straightened up and flung the stick again.

'But if the Pope wants you to?' said Asser, slightly dismayed.

'I don't know. I suppose so. It'll all work out, I'm sure. I'm feeling better now. I will host a celebration. Fire! Come, boy! We're going back.'

The palace had been transformed, its gloom replaced by fresh flowers and gaily dressed servants plucked from far and wide. There were jugglers, musicians, tightrope walkers, a bold athlete dangling from the ceiling swinging back and forth, and even Modena's courtiers had shed their despondent demeanours and were skipping to the music of the fife and drum.

The seneschal was delighted. 'All this at the high aethel's expense? You're a great man, Father Asser,' he said. 'And we have reached a splendid agreement,' he added softly.

'Which will not be discussed further till we reach Rome,' replied Asser.

He sat at the table of honoured guests. A serving woman was offering the diners slices of fruit from a large painted bowl. She spooned plums and pears onto his plate and discreetly dropped a small note in his lap. He teased it open and glanced down at the writing. *Discourse imperative.* There was no seal or signature, only the two commanding words. He folded it, slipped it into his sleeve and looked cautiously around. The woman with the fruit bowl was standing by a side door. She nodded to him, and he stood up and turned to go.

'Are you sneaking off to find a pretty young thing?' enquired Wolf loudly.

'I am a man of God, High Aethel,' replied Asser. 'I'm merely attending to my duty.'

The woman led him outside. Behind the hall, a troupe of mummers was waiting to perform. A young man dressed as a Greek god was being helped onto a pair of stilts; another was passing a colossal papier-mâché head of Zeus up to him.

Asser was glad to see the performers; they might prove useful. Actors were always in need of money, were invariably promiscuous and often prepared to offer their services to the Church when intimate tasks needed to be performed. A young girl was checking the strings on her puppets. She had long hair worn in a topknot and the sides of her head were shaved and painted azure. He nodded to her and she returned his smile.

He followed the serving woman along a covered terrace that led to a series of adjoining guest huts. The drums were becoming increasingly loud and jarring. The woman knocked on a door and left.

'Come!' ordered a voice from within.

He pushed and the door swung open. The room was decked in Arabian drapes. Burning frankincense exuded a sweet, musky odour; a yellow bird fluttered its wings in a small cage. Lady Osburgh sat at a painted table covered in oils and unguents. She was dressed in a many-coloured silk gown of the Eastern style. Her hair was tied back and she was cleaning the paint and powder from her face.

'Discourse imperative, my lady?' Asser enquired.

She turned to him, smiling. 'I trust you've been enjoying the evening's entertainment,' she said.

'A little too feverish for my taste,' he replied.

She returned to her toilette. 'Shut the door,' she ordered. 'Excuse the brevity of my communication. I had considered writing "Please attend me in my room", but it seemed an inappropriate request when addressing a man of the cloth.'

Asser smiled. 'Thank you for giving the matter such careful consideration,' he replied.

She was wiping her neck with a soft cloth now, each stroke revealing the whiteness of her shoulder.

'I was impressed by the ease and confidence with which you tended to my husband,' she continued. 'My informants speak highly of you. I believe I can trust you.'

'You can, lady.' His words surprised him with their forcefulness.

'There is someone in Rome on whom all our futures depend. I want you to find him and take me to him.'

'And he is?' asked Asser, startled by such a bold request.

'My son, Aethelfraed of Wessex.'

Asser paused. So Osburgh knew Aethelfraed was alive, and clearly believed him as vital as Balotelli did to unlocking the future of Wessex. Perhaps Wolf's wife was the ally they had not foreseen. Then again, Asser had seen enough trickery in his time. He would not allow their plans to be coaxed out of him easily.

'Why is finding him so important?' he asked disingenuously.

'You wish Wessex to become the mounting block from which a war can be launched against the Norlanders. My husband's men have told me this and I wish for it too. There are more Norlanders massing in the north than there are herring in the sea. Last year only two ships attacked us, but when they bear down on us in their thousands, they will annihilate us.'

'I'm happy that you understand what great danger we're all in. Many do not.'

'My husband is old, Father Asser. Soon Wessex will need a new leader. There is only one man sufficiently well placed and with the requisite talent – my son, Fraed.'

'But why the secrecy of your proposed meeting with him? Surely all Wessex will welcome a gifted successor.'

'Fraed's relationship with my husband has foundered. It must be repaired so he can return home.'

Asser had always believed diffidence to be a useful tool at such moments.

'I'm sorry. I cannot do what you ask, however intriguing such an invitation might be. I have negotiations to complete.'

'The negotiation has been completed. You know that, as do I. Nothing more need be said on the subject till we arrive in Rome.' She had finished cleansing her neck but her flawless shoulder remained exposed. 'We will leave before my husband,' she continued. 'We will tell him he must travel slowly or he will become exhausted and his gloom will return. That will leave us time to seek out Aethelfraed before he arrives.'

Her resolve impressed him, but was it possible to assist her? Perhaps. He had instructions from Balotelli to keep him informed about the negotiations, but when he'd visited the pigeon messenger the cardinal had recently installed here, the man had told him sorrowfully that his birds had been struck by the blight. Going ahead with Osburgh would allow him to inform Balotelli more quickly, and perhaps find Aethelfraed too. He could leave Father Kennet here in his stead. But he didn't want to champ at the lead, like the hunting dog, Fire.

'My lady,' he said, 'my loyalty is to your husband.'

'No, Asser. Your loyalty is to Christ's victory,' she replied. And her smile seemed to offer a promise Asser dared not name.

On his way back to the dining hall, Asser exchanged a few surreptitious words with the blue-haired puppeteer, who was named Mirandolina. A small purse changed hands, and he returned to the party.

'The evening is to your liking, High Aethel?' he yelled in Wolf's ear as the old man played a drinking game with Rollo and Mountjoy, balancing beakers of beer on their elbows and attempting to drink the contents in one mouthful.

Wolf's reply was incomprehensible.

'Lady Osburgh requests that she leave for Rome in order to visit the great sights of the city before you arrive.'

Asser could only make out one word of his answer: '. . . impossible!'

'I would be happy to escort her. I need to return quickly to prepare for your grand arrival.'

". . . staying!'

Asser gave Mirandolina a tiny nod and she flashed a beguiling smile in Wolf's direction.

'Are you acquainted with that woman, High Aethel?' asked Asser. 'She appears to be looking at you.'

'Who?' Wolf craned his neck, and after a moment his gaze fell on her. 'Never seen her before.'

'You would of course have more freedom to bask in the pleasures Modena has to offer if you weren't constrained by . . .'

Mirandolina approached them. She was operating a marionette in the shape of a mermaid. It was waving its hand at the high aethel and blowing him kisses. Wolf watched spellbound. A seductive voice appeared to emanate from its mouth. 'May I fill your glass, your Grace?' it asked.

'She's very . . . very good, isn't she?' exclaimed Wolf.

'She is, her talents stretch far and wide,' agreed Asser. 'One other matter,' he added. 'If you require more of my healing powder, I'll need to go on ahead as soon as possible to ensure its availability for you in Rome.'

'Would you like to see the other puppets, High Aethel?' the girl enquired. 'There are so many lovely things at the back of the stage I'd like to show you.'

'Take your time,' said Asser soothingly. 'You need to recuperate.'

Wolf made a strange noise, a cross between a sigh and groan, then turned to Asser. 'Osburgh would love to see the Colosseum, wouldn't she?' he said.

THIRTY

Limpspear

When Brocc's ship arrived back in Hamblesea from its odyssey to the Farne Islands, its crew were greeted as heroes. They had survived a terrifying ordeal, wreaked havoc on the heathen Norlanders and brought honour to Wessex, all in the name of Jesus Christ. The ship was blessed with holy water and renamed *The Wrath of Christ.* Brocc was now its proud owner and Red was appointed boatswain. His passion for ships had reached new heights during the voyage, and he constantly regaled Swift with tales of his adventures.

'Our mast smashed and we had to put in at a shipyard north of the Humber,' he'd said excitedly. 'There were all sorts of folk working there, Irishmen, Picts, free Britons, even a few Norlanders. Their carpenting skills were like nothing you've ever seen. And one night some local lads tried to steal our ship while I was keeping watch. I cracked a few skulls and I think I may have killed one of them with our anchor, so we had to leave in a hurry. But I'd do it all again. I can make rope now, hoist a sail and tie a cleat in a gale. Brocc says I'll be able to call myself a ship's master by the year's end.'

Swift was proud of him. He might never be high aethel – he was too guileless and his interests too simple – but word of his exploits was on the lips of all the south coast sailors.

When she decided to sail to the Isle of Sheppey to inspect her new acquisition, she requested that Brocc and Red should take her, and now she was sitting on the top of the Mount, the highest point on the island, basking in the sun, looking down on *The Wrath of Christ* moored below, watching the crew hammering in the last few stakes in a long line that snaked from the Mount to the little beach.

What a fool Hawk had been to cede the island to her! It dominated the Thames estuary, and with a properly manned garrison, she could control the river's shipping from Oxford to the northern sea. Most importantly, it was the perfect spot from which to spy approaching Norlanders as they rounded the coast. Once she had possession of it, and the soldiers and warning beacons she required, she'd be invincible all the way along the south coast.

'What in Christ's name are you doing here?' An old priest was climbing furiously up the slope towards her.

'One day there will be a fort here, Father. These stakes mark the road that will lead to it,' replied Swift.

'There'll be no fort here, nor no road. This is the Lord's land and it will not be defiled,' the man said. He wrested a stake from the ground and flung it down the hill.

'This island is mine, Father, be off with you.'

'Sheppey has been in the possession of the Church since St Augustine planted his staff on its shore two hundred and fifty years ago, and it will continue to be so until the Second Coming of Christ!' the priest said, heaving out another stake.

'I am Lady Swift of the south coast,' she said in as placatory a tone as she could muster, 'and I—'

'You are Lady Nobody of Nowhere,' interrupted the old man as he pulled out a third stake and held it over his head in both hands as if about to strike her.

Rhiannon appeared at a run from behind a boulder. When she was three steps from the priest, she leapt into the air and administered a flying kick. He stumbled backwards, falling to the ground. She stomped on his outstretched arm and the stake sprang from his grasp. She grabbed it and held it over him, ready to deliver a devastating blow.

'Stay your hand!' ordered Swift, and squatted down in front of him. 'I will not tolerate brawling on my land. Tomorrow I will bring a copy of the deeds in my name, which will be lodged with the Sheppey reeve. This is no longer your living. Leave immediately and beg your way to Canterbury!'

But as the priest staggered away, unease crept over her. Why hadn't he known about the island's change of ownership? Had her brother reneged on their agreement? Or was the old man right and it wasn't Hawk's to give away? She'd instruct Brocc to sail further upriver and head for Dagen's Ham to find out.

Hawk's new Essex hall wasn't grand, but he'd never shown much interest in making his homes agreeable, and his wife seemed to care even less about such things, so it probably suited them, even though to Swift's eyes it resembled a miller's sack-store. When she arrived, Hawk was called for, and after a tiresome wait, he burst into the house in such a state of agitation she didn't even have the opportunity to bid him good day. 'Bear is undone!' he shouted, and held his fist high as though he'd won a prize fight. 'He is confounded! He is nailed to the shithouse door!'

'Good morrow, brother,' said Swift calmly.

'Word has spread through Britain like dung on a spring field that Wessex is in disarray,' he continued. 'Do these rumours concern me? Not one jot. I have authority over an area the size of a marrow bed, which I can defend with ease. My brother, on the other hand, has lands of almost infinite proportions.'

'Brother . . .' Swift began again.

'Ten days after our quarrel, the Cornish Britons swarmed into Exeter, and Bear had to muster two hundred local farmers to chase them off.'

'Brother, I've been to the Isle of Sheppey and—'

'The following day, on the other side of his country, the Mercians tried to seize back Didcot, by which time Bear's ability to defend his borders had shrunk considerably . . .'

'Listen to me, brother. The Sheppey priest was unaware that there's been a change in—'

'. . . and today the East Anglians have breached his defences at Wycombe and are running wild all over Buckingham. His realm is in tatters!'

Swift ignored his manic laughter. 'You have broken your pledge,' she said. 'I saved your life and you betrayed me.'

Moira peered round the door. She was a tall, gaunt woman with chapped lips, which she constantly nibbled. 'What's he done now?' she demanded.

'Your husband swore on Christ's name he would give me some property titles. Then—'

'He changed his mind? Of course he did. He's a snake!' She sat down heavily and looked out the window.

'Forgive her, sister,' Hawk said. 'She can't abide company. I was intending to write to you. We all make promises in the heat of the moment that are ill-considered . . .'

She knew it. He was trying to wriggle out of his pledge. Hawk was by far the most unpleasant of her siblings, constantly cheating, shouting, lying like a desperate gambler at a dice game.

'I'll show you something,' he said, and left the room.

Swift and Moira sat in silence for a while. Moira seemed to have shrunk before her eyes. She pitied the woman, and it occurred to her that she might be able to use her to create a little mischief. Swift had deliberately provoked Hawk since they were children and it never became any less satisfying. 'Come and stay with me, sister,' she said.

'Where?'

'Hamblesea.'

'Why?'

'You're bored, you hate your husband, and in autumn the trees of South Hamwicshire have a unique and exquisite beauty.'

'I can't,' Moira replied. 'He wouldn't let me.'

'I'm sorry for that,' said Swift. 'We would have taken pleasure in each other's company.'

Hawk returned, under his arm a sheaf of documents, which he spread before her. 'Here!' he said. 'The deeds to Sheppey since the time of Augustine. The island is tied to a host of oaths and pledges. These show clearly that it's not mine. How could it be? It appears to be pledged to Father in a lease from the Church.' He thumbed through the pages. 'Sub-leases, loan-leases, counter-leases . . .'

She leant forward to examine them, but he snatched them away. 'Believe me or not,' he said. 'It's all the same to me.'

'You are attempting to flummock me with your bundles of documents. If there are problems with the legality of Sheppey's ownership, you must address them, acquire the island yourself and hand it over to me. A dozen aldermen heard the promise you made in the moot house. And I'll require compensation for the time I've wasted while waiting to take ownership,' she added.

'I'm going to South Hamwicshire,' Moira announced abruptly, 'with Swift. In the autumn the trees have a unique and exquisite beauty!'

Hawk stared at her in horror. 'No you're not!' he said.

'I am. I'm bored and I hate you.'

Any composure Hawk had feigned now evaporated. 'I'm not having you colluding with my sister,' he shouted. 'She only wants the shitten island so she can launch an attack on me.'

'Five years ago you borrowed a thousand pieces of gold from my father,' said Moira. 'If I write to Northumbria and tell him how you treat me, he'll send an army to claim it back. He'd welcome an excuse to do so. He might even stay here.'

'Why are you threatening me?' demanded Hawk. 'You want to practise your vile lust, don't you? I've always known you're a tit sucker! You wish to consume your yearnings for my sister on the altar of St Ignatius while being applauded by your fellow sapphics.'

Swift remembered this kind of nonsense from when he'd been thwarted as a child. He'd been prone to sulking, and when anger eventually bubbled out of him, it was wild, disproportionate, like a crazed madman raving on a street corner.

'How dare you!' Moira shouted. 'Swift and I have barely said two words to each other. Do you really think we wish to clamber on top of each other like cows on the way to milking?'

Swift thought she might have been a little too impetuous in her invitation. The next few months would be the most significant in her life, and Moira wouldn't be the easiest of house guests. But her presence would certainly focus Hawk's mind on providing the documents Swift needed, and though she doubted the king of Northumbria could be persuaded to invade Essex, he might lend his daughter a few soldiers, which could help enormously.

'We're leaving for Hamblesea,' said Moira. She grabbed a hat and cloak from an anteroom by the front door, and off they went.

*

As dusk approached and the sun began to sink below the horizon, *The Wrath of Christ* sailed past Sheppey once more. Swift sighed. 'That island would already be mine if it hadn't been for your venomous husband.'

'I wasn't supposed to be his wife,' Moira said. 'Our fathers made an agreement that I should marry Red as part of some pact or other, and I'd happily have done so. He was comely and had a modicum of intelligence, and in those days everyone thought that one day he'd rule Wessex. But he had his accident shortly after I arrived in Winchester with my bridesmaids, so they gave me to that limpspear instead.'

'How sad!' said Swift. 'We must be friends. It's foolish we never have been.'

'Hawk will come for me,' Moira replied. 'He will not be thwarted.'

Swift watched as the sun set and the sea beneath it turned wine-red. 'Let him try,' she said.

THIRTY-ONE

Few Such Intimacies

On the first morning of their journey, surrounded by a twenty-strong escort, Osburgh opened up to Asser like a spring flower.

'Forgive my foolish message,' she said. 'Courtly ways do not come naturally to me. I'm a country girl with a country girl's simplicity.'

Simplicity? thought Asser. She had dazzled him with her subtlety, awed him with her artifice. 'We can be country folk together,' he replied. 'I was raised in the Wessex Summerlands.'

'I too!' laughed Osburgh joyously. 'My father was alderman of Taunton.'

'I've heard tell of the Taunton raid,' said Asser. 'It must have been hard for you. You were very young.' He knew of her tragic early life from the documents Plegmond had prepared for him before he left Rome, but he feigned ignorance.

Her face darkened. 'The Norlanders slaughtered my entire family and many more besides while I was out searching for quails' eggs,' she said. 'For hours I hid in a ditch until Wolf arrived like a conquering hero . . . He was a comely man in those days. He hanged the raiders, lifted me on his steed and told me I was the prettiest girl he'd ever seen. We were married three days later. The crowd cheered and showered us with rose petals. I became the royal consort and was very happy.'

Asser listened, frowning. It sounded like a fairy tale, but Plegmond's documents told a sadder story. She'd been trapped in a palace, barely more than a child, an orphan with no friends or allies, living at the whim of a much older man, a tyrant who soon tired of her.

'You can tell me how it really was,' he said quietly. 'I'm a man of God. I promise you can trust me.'

She turned to him, her eyes like those of a hurt child.

'Yes,' she said after a moment. 'I suppose I can.'

They were to stay the first night in the monastery at Vignola, one of many that catered for the streams of pilgrims making their way to Rome. Rollo and Mountjoy were in attendance. It was extraordinary that for so long he had thought them identical. They might look the same, but their characters were very different. Mountjoy was forthright and uncomplicated and rode ahead to ensure they were treated royally, while Rollo, who attended to their needs on the road, was craftier, with a black mole on his nose.

'I managed to find some scented cloths so you can wipe your faces,' Rollo said, 'and two stream-cooled flasks of wine, some honey cakes and cinnamon sweetmeats. There were hawkers on our path, so I shook a stick at them and they disappeared. Your journey will be as peaceful as a summer sea.'

When they arrived at the monastery, the guards and maids set up camp in a nearby field while Osburgh and Asser ate quail and greens in a small room set aside for high dignitaries away from the hurly-burly of the pilgrims.

'Fraed may appear a little strange at first,' she said. 'Most exceptional boys are. It will take you a while to appreciate his qualities.'

'I look forward to discovering them,' he said. 'Why did his father banish him?'

'My husband can be foolish, obsessed by silly notions. I'm sure he regrets it now, but he's far too proud to ask Aethelfraed to return.'

Her prevarication made the question all the more intriguing. 'You think you can persuade the two of them to become reunited?'

She took a peach from a bowl and examined it. 'I'm sure I can. I believe that deep in his heart he still adores Fraed. I will employ my powers of persuasion.' She cut into the ripe fruit and offered him a slice. 'How strange that we are able to talk so candidly when we hardly know one another. I've shared few such intimacies.'

Not so. She'd had her share, as Plegmond had told him with some relish. He bit into his slice of peach thoughtfully. Was she offering what he thought she was? Would such a liaison be appropriate? There was the issue of his celibacy, although that didn't concern him overly. According to scripture, Christ had surrounded himself with women, and God had created him as a man like any other, presumably that hadn't applied only to praying and tending the sick. And Asser had always tried to follow Christ's example.

They rode south. He'd not been entirely ignorant about matters of the flesh before he met Osburgh. When he was sixteen, he'd been sent to Cologne to study Aramaic, and a kindly Swiss nun had introduced him to the taste of Eve's apple in exchange for lessons in the Saxon tongue. But Osburgh was different. She had a fierce hunger for the act, which at first he'd found intimidating and hadn't been able to reciprocate. But gradually she'd tempered her desires, and he'd become more confident about responding to them.

They talked constantly, although the word *amore* never entered their conversations, other than that they loved what they were doing to each other and did so as often as possible. When their party stopped to water the horses, they'd excuse themselves from the company, Rollo would provide discreet protection, and they'd set off to admire a site of particular interest on the far side of a hill or under a bridge. It was a happy arrangement.

'So you plan to bring Aethelfraed back to Wessex in triumph,' Asser said one day, 'and you'll be your husband's loyal servants until the day when, for whatever reason, your son's time comes?'

'Yes!' agreed Osburgh. 'For whatever reason.'

'You know the throne will never be yours,' said Asser.

'I do. No woman can govern Wessex. The statutes forbid such a thing. But I can become the power behind it,' she replied.

The journey and their adventures tired her. She became wan and coughed a little. She was unpredictable, her mood changing from moment to moment. Sometimes she giggled at his most foolish fancies, at others she was curt and dismissed him from sight before apologising and begging his forgiveness. She wouldn't be an easy ally. Indeed, Balotelli might think her expendable and be happy to nurture the son while discarding the ambitious mother. But that was for another day.

Eventually they rode through the gates of Rome. Asser pointed out some of its sights to her. He'd forgotten how big and rambling the city appeared to those who hadn't seen it before: the crowds, the giant walls built to protect it from Moorish attack, the massive ancient public baths of Caracalla, the theatre of Marcellus, and of course the profusion of dogs and beggars. A sad thought struck him. Once back at the Undercroft, he'd only be able to visit her intermittently. Would she be wounded by this?

As on so many occasions, she answered him as though he'd spoken out loud. 'Father Asser, I must thank you for your company, but I am the wife of a great king and cannot place myself in a position that might give an intimation of impropriety.' She patted his hand. 'We will continue working together and we will find my son. But our friendship must end.'

How fond of her he'd become! It wasn't love, of that he was sure. He had loved his mother and his sweet sister; he loved the Doctore, his friends in the Undercroft, and even, in a strange way, Balotelli; but it was a different emotion he felt for Osburgh, one of gentle tenderness.

'I'll leave you at St Catherine's Abbey,' he said. 'Abbess Clothilde is an old friend. You'll like her, she's a courageous woman who shares our vision.'

The abbey doors bore a charming, freshly painted pattern of holly intermingled with ivy. Clothilde was waiting there with Elswith by her side, in the garb of a novice. The abbess greeted Lady Osburgh cordially, then turned to Asser.

'Father Asser, I've been struck by a pleasant idea,' she said. 'Elswith is a Westsaxon; I will instruct her to attend to Lady Osburgh throughout her stay.'

'The perfect choice,' replied Asser. How charming Elswith looked in her white novice's veil and a linen wimple modestly covering her neck and chin. Nevertheless he was confident she could deal with Osburgh's vicissitudes.

He gave his lover a final glance, but the woman he had known so intimately had already disappeared. The frown had returned to her face, her mouth was tight and downcast, and she was making terse demands of Elswith about the kind of fruit she wished to be on hand at her table.

Balotelli was sitting by the fishpond in the small open garden inside his palazzo. On the flat of his hand were tiny pieces of almond. He took a pinch and held it above the surface, and the fishes' heads bobbed up to nibble the nut crumbs from his fingers.

'I have a tender heart,' he said. 'I decided not to cook the fish the boys sold me. Look how large they've grown. I'm rather proud of my husbandry.' He and Asser watched the hungry creatures for a while. 'You returned early.'

'I did,' replied Asser. 'Modena was a great success, but I couldn't let you know, because sadly all your pigeons are sick.'

Balotelli tutted with irritation. 'My messenger service is not working as efficiently as I'd hoped,' he said.

'Wolf is besotted by the emperor and his family,' Asser continued. 'He's agreed that Wessex should be our battleground. He'll sign an agreement once he's been blessed by the Holy Father, and I've returned to write it in detail and plan his arrival.'

'If your confidence is well placed, I congratulate you.'

'There is another reason for my swift return, Cardinal. I've brought with me Wolf's wife, the Lady Osburgh, who has received similar information to ours about her son, Aethelfraed.'

'He's alive and in Rome?'

'Indeed. And if she allies herself with us and I can find him . . .'

'. . . that could prove very useful indeed,' said Balotelli. 'Wolf's signature on an agreement, and the provision of a talented young prince as his successor. We would appear statesmanlike and give the doubters in the Church hierarchy fresh confidence in our capabilities.'

'We'll still need to persuade them of the necessity for a strong, righteous army. It will be very costly.'

'I agree. We won't announce the concord till it's formally written, but the arguments for such a thing need to be disseminated widely.'

'I'll do my best, Cardinal. Indeed, I set a strategy of persuasion in motion before I left for Modena.'

'Did you indeed? I look forward to its realisation,' said Balotelli. He gave the fish a few more nut flakes. 'Did I understand you correctly?' he asked. 'The Lady Osburgh persuaded you to leave Modena early and you've been in her company for the last ten days?'

'Yes.'

He brushed the flakes from his hand. 'Asser,' he said, 'have you been fucking her?'

'No!' said Asser hotly. 'Absolutely not!

'Good. Well don't,' said the cardinal, and wandered back into his office.

THIRTY-TWO

Sea Dragons and Krakens

Asser was standing in the middle of the Undercroft holding the edge of a voluminous cloth, which obscured a large and mysterious object. He was surrounded by all thirty of Balotelli's priests.

He flung the covering to one side to reveal a magnificent, brightly coloured image, twenty paces long and seven wide. 'This is a mappa mundi freshly commissioned from the great Isadore of Sevilla,' he announced. 'It is made of vellum affixed to neatly abutted wooden slats; it took forty days to make and it cost half my entire papal purse.'

The priests stared at it in wonder. It was a map like no other, depicting a ring of blue sea that was preventing the world from toppling into the infinite abyss. Shoals of multicoloured fish darted through it, and whales, sea dragons and krakens poked their heads above the waves, hunting for lost ships and crushing them in their mighty jaws. Inside the ring were the unknown lands, home to fire-breathing monsters and two-headed elephants. Further towards the middle were the known lands, Asia, Afrique and the Holy Roman Empire; and at its centre, shining like a diamond in the Virgin's crown, was the glorious city of Rome.

Had Isadore painted nothing more, it would have been imposing enough, but what made it so remarkable was the volley of black arrows hurtling towards the Holy City from north, east, south and west, signifying the Norland attacks on Christendom. Observers might have concluded from their message that the world was doomed, had it not been for a small glimmer of light, a sign from God that all was not yet lost. In the far north-west of the map shone Wessex, radiating golden light, the black arrows flying close to it melting under the power of its luminescence and dropping into the sea.

'Isadore is showing us that a righteous Christian army will do battle in Wessex and save us from great tribulation. It is a message that will be preached from every pulpit in Christendom. Copies of our map will take pride of place in all our great churches and cathedrals, and the sisters of St Catherine's will pen a hundred smaller versions that will circulate—' His words were cut short by the sound of splintering wood and twisting metal. Feet were padding down the Undercroft stairs and the curtain was flung aside.

A dozen black-clothed figures with dyed bindings of various hues round their faces entered the room like the dead awakened. Only their mouths and eyes visible beneath holes in their bandages revealed them to be living beings. 'On your knees!' one barked. 'Put your hands together and pray, you sons of whores!'

The priests froze with terror.

'Pray!' roared a second figure. 'Pray now, or it'll be the last prayer you ever make!'

The fathers dropped to their knees, terrified. Asser, who had grown inured to such bullying behaviour in the papal dungeon, knelt with the others, but tried his best to ascertain who the ruffians were. They were commoners without doubt, with a foreign edge to their voices, and the odour of alcohol on their breath was palpable.

'All is ready, sir,' one shouted, and a new revenant appeared. This one sported a silver mask like those worn by lovers at a carnival; he was swaying a little and lasciviously caressing his cudgel as though anticipating the great pleasure of using it.

Asser glanced surreptitiously at the intruders' feet. Some wore crude slippers, others were shod in rags or were barefoot. The masked man had on a pair of fine leather shoes.

'Where's Doctore Guido?' he demanded. 'There, I espy him!'

'Who are you, you ungodly fiend?' demanded the Doctore. 'You have no business here.'

The man laughed, picked up a stone arm from among the pile of discarded statuary and swung it at the Doctore. It hit the side of his head with a hideous smack, and he fell to the floor and lay groaning among the dust and debris.

From behind the mask came a muffled chuckle. 'God's goodness, he's tumbled over! What jinks have you been up to, blackamore? High ones, no doubt.'

'You must leave, stranger,' said the Doctore tremulously. 'We are under the protection of Cardinal Balotelli.'

'That gobbet of phlegm?' the intruder scoffed.

'Take care,' said the Doctore. 'He is a powerful man.'

The masked man hit him in the face with his cudgel so hard his nose split like a ripe chestnut and a cascade of blood splattered on the floor. Asser was torn. He yearned to go to his old friend's aid, but he could not overcome these men, and a struggle would only aggravate them.

'Listen to me, Doctore, and the rest of you mark well what I say. You will not circulate this map, and you will no longer advocate your fantastical war.' The intruder drew a dagger and scored a jagged line across the mappa mundi. 'There are no fleets of invaders bearing down on us, only a few greedy pirates.' He scored the map again. 'This is nothing but an image created by radical neophiles to panic common people into supporting them while they divert the Church's wealth into their own pockets.' He threw the map to the ground, stamped on it, and the wood broke into pieces. 'Any of you who continue to perpetuate this mischievous nonsense will not be allowed to live.'

His men kicked the pieces into a pile, and their masked leader wrested a torch from the wall and threw it onto the heap. The blaze caught immediately.

'We know who your co-conspirators are,' he said. 'The monks and priests, and the pretty little nuns sitting at their drawing tables making copies of it. We will pay them a call. Tell Balotelli we are the masters now.'

The intruders watched the map burn, occasionally coughing as the smoke caught in their throats. Asser shuffled across the floor, took the Doctore's hand and squeezed it tenderly. It was all he could do. When the map had been reduced to a few charred pieces, the attackers left silently, the silver-masked man giving the Doctore a final series of brutal kicks before he disappeared up the stairs.

The priests waited for a few moments, then burst into action, lifting the Doctore gently and carrying him up the steps. Only Asser was left behind, poking among the debris. He drew a charred wooden fragment two handspans wide out of the fire. There was a torn piece of vellum still attached to it, bearing the image of an elephant and the bloody print of a shoe. Who had told the attackers about the Undercroft? How had they known about the map? A dreadful thought coursed through him, and he dropped the fragment among the broken statuary. *Pretty little nuns sitting at their drawing tables.* What was about to happen to the sisters at St Catherine's? And what would that mean for Osburgh?

Asser hammered on the abbey door until his knuckles bled. He could hear nothing from within its thick walls, and his mind conjured dreadful images from the silence. Abbess Clothilde eventually opened the door. Her round, serious face was pallid, and though she spoke calmly, Asser could hear the distress in her voice and his heart sank

'I apologise—' he began.

'If you've come for the drunken thugs, you're too late, Father. They have already left.'

'Are you safe?' he demanded. 'How fares the Lady Osburgh?'

'She is unharmed, but at great cost. Come!'

She led him along silent corridors and through a gardened quadrangle pungent with the scent of trampled herbs.

'Did they threaten you?' he enquired.

'Noisily and with persistence,' she replied. 'They painted a vivid picture of the many acts they'd perform on me if we continued working for the cardinal or copied any document that advocated a great war. They locked me in my study and terrorised my sisters.'

She led him to the library. Tables and benches had been scattered and smashed, scrolls and manuscripts torn to pieces. 'They burnt many of our finest documents,' she said. 'They were particularly keen to destroy the work of Cardinal Balotelli.'

A young novice lay among a pile of blankets. It was Elswith. Her eyes were closed and her face was bruised as though she'd been slapped hard by a man wearing rings. Asser was consumed by guilt. Why hadn't he arrived sooner? Why had this happened now? He'd brought her here to keep her safe.

Two sisters were tending to her injuries.

'Brave Elswith,' said Clothilde. 'Her short time here has been a bitter one. I am sorry I was unable to protect her.'

Asser stared at her, horrified. 'Why did they attack her so brutally?'

'She refused to let them pass through Lady Osburgh's door. Two of the men demanded she unlock it, but she swallowed the key. They held her upside down, punched her in the belly and forced their fingers down her throat. The other sisters begged them to desist, but they called her a stinking Westsaxon wretch and their leader performed horrors on her of which I will not speak. But her defiance bought the sisters time. They went to the garden and gathered scythes and brought knives from the kitchen. They screamed like harpies and drove the men out. I doubt they'll return.'

Asser dropped to Elswith's side and she opened her eyes. They were dull and blank after the terrible ordeal and it took all Asser's strength not to look away. For a brief moment, he saw his sister's face as she was carried off by the Norlanders, that same look in her eyes, the prospect of her fate too much to endure.

'Elswith, it is I, Father Asser,' he said. 'You have performed a heroic service today. You will surely be rewarded with life eternal.'

The girl shook her head. 'I will not, Father, for I cannot forgive the man who did this to me, and that is a mortal sin.'

'You'll not burn in hell for that, but if you do, I'll keep you company, for I cannot forgive him either. I will find him for you, I promise.'

She closed her eyes again, and Asser touched her cold, clammy forehead in blessing.

'I must pay my respects to Lady Osburgh,' he said after a moment, his voice choked. 'She will be overcome by distress.'

'I doubt she heard a single word of the altercation,' Clothilde replied. 'Come and see.'

They went quietly down the corridor and into Osburgh's room. She was lying on her bed, her eyes closed, her breath as shallow as a dormouse. A few of the little things she treasured were on a side table: a garnet brooch and pin, a comb with intertwined woodland animals carved on it, a set of jade beads. 'She's been sick since her arrival. I suspect the journey was not kind to her. My hospitaller gave her a sleeping draught.'

'She's very pale,' said Asser. He wanted to kiss her cheek and stroke her brow. Instead he knelt by her side, held her cool hand and prayed for a while.

'Abbess,' he said. 'You must stop working for us until I can offer you protection.'

Clothilde's face was stark, almost defiant. 'This attack came as no surprise – the violence, the lust, the contempt. It is a woman's lot. You gave us the task of reproducing the mapmaker's image for all to see. We will begin again in the morning.'

THIRTY-THREE

Dinner With Harold

Swift had enjoyed Moira's company over the past two weeks – her dry wit, her perceptive observations, her self-deprecating asides. But she recognised how dangerous she might become. She had nothing but contempt for those in authority, and a single withering remark could damage Swift's relationship with those here on the south coast she wished to ally herself with. She needed to put a little distance between her and her new friend, and a family event offered such an opportunity.

One morning Swift was sitting on a little stool in her Hamblesea orchard reading the day's messages from her supporters. Moira lay under a tree watching a blue tit hopping from branch to branch. It landed on an apple, cocked its head, plunged its beak into the shiny red fruit and pulled out a wriggling maggot.

'See, the bird has found my husband,' Moira said, and they both laughed.

For a while they basked in the autumn sun, then Swift said, 'Red and Winifred are getting married.'

'I should think so,' Moira replied. 'Her stomach is as large as a marrow.'

'And you shall be maid of honour!'

'Me?' snorted Moira. 'I know nothing of weddings. My wedding day was the worst in my life. I was marched to a run-down chapel by a dozen guards, where I met my future husband for the first time. A priest mumbled a few words I couldn't hear, then Hawk took me to a hunting lodge, laid me on the bedroom floor, lifted my skirts and made a sorry attempt to bed me. When I tried to assist him, he lost his temper and called me a whore. He rode off and I didn't see him again for two months! I have nothing to contribute.'

'So you have no wish to go back to him? Even though he's your spouse?'

'You know I don't. I never want to see him again.'

'He has sent me three messages in the last fortnight, each more abusive than the last, demanding your return.'

'I've received four,' said Moira, shrugging. 'But what can he do?'

'He'll attend the wedding and will be doubly persistent.'

'I'll kill him!'

'Don't be foolish.'

Swift was revelling in the predicament she was putting Hawk in. If Moira stayed in the south, he'd lose her and any chance of siring an heir. Swift would only countenance sending her back if he sacrificed Sheppey, which he'd be reluctant to do once he realised its military importance.

'You must make yourself loved by Red and Winifred,' she said. 'You must assist Winifred throughout every minute of the wedding, you must be overwhelmed with excitement about the baby, and when it arrives you must dote on it like a duck on her ducklings. They will desire you to go with them to the Isle of Wight, and it will be your duty to do so.

Hawk won't be able to insist on your return until the baby is weaned.'

Moira grunted. 'I don't like babies,' she said.

'You do now,' Swift replied. 'What will you wear to the wedding?'

The green in front of Winchester Minster was decked out in celebratory fashion, with flowers, branches, banners and flags in abundance. The royal family of Mercia, cousins to the house of Wolf, were in attendance. There were relatively few skirmishes taking place along their joint border at the moment; nevertheless the Mercian men were laden with arms to demonstrate their might. How ridiculous that two families of shared blood should so often indulge in violent squabbling, thought Swift. If she were leading them, she'd behave in a much more subtle manner. She caught a glimpse of her cousin and childhood friend Prince Burgred among them. What a fine soldier he'd turned out to be. Her stomach gave a little skip when he smiled at her. Perhaps one day there'd be the possibility of a liaison between them; one never knew for sure how the future would pan out. Harold Godwin was tending to the Mercians' needs with an obsequious look on his face. Hawk and Bear had put their enmity aside for the day and were seated grudgingly close to each other. Commoners cheered and threw showers of golden autumn leaves.

The groom crossed the grass between the guests in a captain's uniform: a red felted hat, sea boots, and a strong cloak capable of withstanding the fiercest of gales. He was surrounded by eager young sailors, who slapped him on the back and wished him well. Swift was glad to see him among friends. He'd been so solitary after the accident. At least they called it an accident. He and Wolf had been racing their horses. Wolf had feared losing and drove his mount into Red's; horse and rider fell, and the animal had rolled on top of him and cracked his skull.

It had made him slow and solitary, but he had been transformed by the journey to the Farnes. If the tales Brocc had told her were even half true, he'd saved a fellow rower who'd been washed overboard; he'd pulled *The Wrath of Christ* off the rocks when it foundered; he'd even become as drunk as a donkey but had still managed to hoist the sail single-handed. He might still have simple and innocent predilections, but it was little wonder the men of the south coast had flocked to his wedding. They liked and respected him and wanted him to crew their ships.

Winifred looked as pretty as Red was handsome, in an embroidered dress of Maastricht blue, which Swift had purchased for her from a Frankish trader. Red was a good match for her; he'd be the master of the Isle of Wight once they were married, but he'd let her have her way. Swift had watched Winifred pounce on him two years previously, when she'd first realised he was an aethel. He became besotted by her, and it was in Winifred's interests to keep him so.

Behind the bride and groom paraded twenty garlanded little girls in white tunics with Maastricht blue sashes. They were led by Moira, who was walking in an achingly self-conscious way, as though all eyes were on her rather than the bride. As the procession approached the minster steps, twenty oarsmen stepped forward, ten on each side, and held their oars aloft with the blades touching, forming an archway through which the wedding party passed. Red looked as happy as a child on his naming day.

The ceremony was simple. Red produced a ring; a blacksmith cut it in two and affixed each half to a chain, and the bishop placed the necklaces round the couple's necks. He pronounced them man and wife, gave Christ's blessing, then they entered the minster for a brief mass.

Hawk slunk up to Swift. 'You received my messages?'

'I did, as did Moira. You wish her to return.'

'It's been nearly a month. She's my property. It's her duty to come when I say.'

'Indeed. But the bride and groom are insistent that she accompany them to the Isle of Wight. Winifred is young, and Moira will be of the utmost importance to her. I'm sure you wouldn't begrudge the new couple her assistance. The whole family would appreciate it. We could call it your wedding gift.'

'I must have her,' hissed Hawk.

'And I must have the lease to the Isle of Sheppey,' Swift retorted. 'I'm confident some accommodation can be reached.'

'She can stay four weeks more,' he said, 'after which I will send an army to bring her home.'

Later, Swift danced with Burgred. Their parents had once hoped they'd marry. He still had the face of the young boy she remembered from her youth, when she'd visited her mother's Mercian family in Chepstow, but it was lined now and scarred from countless battles, which had made him something of a legend among the Mercian forces. 'We see each other so seldom,' she said.

'My dearest wish is to rectify that,' he said softly.

'Perhaps one day I'll visit you,' said Swift. 'I'd like to see Chepstow again.'

The dance came to an end. She found her brother Bear sitting under a chestnut tree eating a bowl of sweet blackberry custard. 'I didn't expect to see you here today,' she said. 'I thought you were embroiled fighting rebels in the south-west.'

'They're nothing I can't manage, sister,' he replied. As an afterthought he added, 'If you try to make the south your own, I'll destroy you.'

Swift turned to go. 'Eat more meat and drink less mead,' she said. 'You're getting fat.'

'Whereas you, sister, could do with plumping up a bit; you're looking a little gaunt,' he countered. 'Marry soon, or you'll dry up.' He stared down at his custard for a few moments, then threw it into a bush.

Swift spent the night in Winchester, and the following morning took a walk around the compound. It was strange to be the only member of the house of Wolf staying here, but neither she nor her brothers had any affection for the place; memories of their father's drunken beatings were too vivid. Nowadays Bear's hall was little more than a pigsty, Hawk's was empty and cold, hers a convenient trysting place for the occasional liaison. How absurd that Wolf had built them in the first place, given that none of his children could stand each other. Had he harboured the absurd belief that some day they'd all live together in one happy compound?

She climbed the old flag tower, symbol of the might of the house of Wolf. The flags were faded, some frayed and torn. She looked down on the sheep and pig pens, the servants' quarters and the various vegetable patches and herb gardens. As she watched the slaves digging the soil before the winter feed, she turned the day's events over in her mind. Could she truly one day be mistress not only of the south coast but of all the territory these flags represented? She had embarked on a difficult and lonely task. Louis would soon be here to support her, but in the meantime, she needed all the allies she could lay her hands on.

She heard footsteps trudging up the old wooden stairs, and Harold Godwin appeared. 'I believe you asked to see me, my lady,' he said. 'Will you be dining in Winchester tonight?'

'I'm not sure,' she replied. 'I'm always eager to get away from here and return to the south coast.'

'My wife is in Putney, spending time with her mother. It would be good to talk at leisure.'

Swift shot him a smile. 'In that case, we'll eat in the great hall,' she said.

They dined early, attended by five serving women who'd hastily prepared a cold garnished pig and two bottles of plum wine for them. The more they drank, the more Swift felt she'd been too hard on Harold recently. He was attentive, far better company than most Westsaxon men, and possessed commendable authority. She smiled, enjoying the tingle of the fermented plums on her tongue.

'You are a constant mystery to me, Lady Swift,' he said. 'You disappear to the south coast for weeks on end, there are rumours of secret meetings with bishops and aldermen, and when we met on the downs, your language was veiled and circuitous.'

'I want to serve the people of the south. That is all.'

He moved his chair closer to hers. 'I'm sure you do,' he said. 'You are a commendable and fascinating woman.'

'But a cautious one,' she replied, though she didn't move away. 'You must understand the precariousness of my situation. The people of the south are still unhappy about its annexation by Wolf. However loyal I wish to remain to my father, I'm their warden and must represent their interests.'

'You were always his favourite, even when Fraed was with us.'

'Perhaps. But my father has no interest in nurturing the south coast. Potentially it has the finest ports in southern Britain, large forests for felling, a sea full of fish, but the damage wrought by the Norlanders was never repaired, and it has been sucked dry by his taxes. Its people yearn to tread their own path, and I yearn for that too . . .' She broke off and smiled demurely. 'But you are Wolf's chief ally; I should take care what I say to you.'

He pulled his chair even closer and replied softly, 'We both know Wolf hasn't long to live. He struggles to hold Wessex together, and when he's gone, it will fall asunder. Perhaps the best we can hope for is a legitimisation of what we have at present: three separate Saxon states, a league comprising your South Hamwicshire and the Sussex coast, Hawk's lands in the east, and Bear's Wessex, all committed to the common cause of driving out the Norlanders.' He placed his hand on hers. 'If that is your dream, I can help fulfil it. Just tell me what you want from me.'

Swift poured a little more wine into their goblets and examined its colour by the light of the candle.

She had a choice to make, and it wasn't a difficult one. She could detach herself from him again whenever she needed. She leant on him a little, her hand still under his. 'I am a woman alone,' she said. 'I wish only for your strength.'

'Day and night,' he replied.

'The wine is making me a little giddy,' she said. 'I fear I may stumble on my return to my hall. Will you accompany me?'

The following morning, Swift and her band of guards prepared to leave. As they were packing up in the courtyard of the royal compound, Harold strolled out of her hall looking a little smug.

'I will be returning to Hamblesea today,' she said. 'I have pressing matters to attend to.'

'May I join you?' he asked. 'I would enjoy a visit to the coast while my wife is away.'

Was that what Swift wanted? He was a little pompous and humourless, and he'd badger her for information, but his kisses had been comforting and she enjoyed the easy familiarity with which he touched her body. She took him to one side. 'I have guests this evening who care even more passionately for the south coast than I do. Would I be foolhardy to allow you to attend?'

'Lady Swift,' he replied, 'I have already shown you my loyalty by employing the knife you gave me to rend your brothers asunder. Last night I demonstrated the strength of my ardour. We both desire a Wessex free from the Norlanders, and we know this would be best served by a strong south coast. What more can I say?'

Swift studied his expression. She'd trust him, at least for now.

Swift's home in Hamblesea was the largest for miles around. The roof was newly thatched, the walls of bright white plaster. It was thirty paces long, a vast room with an open fire in the middle of the floor; and a small room at each end, one for her, the other for the animals.

Towards dusk, she and Moira welcomed the guests – aldermen, reeves, senior clergy, merchants from the great ports of Southamwic and Shoreham. They drank the proffered mead, and ate the slices of chicken and pickles that Rhiannon offered them, but they became tight-lipped when they realised that Godwin, Aethelwolf's most senior ally, was in attendance. Nevertheless, he moved among them affably.

'How long it took me to ride here!' he complained to the Abbot of Selsey. 'The trackways are pitted with potholes, the bridges collapsing, sheep and cattle wander unfenced. The inability of your people to move freely must be a great hindrance to trading. Even attending mass must be a struggle for many. Something comprehensive should be done to amend the situation!'

This statement was immediately seized upon by the guests. A host of ideas were offered for setting the south coast back on its feet again, and he agreed with every suggestion made. Swift watched with wry amusement. Harold had always been skilled at gaining confidences. He had these people eating out of his hand, like a shepherd boy with his lambs.

Goodwife Bredbaker appeared in the doorway. Some of the guests looked askance, but it was important to Swift that the peasantry should be represented.

'Look at me,' the goodwife chortled, and spun round in a newly dyed smock and a large-brimmed hat she'd found in a field. Behind her were a bevy of common folk dressed in freshly sponged Norland coats and jackets they'd looted from the raiders' bodies. They were greeted with a smatter of applause. Swift set them in a place of honour beside her and began her welcome.

'Fellow Southsaxons,' she said, 'a festivity was recently held in Winchester to celebrate the heroes of the Battle of Hamblesea. Were you there, Goodwife Bredbaker? Were you, Alderman Eadwig?' Her voice turned to scorn. 'Of course you were not. You're from the south coast, which for Winchester folk is an irrelevance! You were the heroes that day, and you will receive a fine reward from me for your bravery, and also one from the Bishop of Chichester . . .'

'And from me too,' added Harold Godwin.

'Thank you, High Alderman!' said Swift. 'Your generosity is appreciated. But from Winchester you will receive nothing.'

'Shame!' cried Goodwife Bredbaker. 'We cannot tolerate such an insult.' She was a tough old woman despite her lowly position.

'I agree,' responded Swift. 'And we are not alone in being outraged by the treatment we receive. All Britain knows of our dire straits, and many of high rank support us. See, we have with us today Moira, princess of Northumbria, who is among our fiercest supporters. I ask you, should we continue to tolerate the slights meted out to us? Who was it who defeated the Norlanders at Hamblesea?'

'We did!' the outraged peasants roared back.

'And what resources were we given to combat them?'

'None!'

'None indeed! On my own initiative I built four beacons to signal enemy attacks,' Swift railed. 'There should have been a hundred and four! Complacent Winchester ignored the danger even though we continually warned of the Norland threat. And while Wessex folk stuffed themselves with ribs and trotters at their Landing Day feast, we risked our lives for them. Do you wish to continue living under their thraldom?'

She spoke for an hour. When she came to a triumphant conclusion, the room was filled with shouting, stamping and demands for liberty. And when Harold Godwin stood on a table and toasted her as the queen of the south coast, Swift could not keep the smile from her face.

Later that night, when the last folk had gone, she and Harold lay by the fire under a bearskin rug.

'You set Southsaxon blood racing,' he said. 'But can the south coast withstand the might of the house of Wolf? Is it truly possible?'

'It is in hand,' Swift replied softly. 'I can raise an army of three hundred fighters. They will have weapons and horses the like of which you have never seen.'

'From where? From Moira's father in Northumbria? From your cousin Burgred in Mercia?'

'I have already told you too much. Know only that I have the means to make such a thing come to pass. Stay by me and you can be part of it.' She kissed the tip of her finger and placed it on his lips.

THIRTY-FOUR

The Flat of His Blade

Cardinal Balotelli sliced the loaves and Asser filleted the trout and spread it on the warm bread. A patient line of ragged Romans sheltered under the Constantinian aqueduct, waiting for the distribution to begin. The cardinal and his men performed this duty every Thursday around the poorer parts of the city. It had been Asser's idea, and the cardinal revelled in it, a series of simple and repetitive tasks that put a smile on everyone's faces, a relief from the other six days of each week spent planning and plotting.

'I've received a message from Kennet, although sadly not from one of your pigeons,' said Asser.

'I know. They all died,' replied Balotelli. 'Ultimately it was not a successful experiment. What does Kennet say?'

'Wolf will arrive in seven days.'

'It's been two weeks since you returned. What's the man been doing?'

'Taking pleasure, I believe,' replied Asser, 'which is a healthy restorative, apparently.'

'Indeed. Considering recent events, you've looked much brighter since your own arrival.'

Asser ignored him. 'Seneschal François will ride on ahead, and he and I will write a formal concord to which Wolf and the Pope will affix their signatures.'

'We must invite the soldiers to the signing,' said Balotelli.

'What soldiers?'

'The ones who wrote me the letter that began this whole enterprise. They're back from Illyria. I think they'll be very happy with the way we're proceeding.'

When there was sufficient food on the table, Balotelli called the crowd forward. Asser gave them their bread and fish, and the cardinal handed out cinnamon biscuits.

'An additional issue has arisen,' said Balotelli softly. 'I've been informed by the Bishop of Winchester that a plot is being hatched in Wessex. It seems Wolf's daughter is planning to marry the emperor's son, Louis the Stammerer, and with the aid of a few hundred of his soldiers they intend to occupy the south coast.' He passed Asser another tray of sliced loaves.

'A fractured Wessex would not be in our interests and would aggravate Wolf mightily,' said Asser.

'It would,' replied Balotelli. 'So you'll squash the idea, will you?'

Asser pressed the flat of his blade firmly into the flesh of a succulent trout.

Asser's hands stank of fish. He washed them in the bowl in his room at the palazzo, changed his cassock and peered round Doctore Guido's door. The Doctore was propped up in bed, wrapped in bloodstained bandages, his eyes half closed. An elderly nun was feeding him pieces of bread soaked in milk and honey.

'Why are you back so soon?' he mumbled between mouthfuls. 'You sat with me all night.'

'Someone had to read to you,' retorted Asser. 'I chose the Book of Deuteronomy because I knew it would put you to sleep.' The nurse glanced at him reprovingly. 'How is he, Sister?'

'His nose and several ribs are broken and he is passing blood. I suspect his back was kicked several times.'

'It was,' replied Asser. 'The perpetrator will be found and severely punished.'

The Doctore shook his head.

'He will,' said Asser. 'I swear it, my friend.'

'You are not to pursue him!' the Doctore said forcibly.

'The man savaged you.'

He sighed. 'Sister Clara,' he said, 'fetch me some more squares of linen. These are bloodied.'

The nurse looked at the two men suspiciously and left the room.

'Come closer,' the Doctore whispered. 'I know who attacked me, Asser.'

Asser stared at him. 'How? We must immediately—'

'No.' The Doctore coughed and his face crumpled in pain. 'To punish him now would destroy everything we're working so hard to achieve. He will receive his deserts, that I swear, but for the moment, in the name of Christ, return to your work, write the concord and leave him be!'

Three days later, in the emperor's home in the hills overlooking Rome, Asser flung down his pen and stretched his aching fingers. A serried row of scribes and advisers did likewise and leant back in their chairs. Plegmond cleared a space among the crumpled parchments and set down towels and scented water so they could wipe the exhaustion from their faces.

'Day has broken!' said Asser, and yawned. The concord had

been completed. The secrecy surrounding its contents could be lifted, and Wolf could publicly sign it in front of representatives from all over Christendom. The details had been endless, and he was proud of what he and the seneschal had achieved. He crossed to the window and observed the sun rising over the city. This little palace was known as Caesar's Haven and was where the Emperor Julius and his paramour Cleopatra had once disported. It was luxurious, quiet and discreet, the ideal location for such complex negotiations.

'Let us hope Aethelwolf isn't alarmed by the concord's length,' said the seneschal.

'It's written in the gentlest of tones,' replied Asser. 'It wouldn't startle a hare.' He liked François; underneath his flummery lay a fine mind.

The seneschal stood up and yawned. 'We'll be glad to be abed, I think.'

Hands were shaken, there were a few murmurs of congratulations and the entire company moved towards the door – except for Asser, who remained seated as he'd planned. 'There is one problem,' he said.

'I don't think so,' replied the seneschal suspiciously. 'Every page has been agreed. Every line.'

'There's a small but profoundly important issue that still needs resolution,' replied Asser. 'It's an infuriation! But may I explain?'

The seneschal gave his reluctant acquiescence and signalled to his scribes to return to their places.

'Six years ago, Lady Swift of South Hamwicshire stayed at the emperor's palace in Amiens, and it was rumoured that she and Charles's son Louis . . . you'll be familiar with this allegation, I'm sure . . . it was said they shared an intimacy.' He looked slowly round the room so everyone would be quite sure what he meant.

'That is not true,' said the seneschal. He sounded a little weary at the introduction of what he clearly considered to be trivial gossip.

'I'm sure you're correct. Nevertheless, words of love were allegedly spoken, marriage was discussed.'

'A fairy tale,' said the seneschal. 'Malicious and baseless!'

'I agree. And even if it were true, which it's clearly not, it would have been of little import. The two parties have seen nothing of each other for many years, other opportunities might have presented themselves, fresh dalliances may have been considered. I suspect no one has given the relationship a moment's further thought.'

'Exactly.'

'Unfortunately, though, vicious tongues are now saying that not only is Prince Louis about to marry Lady Swift, but accompanying him to South Hamwicshire will be an army of three hundred men, which will of course be interpreted as a threat to the stability of all Wessex, even if it's purely an arrangement to keep the lovers secure from the occasional deranged assassin.'

'There is no such army.'

'I know. It's complete nonsense. But you'll understand that however important this concord may be, we couldn't possibly give it our support if such a rumour were still abroad.'

'Father Asser,' said the seneschal, 'I give you my word. Louis will neither marry Lady Swift nor send fighting men to south Wessex.'

Asser adopted a smile brighter even than the morning light now flooding through the windows. 'Thank you!' he said. 'That is a great weight off my shoulders.'

Once more the seneschal's advisers stood to leave.

'Of course,' said Asser, 'you'll understand that the Pope will want this in writing.'

*

Eventually Asser returned to the Undercroft bearing a copy of the newly drafted letter to the Pope guaranteeing that relations between Louis and Swift would be broken off, and that no Frankish soldiers would be crossing the Narrow Sea to support her.

Clothilde and Balotelli were discussing the number of copies of the concord needed for circulation to the foreign dignitaries attending the signing.

'How is young Elswith?' enquired Asser.

'She is possessed of a fierce anger,' answered Clothilde, 'but with Christ's help she'll defeat it.'

Asser turned to Balotelli and presented him with the seneschal's letter.

'The business of the Lady Swift has been resolved?' the cardinal enquired.

'Indeed, the seneschal has promised that Prince Louis will write to her to disabuse her of any notion that a Frankish army will be coming to her aid.'

'Yes, that should nip it in the bud. We must tell the Bishop of Winchester, of course.'

Asser nodded. 'I've already sent word on.'

'Good work,' said Balotelli, and went back to his conversation with Clothilde.

Asser looked round at the freshly scrubbed Undercroft. All that remained of his magnificent map was a few burnt pieces of wood. How profoundly frustrating it was that those who had perpetrated the attack had so effectively disguised their identity. He squatted in front of the pile. The small remnant of the map with the Doctore's blood on it was still there. He turned it over and stared at it for a long time.

In the House of Illusion, Abdulalah peered over Asser's shoulder at the bloodied footprint on the broken piece of the mappa mundi.

'You see how fine the shoe must be?' said Asser. 'The edges are crisp. There are intricate and finely crafted patterns etched into it to prevent the owner from slipping. They are hand-cut. The pattern is unique.'

'And you want me to find the shoe this print came from?' said Abdulalah.

Asser nodded and smiled at him. He'd known the old rogue since he was a boy. He'd been sent by his seminarium to a dilapidated church to assist Father Chrysostom, an ancient priest hampered by the rheum. Though shaky of leg, Chrysostom was remarkably sprightly of mind, whereas young Asser was constantly on the verge of sleep, particularly when forced to spend hours polishing brass, copying sermons and sweeping floors. One afternoon, the priest found him slumped in the pulpit face-down in St Paul's Second Epistle to the Colossians. The kindly father had sent him to Abdulalah to collect his weekly medication, and on his return had given him a tiny pinch. After that first experience, Asser had struck up a close bond with both Abdulalah and his medication. It was a friendship that had lasted years. Even when Asser was thrown in the papal dungeon, it didn't fade. Abdulalah visited him three times, twice with small smuggled packages of the medication and once, when his supplies were low, with a slice of fig and date pudding.

The old alchemist turned the wooden fragment from side to side and pulled a series of exaggerated faces as though considering the matter deeply. 'It'll cost you,' he said finally.

'I know.'

'Clovis!' he called. His assistant appeared, a willowy young man with olive skin, crafty eyes and an expressionless face. He reminded Asser of the boys who smiled beguilingly at pilgrims, lured them into back alleys and took their purses at knifepoint.

'Find the fancy bootmaker who made this shoe, would you, and frighten him a little so we can discover who it belongs to.'

Clovis put the bloodied board in a sack, winked and walked away.

THIRTY-FIVE

Stumphand

Guthrum stood on the stark black cliff overlooking his settlement and stared out to sea. He was soaking his stump of a hand in a barrel of vinegar. Mighty Odin, how the mixture stank. The ocean was empty save for his two longships and a few coasting fulmars. 'How many clans did we send word to?' he demanded. His young cousin Sigurd didn't answer. 'How many?' He lifted his arm from the barrel and watched the vinegar drip onto the grass.

'Twenty-one, I think,' replied Sigurd.

'And only two have answered?'

'Perhaps there's a storm.'

'There is no storm,' said Guthrum.

Sigurd wrapped a leather bandage round the stump and pulled it tight. He was a dangerous young man who'd lived wild after his mother had died and had been pegged out on the shoreline many times for fighting and stealing. But he was devoted to mighty Guthrum and served him well.

'We could bring the house of Wolf to its knees if the clans

would join us,' Guthrum continued. He thought back to the rolling downs of Wessex, the wide rivers brimming with fish, the slow, fat kine. They could make all that their own if they were so minded, build ports fit for their ocean-going vessels, trade with Salamanca and Constantinople. It was hard to imagine how it would ever happen, but it was a dream worth dreaming. 'Why won't they fight?' he snapped. 'Our people are cowardly fools!'

'Calm yourself, big man,' Sigurd cried suddenly, and pointed out to sea. 'This is a good day!'

The outline of a ship had appeared on the horizon. Slowly it approached them.

'Save your cheering, lad,' replied Guthrum, gesturing to a black pennant now visible high on its mast. 'It's Haakun Haakunson.'

'Don't let old enmities play your mind false,' replied Sigurd. 'He may be a whore's snatch, but you need his ships.'

Guthrum flexed his one, strong hand. He'd known Haakunson since they were young. He'd been a noisy, foolish man even then, and Guthrum had made no attempt to disguise his disdain after their falling-out over a slave woman. Now, Haakun was clan leader of the Shieldsmen, and had boatbuilders at his disposal. But the issue between them wouldn't go away, nor did he want it to.

They walked through the settlement and towards the sea, past the longhouses with their turfed roofs sloping almost to the ground, ducking under the strings of dried herring slung between them. It was Guthrum's island now. He had no wish to see Haakun here.

Nevertheless, they waited at the water's edge for his boat to land, and when it pulled in, he put his arm round Haakun's shoulder as he was obliged to and led him to the fire.

Haakun sat on a log, his crew behind him. Someone handed

him a beaker of ale, and he gossiped with the islanders about fish and tides, and told them about his fine new fighting ships. He was a strange-looking creature, thought Guthrum. Three times he'd won the wrestling contest at the Yorvik fair, but he was ungainly and cumbersome, as though the gods who'd made him had used clay that hadn't set as it should.

'Eat with us,' Guthrum said, 'and I'll tell you my plans. No Norlander has ever overwintered in Wessex, but in a few years we could be ploughing our own furrows and tending our cattle.'

'I have no interest in your fields and cows,' replied Haakun. 'We're fighters, not dull-witted graziers.'

There was silence, broken only by a mewing kittiwake.

'This is my campaign,' Guthrum said.

'Your campaign?' scoffed Haakun, rising to his feet. 'You were out-thought and out-fought in Wessex, yet you wish to return there?' He paced round the fire with a smile on his face. 'You stink of defeat and wear a glove as empty as your addled head. Men of the Farnes, I've sailed here to invite you to join me. Guthrum can stay home and tend the pigs.'

'Haakun!' Guthrum said calmly. 'You think you can insult me on my own isle?'

'I do,' Haakun replied. 'You're no fighter. You're fit only to stand stock still in the mud and scare the ravens.'

'You wish to provoke me,' said Guthrum. 'I'm happy for you to succeed. We will hold a sorting. You and I.'

'A sorting?' laughed Haakun. 'You jest. There's no honour in combat with a stumphand. Sit down!'

'We will hold a sorting,' repeated Guthrum.

Haakun shook his head.

'A sorting!' Guthrum said, and spat in his face.

The Norlanders gathered round a worn circle on the cliff. Guthrum and Haakun stood outside it with their supporters.

Sigurd offered Guthrum two swords.

'The choice is of no consequence,' Guthrum said. 'You decide. Is my bandage tight?'

'It's as you wanted it,' replied his cousin.

Carl Carlson, an old man bruised and battered by decades of combat, had been assigned to judge the fight. He began the proclamation. 'Haakun Haakunson . . .' Haakun walked into the circle to much cheering from his crew, one of whom walked behind him carrying his sword and axe. 'Guthrum Guthrumson . . .' Guthrum entered accompanied by Sigurd. The cheering was more subdued, and Guthrum felt a twist of irritation. His islanders were wary of showing him support; they had little confidence that he could win.

The two combatants stared at each other contemptuously. Haakun's man and Sigurd plunged the blades of the fighters' swords and axes into the ground.

'Combatants, greet one another for a final time,' called Carl Carlson.

Haakun smiled and held out his hand.

'When the horn sounds, the combat will begin.'

Guthrum's uninjured fingers wrapped themselves tightly round his opponent's wrist. Haakun attempted to shake himself free, but Guthrum held him like a vice.

'You have agreed to fight to the—' began Carl Carlson.

Guthrum smashed his leather-wrapped fist into Haakun's right cheek, and there was the sound of bone shattering. As Haakun attempted to steady himself, Guthrum delivered a blow to his other cheek, then let go of his hand. Haakun staggered backwards, away from his weapons, his face bleeding copiously. Guthrum followed and hit him twice more in the face, then drew a short seax from his jacket and jabbed at him fast and hard like a chicken pecking corn. Haakun retreated through the ring of Norlanders, but every time he tried to steady himself, Guthrum administered another blow. Haakun's man grabbed his sword and raced towards him. Sigurd sprinted to the man's side, sliced into his arm with his war-axe, and the sword dropped to the earth.

'A helping hand is forbidden, cheatling!' Sigurd cried.

Guthrum was humming as he did when planing wood in his yard. The Farne men were shouting encouragement. Haakun's crew stood frozen, overwhelmed by the speed of the attack.

The fighters were well outside the circle now, heading towards the verge of the cliff. Haakun staggered back under the never-ending rain of blows until they reached the edge. Guthrum thought of all the years that had passed since the squabbles of their youth. How insignificant they seemed compared to this moment. He grinned, and a little hope dawned in Haakun's eyes.

Guthrum kicked Haakun ferociously in the midriff. His opponent's arms flailed wildly; he toppled backwards and plunged down onto the rocks and the swirling water below.

Guthrum turned to the Norlanders and gave a deep-throated roar. 'Who will lead this campaign?' he yelled.

Every Norlander dropped to their knee.

Cuts and swellings had appeared on Guthrum's stump. Sigurd tended them and picked out the small pieces of broken rock.

'The stone in your bindings has shattered,' he said. 'You hit him with more force than I expected. They'll be calling you Guthrum Strong-in-the-Arm now.'

'It'll be a month before I can fight again,' Guthrum said.

'In future we'll use metal blades, not stones,' said Sigurd. 'They'll leave pretty patterns on the faces of our enemies.'

Guthrum stared out to sea. He took pleasure in his win, but he'd only be truly content when he rounded the chalk cliffs of the south once more. He was tired of the bleak north-east, the endless wind and the dull taste of winter blubber. One day, he'd sit on the Winchester throne surrounded by buxom girls smelling of roses and cows' milk, and Aethelwolf would be blind and earless at his feet.

THIRTY-SIX

The Letter From Frankia

As soon as Hawk crossed the border into Swift's territory, the drumming began: spoons on kettles, knife hilts on platters, hammers on wooden stakes. In every village it was the same: men, women and children with anger on their faces. It was deeply disturbing. His soldiers were Essex farmers in borrowed helmets; he didn't want them unnerved by this terrible din.

They stopped at the Giant's Cave on the side of Bevan Hill, a league short of Hamblesea. As children, he and Bear had played in its dark recesses, entrapping and slaughtering imaginary half-naked Britons. It had been chosen as today's meeting place, because although it was well hidden, you could see through the trees across the southern downs all the way to the south coast and the Isle of Wight beyond. No one could sneak up on them unnoticed.

The cave was no longer the place of adventure he remembered from his childhood; it was caked in moss and gull shit and smelt like something had died in it.

Standing at its mouth was Harold Godwin, wearing his usual ingratiating smile. A surge of contempt welled up inside Hawk.

'I have ridden all night because your message told me I would learn something to my advantage if I came here in haste. I trust the journey will have been worth my while.'

'Please sit beside me,' replied Godwin, and laid his cloak courteously over a mossy rock.

'I'll stand,' said Hawk.

'Very well,' said Godwin. 'Your sister has become betrothed to the emperor's son, Louis the Stammerer, who has pledged her three hundred Frankish warriors. They plan to seize the southern coast and create a new kingdom separate from Wessex.'

He paused to allow the effect of this news to sink in.

'Why am I not surprised? They must be stopped immediately,' replied Hawk. He felt a little panicked. Would he be called upon to prevent such a thing from happening?

'The situation is being addressed,' replied Godwin reassuringly. 'Bishop Humbert learnt of the plot some time ago. He wrote to the Pope's people, who have persuaded the emperor to put a stop to it. A letter is even now on its way to your sister from Louis, apprising her of the termination of their relationship.'

'I am pleased to hear it,' said Hawk, 'though I would rather have quashed the invasion myself. But why did I have to traipse halfway across Wessex to hear all this?'

'I have always been your loyal servant, Aethelhawk, even when the misunderstanding arose over Lady Osburgh's honour.'

Hawk squawked with laughter. 'And my brother and I had you dumped on the floor of the Kingsworthy whorehouse,' he said, revelling in the memory.

'Exactly,' said Godwin. 'Such upsets occur, and it is our Christian duty not to dwell on them. I have people on the Frankish coast who have informed me that the letter will be arriving at Southamwic on one of the emperor's ships in two days' time. And if you are able to apprehend her with this letter in her hand . . .'

'. . . she will be hanged for treachery,' said Hawk, gleeful that such a glorious opportunity had suddenly dropped in his lap.

'She may well indeed.'

'But how can this be arranged?' said Hawk, his eyes shining. 'We can't snatch the letter from the hand of the emperor's messenger as he passes it to her – that would create a diplomatic furore – and we can't wait till he's returned to his ship. Swift will burn the letter as soon as she's read it. So how can we ensure she is caught with it in her hands?'

'I have always thought I would make a fine Warden of South Hamwicshire and the Sussex Coast,' Godwin said softly.

'You know how we can do it?' asked Hawk eagerly.

'I do,' replied Godwin. 'Although I have already incurred considerable expense in bringing this about.'

'You want wardenship of the south coast and a sum of money in return for exposing my sister?'

'If that's what you think appropriate, I will gladly accept it,' said Godwin. 'I have told the Lady Swift that a message is on its way to her from the emperor bearing good news, and I have recommended that it be collected by her man, who will take it to her at a secret location.'

'And I will follow that man,' said Hawk, 'and when he hands it to her, I will seize her and the message.'

'Exactly.'

'Good, very good. There'll be no objection from my brother, Bear; he loathes her as much as I do.'

'Well then, let us proceed,' said Godwin, and held out his hand.

Hawk smiled at him, remembering with pleasure the day he and Bear had instructed the guards to have him abducted.

Had the obnoxious ingrate really thought he could seduce their stepmother, assassinate their father and seize the throne without their being informed? Even Bishop Humbert had wanted him given a beating. But they'd agreed to let him live because the bishop had said he could be useful, and he'd been proved right. Godwin was now their puppet. He'd wormed his way into their sister's gash and had told Hawk everything he needed to know in order to bring her down. He returned the handshake.

On the day of the ship's expected arrival, Hawk placed his men at the crossroads and ferry crossings around Southamwic and waited. The most imposing building in Southamwic was the quay owner's house: solid stone from the old Roman times, three storeys high and with a walkway round the top floor from which the comings and goings of town and harbour could be observed.

'An excellent vantage point,' he said.

'Indeed. Do have some more wine,' said the quay owner, his face twitching. Doubtless he secretly supported Swift, as so many of these petty officials did, but with his wife and children downstairs under guard, the man wouldn't betray him.

The harbour was busier than ever. Logs were being unloaded, iron, tin, slate, slaves and barley. Hunting dogs were yelping incessantly in their cages, foreign traders were squabbling over bundles of cloth and baskets of trinkets.

Kretch, his strong, dull-witted sergeant-at-arms, gave him a nudge. Swift's man Wigan was riding down the crowded street. He drew up at the harbour-workers' drinking shop, tied his horse to a post and disappeared inside. He'd been one of the finest fighters in Aethelwolf's army, but time and battle had taken their toll; now he was slow and limped a little. But he was still canny. Swift had made a wise choice entrusting him with collecting the Frankish letter.

Time passed. As dusk approached, a fine ship bearing the

imperial double-headed eagle dropped anchor in the middle of the harbour. A skiff was lowered and headed shorewards bearing a single passenger. Hawk watched from the quay owner's house as the man climbed a ladder up to the dockside. He was well dressed, a Frank from the shape of his beard and the cut of his cloak, with a leather satchel over his shoulder. He strode out of the dock through the mêlée of carts, horses, seamen and porters and into the drinking shop. Two of Hawk's men were already inside it dressed in rough clothes to disguise their identity. Once the letter had been handed over, they'd follow Wigan to wherever his mistress might be. This would be simple.

Suddenly there were cries of alarm, then Wigan was rolling backwards out of the shop window into the street. He untied his horse and made to ride off, but as he did so, a cart loaded with timber swung round the corner and horse and rider crashed into it, sending them tumbling to the ground. Wigan heaved himself back up and remounted, though now the animal was limping and he was bleeding profusely. Hawk looked on helplessly. Where the hell were his men?

Eventually they staggered out of the shop, but Wigan was already weaving his way through the throng and in moments had disappeared.

'What happened, for Christ's sake?' Hawk shouted down to them.

'He must have had his own people in there,' one called back. 'They attacked us without warning.'

Hawk roared with frustration. 'Why are you still here? Go! Stop him at the ferry crossing.' Why did misfortune continually befall him? Whenever he attempted to assert his authority, he was thwarted by the Fates. He wouldn't fail this time. His sister would not make a fool out of him again. He would unmask her as a traitor and her punishment would be terrible.

*

Hawk rode to Hamblesea. He had hated the crone Agneta since he was a child – her short stature, the hair above her lip, the look of withering contempt she'd constantly directed towards him even though he had been an aetheling and she a mere drudge. But if anyone knew where Swift was, it would surely be her.

He and his men burst into the village and burnt down three or four huts to set the tone. There was the usual sobbing and wailing, but once they'd cuffed a few villagers, the noise quietened down.

Kretch dragged Agneta out of her hovel and threw her at Hawk's feet.

'Where's Lady Swift?' he demanded.

The tiny old woman said nothing.

'Where's my sister?' he repeated.

'Eat my shit,' the old woman replied. Kretch silenced her with a single blow.

'Tie her to a gate,' Hawk instructed.

His men did so, and lashed her with a whip, but still she didn't say anything.

Hawk was growing frustrated. 'Torch her hut too,' he said, 'and kill her goat.'

Alderman Eadwig came running down the hill, shouting and waving his arms. He dropped to his knees in front of Hawk and begged him to stop.

'Cease your gabbling,' said Hawk. 'I have no time for niceties. If my sister's not at home, where is she?'

'I don't know, Aethel. I've no idea. I swear to God.'

Kretch hit his arm with the hilt of his sword and there was the sound of bone snapping.

The old man yelled in agony. 'I beg you, leave my village be and I'll tell you what I know,' he said, tears of pain falling down his cheeks.

'Mouth shut, Eadwig,' ordered Agneta, and Kretch hit her again.

'She could be in Nutley,' Eadwig cried, 'at your family chapel. She's trying to make the monastery habitable again.'

'What a good woman she is!' replied Hawk. 'We will go and assist her.'

Hawk and his men rode off; Agneta lay on the ground bloodied and cursing.

My sister's dreams are about to be shattered, he thought. Once they'd climbed Dover's cliffs together, swum in Swanage Bay, swung on ladders made of rope. Now he would be the one to have her executed. He felt the tiniest twinge of remorse, but it didn't last.

Swift was confident Wigan would collect Louis' letter without too much difficulty. He'd called on the services of some of his old army companions, who would come to his aid if necessary. She had agreed to meet here at Nutley because she had a key to the family chapel, and it was the perfect place for a secret assignation.

Her servants had loaded up a cartful of furniture and cleaning materials at Hamblesea Hall, Rhiannon had driven the cart and Swift had hidden under a carpet. They'd left the cart and its contents at the encampment the monks had set up while rebuilding the monastery, and in the fading light had made their way to the chapel. As they came close, they could see a brazier's faint glow through the tiny window slit. Alderman Eadwig had arranged for it to be lit to keep her warm and provide the means for the letter's destruction. They went in and locked the door.

This would be the night she'd planned for so long. The south coast clergy were waiting on her word. Once they knew the Frankish soldiers were on their way, they'd announce from every pulpit that it was God's will that she should become

High Aethel of South Hamwicshire and the Sussex Coast, and the insurrection would begin.

It was pitch dark now. Rhiannon was sitting by the brazier, humming. The chapel was as it had always been: musty, a little damp, but strangely reassuring. When they were young, Swift and Bear had sat in here on each side of their father, listening to the chanting of the priest, and sometimes Father had put an arm round them. Hawk would lie with his head in their mother's lap, sobbing over some imagined slight; she'd gently straighten their clothes, wipe the specks of dirt from their cheeks and poke their father when his snores broke the silence.

An owl hooted, a fox screeched, and she heard a limping horse on the path outside.

'I have it,' Wigan called. 'Make haste.'

She unlocked the door, and he fell from his mount and stumbled towards her.

'You're wounded, poor man,' she cried. 'Let me attend to you.'

'There was trouble in Southamwic and Hawk's men were patrolling the river crossings. I had to ride inland, but I fear they may have followed me. Take the letter quickly,' he said, and drew it from his coat.

But the moment she took it, there was a fearful commotion, and men came bursting out of the bushes bearing weapons. Swift's worst fear had been realised. She'd been betrayed.

Hawk's men attacked the injured and exhausted Wigan ferociously. They threw him to the ground, stamped on him and kicked him in the ribs, the back, the head. There was a howl of rage, and out of the chapel burst Rhiannon, wielding her knife. But as she raised her arm to bury the blade into the back of one of the attackers, Hawk's sergeant-at-arms wrapped his big arms tight round her, lifted her high into the air and flung her back into the little church. She skidded across the floor, hit the wall with a crash and lay still.

Hawk stepped from the shadows and snatched the letter from his sister's hand. 'What a night this has been,' he said, 'but we've found you now, that's the important thing, and your letter is safe. Let me read it to you.' He tore it open and scrutinised it. 'Ah! It's from Prince Louis, the son of the Holy Roman Emperor. You do have grand friends, don't you? He says he's deeply sorry he's taken so long to reply, but matters of state have inhibited his decision. Now, though, he realises he cannot put in peril the recent agreement between Aethelwolf and the emperor – a new agreement, how lovely! – though it breaks his heart to decline your request. Likewise he must regretfully withdraw his proposal of marriage, and the three hundred men he promised you will no longer be forthcoming ... What in God's name did you want with three hundred men? Surely they can't all be your lovers? He knows you'll understand his predicament. You do, don't you? Yes, I can see from your face that you do.' Swift said nothing. 'How is my dear Moira, by the way?' he persisted. 'She'll return to me once you're dead, of course.'

'How did you know?' she demanded.

'Know what, my dear?'

'That a letter was coming for me from Frankia. Who could possibly ...' She stopped and gave the rueful smile of a gambler who'd lost all on their last throw. 'It was Harold Godwin, wasn't it?'

How stupid she'd been to accept the word of such a devious wretch simply because he'd smiled at her kindly when he held her in his arms.

'I couldn't possibly say,' replied Hawk.

THIRTY-SEVEN

The Shoe

'A little sniff?' enquired Abdulalah jauntily.

'That's what I came for. And a mug of fortified wine, if you have such a thing.'

The old man disappeared into his House of Illusion and returned with two steaming beakers. Asser would happily have sat drinking all morning, but the old man began bouncing about excitedly.

'Do you love me?' he asked.

'Yes . . .' replied Asser tentatively.

'More than life itself?'

'Possibly. Why?'

Abdulalah gave a shout as glorious as the disciples witnessing the risen Christ. 'We've found him. We've found him. The man who wore your shoe!'

Asser's aching head, his anger, the feeling of duty that had weighed on him so heavily instantly melted away. 'You will go to heaven,' he said. 'I will write to St Peter personally. How did you do it?'

'Clovis!' Abdulalah called, and the taciturn boy appeared. 'You discovered the bootmaker, didn't you, lad?' Clovis nodded. 'You hardly had to touch him and he told you our man's name, right?' Clovis smiled. 'And you broke into his house, didn't you, and the naughty fellow had lots of fancy shoes, but there was one particular pair in an old sack he'd pushed to the back of his garderobe, and they had the exact same carving on the soles, just like we wanted. But then . . . tell Father Asser what else was on those shoes, lad.'

'Blood,' said Clovis coolly, and shrugged.

'Spots of blood!' repeated Abdulalah. 'So do you want the shoe? Do you?'

'Of course I do!'

'You have two silver pieces?'

'Tell me the man's name or I'll likely die on the spot,' Asser said, and passed over the money.

The old man plunged his hand into the recesses of his voluminous gown. 'The villain who owns this lovely shoe is . . .' he pulled it out and presented it to Asser, 'Signor Fabio Gilotti.'

'Fabio Gilotti?' The Doctore was looking a little better, sitting in his favourite chair in his rooms overlooking the palazzo garden, holding the shoe disdainfully between his fingers. 'You wish Balotelli to show this shoe to the assembly of cardinals and tell them it proves Fabio Gilotti attacked me?' he said.

'Yes,' replied Asser. 'You told me not to search for your attacker, and I didn't. A young boy at the bazaar gave me this shoe.'

'The High Aethel of Wessex is about to arrive in Rome, Father Asser. After a month of wheedling and cajoling, the Pope has managed to persuade every cardinal, even the Notarii, to attend the signing of the concord. For the first time since Benedict's investiture, the Church will be united under the watchful eye of the kings and princes of Europe. And you want to undermine all that with this incendiary accusation?'

'I do.'

'You know who Fabio Gilotti is?'

'I do! He was the man who attacked you.'

'He is the brother of Cardinal Gilotti,' continued the Doctore, as though Asser hadn't asked, 'who is the most senior member of the Notarii. To accuse Fabio of such horrible crimes would be to declare war on the entire cardinalate. Do we wish him torn apart by wild horses? We do. But could he offer a thousand reasons for the presence of the shoe in his room? He could. Without further evidence, his brother would have the allegation summarily dismissed, we'd be accused of blackening the reputation of a senior Roman figure, the Undercroft would be shut down and reprisals would begin.'

Asser sighed with frustration. 'Without further evidence?'

'Exactly.'

'What kind of evidence?'

'I doubt such evidence exists. Now wheel me into the garden. The doves in our aviary are in need of seed.'

THIRTY-EIGHT

Rhiannon

Rhiannon came to and shook her throbbing head. When she put her fingers to the back of it, she could feel a bump, and dried blood in her hair. Were the men still outside? Where was Swift? She listened hard, but all was silent. She pulled herself to her feet and tried the chapel door, but it was locked. She peered around and her gaze fell on a little window above the altar. She climbed onto it, prised apart the shutters with a small wooden cross, wriggled through and jumped out onto the ground. It was dark, but she could make out the shape of Wigan's body on the path. She shook him, but there was no sign of life. She put her fingertips to his cheek; he was cold to the touch. He was probably dead, but she wasn't sure. He'd whipped her once or twice, but he gave her titbits and let her sleep all day when she had the fever. She'd find someone to take care of him.

Some way off, she could see a light flickering in the monks' encampment. She made her way towards it and came to a shack with a lamp burning in the window. 'Help!' she yelled. 'There's someone down by the chapel! He's been attacked!'

She ducked into the shadows, and a few moments later two monks stumbled out. She followed them at a distance as they headed towards the little church. When they found Wigan and she was satisfied they were tending to him, she began the long tramp back to Hamblesea. She knew the way even in the pitch dark, through Cheadley, Spode and Little Rampton, the journey she'd made with Swift many times before.

When dawn broke, she found a little copse with a stream running through it. She picked a few handfuls of berries and ran her hands through the earth looking for cob nuts the squirrels might have buried. She drank from the stream and ate the nuts and berries, then dug a shallow resting place, covered herself with leaves and fell asleep.

She woke after noon, brushed the leaves aside and lay looking at the starlings flocking. Then she yawned, stretched, and headed to Swift's hall.

Back in Hamblesea, while she waited for Swift to return, she slept in a ruined barn so the servants wouldn't spot her and try to force her into dreary labour. For two days she watched them cleaning, cooking, plumping and primping, and the slaves mending the roofs and tending the gardens as they always did. In the daytime she hunted hedgehogs and shrews in the woods; at night she slipped into the house and stole bread and curds.

By the third day, the servants were becoming uneasy. 'When will Swift be back?' she heard the cook say. On the fourth day, the restlessness had become anxiety. 'They say she's been put in prison. Maybe she's not coming back at all.'

It was then that it dawned on her. She had no need to stay. All she had here was the vague promise of freedom in five years' time, but with Swift and Wigan gone, that pledge was worthless. A strange feeling crept over her, one she could not quite name. It made her skin prickle. Where should she go?

Her people were few around these parts, most of them sold into slavery or pushed out onto the edges of the land. But she'd heard tell of whole villages of them in the far south-west. Yes, she'd leave here and find the free Britons in Cornwall.

She'd need a few trinkets she could exchange for food and shelter. She rolled up her sleeves, plunged them deep into the garden privy and fished out two old spoons, a broken brooch and a handful of copper coins. She put them in a sack along with some magic stones she'd found down the well. She strengthened her worn-out shoes with pieces of leather from the stables, and found a flask of sour peach wine buried in the hay loft. She lay down in the hay, drank half the wine and waited for nightfall and her escape.

She was woken by the sound of men yelling. Her head was thick, her mouth parched. Light streamed in through the slats. She crouched low in the hay and listened to them stomping about and giving orders. 'We're taking everything,' one was shouting. 'The furniture, the carpets, all of it.'

'What right do you have?' the cook replied tearfully. 'This is the property of Lady Swift.'

'Not any more,' said the man. 'She's to be hanged. They're Lady Winifred's possessions now, bound for the Isle of Wight.'

'What will become of us?'

'That's not my problem,' the man said gruffly. 'Where's the slave they call Rhiannon, the one with the brand on her face? I have special orders to bring her with me.'

Rhiannon started. She would not go back to slavery, not now, not ever.

She grabbed her pack and pushed open the old barn door. The garden stretched ahead of her, beyond it was the wood. She glanced about her but could see nobody. They must all still be inside the house. She ran.

*

A long time later, she came to a drovers' road, dusty, well travelled, fifty paces wide, snaking its way through the landscape. She remembered what an old Briton had once told her, *If you keep the sea in sight and walk towards the sunset, you'll find freedom.* She strode along confidently for a while, then ran, then strode again. When the sun was high, she slowed a little; she was thirsty and there was a stream close at hand. She stopped and knelt to take a long draught, and as she did so, a high-pitched Saxon voice said, 'Come here, slavey.'

She glanced over her shoulder, ready to attack. Out of the trees came a bare-legged boy wearing a battered black conical hat and a long hessian coat. 'Unless you want a thrashing, give me your pack,' he said, and waved a stick at her.

In the brook was a large round stone. She picked it up, turned round, holding out her pack with one hand, and as the boy leant forward to take it, she brought the stone down hard on his skull. With a grunt, he dropped to the ground, and when she poked him with her foot, he didn't move. She tore off his coat, grabbed his hat and put them on, then peered into the stream. 'Come here, slavey,' she said to her reflection.

She kept close to the side of the road, and when anyone came by, she adopted the boy's strut. It was very busy. Ox carts loaded with wheat and kindling creaked along; there were flocks of sheep driven by listless girls with yapping black and white dogs, farmhands on donkeys, the occasional rich man on a fine horse. A dog cart overtook her with a half-clad body in it. Was it the boy? She hoped it was and that he was dead. She'd no longer tolerate being threatened by Saxons. She came to a place where ditch diggers were at work. They'd thrown up piles of mud along the road as far as the eye could see, but had left a gap for access to a hut with rickety tables in front of it where wayfarers could stop for bread and ale. She wondered whether a spoon might buy her a loaf, but when she stopped to search her pack, she realised that among the carts tethered up by the side of the hut was the dog cart that had passed her.

'That's her! That's my hat!' The boy stepped out of the hut and pointed at her in an agitated fashion. He had a crude bandage round his head. 'It's the slave girl with the brand,' he yelled. 'The one they're looking for.'

She turned and ran as fast as she could, but another voice rang out. 'Stop her. There's a two penny reward for her!'

The diggers appeared out of the ditches, huge and muddy, like clay giants, two-score or more, on both sides of the road. She had nowhere to run.

She was whipped, returned to Hamblesea in the dog cart and flung into an open boat, her arms and legs bound to prevent her from jumping over the side. She barely noticed the pain: her fury consumed it and everything else.

A while later, a large island came into view and the boat pulled into a stony bay. A rope was tied round her neck, and she was led up a succession of steep steps to a cluster of pens and locked in with fifty or so other women. Some were Moors from Afrique and Spain; most spoke languages she'd never heard before. A few were from Swift's hall, though she ignored them and they her.

It was cold, she was given no food, and she kept as far away as she could from the overflowing shit pit in the corner. The women in the next pen had a vomiting disease and two died in the night.

Next morning, she was stripped and washed, taken to a big hall close by and flung on her knees in front of a woman she recognised: Lady Moira, Swift's friend, who looked like a sorceress. Moira stared into Rhiannon's eyes and Rhiannon stared back. There was no use trying to hide from such as her.

'She's the one,' Moira called. 'See the brand on her face.'

Another woman appeared. Rhiannon remembered Lady Winifred's wedding well, because it was the day she'd found a blackberry custard in a bush and eaten it all without being whipped. Lady Winifred had been a foolish rosy-cheeked girl then, barely a woman at all, constantly snuggling up to Swift's halfwit brother. Now, though, she was fatter in the face, had a baby by her side and looked fearful. She gripped Rhiannon's wrist tight, pulled her to her feet and whispered fiercely in her ear. 'Moira has told me about you. You guarded my husband's sister, didn't you? You were taught by the old soldier.'

Rhiannon shrugged.

'I need someone like you,' Winifred continued. 'My husband's gone to sea, I have a new child, and the Norlanders are coming back. You must stay close to me. Very close. Day and night.'

THIRTY-NINE

The Road to Emmaus

It was dawn, and the bazaar was beginning to awaken. Whores were leaving their places of work, yawning and scratching. Two were giggling at a man whose parrot had shat down his tunic, but mostly they were tired, their face paint smudged, and they made little attempt to comb their hair or cover the bruises on their lips.

Late the previous night, a ragged boy had knocked on Asser's door and told him that Abdulalah requested his presence at the bazaar again at first light, and that he should bring with him another piece of silver.

'Why have you summoned me at this horrid hour?' Asser demanded now.

'I have something I think you'll be interested in,' Abdulalah replied, and handed him a torn piece of parchment. 'Clovis has done more digging for you. It's a list of Gilotti's associates. Degenerates all!'

Asser handed the old man his coin and cast his eyes across the scribble. *Leonardo of Calabria, Aldo Massini, Petr of*

Macedon, Giuseppe the Catamite . . . He looked up, distracted by a voice he recognised. A Saxon girl was asking a friend if she wanted to go with her to buy some cherries. It was Elswith; she was alive and well! Asser's heart leapt with joy, then fell again. What was she doing leaving a whorehouse, no longer wearing her drab novice's habit but dressed in a short gay tunic that showed her arms and would have turned any man's eye?

Her eyes met Asser's, but instead of greeting him, she walked in the opposite direction. He called her name, but she didn't look back. He called her again.

'Leave her be, Cuckoo!' said Abdulalah. 'She's been working hard.'

'In this place?' retorted Asser. 'That cannot be. She's given herself to Christ!'

Abdulalah laughed so hard it brought on a fit of wheezing. 'And to several other gentlemen too!' he said eventually.

'Elswith,' cried Asser. 'Please, my heart breaks for you. What have you done?'

She turned and came back towards him. The heat of shame was on her cheeks, but a defiant look burnt in her eyes. 'I'm sorry to distress you, Father,' she said, 'but I cannot pretend any longer to be one of the abbess's blessed sisters, living by the precept of forgiveness. I wish to work among women who, like me, cannot forgive.'

'You must not do this!'

'I must, Father. I wish to stay.'

'But sweet girl, you could work with them in other ways,' he cried. 'Care for them, cure their ailments, listen to their tales of distress.'

'You can't make money doing that, Cuckoo!' said Abdulalah.

Asser thought of his sister, thrown into a Norland slave ship, and what she'd doubtless endured in its hold. 'I will pay,' he said. 'I will pay double what you receive here if you will agree not to sell yourself.'

'That papal purse of yours is getting a kicking today, isn't it?' said Abdulalah.

Elswith held Asser's gaze. 'What I do for coin is of no importance to me, Father,' she said. 'One thing only matters: to find my abusers. I will do as you wish if, and only if, you help me do so.'

'I am close to the guilty ones, Elswith,' he replied passionately. 'I am very close. I swear it.'

Back at the Undercroft, the soldiers from Illyria had arrived, those who'd written to the cardinal all those months previously proposing a righteous army, and they vexed Asser enormously. Balotelli had thought it important for them to see the progress he'd made, but they were openly disdainful.

'We expected more of you, Balotelli,' their leader said. 'You gave us such fine promises. You said you'd transform the Church and muster a Christian army, but all you've got to show us are a few documents.'

'Change takes time, brothers,' replied Asser. 'We need to plan carefully and harness support.'

The man raised his eyes wearily, as though he'd heard such excuses a thousand times.

'Don't disappoint us,' he said a little menacingly. 'We'll be watching you.'

After much sighing and pulling of faces, the soldiers reluctantly shook the priests' hands and left.

'Why do they make me feel so guilt-ridden?' Asser said. 'I can endure the hectoring of our enemies, but these are supposed to be our friends.'

The Undercroft grew calm again. Pens squeaked and were resharpened, pages were turned. There was the occasional murmur, nothing more.

'Hallelujah!'

Plegmond, quiet, serious Plegmond, had climbed on his bench and was waving a parchment triumphantly in the air.

'What is it?' said Father Philip.

'It's Aethelfraed! Only his name isn't Aethelfraed.'

All work was forgotten. The priests left their tables and huddled round Plegmond like puppies round a fresh bone.

'I was lost! I was frustrated!' he said. 'I had come to the conclusion that there was no such person in Rome as Aethelfraed, but then it occurred to me that he could have changed his name. If so, why would he have done such a thing? And then I thought about the fact that I had done exactly the same when I entered the seminarium. Plegmond isn't my real name. I took it because I thought my birth name was ridiculous.'

'Why, what was it?' asked Father Philip.

'That's not important,' replied Plegmond. 'Many of you did something similar, did you not?' At least ten of them nodded. 'So I looked through the letters of those who had recently recommended boys and young men to our various seminaria, and I found one from the Bishop of Winchester, who not only recommended a young Saxon of the right age, but paid his fees. When I saw the original name of the boy, I almost cried. But that isn't all. His name had been scored through and another written above it. And that name was . . .' He paused like a trickster about to produce a copper piece from a hat. 'Alfred! We need to find an Alfred!' He looked around the little crowd, relishing his moment of glory.

Asser ruffled his spiky hair and kissed the top of his head. 'Excellent,' he said. 'Plegmond, you are rapidly becoming the finest and wisest of us all. Which seminarium does this Alfred attend?'

Plegmond took a nervous breath. 'The Emmaus.'

Every iota of excitement that had filled the room was sucked from it. The Emmaus had left scars on the souls of all who had passed through its portals. Asser had sworn he would never set foot in it again.

The cardinal was observing them from the far side of the room. 'How strange that you should loathe the Emmaus so much,' he said wryly. 'It worked well for me. It produced all you wicked young men who climbed out of its windows to come and listen to my sermons. But you're right, we should remove him from the vile place. You may put aside your work for today, Father Asser, and take the road to Emmaus!'

'Not me!' replied Asser. 'Please don't think I'm going, because I'm not.'

After his parents died, Asser was sent to live in the house of the local priest, who had bad breath and seldom spoke to him. He was profoundly lonely and very bored. He slept on the floor and amused himself all day looking at the scraps of parchment the priest had discarded. He could neither read nor write – no one had shown him how – but he copied the priest's writing, deduced from a discarded list of purchases what some of the letters represented, realised that most of the scribbles were quotations from the Bible with which he was familiar, and was soon writing simple sentences in Latin.

When the priest discovered what he'd been doing, Asser was immediately transformed from an orphaned pauper into the biblical boy David reborn. The man gave him pottage and watered wine, and devoted every spare moment to instructing him. Within a month he was reading whole chapters from the Gospels.

He was summoned into the presence of the Dean of Bath and Wells, who instructed him to read out loud extracts from the Book of Ezekiel. A bell rang, the dean was called to matins and Asser was left alone. While he was waiting, he wrote a short piece on the parable of the wise and foolish virgins, partly to amuse himself but also because he thought it might impress. That evening, he was returned to the halitotic priest, who appointed him his altar boy.

A month later, he was summoned back to Bath. The dean said he was to be sent away to the most famous seminarium in Italy, paid for by Bath Abbey, because he was blessed with a rare gift of intelligence. He refused to go – what if his sister returned and came looking for him? – and he ran off, but was caught, spanked and put on a ship across the water, and then on a series of carts bound for Rome. When he finally arrived at the Emmaus, he curled up in a ball and refused to speak for weeks. There were harsh words and beatings, but he never showed his wretchedness, even when he was forced to lie on cold flagstones in front of the altar for hours on end with his arms outstretched in the shape of the cross.

And now he was back at his old seminarium, heading towards the long, thatched huts in which he'd worked and slept for so many years, which radiated in the shape of a sundial round an ancient brick tower, the house of his nemesis, Master Spinoza. He climbed its stairs, knocked on the sturdy oak door, heard the once-familiar command to enter – and there in front of him was the architect of his youthful misery, his face flushed with anger.

'You're back,' the master said, a hint of triumph in his voice.

He was a thin-faced man with bulging eyes. As a boy, Asser had found the head of a cockerel lying in the road after it had been severed by the wheel of a cart. Its benighted face looked exactly like that of the master.

He stood in front of Spinoza and explained calmly that a member of the Westsaxon royal household was a student here, and that he and Cardinal Balotelli wished to remove him from the school and . . .

Spinoza cut him short. 'You are as arrogant, as confident of your own rectitude as you always were,' he said. 'You and your henchmen drag Mother Church into the gutter, you accuse our most capable churchmen of greed and corruption – why shouldn't they receive the riches due to them? – and now you come here and demand that I hand over to you one of my seminarians?'

'I have demanded nothing,' said Asser.

'But you are about to?'

'I am,' he agreed.

'No!'

'With respect, that answer is unacceptable.' Asser produced a small roll of parchment from his leather bag. 'I have a letter for you.'

'I don't care if it's from his Holiness the Pope.'

'It is from his Holiness the Pope.'

Spinoza paused, and for a moment Asser thought he was about to relent. Instead he said: 'I cannot hand him over because he's not here. He left a month ago. Tell Cardinal Balotelli he's too late.'

Asser took a deep breath. 'Where did he go?'

'I've no idea,' replied Spinoza. 'Good day.'

Asser trudged back down the long, winding flight of stairs. Above him, he heard the slam of a door, the hurry of footsteps along the landing and Spinoza's voice hurtling down towards him. 'I know what you and your little cabal are planning. Women administering the sacred host, our finest art being sold to feed criminals and whores, our princes and kings being laid low. A new vision? It's the devil's vision!'

He left the building shaking. Spinoza was still berating him from a high window. 'One day you and Balotelli will burn. God grant they let me light the fire!'

He sat down in the seminarium garden and waited for his

agitation to dissipate. A grey-bearded slave was pulling carrots, lopping off their tops and throwing them on a compost heap.

'Hullo, Trug,' said Asser.

'You're out of jail then,' replied the slave.

Asser nodded.

'How did it go upstairs?'

'Deep down I think he's in love with me.'

The slave laughed. 'You once told me you'd never come back,' he said.

'I wish I hadn't,' replied Asser. 'You remember a Wessex lad . . . he was here until recently?'

'Aye,' replied the gardener, and lopped the top off another carrot.

'Where did the little bugger go?'

Asser strode purposefully up Rome's Via Gallinaceo, accompanied by Plegmond and Father Philip. Plegmond had been very nervous about coming. 'It's a place of sin, where publicans, sinners, whores and gamblers abound,' he'd said.

He was right. Men and women kissed openly, as did men and other men; tricksters played Find the Pope's Cock surrounded by crowds desperate to double their money; drunkards pissed and swore, fights flared, children stole gewgaws and plums, lewd songs echoed from every window. The smell was overwhelming, an intoxicating concoction of myrrh, frankincense and human excrement.

In the side alleys, the excitement and gaudy hues gave way to bleak poverty. The faces of the women working the streets were no longer brightly painted, but grey and tired, with unfocused eyes and mouths covered in sores. The children were listless, the men sly and hostile.

Trug the gardener had told Asser to look for a crumbled, rambling building bearing the sign of a young boy's head. After some time searching, they found it. Plegmond went round one side, Philip round the other, and Asser approached the front door, which was half open and covered in greasy hand-marks. 'Hello?' he called, and stepped inside.

Excitement welled up in him. Was he finally about to meet his sweet Osburgh's son, the prince who might one day transform Wessex? What kind of man would he be? How should he address him, by his assumed name or his real one? The room was illuminated only by a narrow gap in the flimsy curtains at the window.

'Aethelfraed!' he called into the darkness. There was no response. 'Aethelfraed!' he called again.

A fierce blow struck his head and Asser fell to the floor. He felt no pain, only a strange thickness in his brain, as though his thoughts had turned to pond sludge. Standing over him in the half-light was a large man holding a baker's rolling pin. He had the build of a carter, but his eyelids were painted blue and he was wearing a large headdress in the shape of a buttercup.

'I am not Aethelfraed. My name is Alfred,' he said.

'Alfred?' Asser repeated. 'Great!' he said, and plunged into the black hole of unconsciousness.

PART THREE

FORTY

Alfred

'I was in Hamburg,' Alfred said. 'No, that was earlier – it was Lübeck.' He talked incessantly, barely pausing for breath. 'I was in Lübeck, teaching the monks and merchants how to translate Hebrew into Latin, Latin into Greek, this into that. It kept the wolves from the gate, but it was as boring as purgatory. And of course my reputation preceded me.'

'Your reputation for what?' enquired Father Plegmond.

'Awful things! Awful!' Asser noticed that Alfred did not attempt to refute them. 'And I was being watched. I was sure. By strangers. Wessex men.'

'Why would they be watching you?' asked Father Philip. He and Plegmond were captivated by his story.

'I know! It makes no sense. I wasn't doing anything wicked. I certainly wasn't going back to Wessex. Have some more wine.'

The first thing Asser had been aware of on regaining consciousness was his friends hovering over him and Alfred apologising profusely for having hit him.

'Sometimes I forget how strong I am. It's not an attractive quality,' he'd said. 'I thought you were a spy.'

He'd asked them if they'd like to stay and share a beaker of camomile and honey while they waited for Asser to recover. The infusion had become wine, Plegmond had left and returned with a mutton pie, and now Plegmond, Philip and Alfred, still wearing his buttercup headdress, were sitting around, deep in conversation, while Asser lay on the floor with a cold compress on his head.

The room was small and cluttered, with large, half-painted wooden cut-outs of farm animals and buckets of white and yellow paint. A battered string instrument was propped in a corner.

'So after I'd been in Heidelberg for a while, I got restless,' continued Alfred. 'I wanted to go to the Pyrenees to look at a Gospel of St John that had been rescued from Lindisfarne and apparently contained lots of interesting textual inconsistencies, but I had no money, I mean no money, and no one cared that I was a prince – every other foreigner in Heidelberg is a penniless son of some royal family or other – so because I'm quite strong, you know that of course, I'm so sorry, I was offered a job overseeing the transport of lumber to Andorra . . .'

Quite strong? thought Asser. The blow Alfred had dealt him had been like a kick from an angry ox.

'. . . and when I was there, I found a position as a guide – have you seen the mountain of Coma Pedrosa? It's wondrous, like a pyramid capped in snow – but more Saxons arrived in the little village where I was staying and began asking questions about me, and I wished I was dead, I truly did.'

Asser prayed Alfred would come to the end of his story soon. His head pounded, he wanted to go to sleep and he still hadn't had the chance to talk to this strange man about meeting his mother and returning to Wessex.

'Then, and I swear on Christ's bones this was meant to happen, there was a blizzard. And I went out to search for snowbound travellers, and I was on my own, and I came across this dead man buried in the snow . . . and I know it was a sin, but I put my ring on his finger and covered him up again, and I thought, where shall I go now? And it occurred to me – Rome! My destiny! So here I am.'

'And you changed your name?' said Plegmond.

'Wouldn't you if you were being chased all over Europe? And I've always hated the name Aethelfraed. I've no desire to be anyone's aethel.'

'Why Rome?' asked Asser, and immediately cursed himself. He was desperate for the story to come to a conclusion, but even so he had asked another question. Yet he had to admit he was intrigued by Alfred's guileless account, and by the fact that he showed such disdain for his antecedence.

'Well, I knew it was the most glorious city in God's creation, even if it is fraying at the edges, and I wanted to learn more, and the Emmaus was supposed to be the best seminarium in Christendom. Everybody said it. So I wrote to a friend in Winchester and he obtained a position for me there, and I went, and it was dreadful. So dreadful!'

'We know,' said Asser.

'I mean, I could stand it for myself, but those poor young boys! I swore I'd never be that kind of teacher. I've always loved teaching, and I had this notion of establishing a school for common boys. I mean, no one does that, do they?'

'Not for common boys,' agreed Philip. 'How extraordinary.'

'And suffer the little children, you know what I mean?' continued Alfred. 'So I started this school for young Saxons, and it's nothing much, but the children love it, and I'm really good at it!' He paused for the tiniest of breaths, and slapped his hands on his knees. 'Only now you've ruined my plans. I spent all this time and trouble keeping my name secret and you found out who I really am, so I'll have to tie you all up and—'

'There are three of us,' warned the burly Father Philip. 'You'd have trouble doing that.'

Alfred glanced at them. 'No, I don't think I would,' he said, 'but I don't want to. You're my new friends. I'll kill myself instead.'

'Don't jest,' said Plegmond.

'I'm not,' replied Alfred. 'I've thought about it often.'

'But what of your students?' said Plegmond. 'You said teaching is of the utmost importance to you.'

'You're right,' said Alfred. 'I have a festival to organise. But I'll pour another jug first. It'll have to be mead, I'm afraid.'

'No thank you, we're fine,' said Asser, propping himself up on his elbows. Was this jabbering boy, dressed like a little girl at her first communion, really the person on whom all Europe's hopes rested? Could this whole exercise be an enormous waste of time? 'We should be—'

'What kind of festival?' asked Philip.

'A flower festival, of course!' retorted Alfred. 'You surely don't think this is my usual garb? What kind of a man do you think I am?' He threw off his buttercup headdress, then prowled round his tiny room looking for more beverage. 'So, my boys are taking part in the singing competition. They're working really hard, bless them! The church has hired a singing teacher for a few weeks so the children can learn to sing sweetly, and he says they're bound to win. He's called Petr the Greek. Well, he says he's Greek, but I think he's Macedonian.'

Asser was suddenly wide awake. 'Petr of Macedon?'

'As you like. Anyway, it'll be held at St Agatha Angelus on All Souls' Eve. You must come!'

'We will,' said Asser. 'We definitely will.' *Petr of Macedon.* It was one of the names on the list Abdulalah had given him. He glanced at Philip, who stared back quizzically, far too full of wine to understand the import of what Alfred had said.

'How vexing,' said Alfred. 'I've no more ale, no mead, no wine, nothing!'

'Good!' said Asser, climbing tentatively to his feet. 'Very good! The frivolities are over. These men of God must be at prayer within the hour. Off you go!'

With a firmness and speed that astonished even Asser himself, he ejected the priests from Alfred's quarters. They scarcely had time to protest before he'd slammed the door behind them. At last!

'You must be wondering why I'm here,' he said.

'I suppose so,' replied Alfred doubtfully.

'It's about your mother.'

Asser looked at the expression darkening Alfred's face. It did not bode well.

FORTY-ONE

Alfred Is Made an Offer

Alfred's line of young boys wended their way back from St Agatha Angelus through the burnt rubbish and looted graves of the Colosseum. He loved it here. How extraordinary the ancients had been. Their ambition, their imagination, their organisation. He'd once made a list of all the skills he thought had been required to build it, how much it had cost, the materials necessary, the time involved. It would have been a monumental undertaking, the result of which was still rooted here in the landscape eight hundred years later. It was a miracle, yet the sight of it depressed him too. Great heroes had once wandered among these mighty arches; now they were home to the drunk, the homeless, and gangs of bully boys looking for someone to assault.

'Look closely, children,' he said, spinning in a circle and gesticulating towards the crumbling terraces. 'Imagine this wonderful edifice as it was long ago. Thousands of spectators, the emperor and his family waving down from the royal box, circuses, battles, saints torn to pieces by hungry lions ... Concentrate, Cuddie, put that thing down, it's filthy ...'

He guided the grubby little boy back into line and they continued their walk through the decayed remnants while he recounted tales of the city's former glory. Rome had once been home to a million citizens. Now there were barely fifteen thousand, half in poverty, the lucky few decked in finery.

He thought back to the previous night. It had started well enough. Yes, he'd hit the priest, but the man had been skulking around like a feral cat, and called him Aethelfraed, which was intensely irritating. They'd drunk a great deal, and laughed a lot. But the moment the other priests had left, the evening had turned sour. What was his name? Father Asser. He was unpleasant, and far too forceful. *Your mother's in Rome! She needs you! You must apologise to your father!* Really? Apologise for what? *You must return home.* Why in the name of Christ's saints would he want to go back to Wessex?

'Mind that cart, Cuddie.'

He'd explained that he couldn't go back, that he was busy trying to raise money for a new school roof, but Father Asser had yelled at him again, and he'd felt his chest tighten as though he was being squeezed by a bear. Yes, he'd promised to visit his mother, but only to get the priest out of the room, and when he was finally alone, he'd lain on the floor and done his breathing exercises for a long time.

He felt better now. The boys always cheered him up. The sons of penniless traders and drunken seamen, who'd fled with their parents from faraway lands, they meant more to him than anything.

They'd sung well this morning, although Petr was a trial. Alfred couldn't understand why the church employed a singing teacher who let the children run amok. So Alfred had offered to help control them, which was not a good use of his time but at least the boys had begun concentrating.

He was determined their childhood should be better than

his. As a boy, if he'd made a mistake in his reckoning or miscopied a psalm or smudged his writing, his mother had beaten him and locked him in a cold, damp cellar. There was always another exercise she'd wanted him to do. His half-brothers hated him. He made them look stupid, though they were much older, and his sister ignored him, which was very cruel. He'd been desperately lonely and wasn't allowed friends; even his full brother, Red, wasn't permitted to associate with him. He took a knife to his arms and legs, which made him feel better. Then his father had accused him of terrible things and sent him away.

They were getting close to the school now. It was shabby and neglected, and he was a little ashamed of it.

They turned into the courtyard and were greeted by the school caretaker, John of Old Saxony. 'Home again!' he chortled. 'Wash your hands at the pump! Hurry up, you've got guests.'

Alfred picked out some flat pieces of wood from a pile of debris and gave one to each boy. Inside, he passed them dishes of white daub and showed them how to make crude brushes out of straw, and they began painting on their wooden boards.

Only then did Alfred notice the two clerics sitting on the bench at the far side of the room. One was Father Asser.

'I've nothing to say to you. Nothing at all!' he shouted.

The other man was dressed in church finery. Alfred wasn't impressed by his garb. He cared little enough for his own rank, let alone anyone else's.

'Good day,' the man said. 'Father Asser has something to say to *you*, though, don't you?'

'I do,' said Asser, although he seemed a little reluctant to speak. 'I apologise. I became overexcited and should not have spoken as I did. I had suffered a blow to the head, which may have affected my behaviour, but that is no excuse.'

Alfred felt obliged to curb his anger, at least for the moment.

'I'm not going back to Wessex,' he said as calmly as he could. 'You can't make me.'

'We're not here to discuss your travels,' said the finely dressed man. 'You will go where you will. I wish to talk about your new school. Does that not merit a little attention?'

'What new school? I've planned a new roof, 'tis all.'

The man tilted his head as though considering Alfred's reaction. There was something about him that made Alfred curious. Why was he talking about a new school?

'Clean your brushes, boys, and put them away,' he said, 'then go outside and play, but not too roughly.' He ruffled Cuddie's head and his charges ran from the room.

'You care for the children well,' continued the man. 'I admire that. Let us begin again. I am Cardinal Balotelli, chief adviser to our Holy Father.'

Balotelli! He knew that name. There had been a poet, a very good one, called Stephen Balotelli. This couldn't be the same person, could it? 'What is it you want, your Eminence?' he said, a little more cordially.

'You're acquainted with a man you know as Petr the Greek, are you not?' said Balotelli. He was confident, well-spoken, charming almost. 'Here in Rome there is a Macedonian called Petr who we believe may be pursuing the devil's work.'

Alfred stared at him. Petr might be an incompetent singing teacher, but a heathen and a scoundrel? 'Not my Petr, surely!' he said.

'It is not yet confirmed. But a senior churchman has been violently attacked, and this Petr of Macedon is on a list of those who may be culpable. You are a man of God?'

'Of course.'

'You appear to have won Petr's trust. We wish you to establish whether he is the man we're looking for. We need you to watch him, tell us what he says, and most importantly, who he meets.'

Alfred scoffed. Even if this was Stephen Balotelli, the great poet, he wouldn't be badgered when he had so much work to do. 'I have no time for that! I have my duty to the children.'

The cardinal's voice became a little harder. 'Alfred, your father will shortly be visiting Rome,' he said. 'I am considering the possibility of building you a new school to which the high aethel will affix a plaque in order to help cement relations between Wessex and the Church. If you do as I ask, this possibility will become a reality.'

Alfred was stunned. An entire new school? Where the boys wouldn't freeze in winter or fall asleep in the heat of summer? But was he prepared to pay the price of a visit from his father? His chest was tight. 'Did you write *A Meditation on the Touch of Christ*?' he blurted out.

The cardinal's face softened. 'Long ago,' he replied.

'It's very good,' said Alfred. 'It's vivid, evocative, and the metre is rigorous but unlaboured.'

'Thank you,' said Balotelli, looking mildly amused.

'So we've come to an agreement, have we?' said Asser.

Alfred gave a reluctant nod and stared at the little priest pensively and a little suspiciously. He did not like him, and from the expression on the man's face, the feeling was mutual.

FORTY-TWO

The South Shields

Guthrum trudged across the sand towards the battered old sea hall where the sailors of the South Shields wintered their ships in the lee of the butter-coloured cliffs. The wind was whipping across the great northern sea, the waves were wild, the seabirds silent.

He had already paid his respects at the other Shields settlements, had been greeted cordially, listened to seriously and offered fighting men, but no ships were forthcoming.

He opened the sea hall's massive door and the wind all but tore it off its hinges. He leant against it hard and forced it shut. Outside, the gale howled.

The hall was full of ships' gear: massive gutted sea-ships, half-built thirteen-bench karves on wooden blocks, two long, pristine war vessels scrubbed and sealed ready for the next fighting season, piles of split planks, boxes of rivets and roves. The local men, two dozen of them, sea-blown and taciturn, stared at him suspiciously.

He picked up a rowboat that had been leaning against a

wall, lugged it across the floor and stepped up onto it. He was the tallest of them anyway, but now he loomed over them like a Jötnar battling the gods.

'Fellow Norlanders, you know who I am,' he said. 'Guthrum Guthrumson of Clan Farne. We have had our differences in the past; tempers have been lost, blood spilt, but all has been resolved in true Norland fashion. I defeated Haakun Haakunson; now I am your clan leader, and it is an honour so to be.' He paused, waiting for a challenge, but none came. 'Many of the fighters I admired most as a lad were Shieldsmen – Njord Thorson, Halfdan Harlson, Einar Einarson – and I pledge I will lead you as ably as they did.' He felt them soften a little at the acknowledgement of their heroes. 'You offered Haakun Haakunson two warships for his summer campaign.'

'We did,' a scarred, one-eyed sailor said, and the others nodded.

'I wish to renew that request, but I ask another, too. I will not have my fleet under-manned and under-victualled as Erik Longshanks' was. I need a support vessel – bigger, a little slower perhaps, but nonetheless a fighting ship, crewed by rowing slaves if necessary, and by shield women who'll tend to our needs, strong lassies who'll act as our last line of defence. You understand?'

The men nodded.

'You can provide such a ship?'

He waited while they conferred, his face stony.

'We have a knarr built for the open water,' a grey-bearded captain said eventually. '*Sea Cat* is her name. She's hauling timber in the Orkneys.'

'I've seen her many times off the Farnes,' replied Guthrum. 'A fine vessel. She'd serve us well.'

'If she were to join you, we'd ask an additional one tenth of the spoils.'

'I cannot give you that,' said Guthrum firmly. 'Nor would you wish me to. Your share will be proportionate to the number of men you send. All Norland fighters are equal before the prow.' He wouldn't barter, even if it meant he had to walk away.

The men conferred again, then the captain said, 'You speak true. You can take *Sea Cat*, forty of our fighting men and our new vessels *Sea Vulture* and *Raven*.'

'That is good,' said Guthrum tersely, though his heart was singing. 'Now pour us all a drink, and we'll talk about the old days.'

Later, he tramped up the hill to the settlement, a sack over his shoulder. Sheets of rain swept over him; tiny shards of ice stung his face.

He came to Haakun Haakunson's hut, big and brutal like its former owner. He hammered at the door.

'May I enter?' he called. 'It is I, Guthrum Guthrumson.'

'Pull the door fast behind you,' a voice called back.

There was no sign this had once been the home of a chieftain. The clay walls were bare, as though every memory of Haakun had been torn down and discarded. Indeed, there were few signs of habitation anywhere, apart from a blazing fire in the centre of the room, a few cooking utensils piled up next to it, an ale barrel, and a crib in the corner. Astrid Haakunson stood by the fire, her arms folded. She was strong of body, her jaw set, her eyes heavy.

'You are clan chief now, they tell me,' she said, looking at him coldly. 'Must I curtsy to you?'

'No, Astrid,' he replied. 'But you can pour me a drink.'

She went to the barrel, ran two mugs of ale and set them on the table while Guthrum warmed himself by the fire.

'How many years since we last met?' he asked. 'Ten?'

'Eleven,' she replied. She was tying a sleeve string and barely looked up.

'You've lost your smile, I think,' he said.

'And you your fingers.'

He looked at his hand and shrugged. 'You have children?'

'Three.'

He was not prepared for the wave of sadness that washed over him then. 'This will be the last gale of winter. We'll sail soon.'

'So they tell me.'

'Will you come? I need a mistress for my shield women.'

She laughed scornfully. 'My fighting days are long over,' she replied.

'You were the finest of the shield maidens.'

She looked at him steadily. 'You are my husband's killer,' she said.

'I fought him fair and true.'

'Not so. You struck the first blow before the signal came. You hid rocks in your bindings.'

'For Odin's sake, Astrid,' he replied, 'I'm not a Christ worshipper! I don't fight to save my soul. I do so for gold and land and the joy of the kill. And I settle my disputes the Norland way.'

'That doesn't give you the right to take a man's wife.'

'I'm not asking for your body,' he said. 'You'll fight with me, that is all.'

'I have a baby, Guthrum,' she said.

He glanced at the cradle and the sleeping child in it. 'A son, I think? Is he weaned?'

'He is not.'

If things had come to pass another way, if he'd not let her go all those years ago, the child could have been his. For a fleeting moment he allowed himself to feel the pain. 'Can you find a wet nurse for him?'

'You press me hard, Guthrum,' she said. 'What if I refuse to come?'

'I have a gift for you,' he replied. He pulled open the neck of his sack and tipped out its contents: a polished shield, a short sword, a helmet bearing the image of a flying crane.

'I know this gear,' said Astrid. 'It was your mother's.'

'It was,' said Guthrum, handing her the helmet. 'Try this. It'll look fine on you.'

FORTY-THREE

Like Poisoned Darts

Guthrum's ships sailed south, but they were not alone. Every day more Norland vessels hove into view, from Dunbar, Cockburn, Berwic, Hartlepool, Durham and the other north-east settlements, each one looking for a church to despoil, a monastery to suck dry. In Guthrum's youth, raiding parties would sail fifty leagues or more in search of prey, but now most of them pulled in half a dozen leagues from home, revisited a church they'd raided the previous year, and were back in the soft arms of their women within a week. Indolent cowards! A few days later, nearly all the boats had disappeared, only the most adventurous still keeping him company.

He could no longer grasp an oar with both hands, so he stayed aboard *Sea Cat* and Astrid taught him Saxon. She made him chant the same words over and over, then strings of words. He hated the sounds they made, soft like a chick's feathers and so cloudy he could hardly tell one word from another. But they possessed the power he wanted to wield, and he would do so very soon.

After seven days, they pulled into the eastern seaboard town of Gipswic. The folk there were terrified. They drove their animals indoors and locked and barred their houses. But Guthrum had no intention of sacking the place. He didn't want his ships filled with the dead weight of loot at the start of his summer campaign. He needed fresh provisions, and would pay for what he took. He'd return here on the way home, and if he still had room for church gold, he'd take it then.

There were Pictish sailors in the town, a boatful of Irish pirates, a few renegade Norlanders planning to row upriver to raid deep into Mercia. On the second night, they caroused together. The town was drunk dry, women were roistered and a few houses were burnt down. It was a memorable night.

In five or six days they'd arrive at the Isle of Wight. They'd sail round the southern side, where they'd not be noticed by passing ships, and set up camp. He'd use his new Saxon words like poisoned darts, and the islanders would quake.

'They've landed!' 'They've slaughtered our patrol!' 'There must be two hundred of them!' cried the Wight islanders. They're blarting like children, thought Rhiannon, who had never seen such terror. Shankalin Hall reverberated with a deafening wailing. Even Winifred's guards had the fear of death etched deep in their faces.

'They're coming up the path!' someone shouted. 'They're almost on us!'

Rhiannon wasn't concerned about the lives of the islanders – all Saxons were the same to her – but she was vulnerable too. The Norlanders would either kill her or consign her to brutal labour. She scoured the hall, but there was no means of escape, no side door, no privy chamber.

They waited for a long time, but no attack came. The hysterical chatter died away and was replaced by a terrified silence.

Rhiannon pulled the key from the lock on the big door and peered through the hole. 'They're here,' she whispered.

'Let me see,' said Lady Moira, the only Saxon who seemed unflustered. 'They are. But they're not moving.'

Rhiannon felt a hand seize her shoulder and turned to see Winifred's face, pale and wide-eyed with terror. 'Where's Helm?' she gasped. 'Where's my little boy?'

Rhiannon glanced about the Saxons assembled in the hall. Sure enough, the child was not among them.

'The sweet boy's safe,' replied Moira. 'He's with his nurse on the far side of the bay.'

'I will go to them,' Winifred said nervously. The islanders stared at her. 'I will go to them,' she repeated a little more loudly. 'It is my duty to . . .' She couldn't complete the sentence.

'I'll come with you,' said Moira. She took Winifred's arm. 'Rhiannon, you too. Stay close.'

Moira pulled open the door, and the three women walked into the bright late-spring light, Rhiannon at Winifred's shoulder, her right hand by her side, resting on the knife hidden in her skirts.

Thirty steps away stood the Norlanders, perhaps two hundred of them, sporting fancy Spanish coats and dyed feather caps. Some had jewellery hanging from their ears and noses. Had it not been for the weapons dangling from their belts, they could have been a band of wandering players at a harvest fair. Rhiannon was confident she could outsmart them, if not outfight them, until she spied the man at their head. Blessed goddess, it was him! The giant whose fingers she'd hacked off that day on Hamblesea beach. But it couldn't be, because she'd seen his battered, lifeless body. Was this his spirit? Had conjuring men resurrected him like the crucified Christ? Was he a ghost? Whatever he was, he'd recognise her, and when he did, his vengeance would be terrible. She took a step back behind Winifred.

The giant looked from one Saxon to the next, then began to speak.

'I am Guthrum of Clan Farne,' he said, his voice so loud even his own men seemed startled. 'Who is your head man?'

A Norlander speaking Saxon, how could this be? Rhiannon kept her eyes lowered to the floor. This was no ordinary Norlander, whatever he was, even if his Saxon was heavily accented and a little slow.

Winifred stepped forward. 'I am Lady Winifred of the Wight isle,' she said. 'My husband is at sea. You may address me. I hold his authority until he returns.'

A fine-looking Norland woman was standing a little way apart from the giant. He turned to her and they conferred in the Norland tongue for some time.

Rhiannon stared at the giant ghost-man, waiting for him to breathe fire or turn into a monster. She feared no one; what could a man do other than beat you and kill you? But demons and ghosts could torture your soul, they could haunt you for ever, they could eat your body from the inside.

Finally the Norland woman spoke in a clear Saxon tongue, as natural as Winifred's, and far better than Rhiannon's. Where had she learnt it? Rhiannon wondered.

'We will over-summer here,' she said. 'You will provide us with all we need. In return, Chief Guthrum will leave you and your people unharmed.'

'I must confer with my councillors,' Winifred said, desperately trying to appear confident, even though every part of her was shaking like a child with a chill.

The giant man gave a low, mocking bow. Winifred and Moira headed back to the hall, but Rhiannon stayed staring at him, watching him talk to the woman by his side, till she realised she was alone, shook herself free from her torpor and ran after them.

In the hall, everyone was speaking at once, but Rhiannon had no interest in their terrified chatter. The giant hadn't seemed to notice her. Had he forgotten who she was? No, he was busy, that was all. He had killing to do, islanders to butcher, rape and torture. Winifred turned resolutely towards the door again and the prattling came to an end.

'You must tell them clearly what you demand,' said Moira.

'I must,' replied Winifred faintly.

'Don't be afraid. If they kill you, you'll become a saint and have life everlasting,' added Moira.

They went back outside and faced the Norlanders again. Rhiannon kept her head bowed, only raising her eyes to glimpse the exchange.

'I cannot countenance your proposal unless my mainland estates are left unharmed,' Winifred said.

The Norlander woman conferred with the giant, and he nodded. 'You have Chief Guthrum's word,' the woman said. 'We will exchange hostages. He will place with you the one he loves most.' A young man stepped forward. 'This is his cousin. Sigurd is like a son to him.'

Sigurd looked brutish and arrogant; he was chewing a piece of dried venison and looked Winifred brazenly up and down as though deciding whether to bed her. Rhiannon had no affection for Winifred, but her stomach knotted in contempt.

'You love your little boy, don't you?'

Winifred gasped and raised her hands to her mouth in horror.

'Don't concern yourself, you have no need to fetch him,' the woman continued. 'We already have him.'

'Helm,' added the giant. 'Helm.'

'But . . . but . . .' Winifred stammered.

'He will be safe unless you refuse our offer,' said the woman. 'If you do, your people will be slaughtered and you will become a slave. But our leader has respect for you, Lady Winifred. You have fire. He does not wish such a thing to befall you.'

Winifred's bravado crumbled to dust. She dropped to the ground and pled mercy for her and her child. She looked like a little girl begging to be spared from punishment, not the wife of an aethel. Rhiannon was almost embarrassed for her.

The Norlander looked at her a little contemptuously, then he and his men turned and left.

A voice whispered in Rhiannon's ear. It was Moira. 'Find me a fisherman who'll smuggle me to the mainland and I'll give you a penny,' she said. 'I must leave this place and warn the Westsaxons.'

FORTY-FOUR

Metal Implements

'I am not what I seem,' said Petr. He had a gaunt, stubbly face and the teeth of a weasel.

'Are you not?'

'No.'

It was a few days since Balotelli had asked Alfred to ascertain the truth about Petr, and it seemed the priests were right about him. The two of them were sitting on the floor of the little Church of St Agatha Angelus with their backs to the wall, sipping from a flask of burnt wine. It was very strong – Petr was so drunk it was difficult to understand what he was saying.

'You're not Greek?' suggested Alfred.

'No,' replied Petr, 'nor a Christian.'

Alfred offered him the last drops. 'Are you not?'

'I hold fast to the one true faith. I am an Antonil.'

So he was a heretic, the first Alfred had ever met. He felt very excited. 'And what is that faith, Petr?' he enquired.

'Do you really wish to know, or will you use what I say to have me locked up?'

'I wish to know,' said Alfred, and he truly did.

'I have no love for pomp and money or bread and wine as you Catholics do. The world is a battlefield on which God and the devil wage war, and we are mere clay figures suffering the consequences of this never-ending struggle. Life simply unfolds; all we can do is endure it and grasp a little pleasure where we can.'

Alfred shuddered with revulsion. How offensive such a notion was, blind to the beauty of Christ's suffering and ultimate sacrifice. Yet there was something intriguing about it too, like staring into the eyes of a viper.

'And do you truly believe that Jesus and Satan were brothers?' he asked.

'I do,' replied Petr.

'And that the Pope is an agent of the devil, and that men and women should lie with each other regardless of their marital bonds?'

'Marriage is the sacrament of the Antichrist,' slurred Petr.

'I have always wanted to talk with a heretic. I've been intrigued by such philosophy since I was a child,' said Alfred.

'We are good men. Very good,' Petr went on. 'You are welcome to come and meet my brothers in faith.'

'I should! I will! Tell me, why did you come to Rome?'

Petr rose unsteadily to his feet. 'We were driven out. As we always are.' He sighed. 'From Macedonia, Greece, Bulgaria. We had nowhere to go.' He stumbled to the altar and began urinating on it. Alfred winced. 'We found places to stay among the city ruins, we played music in the squares for the pilgrims . . .'

'But it went badly, didn't it?' said Alfred. 'You became involved in a fight at the Undercroft.'

'What?' Petr's movements had been slow, drunken, but his reply now was quick as a dart and laden with suspicion. He glowered over his shoulder at Alfred. 'How did you know?'

'You told me. Just now.'

'Did I?' He frowned as though trying to recall what he'd said. 'Yes, perhaps I did.' His expression relaxed, and he turned back to his business. 'Anyway, we were paid to frighten the priests. They were wicked. They had a map of all the houses in which our brothers and sisters meet, and they were going to kill us. We were given alcohol and some money . . .'

'And you thrashed them?'

Petr shook himself dry and turned back to face Alfred. 'Some did, not me.'

'Fascinating, Petr. And who was it who told you to do this? He wore a silver mask, didn't he?'

A shadow crossed Petr's face. 'I can't tell you.'

'Please. You must!'

'I've already said too much. He has friends . . . in high places.'

The man was becoming almost incoherent. It was time for Alfred to drop his affable tone. 'So do I,' he said quietly. 'I will be frank. I am not what I seem either. It's terrible, I know, but you will be cruelly used if you do not tell me.'

'I knew it!' said Petr. 'You are an agent of the devil. You lied to me! You . . . you . . . I will not . . . not . . .' His head rocked and he slumped forward.

'That was not supposed to happen,' said Alfred. He grabbed him and shook him. 'Petr! Petr!' he called urgently, but the Macedonian was in a deep stupor. Alfred turned towards the vestry. 'Sorry!' he said loudly.

Its tiny door swung open, and Asser and Philip appeared.

'Well done,' said Philip. 'We will take care of him now.'

'Go home and pray for your soul,' said Asser, and Alfred couldn't miss the mockery in his tone.

'No,' said Alfred firmly. 'The cardinal charged me with obtaining information from him. I will stay to the end.'

'You may not like what you see,' said Asser.

In the Pope's dungeon, they were confronted by a man whose face was so disfigured by the pox it was hard to discern any of his features at all.

'Hullo, Halfnose,' Asser said. 'Remember me?'

The man shook his head. 'No,' he replied. 'We used to have a little cunt in here who looked a bit like you, but he didn't have your fat purse.'

Asser chose not to rise to this cheap provocation.

'The man we brought in last night. Is he sober yet?'

'He is.'

'And you haven't touched him?' asked Father Philip.

'Not yet.'

'We don't want you to hurt him,' said Alfred quickly. 'We merely want to find out what he has to say.'

The dungeon master snorted. 'Fine,' he said. 'I'll play with him for a while. Show him my tools.'

He disappeared into another room. The prisoners began shouting vile curses at the priests, making Alfred uneasy, but Asser produced a keg of ale, which he tapped and poured into dirty clay beakers, and soon they were all drinking and blessing the holy fathers for their kindness. One sang a song about the Virgin Mary lying on her back with her legs apart and the others joined in the chorus. They were blasphemous men, schooled in the language of the streets, but Alfred felt pity for them.

There was a cry of pain from the next room.

'Should we go in?' he asked anxiously.

Asser shook his head

'Wait a while,' Philip said.

Eventually Halfnose reappeared, wiping the sweat from his face. 'Your man talked,' he said.

The torture chamber was empty save for a long table. At one end various complex metal implements had been laid out; at the other, a drunken man was sitting with a pen and parchment in front of him. In the centre of the room was what at first glance appeared to be a church lectern. Petr was kneeling at it on a small step, his wrists strapped to it, allowing Halfnose full access to his back and face. Blood trickled from the corner of his mouth, and a few of his teeth were missing.

'We told you not to hurt him,' cried Alfred, horrified.

'What's he been saying?' Asser demanded.

The scribe picked up his parchment, his voice as squeaky as a rusty hinge. '"My friends and I worked as street musicians. We would bind ourselves with coloured cloth to appear uniform. We attended large gatherings, hid among the crowd and at a signal we would appear as if from nowhere and dance in concert."'

'Lovely!' said Halfnose. 'I only wish I could have seen such a thing myself.'

'"On the day in question we were given money and strong drink and disguised ourselves as we used to. We were told certain priests wished to persecute us and we were sent to where they were lurking to admonish them. But they became surly and my friends castigated them. I watched as they did so, but I took no part. I'm not a violent man. I left and went home as fast as I could."'

'So he didn't go to St Catherine's?' said Alfred.

'Apparently not,' replied Halfnose.

'One moment,' said Asser. He left the chamber and returned almost immediately with a young woman, modestly dressed and with her eyes lowered. 'Thank you for coming as I requested.'

'Please, young lady, tell them to stop hurting me,' Petr pleaded. 'For the love of all you hold holy!'

'Elswith, do you know this man?' demanded Father Philip. 'Was he at the abbey?'

'He was,' she replied. 'His voice is unmistakable.'

'You dissembler!' Alfred cried. 'You monster, Petr.'

'Oh dear!' said Halfnose. 'You are in a pickle, you naughty fellow.' He turned to the three men. 'Leave me alone with him a while longer, why don't you?'

'It wasn't me, I didn't plant my seed inside her. It was Fabio Gilotti,' the panicked Petr screamed. 'He's the man who paid us. He made me hold her down. Ask any of my friends, they'll tell you!'

Asser and Philip glanced at each other. 'Find out everything he knows,' Philip instructed Halfnose. 'Everything!'

The two priests guided Elswith out of the room and Alfred followed. The door slammed shut behind them. They were back in the main dungeon, but Alfred couldn't bear to look at the drunken prisoners. He leant an arm against a wall and was sick in a corner, only half hearing the conversation behind him.

'Will he be executed?' Elswith was saying.

'He will,' replied Father Philip.

'Good,' she said. 'And the man who violated me?'

'It's hard to say,' replied Asser. 'His family has influence.'

'I couldn't bear for him to live,' said Elswith.

'We will do our best. In the meantime, you can take comfort from the fact that his accomplices will suffer terribly.'

Alfred stared at the little pool of vomit at his feet. How could anyone witness what they had seen and find satisfaction in it? The more time he spent with him, the more he disliked Balotelli's little priest.

FORTY-FIVE

Mother's Blue Dress

Swift stood in the nuns' washhouse at Bath Abbey, scrubbing herself with a badger-hair brush while Sister Dominica poured cold water over her from a bucket. She would wear the blue dress today; it had belonged to her mother, Agnes.

Dominica dried her with a handful of cloths. It wasn't one of her duties; she was there only to ensure Swift didn't escape or attempt to kill herself, tasks to which, given her muscular physique, she was particularly well suited.

Was it maudlin to wear this gown today? Swift doubted her mother would have thought it so. She would have found it wryly amusing.

She slipped on a light coat and the two women returned to her room. It was clean, simply appointed, with pictures on the walls of female saints suffering various torments in the name of Christ. She stared at their pained, adoring faces with distaste. This was the guest quarters for those of high rank, but with sturdy locks on the door so that, as at present, it could be transformed into a place of detainment. Initially, Swift had been surprised by the speed of her fall from grace, but six weeks on, she had become more philosophical. She had reached high but had fallen. So be it.

The previous week, Moira had come to visit her, or at least had tried to. She'd smuggled herself off the Isle of Wight and had somehow found her way to Bath. But the abbess had told her she must leave or she'd face severe consequences. Moira had refused, and had shouted up to Swift's window, 'The Norlanders are here. I will lead an uprising of the people of the south coast and we will set you free.' Three nuns had crept up behind her, pinned her to the ground and told her she was mad. Moira had broken free, and when the abbess had remonstrated with her, she'd hit the poor woman with a branch. Eventually she'd been dragged off. Swift had called out that she loved her, which for that moment she truly did, but Moira was already out of sight.

Sister Dominica laid out her dress and a simple shell pendant.

'The woollen shift first,' Swift said. She didn't want to shiver. She would look proud and disdainful in front of the crowd – her dignity was all she had left.

When Swift was clothed and perfumed, Dominica called for the small team of hired hands who were waiting respectfully in a corridor with a pile of furniture: seven additional chairs, some small tables and a larger one, which they lugged in and placed in front of the window. A nun entered with an elaborately embroidered cloth, the kind brought out only on formal occasions, and which smelt of lavender and mildew. Another nun brought in polished wooden boxes containing the seals of Sussex and South Hamwicshire and the great seal of Wessex. She took them out carefully and laid them on the table. A silver inkwell in a granite stand was placed in front of them, along with several piles of documents and two large candlesticks.

Three clerks appeared and bowed low to Swift. They set their pens, ink and parchment on the small tables, sat down with their hands folded and waited patiently. Sister Dominica sat discreetly in a corner working her rosary beads. A few moments earlier, the room had been neat, tidy and virtually empty; now it was full of purposeful clutter.

There was the repetitive tap of a walking stick and Bishop Humbert entered, supported by a young priest, who helped him into the most elegant seat behind the table. Swift hadn't seen Humbert since he'd been stroked by the angel's wing. He was deathly white, and every muscle in his face appeared to have sagged; his left eyelid didn't blink and the eye itself was blood-red. How sad that the man who had been at the centre of Westsaxon affairs for so long should be brutally stricken down. She admired his fortitude in being here today, but he would doubtless be the bearer of bad news.

Hawk and Bear arrived next, momentarily united. She wondered how many letters had been sent, how many fraught conversations had taken place between their intermediaries before her two brothers had been prepared to sit at the same table, albeit at opposite ends.

The last to appear was Harold Godwin, neatly dressed in a long grey coat with stoat-fur trim. He assiduously avoided her eyes. She was about to be charged with treachery and these were her judges. Swift felt a little of her forbearance slip away. How ridiculous they all were.

'Please . . . stand,' said the bishop, his voice little more than a murmur. She did so, and he passed a parchment to his assistant, who cleared his throat and began to read out loud.

'Lady Swift of the house of Wolf. We are gathered here in the sight of God to hear accusations against you of the gravest import.'

How absurd it was to hear these portentous words issuing

forth from the mouth of a boy whose voice had barely broken. He read for some time, his hands shaking, stumbling over the more complicated words, as he outlined the heinous crimes it was alleged she'd committed. When he'd finished, he sat down, then quickly got up again and asked her if she had anything to say. She shook her head. What she had done, she had done. She would accept the consequences.

The judges spoke one by one.

'Sister, you have behaved in a treacherous manner since childhood,' said Bear. 'You stole from me and told lies about me; our father punished me because of your false accusations. A lesser man might well have been undermined by your malice, but I bore it with fortitude. I had a puppy, Fighter was his name, and you took that puppy and . . .'

It was all Swift could do not to laugh. Did he not realise how foolish he sounded, introducing such childish slights as if they were proof of anything? In his agitation Bear dropped the pen with which he was gesticulating. He bent down and retrieved it from under the table, talking all the while. Swift looked round the room and her eyes fell on a painting of the death of St Agatha, the torturer's tongs clamped round her breasts. She waited for Bear's speech to come to an end.

Hawk was next. He said a great deal, but it was empty noise. She felt little resentment towards him. She'd made him look a fool by taking Moira from him, and her rush to marry Louis had made her vulnerable, so he'd taken advantage of her mistake. Wouldn't she have done something similar had she been in his place?

Finally Harold Godwin rose to his feet and spoke in an urgent and businesslike fashion. 'As Delilah lured Samson, so we have been guiled by Lady Swift.' His eyes were looking somewhere between the ceiling opposite and the top of the wall. 'We thought that in her role as Warden of South Hamwicshire and the Sussex Coast she was dedicated to a unified Wessex, but she secretly plotted to create a new kingdom, of which she would be high aethel. We believed her to be chaste, but she was consorting with her Frankish paramour and promising him swathes of our beloved land. She is not only a traitor, but a conniver and a seducer, and she has persistently kept company with witches and spellbinders.' He picked up a handful of documents and flung them dramatically on the table in front of the bishop. 'These letters, in her own hand, prove her guilt beyond doubt. I bear her no ill will, but as an example to all those who might be seduced into following in her footsteps she must be put to death, now, without further delay.'

There was a murmur of agreement and Bear beat the top of his leg with his open hand by way of applause. Swift's accusers turned to Bishop Humbert, who scribbled on a piece of parchment. His assistant read out his words.

'You have committed the most heinous of crimes and there is no mitigation. None. I will burden you with no homilies, no words of comfort or balm. You will be hanged by the neck on the morrow.'

'May God . . . have mercy . . . on your soul, child,' said the bishop. He had always called her *child*.

Swift stared out of her barred window into the garden. Her room was now empty save for Sister Dominica. Her brothers had left without a word, though she'd heard them giggling in the corridor. Dominica unlocked a small cupboard and produced a bottle of Malvasia wine, the finest the abbey possessed, but Swift declined the proffered goblet. She needed a clear head.

She heard the tap of Humbert's stick in the corridor once more. The door reopened; he had returned with his young assistant.

'They're . . . gone,' he said, sitting down heavily at the table.

'So today will be my last?' said Swift.

'I trust not,' said the bishop.

She stared at him. 'Then when will I die?'

He gave a wheezy laugh, then picked up a pen and wrote a few words. Passing the note to her, he put his forefinger to his lips.

Despite your brothers' opposition, I have ruled that you shall be kept here till Wolf returns. Whether or not to implement the sentence will be his decision.

Swift breathed a little easier. Was she safe? Apparently, at least for a while. She'd not been frightened of dying – it happened to everyone eventually – but now that she had her life back, she felt an overwhelming sense of relief. She'd remain imprisoned, of course, with only the Amazon Dominica for company, and that itself would be a torture. Perhaps she'd learn to draw or paint. No, that would be repugnant. Something would occur eventually, something that would be to her advantage.

'What will happen to the south coast?' she asked.

Humbert scribbled again.

Harold Godwin has become its warden. There will be executions and minor mutilations. The dissenting bishops and merchants will be fined, the noisiest drummers will have their hands removed. But the dream of freedom will be easily extinguished without you.

'And my estate in Hamblesea?'

Gone to Red and Winifred, along with your wealth, orchards and slaves. A fine project for Winifred.

Swift looked up and smiled. 'I agree,' she said. 'Winifred is young and ambitious, and I admire that in a woman, however difficult it might sometimes be.'

'As . . . you have . . . discovered,' said the bishop softly.

She had always liked him. He was duplicitous, probably the least trustworthy of all of them, but only in order to advance the interests of the Church and the House of Wolf. And he had a deep affection for her, of that she had no doubt, particularly after today. He was like the uncle who slapped your leg to punish you but left a shiny coin under your pillow.

Nevertheless, she felt the relief of her temporary reprieve fade a little. She was still imprisoned until her father returned. And after that who knew what would be?

There was a knocking of the pen on the table. The bishop was drawing her attention to yet another note.

There is a problem with my ruling. Your brothers loathe and detest you. They will kill you if I leave you here. So you'll escape. And because I love you, I will give you a few of my monks. They will be armed in case you are endangered.

'Fighting monks?'

He nodded.

'How droll,' she said.

She couldn't believe it. She felt like a trapped bird faced with an open window. She wasn't safe, nor did she have what was rightfully hers, at least not for now, but she was free. She'd have no need of a paintbrush after all.

The question was where to go. Her alliance with Louis was no more, Godwin had proved himself a cheat and a fraud. Then it came to her.

'Thank you. I will go to—'

'Shh!' The bishop put his finger to his lips again, more urgently this time.

'I will stay silent, old friend, and offer you only my gratitude,' she said.

The corner of his mouth showed her the hint of a smile. His assistant produced a key and a small purse, which he put on the table, and the two men slowly left the room.

Sister Dominica darned in the corner for a while before she

too departed. Swift looked round the room one final time, then drained the goblet of wine and picked up the key.

Swift rode west, the bishop's fighting monks trotting behind her. For the first time in weeks, she threw her head back and laughed out loud.

FORTY-SIX

The Cross I Bear

There was a hammering on Asser's door.

'Who is it?' he demanded.

'It is I, Alfred.'

Asser groaned. The time they'd spent together had done nothing to lessen the irritation he felt towards Wolf's estranged son. He was becoming increasingly doubtful that this boy was capable of solving anything.

'What do you want?'

'I need your help.'

Asser heaved himself out of bed, turned up his lamp and let him in. Alfred almost filled the entire door frame, his hair awry, his face anxious.

'I've written a report on our interrogation for the cardinal. I've included background documents on Fabio Gilotti and the Antonils,' he said.

'So?'

'Will you cast your eyes over it?'

'It's the middle of the night.'

Alfred grimaced. 'Believe me, I'd rather not have come. But you know better than anyone how Balotelli works.'

'I've no interest in helping you ingratiate yourself with Balotelli,' said Asser.

'It's only the opening I need you to look at. After that, it's fine.'

Asser snatched the bundle from him and scoured the first page.

'You need an introduction,' he said. 'Balotelli's a busy man. He must know precisely what he's going to be reading before he starts.'

'Yes, a very good idea.' Alfred put out a hand to take the document back, but Asser held onto it.

'The second page is laboured. Can you not write in a more sprightly fashion?'

'Sprightly? I will.'

Again Alfred reached for the document, but Asser turned away from him, still reading, and climbed back into bed, letting each page drift to the floor after he'd perused it.

'It's terrible,' he said. 'It's truly bad.'

Alfred groaned. 'I'm an idiot.' He scrabbled around on the floor picking up the pages.

'Is Fabio guilty?' asked Asser.

'He is. We have witnesses, a signed statement, the footprint, the shoe . . .'

'And Petr, is he guilty too?'

'Yes.'

'And what of the other Antonils who attacked us?'

'Yes, guilty, of course,' said Alfred. 'But they were drunk and under the influence of a wealthy man.'

'So they shouldn't be burnt, or torn to pieces?'

'Holy St Michael, no! They are profoundly misguided, but most common people are. They should be severely punished, but not killed.'

'Then make that argument, and do it subtly. Don't tell Balotelli what to think. Let him come to his own conclusions. Wake me up again when you've sorted it out, but not before first light, and bring me an apple infusion. Now go away.'

The next morning, Balotelli sat at his table in the palazzo with Alfred's document in his hand.

'The Doctore thought the footprint and the shoe weren't on their own sufficiently compelling,' said Asser. 'But we now have more evidence and it has all been collated into this single document.'

'The Doctore was probably right,' agreed Balotelli. 'We needed something sufficiently robust. It won't only be the Gilottis who'll spring to Fabio's defence. The other wealthy families and the Notarii will too. But we still have cardinals in our midst with sense and integrity, and what you have produced is cogent and convincing. Who wrote it?'

'We both did,' said Alfred.

'He did,' said Asser. Alfred glanced at him, surprised at his magnanimity.

'You're learning fast, Alfred,' said Balotelli. 'This demonstrates the culprit's guilt beyond doubt, and you make a good case for the need to temper our response to the Antonils – punishment tinged with a little mercy. As for Gilotti, we have no alternative other than to apprehend him, but it won't be easy and may not end well.'

The arresting cohort comprised Asser, Alfred, Philip and six papal guards. Balotelli also insisted on being present. Asser had thought such a task beneath the cardinal, but he would not be dissuaded. 'I have known the Gilottis all my life,' he'd said. 'It is my duty to ensure the apprehension is conducted with propriety.'

The Gilotti residence was one of the finest in Rome, a network of turrets, thatched towers and wattle-and-daub extensions surrounding an ancient brick villa. As they approached the towering edifice, Asser found it difficult not to be awed by the wealth of Enzo Gilotti's family. It was little wonder he thought he could run the Notarii as he pleased. Still, they were about to show the Gilottis they were not unimpeachable, and how satisfying that would be.

But to Asser's surprise, Fabio was already in the courtyard, dressed in a stout cloak and clutching travelling bags.

'Fabio Gilotti!' called the captain of the squad. 'On behalf of his Holiness Pope Benedict, I have been instructed to investigate your participation in—'

'You will do no such thing,' snapped Fabio, and continued heaving his bags onto his horse's saddle. He was a man of middle age with the bloated face, broken veins and heavy eyelids of a dissolute. 'Anything you wish to enquire about should be discussed with my brother, the primicerius. I have business to attend to.'

Balotelli observed the scene discreetly from the gateway. 'Fabio! You cannot leave,' he called. 'We have eight witnesses who will attest to your presence at the Undercroft and St Catherine's Abbey on the night of the attacks!'

Fabio began mounting. 'Who are they?' he replied. 'Heretics and whores, no doubt.'

'And we have the bloodied shoe you wore that night.'

'I've been combative all my life,' he retorted. 'Every shoe I own is bloodied.'

'But no other of your shoes left a footprint in the Undercroft,' retorted Balotelli.

'You are a fanatic, Stephen, bent on attacking good Christians. Go eat your own shit!'

'You are guilty without doubt,' replied Balotelli. 'Arrest him!'

The guards surrounded Fabio's steed.

'Let him go!' A gatekeeper with the build of a prize-fighter appeared from his hut by the entrance to the courtyard. Before anyone could stop him, he had pulled Balotelli to him and rested the point of his sword against the underside of the cardinal's chin. Asser was aghast. Would the man really kill a cardinal in cold blood? The retribution would be terrible. For a moment, no one moved; it felt as though the entire city had come to a halt.

Then an authoritative voice said, 'Don't be foolish. Drop your sword, please.' Alfred was walking unarmed towards the gatekeeper, his arms spread wide. Asser couldn't believe what he was witnessing.

'As you can see, I have no weapon,' Alfred said, 'but listen to me, I beg you. The man you are threatening is the finest of all our cardinals. He will ensure your master is treated fairly. You believe you are doing your duty, and I commend you for it, but stay your hand, I pray you. You don't wish to be apprehended for assaulting such a powerful churchman, do you? Here, let me take your weapon.'

The gatekeeper was staring at the tall, earnest young man, his eyes narrow. Asser was convinced he would strike Alfred down, but to his amazement, he slowly lowered his hand and with a nod gave the young man his sword. A sigh of relief echoed round the courtyard.

'Thank you, Alfred,' said Balotelli briskly, and brushed himself down as though he'd discovered a scatter of grass seed on his robe. 'Fabio, come with us,' he ordered. Two guards seized him, and the gatekeeper was led off too.

Alfred smiled diffidently and put the sword back in the gatekeeper's lodge.

But even as the excitement began to dissipate, Father Philip appeared from inside the house. 'Pray forgive my foray into your home, Fabio,' he called. 'I wished to admire your magnificent friezes. But look what I discovered mounted on the wall above your bed.' He held up a silver carnival mask. 'It's exactly as our witnesses described. How foolish of you not to have discarded it!'

Back at the palazzo, Balotelli put an arm around Alfred and hugged him. 'My new hero, you saved my life,' he said. 'You have become one of us.'

'I am happy to serve,' said Alfred, looking abashed. 'It was nothing, truly nothing.'

Asser raised his eyebrows. The cardinal always became excited when promising young men entered his orbit, particularly those who were well favoured and dabbled in music and poetry.

'I had no idea you were capable of asserting such command, Alfred,' he said. 'For a moment you looked almost like a king.'

'It is the cross I bear,' replied Alfred. 'I come from a family of kings. It's in my blood. I wish it were not.'

FORTY-SEVEN

Offa's Dyke

Swift sailed across the mighty River Severn with her party of monks, ten young men who loved Christ but were only too glad to carry sharp swords in their belts. Ahead of her was the kingdom of Mercia, where her mother had been born; to her west was the great dyke.

She knew it well; a colossal bank of earth that wove its way league after league along the Mercian border. It had been thrown up by the mighty King Offa to keep the Welsh at bay, but mudslides, floods and complacency had worn it down over the years, and now it occupied the landscape like a row of gigantic rotting teeth.

They rode along in its shadow till they arrived in Chepstow. She'd stayed here with her cousins many times as a child. She remembered it as a tidy place of neat houses, huts with painted doors and tubs of flowers in the doorways, and a big market brimful of cheeses and fresh fish. Now, though, it was mean and oddly silent. Homes had been burnt to the ground, gates and fences smashed. There was barely anyone to be seen, and the few brave souls who did venture out scurried along nervously. Her monks were wary, scanning windows and alleyways for signs of danger.

A figure sprinted across the road a little way ahead, wearing nothing but a scanty loincloth. It was daubed from head to foot in black and blue woad, had spindly arms and legs and wild, unkempt hair, and was wielding a short sword. No sooner had it appeared than it vanished again among a jumble of tumbledown shanties on the far side of the road. Had it been an apparition? The Welsh Marches were full of strange creatures. Several of the monks crossed themselves.

Swift glanced at the monks' captain, a veteran of foreign wars known as Brother Hercules on account of his immense shoulders. He shrugged. All seemed quiet enough. But as he was about to give the order to proceed, six more spectres burst out of an alley and ran screaming towards the shanties, evidently oblivious to the presence of Swift and the monks. There was the sound of swords and shields clashing, yells of pain and Saxons shouting in thick middle-land accents. One voice in particular Swift recognised.

'There are Mercian soldiers in there under attack,' she said. 'We must go to their aid.'

Brother Hercules nodded. But suddenly the apparitions reappeared, only now they were running away from the shanties back towards the dyke, two or three of them clasping wounds and dripping blood. These were no ghosts.

Twenty paces ahead, a soldier appeared from the ruined shanties.

'My Lord Burgred!' Swift cried.

'Who is it that calls my name?' he replied.

'It is I, your cousin Swift. I told you I'd come.'

They sat in a burnt-out basement along with two-score exhausted Mercian soldiers eagerly chewing strips of boar meat and drinking from waterskins the monks had fetched from their saddlebags. The walls had all fallen away, and they could see the dyke dominating the blighted landscape.

'Who are those terrifying creatures?' Swift asked once the Mercians had been sated.

'Ignorant heathens who were driven into Wales long ago,' replied Burgred. 'They call themselves Britons, but there aren't many purebloods left; they've been reinforced by Irish thieves, runaway slaves, even Norlanders banished from their clans. They're all along the border. The Welsh kings despise them but hire them to do their killing. This particular mob of half-breeds are in the pay of Rhys of Gwent, who claims Chepstow is his and wants to drive us further back from the dyke. Our Mercian king, Burrt, sent us here to pacify them, but we're hopelessly outnumbered. They attack us at will, then scamper back to safety.'

Swift could see the creatures moving about at the top of the slope. They reminded her of the black lice that crawled over the heads of the poor. 'They're a vile scourge,' she said. 'You must rid yourselves of them. Have you requested more troops?'

Burgred laughed bitterly. 'Our king is too consumed by his own troubles to worry about us,' he said.

Two of Swift's monks returned from scouting the surrounding area. 'We found four-score local folk in a cave up the hill,' one said. 'They're hungry and frightened.'

'There's a monastery close by, is there not?' enquired Hercules.

'St Columb's,' replied Burgred. 'A league south. But the monks there are terrified of the Britons too. They're hiding in the forest.'

'Shame on them!' said Hercules. 'They should be supporting you, not cowering among the leaves. I'll fill their hearts with God's righteous anger! They can supply you with food, and we'll bring their smithy back to life and forge swords and daggers for the villagers. They'll be roughly made, but strong enough.'

'You'll teach the Chepstow folk to fight?' exclaimed Burgred.

'Indeed,' replied Hercules. 'If you let us.'

'I'd welcome your aid, Brother,' replied Burgred gratefully. 'My men are exhausted.'

'Movement up the street!' called a Mercian guard. 'Another wave of the bastards.'

'We'll work our way round their flanks, attack from behind and confuse them,' said Hercules. 'Then you should be able to advance on them unhindered.'

Swift jumped to her feet, but Burgred grabbed her arm. 'Stay here, cousin,' he said. 'It's too dangerous. I forbid it.'

'I am not yours to be so instructed, Burgred,' she said. 'Please stand aside. Like you, I have Britons to slaughter.'

FORTY-EIGHT

Nunc Dimittis

Alfred picked up an old knife handle from a battered box, then threw it back again. 'So there is no escape,' he sighed. 'I have to call on my mother.'

'If you want your new school,' replied Asser tersely.

For days Alfred had found excuses for delaying his visit to St Catherine's – a headache, a sick schoolchild, a leaking roof. Finally Asser had told him that if he didn't go today, the plans for the new school would be torn up. He was now leading Alfred through a desultory market where the poor came to sell the few miserable objects they'd found in the fields: old arrowheads, a few beads, carved bones dug out of a barrow.

'You don't understand,' said Alfred. 'She's vicious, manipulative, bullying, vindictive . . .'

'I rode with her for ten days. She was never less than charming.'

Alfred hooted like a spring goose. 'You fell under her spell,' he said. 'Men do.'

'Show a little kindness,' said Asser, irritated by his scorn. 'She has a bad chill.'

Alfred didn't reply.

'She told me how her family were slaughtered by the Norlanders,' Asser continued. 'How Wolf rode in and killed them all, married her three days later, then left her trapped and friendless in his great hall ever after.'

'You are not the first man to hear that tale,' retorted Alfred, 'nor the twenty-first, but the story always changes.'

'Whatever animosity you have towards her, you must see her. There's nothing else to be said.'

Asser knew Alfred had good qualities. He had shown himself to be brave, his script was elegant, and he knew his Bible better than Asser, which few did. But when his chatter erupted, it was as though the prospect of silence terrified him, and there was something about his manner – his self-confidence, his righteousness, his excited enthusiasm – that irritated Asser beyond measure. With his curly blonde hair, his huge shoulders and his ungainly gait, he looked like a farm boy at his first dance.

'Your mother loves you,' Asser said. 'She has poured her ambition into you. She believes you'd make a better leader of your country than any of your brothers. Can you not respect her for that?'

Alfred gave a start. 'I'll need a fine coat,' he said. 'I can't let her see me in my commonplace clothes.'

'I've already arranged for one to be made available for you,' said Asser.

A bell was tolling some way off, like single drops of rain into an empty pan.

'I hate them both!' Alfred said suddenly. 'My mother and my father. If I heard anyone else say such a thing, I'd think it a sin, but I do. I truly do.'

As they approached the abbey, they could hear the nuns singing the Nunc Dimittis: *Lord, now lettest thou thy servant depart in peace.*

Clothilde and two of her sisters were walking towards them solemnly, their hands clasped. Asser recognised the look on Clothilde's face, and was overwhelmed by bitter coldness. It was the demeanour God's servants invariably wore at times of sorrow. It was why they were singing the Nunc Dimittis.

He looked up at the sky, the unremitting grey, a single black bird wheeling and curving.

'I'm sorry, Alfred,' the abbess said. 'She's dead. Your mother is dead.'

Osburgh was lying in her room. She looked like a saint with her crossed hands resting chastely on her lap, her hair neatly combed, her eyes gazing towards the heavens. Two nuns were in attendance, praying for her soul. Clothilde said she had died peacefully.

Asser cried, of course, discreetly but profoundly in the abbey garden, but even though the pain was deep, he understood there were more important things than his sorrow. Osburgh's greatest wish had been that her son should return to Wessex. His last gift to her would be to devote himself entirely to that wish.

When he returned, Alfred was sitting looking at her, erect and still as he had been when Asser had left him, not a tear in his eye.

Sister Mercy arrived from the abbey hospital. She was the oldest nun; her sight was failing, she was a little deaf and very irritable. She gave Osburgh the briefest of examinations, closed the dead woman's eyes, announced that it had been God's will to take her to his bosom and turned to go.

'Perhaps, Sister, you might elaborate a little,' said Asser.

'There is nothing more to say,' the old woman replied.

'Sister Mercy,' said Clothilde gently, 'the Lady Osburgh was the wife of a king and a guest of his Holiness the Pope. It would be easier for us all if we were able to explain her passing with some clarity. You wouldn't want her death to reflect adversely on the abbey, would you?'

The old nun sighed like a bad-tempered mummer. 'Look at her,' she said. 'Is she bleeding or drooling from the mouth? Did she shit or vomit, can you see pustules or boils?'

When Asser had first been confronted by Osburgh's lifeless body, he'd done his best to satisfy himself that her death was as innocent as it appeared to be. 'There are a few bloody specks on the whites of her eyes,' he said.

The old nun looked at him as though he was the village idiot.

'Specks, Father? Were there indeed? How could I, with my sixty years of attending the dead, not have perceived that? Look at my eyes.' She pulled her lower eyelids down with her fingers. 'Do I have specks? Of course I do. We all do. Specks!' She spat the word as though it was a small fly she was expelling from her mouth. 'Dust blew into her face, Father, or she sneezed so hard that tiny motes were let loose. Do you wish us to tell the world she died of the plague, or was cursed by a witch, or caught a pox while she was in our care? Do so, and may God forgive you. But I'm telling you she was a woman in her middle years who caught a chill and Christ took her as he will take us all. Adieu!'

There was nothing more to say. And though it was hard to believe that the end of Osburgh's life could be so easily accounted for, Asser told himself to take comfort. She hadn't died in great pain or been killed by an assassin. She would be interred tomorrow, and once Wolf was in Rome, she would receive an appropriately dignified memorial service.

Alfred, Asser and Sister Clothilde waited anxiously for Balotelli in the abbey entranceway. He arrived abruptly and urgently. 'Every sister must attend me now,' he barked.

Alfred had expected him to show a little compassion for his loss – an arm round the shoulder perhaps, or a few kind words. But no such gesture was forthcoming. Balotelli walked straight past him into the abbey, shouting his orders.

The abbess was as composed as ever. 'We thought it prudent to say nothing about today's events till you arrived,' she said. 'No one outside the abbey is yet aware of the Lady Osburgh's passing.'

'Good! Good!' Balotelli's relief was palpable. 'I'd have expected nothing else from you, Clothilde.'

Soon all twenty nuns were gathered in front of him. 'We will bury Lady Osburgh tomorrow,' he announced. 'But there is a pressing problem concerning Aethelwolf's signature on the Norland concord. In three days, he will arrive in Rome. He has been suffering from profound attacks that have prevented him from addressing even the simplest of tasks. The signing cannot be undermined by any paralysis of mind that might occur were he to hear of his wife's death. You will divulge nothing of this matter till his ink is dry on the parchment.'

'The high aethel may wish to see her when he arrives. She is his wife. It could be uppermost in his mind,' said Clothilde.

The cardinal looked aghast and turned to Asser, who nodded thoughtfully for a few moments then said, 'She has a chill. It would be wise if she were placed in quarantine.'

'Quarantine!' agreed Balotelli eagerly. 'Good! Yes! Quarantine! Now go about your business, all of you.' He paused and looked intently at each nun to emphasise the seriousness of his instruction. 'Thank you for your understanding,' he said. 'May Christ bless you.' Then he turned to Alfred and pulled him close, holding him tight for a brief moment. 'I'm so sorry, my son. I truly am.'

How strange, Alfred thought. In that moment he could summon no emotion for the death of his mother. All he could think about was the warmth of Balotelli's skin next to his cheek, and the rose oil on his robe.

FORTY-NINE

The Island on the Lake

The southern Marches had become quieter in the weeks since Swift had arrived. The local people were learning how to defend themselves, and their confidence had grown. Chepstow market had reopened and the children were allowed out to play. But there were still skirmishes with the Britons, and though Burgred had more successes than defeats, he was sacrificing men he could ill-afford to lose.

It had been Swift's idea to keep some of the captives alive; she thought they might come in useful. Her fighting monks reinforced a few old cattle pens and shut the prisoners in under guard. Their war paint soon wore off, and their features became recognisable. There were young men with vacant faces and blemishes on their skin; older, swarthy ones, always angry, their eyes looking around for a means of escape. There were women too, and one in particular took Swift's attention. She looked serious, dangerous even, and the others deferred to her and kept out of her way. For a week or two Swift watched her closely. Occasionally their eyes met, then the woman turned away contemptuously. One day, Swift produced a crust of bread, held it up, and deliberately placed it on the ground close to the fence where the woman was standing. It was still there the next day. She replaced it with a fresh piece, which was also ignored, but on the fourth day, the bread had disappeared. She repeated this ritual for a week or so, sometimes sitting by the food and waiting for a while, but it was never taken till after she left. Eventually the woman sat down opposite her, snatched the bread and said in a clear, north Saxon voice, 'What's this pissin' bread for? What does thee want?'

'I want to get you out of here,' Swift replied.

'Then open the shittin' gate,' the woman said, and Swift laughed.

The days went by and the woman began to talk to her. She said her name was Fria, and she complained about their meagre food and scant bedding. But soon she began to unburden herself. 'When I were a little 'un, we lived on the Wirral,' she said. 'It were right cold up there. Pa caught fishes in the big river, but Ma died of plague an' he sold me for drink.'

Swift suspected the woman hadn't talked this candidly for a long time.

'I had three babbies,' Fria went on, 'but they got plague too. Their da said I'd poisoned them an' I were locked up. But I found a broke saw-blade an' cut the guard's throat when he were pullin' down his cacks. I ran away, crossed the border into Wales, and now I'm here cussin' Jesus and killin' Mercians.'

'But you'd kill Welshmen if the price was right?'

'I'd kill anyone if the price were right.'

Swift nodded thoughtfully. She didn't need Fria as her ally. Allies were dangerous, she'd discovered that. But she was sure there'd be a time when they could be of use to each other.

*

Chepstow Long Hall had been the heart of the town. It was where the elders used to meet, where sombre festivities had been held for the souls of dead children, where pedlars had sold necklaces of shiny stones from across the sea. But when the Britons' attacks grew fiercer, it had fallen into disuse, and by the time Swift and the monks arrived, it was little more than a store for old farm tackle.

But Hercules and his men had brought it back to life with new benches and coloured washes, and today the first wedding party for five years was being held. A crowd spilt out of the door and there was dancing in the streets.

Burgred sat in the far corner of the hall with his feet on the table and his arms round the waists of two of Chepstow's grateful daughters. He looked to be the perfect leader: strong, kind, speaking words of wisdom to the bridegroom, patting the bride's hand, receiving compliments from the fawning local gentry. But in truth he had been a disappointment to Swift. Unlike her, he had no ambition. He was here because he'd been instructed to be, and when the battle was won, he'd return to the royal seat in Tamworth. He'd receive the next set of instructions from his king, continue to do so until he was old, and spend his dotage reminiscing with other old soldiers about glories past.

She'd thought they could create something of significance together – it was why she'd come to Wales and sought him out – but he wasn't equipped for kingship.

A drummer was half singing, half chanting the story of Beowulf and the monster Grendel, and the audience were joining in the chorus and pointing at Burgred.

I tell you right, when it comes to a fight
You're as mean a man as Grendel.

She'd stay a while. She wanted to help bring peace to her mother's land, but once that was accomplished, she'd move on.

The chanting ended, fresh jugs of mead were passed round, and conversation began again.

'I'm considering a parley,' Burgred said, still ensconced between the two girls.

'With Rhys of Gwent?' Swift exclaimed. 'A local chiefling with a fat purse? You're the nephew of a great king. Why would you show such weakness? Every day we kill more of his men and drive them further back from the dyke. Do you want to remind him we're a hundred leagues from Tamworth with only a handful of fighters?'

'You don't understand men, cousin,' replied Burgred. 'He'll want this war over as much as we do. His purse isn't limitless. I've already sent a messenger. We are to meet in two days.'

Swift's worst fears had been confirmed. She looked contemptuously at him speaking of appeasement so casually.

'He'll not listen to you. He thinks he has no need. He can call on all South Wales to fight for him if necessary. Strike hard and suddenly. Don't curtsy before him like a blushing milkmaid.'

But the bard had begun chanting the story of Beowulf's final victory. No one was listening to her, not even Hercules.

Four leagues from Chepstow lay an island in the middle of a lake made by forgotten men long ago. The branches of five hundred trees had been woven together, turf and mud weighed down on them, and on top of this earthen platform a mighty hall had been built. It was an awesome sight, like a palace in a fairy tale, surrounded by a painted stockade, the lake teeming with chattering geese. But swarms of tiny black flies rose from its surface in their tens of thousands, stinging Swift's face and crawling under her eyelids and up her nose. She would rather have lived in Fria's pen than in this dreadful place.

They rode cautiously along the long wooden causeway towards the hall. At the far end stood King Rhys, dressed in a leather jerkin and skirt, his hair to his waist, a bronze crown on his head, and behind him twenty or so of his Welsh fighting men with two curious young boys peering between their legs. Further back stood a small crowd of Britons, barely clothed and in their warpaint. Burgred's way was barred.

'It is I,' he called. 'Burgred, landliege of the southern Marches, bondsman of King Burrt of Mercia. I wish to parley.'

'Parley?' The king spat out the word as if it was a mouthful of his black flies. 'Your ancestors stole our land, threw up a barren wall, denied our people access to Chepstow and our villages beyond it, encroach ever further into my kingdom, and you wish to parley? Away with you! Do not waste my time!'

Burgred ignored the man's tone and began to reply in a courteous fashion, but Rhys interrupted him.

'You buy the services of a band of Westsaxon monks to do your fighting. You spend your days with your cock in the cunny of some lascivious princess-whore, and you wish to parley because you cannot defeat us in battle!' He took the two little boys by the hand. 'Ithael! Maurig! Mark this man, if man he be. One day you will kill his children. They'll be cowards too, like all Mercians. They'll run away if you cry boo and beg to parley. Burgred, lackey of the southern Marches, leave my island before I have you whipped!'

He turned his back on them, his doors slammed shut, and Burgred and his men were left to perform the ungainly manoeuvre of turning their horses around on the narrow causeway and returning to land.

They rode in silence for a while, then Burgred let out a string of expletives.

'Calm yourself, my lord,' said Brother Hercules. 'We have

learnt a great deal. Rhys is complacent, he's relying on the Britons to defend him, his palace is vulnerable to attack . . .'

'And his greatest vulnerability,' added Swift thoughtfully, 'is those two boys.'

'You want gold, Fria?' enquired Swift.

'Aye,' replied her captive. 'What else is there?'

'So if someone were to give you more gold than Rhys of Gwent, a great deal more . . .'

'Who would do that?' demanded Fria.

'I would,' replied Swift. 'In return for which your people would burn down Rhys's palace and move further west towards the Great Sea.'

Fria said nothing, but the following day when Swift came down to the pens, she was waiting. 'You aren't my friend,' she said. 'We make idle chatter, 'tis all and I don't trust the bones of you. If we're to do what you bid, you'll have to show me the gold first.'

Swift smiled. She liked this woman who conducted her business as Swift would have done in her place. 'I will give you a quarter now, I will let you out of this gate, and you will take it to your people beyond the dyke. When your task is completed, I'll free the prisoners and give you the rest of the money.'

'Half now.'

'Very well, half.'

Fria considered. 'When?' she said.

'When the time is right.'

'What if you play us false?'

Swift laughed. 'We won't. If we do, your people will make far more trouble for us than ever before, I'm sure of that.'

'How much gold?' demanded Fria.

Swift had insisted on a purse sufficient for the task, and Burgred had given it to her. She opened it and showed it to the woman.

'We'd need more than that!' she said.

'I have no more. Take it or don't take it, it's up to you.' Swift put the purse back in her pocket. 'And while you're deciding, tell me what you know about the sons of King Rhys.'

FIFTY

The Blessing

Asser walked ponderously two steps behind Wolf; he was not a lover of formality. The high aethel, though, was as happy as a child with a plum in its mouth, treading barefoot through Rome dressed in nothing but a thin shift, accompanied only by his sergeant, Stub, and Cardinal Balotelli. Passers-by ignored the sight. The city was accustomed to witnessing the deranged and penitent as they trudged towards the Pope's Lateran Palace on the Caelian Hill to meet him, but for Wolf these were the most significant and glorious steps he had ever undertaken, his journey to Calvary.

'At last, the Holy City!' he murmured to Stub out of the corner of his mouth. 'I will receive the soft touch of the Pope's fingers on my brow, I will kiss his ring and bask in his blessing.'

Asser and Balotelli glanced at each other, so many months of planning finally coming to a happy conclusion.

At the top of the steps, Asser nodded to the papal guards and the great doors swung open. The four men walked at an even pace past the mural of St Peter fishing in the Sea of Galilee, denying Christ three times and weeping bitterly in repentance, being crucified upside down by the Emperor Nero, and finally seated next to Christ in all his glory.

'How inspiring!' whispered Wolf reverently. 'The great saint's life is passing in front of me as if in a story. I will dedicate the rest of my life to becoming as fine a Christian as he.'

They came to a halt in front of the doors of the Pope's receiving room. Balotelli knocked discreetly, then he and Asser stepped back. The doors opened. Wolf gave an audible gasp and stepped inside, and they closed again.

Balotelli and Asser sat on a bench in the corridor and waited for Wolf's return. Stub sat a little way off, staring at the door. Asser ordered bread and sausage from a passing servant.

'How is Alfred?' asked Balotelli quietly.

'Surprisingly sanguine,' replied Asser. He glanced at Stub, but the man didn't appear to hear them. 'Remember we promised Lady Osburgh we would set up a meeting between him and his father. We must fulfil that promise.'

'Can we do so? Alfred has been resistant to the idea.'

'He has, Cardinal, but he is besotted with you . . .'

'Don't be ridiculous!'

'He is and you know it. I think you can persuade him to attend such a meeting.'

'But is he ready to leave Rome yet?' the cardinal said. 'He has authority, but he can be foolish, almost like a child. Should we offer to keep him for a year or so and train him in the art of governance?'

'You have trained him well,' said Asser. 'As you do every bright young man whom you welcome into the palazzo. But you must let him go.'

The servant returned with a mug of water.

'The sausage?' Asser enquired, and the man scuttled off again.

The cardinal began picking at a small lichen that had lodged itself tentatively in a crack in the fluting of a pillar. 'Fabio Gilotti,' he said thoughtfully. 'I saw him often as a child. He was a monster even then. I should have predicted the direction in which his life was heading.'

'He'll receive his just reward in hell,' said Asser.

'Will he? If so, I doubt it will be for some time. His brother has refused to let him be confined to the papal dungeon; he's under guard at their summer home in Tivoli. Doubtless he has his own cook, and a slave to ease his aching limbs. He'll be exiled, I imagine, somewhere not too unpleasant.'

'Did he act on his own?' mused Asser. 'He's not very bright. Could someone else have been orchestrating all this? His brother Enzo, Ponti, one of the other Notarii – perhaps someone who hasn't even crossed our minds?'

Balotelli shrugged. 'Perhaps. Time will tell.'

It was growing dark when the door to the Pope's quarters swung open again and Wolf appeared, a beatific smile on his face. 'His Holiness looked deep into my eyes and lifted the weight from my troubled soul,' he said.

'It has been a difficult journey for you,' said the cardinal, 'but worth the arduous travel, I think.'

'He embraced me. He said I can return home free from doubt and sorrow. Christ will give me the strength to become a great and glorious Christian king.'

'And did he say he looked forward to witnessing the official signing of the concord in four days' time?' enquired Asser.

Wolf had no time to reply. As if by chance, Undersecretary Ponti came bustling round the corner. 'High Aethelwolf,' he said, 'you startled me. I didn't expect to happen upon such an important personage. What an honour to meet you. I trust the Holy Father has laid balm on your soul to help you bear your tragic loss.'

The smile vanished from Wolf's face. Asser glanced at Balotelli, who was staring at Ponti in horror.

'What tragic loss?' demanded Wolf.

'Your wife.'

'What about her?'

'She's dead. Has no one told you?'

'No she isn't,' said Wolf stoutly.

Ponti's eyes widened in mock concern. 'I thought your friends here would have broken the news to you.'

Wolf turned to Balotelli. 'Is this true?' he demanded.

The cardinal struggled for words. 'I . . . had planned to acquaint you with your loss later today. I didn't want the news to mar your papal audience.'

Wolf let out a howl worthy of his name, an achingly sad sound that echoed down the corridors. 'My beautiful wife has been cut down in the prime of her . . .' He punched the wall with a force that made Asser's knuckles twitch. He had expected Wolf to be upset, perhaps to use his wife's death as an excuse to delay signing the concord, but he hadn't thought he'd witness quite such sorrow after all Osburgh had told him about their marriage.

'I believe you are staying at Caesar's Haven; I'll escort you back,' Asser said gently.

'You won't,' Wolf retorted. 'Stub,' he called. His sergeant leapt to his feet, took his arm and led him back down the corridor. Balotelli and Asser stared after them, speechless.

'You should have told him sooner, your Eminence,' said Ponti reprovingly.

The sausage arrived, Asser broke it in two, and he and Balotelli sat chewing and ruminating.

The Pope's doors slowly opened. 'Has he gone?' Benedict enquired.

'He has, your Holiness,' replied Balotelli.

'He's very noisy, isn't he?' the Pope continued. 'He wanted to hug me, which I found a little disconcerting. May I sit with you?'

Asser moved along the bench and the three men sat quietly for a while.

'He was inspired by your words, your Holiness,' said Asser eventually.

The Pope sighed. 'Adrianis is a good man at heart,' he said.

'I meant Aethelwolf. The one you just blessed.'

'That was Adrianis of Sardinia.'

'No, it was Aethelwolf of Wessex, your Holiness.'

'Was it?'

'Definitely.' Asser felt as though he'd swallowed a giant lead weight. 'So you didn't tell him you were excited about the concord? You didn't say you were eager to attend the signing in person?'

'Was I advised to do this?'

'You were, your Holiness,' replied Balotelli. 'Several times.'

The Pope stood up, his irritation palpable. 'I can't be expected to remember everything,' he said. 'You'll have to sort it out. Clearer instructions, that's what's required.' He returned to his quarters grumbling, a small, angry figure.

Asser and Balotelli walked back down the palace steps.

'The papal crown weighs heavily on Benedict's head,' said Asser bitterly. 'All our work has come to naught.'

'It's a disappointment,' agreed Balotelli, and though his voice was calm, there was a furrow of anxiety on his brow. 'We did our best to keep his wife's death from him so he wouldn't become distressed at such an important time; let's hope he will take it as a kindness. I'll instruct the Pope to send him a letter saying how much he's looking forward to their meeting again at the signing, and we'll pray no harm has been done.' He gave a tiny groan of frustration. 'But how in the name of Christ did Ponti know Osburgh was dead?'

'It was a strange encounter,' replied Asser. 'Wolf's display of sorrow was extraordinary, all that noise and punching, but not a single tear. It seemed counterfeit. It was almost as if . . .' He stopped abruptly, the truth of the situation suddenly clear to him. 'He already knew his wife was dead, didn't he?'

FIFTY-ONE

Buffleheads and Shovelers

Swift crouched deep in a hawthorn bush, Hercules squatting by her side. The early-morning light leached through the trees, the smell of forest leaf-mould fresh and exhilarating. There was a crash a way off, a wild boar perhaps, but it wasn't close enough to be troubling. This forest was a place of dark magic, far more menacing than a handful of painted Britons, yet Swift wasn't fearful; she loved the quiet, broken only by the occasional flutter of a tiny bird.

They'd been waiting since before dawn, hidden in the bushes surrounding a little pond where the tribal chief's boys came to hunt waterfowl, a sport so pleasurable, Fria had said, that they were here every morning at this time of year. Swift could see plenty of birds now: pochards, buffleheads, shovelers. A tufted duck started, and flew off with his mate, and Swift's hand tensed round the hilt of her sword. There was a muffled cough, but it was only a fox. Finally, when the light was full, the fowling party arrived: six guards, two slaves and the princes.

Her men had practised their assault well. It was conducted

in complete silence. One moment Rhys's guards were standing at the water's edge; the next their bodies lay face-down in the pond and the two little boys were gagged and blindfolded. It was a good morning's work, quick, elegant and effective.

Late that afternoon, Rhys of Gwent galloped into Chepstow with a band of his men. Swift and Hercules, who had been looking out for signs of their approach, stepped from the long hall to meet them. The king was white-faced and shaking.

'Where are they?' he said. 'Are they dead?'

'Come to parley, have you?' replied Swift coolly. 'You would appear to have very little to parley with.'

'I want my sons, nothing more.'

'They are with Landliege Burgred,' Swift replied, 'many leagues away on their journey to Tamworth.'

Rhys waited for her to continue, but she remained silent. Let him quake a little longer.

'What is it you want?' he pleaded. Gone was his superciliousness, his jock-the-cock demeanour. Curious, Swift thought, how two small boys could make this large man so soft.

'I want almost nothing at all,' she replied. 'You will pledge to cease your attacks on Mercia, and from today you will deploy none of your men within three leagues of the dyke. Your sons will remain with us. They will be fed well, taught wisely and treated royally. But if you break your pledge, they will be executed.'

'Please!' stammered the king. 'I beg you, do not harm them!'

'To whom is it you beg?' enquired Swift, feigning puzzlement. 'I see no one here but a lascivious princess-whore.'

For a moment he didn't grasp her meaning, then he dropped to his knees. 'Please, Lady Swift, blessed daughter of Aethelwolf of Wessex, I have nothing but respect and admiration for you. My words two days past were doltish and spoken only in anger. I apologise.'

'I accept your apology,' said Swift gracefully. 'Now make your pledge.'

He nodded. 'I will do as you say.'

'You may go.'

He rose and turned to leave.

'One thing more. When you return home, you'll find your kinsmen slaughtered and your palace burnt to the ground. Your words offended me a little. I'm sure you'll understand.'

FIFTY-TWO

The Saxon School

Wolf would enjoy himself, Asser was determined of that. He would be so well entertained he'd forget his fear, his madness, their failure to tell him about his bereavement, his anxiety about the long journey home, anything that would inhibit him from signing the concord. For the next few days his life would be a fount of unadulterated pleasure.

Asser arranged a memorial for Osburgh in the grand Lateran basilica on the far side of the city, and Wolf was given the place of honour, sitting on a jewelled canopied throne with five hundred voices singing his name. After the final prayer, Asser returned him to Caesar's Haven, where dancing girls from the finest bordellos in Rome entertained him with their dextrous skills. A vast tank was erected in the garden, and naked boys and girls swam in synchronous fashion to the accompaniment of harps and drums. He organised a rendition of *The Comedy of Asses*, performed by the finest comic actors in the city, with a party afterwards for the players, which little Judith hosted. He administered Wolf's medication twice every day, sometimes thrice, and all this attention seemed to have the desired effect. Asser had never seen the old man so happy.

Seneschal François was enjoying himself too, now he'd been liberated from the responsibility of negotiating an agreement. Judith, Asser, Wolf and the seneschal became a little family, feeding ducks in the Haven's garden, drawing foolish pictures, playing Hook the Hat. But all this changed when a band of Frankish courtiers arrived: the emperor's representatives at the signing. François was forced to excuse himself from childish pursuits and confer in private with these serious men for hours on end.

They were pleasant enough, as courtiers usually were, but they treated Asser with mild disdain.

'Is all well?' he enquired. 'Are the arrangements for the signing to your liking?' By way of reply they offered only empty smiles. François assured him nothing was amiss, but Asser became a little concerned.

He and Wolf embarked on a tour of the great city. Rome was at her most magnificent; the sun was shining beneficently, glorious blue and purple bindweed swathed its innumerable ruins. He showed Wolf the gigantic statue of the Emperor Constantine's foot and the colossal sundial that cast its shadow over all Rome and was known as the Horologium Augusti. They visited the Saxon Quarter and ate a beef pudding the like of which Wolf said he hadn't savoured since he'd left Winchester, but as they were about to return to the Haven, they came upon a group of ragged children throwing stones into a chalk-drawn circle. Wolf stopped, watching them with charmed fascination.

'I want to go to the Saxon school,' he announced.

'We'll be visiting the school after the concord has been signed, High Aethel,' replied Asser nervously. 'There will be a concert, you'll unveil a plaque, and you've also generously agreed to make a speech to the local officials.'

'Now!' Wolf insisted.

'I haven't written the speech yet,' said Asser.

'I wish to play with the children without the encumbrance of fawning dignitaries. Are you telling me I can't?'

'Of course I'm not, High Aethel,' said Asser. 'It's just that . . .' Wolf must not see his son yet. Nothing had been prepared for the meeting.

'That's settled then. Come on.'

Alfred's new school consisted of five gaily coloured roundhouses. When Wolf and Asser arrived in its neat and tidy grounds, there was no one about.

'I suspect it's some local saint's day,' said Asser. 'Let's go back to Caesar's Haven. Judith will be waiting for us.'

But as he was turning his horse around, an elderly man appeared and introduced himself as John of Old Saxony, the school caretaker. On realising who Wolf was, he became very excited. He clapped his hands vigorously, and out of the huts tumbled and scampered forty or so Saxon boys.

'What fine young men,' said Wolf.

'Very,' replied Asser, looking around desperately for Alfred. If he and Wolf encountered each other without prior warning, there'd be pandemonium. He cursed Balotelli for having failed to make the necessary arrangements.

Wolf was now standing among the boys, patting their heads and giving their cheeks a squeeze.

'Do you know who I am?' he bellowed.

'No,' the boys shouted back, and everyone laughed.

'I am the High Aethel of Wessex. Follow me,' he said, and embarked on a strange, jogging shuffle across the courtyard. 'Come on!' he called, and the children trotted after him. John of Old Saxony smiled benignly, then produced a whistle from his belt and began playing 'The Wessex Boatman'. Wolf and the children joined in the chorus, and they all danced in a long procession round the huts, John hobbling along behind.

Come all you fine young Saxon men
And listen to my tale,
It tells of Brit the boatman
And a giant of a whale.

Asser had searched everywhere for Alfred, but to no avail. His one remaining hope lay in a small child who hadn't joined in the dance and instead was standing staring quizzically after his fellows.

'Boy, where's your master?' he whispered. The child looked at him blankly. 'Where's Master Alfred?' he asked again, a little louder. But there was no reply. 'This is very important,' he shouted. Tears appeared in the boy's eyes and a moan issued from his mouth like a solitary goose flying across a misty marsh.

'Calm yourself, please,' said Asser, a little desperately. 'Would you like a cob nut? I believe I have one.' But as he searched his bag, Alfred appeared at the school gate carrying a pile of logs.

'What have you done to Cuddie?' he demanded, dropping the wood and putting his arms round the boy. 'Why have you distressed him so? What are you doing here?'

'Alfred, you must leave immediately,' said Asser urgently.

'I've only this moment arrived,' replied Alfred.

Asser gesticulated at Wolf and his train of boys, who had completed their circumlocution and were arriving back where they'd started.

'Look who is here,' he hissed.

The song had come to an end and the boys were excitedly quizzing Wolf about what being high aethel was like.

'Hush, children,' he said. 'One question at a time, please.' He glanced up at Alfred, who was looking at him appalled. 'And who is this fine fellow, boys? Is this your master?'

'It is I, Father,' said Alfred.

'There appears to be some confusion,' Asser interjected. 'I'll take the young man away, shall I?'

Wolf looked momentarily puzzled, then realisation dawned. 'You?' he exclaimed. 'The profligate? The dissolute?'

Every iota of jollity had disappeared from the courtyard, replaced by the angry voice of a red-faced old man. The boys stared, overawed.

'You who brought shame to the house of Wolf,' he went on. 'You whose face I swore never to lay eyes on again. Crawl back to the city of Sodom and make sport with your own kind, you buggerer.'

Alfred said nothing, but his initial surprise had given way to another almost wistful look. Asser had no idea what he was thinking.

The following morning Asser stood apprehensively at the gates of Caesar's Haven carrying a large, freshly bound book. Had Wolf realised he had known Alfred would be at the school? Would he thrash him, ignore him, pretend the meeting with his son had never occurred?

His thoughts were interrupted by a finely dressed woman in a long peplos decorated with jewelled brooches, who was leaving the Haven. She wore a hat so large it was impossible to tell how old she was or what she looked like. She hailed a dog cart, and when it pulled up beside her, she threw a large bag and her hat into it, revealing cropped hair dyed blue at the sides. It was the puppeteer from the palace at Modena.

'Mirandolina, however did you get here?' Asser exclaimed.

'My, Father Asser, you're looking handsome,' she gushed.

'What are you doing here?' Asser insisted.

'I'm making haste to leave this place,' she said. 'What a pleasure it is to see you again, my dear man.'

'You're a long way from Modena.'

'Indeed I am. The introduction you gave me to the high aethel proved very lucrative. He quite fell in love with me, wanted me to come to Rome with him, and I was more than happy to do so as I've wished to live here for a long while. But I grew tired of his slobbering amore, and was desperately relieved when he decided to spend the journey playing Snake-Hole-Elbow with his little princess rather than constantly pressing his nose into my boobies.'

'And now you're making your escape?'

'Indeed I am. First, though, I'm off to the market to sell the ridiculous clothes he gave me. Even the jewellery is vulgar.'

'Where will you stay? You gave us great service in Modena. I'm sure we could find you lodgings for a while.'

'Thank you, Father, but I have an old lover who I know will accommodate me. He lives among the Antonils. I see from your face that you know of them.'

'I do indeed. They're heretics and are a little crazed.'

'As am I. I'll enjoy their company.'

'Perhaps, but I would urge you to stay away from them,' replied Asser. 'They are not popular here. Most are harmless, but a few are tainted with evil and are currently being sought out by a vicious man of some authority.'

'Don't concern yourself about me,' she said, and climbed into the dog cart. 'I am popular wherever I go.' She blew him a kiss, and the cart set off into the city.

Asser found Wolf, still dressed in his night attire, laughing and playing dice with Judith. 'Would you like a spin?' she asked him, and burst into a fit of the giggles.

'No thank you. I have much to arrange for tomorrow's

signing,' replied Asser, his concern somewhat allayed now he sensed that the events of the previous day hadn't plunged Wolf back into a dark place. Judith was laughing uncontrollably. He felt as though he was the butt of a joke he didn't understand. 'I apologise for the confrontation yesterday, High Aethel,' he said. 'It must have been a shock. I was very angry on your behalf. Someone in authority should have warned me your son was teaching there. Nothing like this will happen again, I promise you.'

'It's not important,' Wolf said.

Asser breathed a sigh of relief, and felt confident enough to proffer the book he'd brought with him. 'This is rather wonderful,' he said. 'It's the concord and it has the most magnificent frontispiece, fashioned by our finest mapmaker. Isn't this the most glorious picture? See how he has portrayed Wessex and Rome as the great stars of the firmament, surrounded by the lesser stars of the other nations. Perhaps you'd like to look through its elegantly fashioned pages?'

Wolf grabbed the book and smote Asser round the head with it, sending him stumbling across the room. 'Pages?' he roared. 'I don't want pages. Are you mad or deaf? I agreed to sign one page to appease my friend the emperor, just one! What is this snare of words you are weaving for me?'

'I'm not, I promise you. It's too long, I agree,' said Asser, his head smarting from the blow. 'I will ensure its size is reduced.'

'I'll ensure *your* size is reduced, you little shit,' retorted Wolf. 'Now fuck off!'

'I will,' said Asser. 'Immediately.'

'And tomorrow bring me more medication,' Wolf added.

Judith was laughing so hard that Asser had an overwhelming desire to slap her.

FIFTY-THREE

Yesterday's Bread

The following morning, Balotelli's coterie of priests met at the front of St Peter's Basilica an hour before sunrise, yawning and wiping the sleep from their eyes. Asser had thought it a foolish idea to mount the signing in the half-restored church, but Pope Benedict had insisted that its one hundred and eight newly refurbished columns signified the transformation that was taking place under his papacy, and that it was thus the perfect location for the event.

On Asser's instructions, fifty servants and slaves had worked through the night scrubbing the floors to keep the dust down, and had hung a panoply of linen drapes from the balcony to obscure the building work. Trees in large pots were brought in, painted screens were set up on the walls with garlands of flowers affixed to them to add colour to the proceedings. He was determined that this would be a memorable day, and had put Kennet in charge of ensuring that all those taking part were in the correct place at the correct time. Philip was responsible for guaranteeing that no uninvited citizens could enter the building, and Plegmond and his team were taking care of the representatives from faraway lands who would hopefully be signing similar concords very soon.

Balotelli led the priests in a brief prayer on the basilica steps, and everyone set about their allotted tasks. Asser and Balotelli headed off for Caesar's Haven to greet the high aethel and ensure he was happy, confident and ready to leave on time. The town guards were putting up barriers to prevent the crowds from spilling onto the roads, vendors were erecting their stalls, pushing sticks through honeyed apples, roasting chestnuts and the like, and large crowds had arrived early to ensure they obtained the best view of the processions, some of the children wearing Saxon costumes and waving the blue Wessex pennant.

'My only anxiety is the emperor's men,' said Asser. 'They are profoundly unhelpful. I didn't hear a word from them yesterday and I left countless messages.'

'Don't concern yourself,' replied Balotelli. 'They are not our responsibility. The seneschal is in charge of Wolf's entourage and I have every confidence in him. It is in his interest that the day goes well.'

The early-morning cloud was dissipating, and as the sun tentatively began to break through, they could feel a little warmth on their faces.

'It's going to be a good day,' said Asser.

But when they arrived at the Haven, they found the big front gates locked. Balotelli's men shook them several times and shouted for attention, but no one responded.

'Perhaps they fear the crowds will come here in advance of the ceremony and disturb the high aethel,' said the cardinal.

Asser thought that unlikely, since the ceremony was taking place nearly a league away; nevertheless, the barring of their way was very odd.

Two of the cardinal's men clambered over the wall and

unlocked the gates from the inside, but the puzzle continued. When they finally gained entrance to the grounds, they discovered the stables were empty.

'Could they have left for St Peter's already?' suggested Asser.

The gardens, which had been humming with jollity for days, were now completely deserted. There wasn't a single servant about, and the front doors were firmly closed and the windows shuttered. They attempted to peer through gaps in the wooden slats, but there was no sign of movement. The guards walked round the side of the house knocking and calling.

'It's as though it's been shut down for the winter,' said Asser.

'Nonsense, it can't be,' replied Balotelli.

Someone at the back of the house yelled, 'Your Eminence!'

They walked briskly round the building and found a guard gesticulating towards a half-open servants' entrance, which led into an eerily silent kitchen. They wound their way through empty corridors towards the front entrance, shouting for attention, but there was no reply other than the echo of their own calls, until they came to a large shadowy reception room and heard a familiar voice.

'I thought you'd come. Have you broken your fast yet?' A solitary figure was ensconced in a comfortable chair. 'There is a loaf of yesterday's bread and some water, I think.'

'What are you doing here, Ponti?' said Balotelli. 'Where has he gone?'

'Gone? Who?' replied Ponti. 'Oh, you mean the high aethel. I arrived here a little while ago on behalf of the Notarii with a gift for him to wear on his great day: a golden pin bearing the image of our great city's founders Romulus and Remus. But he was in the process of leaving, as were the seneschal and his retinue. There will be no signing. Your plan is undone. They wish me to send their apologies, but they've made other arrangements.'

'Apologies?' said Balotelli, barely able to contain his outrage. 'What other arrangements?'

'I wouldn't know,' replied Ponti, 'but apparently they don't involve you. He loved our pin, by the way.'

Asser stood in the middle of the garden, consumed by so many emotions he couldn't begin to count them. The hopes they'd shared, the endless work, the thirteen-month incarceration, all brought to nothing by this inexplicable flight. And the seneschal, why had he sneaked off? What in Christ's name had made him walk away from an agreement into which he'd put so much time and trouble?

Balotelli was sitting on a garden bench with the tips of his fingers resting on his nose. 'We summoned kings, princes and ambassadors from twenty-three kingdoms to St Peter's. What will we tell them?'

Asser welcomed the challenge of solving any problem that might help him forget his pain. 'We'll tell them . . .' his mind was churning like a small boat in an angry sea, 'that St Peter's is unsafe. There's been a threat . . . a violent threat . . . from heretics – from the Antonils, perhaps?'

'Excellent! Yes. The Antonils,' agreed the cardinal. 'They've attacked us before and they're threatening to do so again. We'll arrange the signing for another day and hope to Christ we can salvage something from this mess. In the meantime, find Wolf. Find the seneschal. Find out what the crafty bastards are up to. The future of the entire papacy is at stake.'

FIFTY-FOUR

Home

Alfred was watching his boys as they sat in a circle in the school courtyard, concentrating hard on a burning candle with black lines drawn round its circumference.

'What time is it when the candle burns down to the first line?' he asked them.

'Pear time!' chorused the boys.

Out of the corner of his eye he saw Balotelli arrive. He was carrying an intriguing cloth-wrapped package. Alfred gestured to John of Old Saxony, who produced a small stool and placed it next to him. Balotelli sat on it with a grunt.

'I'm sorry the signing failed to take place. I hope it wasn't my fault,' said Alfred.

'It was your father's,' replied Balotelli. 'Asser is scouring Italia for him, but I suspect the old man is trying hard not to be found. The Pope thinks I'm to blame, the Notarii are giggling like foolish virgins, and I'm the butt of all Rome's jokes. It is not my finest moment.'

The flame on the candle had reached the first line. 'Pear time!' shouted little Cuddie, and blew it out.

'Go to the storeroom and choose your fruit,' said Alfred. The boys raced off squealing.

'In truth, the fault *was* partly mine,' said Balotelli. 'I was supposed to propose to you that a meeting should take place between you and your father, but I had so much else on my mind I forgot, even though I was constantly prompted.'

'He said I was a buggerer,' replied Alfred.

Balotelli laughed. 'I've been called far worse.'

Alfred was thinking about the humiliation of his banishment, something he'd pushed to the back of his mind long ago. How absurd his father had been, and how hypocritical. Every soldier did what he'd been accused of when they were cold and loveless and far from home. It was a Saxon jest – *What happens before a famous victory but is never spoken of thereafter?* It didn't matter. He had his school, his new friends, Balotelli. The extraordinary thing was that he'd found the confrontation with Wolf a blessing. The father he remembered, the one who'd spoken to him so cruelly on the day of his banishment, the ogre who had loved him certainly but with the fierce ebb and flow of a squally sea, that father no longer existed. And the new one, shuffling around his school grounds with a gaggle of children in his wake, held no fear; he was old and foolish, a once great man whose mind had withered away. Wessex seemed less terrifying now, not somewhere Alfred wished to return to, but he knew he could if he wanted to.

The boys came running back, sat down and bit enthusiastically into their fruit.

'I have a gift for you all,' announced Balotelli.

He handed Alfred the package, and the boys looked on curiously as he unwrapped a large, round, flat object with two wolves painted on it.

'It's just a plate,' said one of the boys, his voice tinged with disappointment.

'It's a plaque,' said Balotelli. 'A very special royal plaque. High Aethelwolf of Wessex was going to give it to you. The red wolf symbolises Rome, the blue one is the high aethel, above them the Pope's golden crown. Rome and Aethelwolf in perfect harmony.'

'May we hold it?' the boy said.

'Lick your fingers first,' said Alfred, 'or you'll make it sticky.'

The boys passed it round.

'Why didn't he sign the concord?' asked the cardinal.

'My father? Isn't it obvious?' replied Alfred.

'Not to me.'

'He can't read. He didn't know what the words meant.'

'Why in the name of St Matthew the scrivener can't he read?'

'None of the old kings of Britain can,' said Alfred. 'They don't milk cows, they don't bake bread and they don't read books. They haven't yet understood that times have changed and the storyteller's lyre has been replaced by the turn of a page.'

'But Wolf and Father Asser agreed on what the concord would say when they were in Modena,' Balotelli said. 'Even if he couldn't read it, he knew what was in it.'

'Perhaps he didn't believe that the written words were a true reflection of what they'd decided.'

'Or . . .' Balotelli frowned, 'perhaps someone made him a better offer.'

'Like what?' said Alfred.

'That's the question, isn't it? What could be more attractive than the promise of the greatest army in the world?'

Asser and his small band were in hot pursuit of the high aethel. Mountjoy had received intelligence that he was heading for

Modena, but it proved false. When they arrived, they were told Wolf was on his way to Aix, but they couldn't find him there either. After much bribery and a little shouting, the Bishop of Aix admitted that the high aethel was heading for the Frankish coast on his way home to Wessex, but though they hired countless sets of fresh horses, they were unable to catch up with him.

In Brettony, they came upon long, desultory lines of retreating soldiers wearing the colours of the Holy Roman Empire. They were exhausted, dirty, many of them injured. Asser ordered his men to give them water and what little provisions they had left.

'We took a drubbing in the Lowlands,' one man said. 'We were outnumbered and outmanoeuvred.'

Asser was shaken by the sight of them. When he'd envisioned an army of the righteous, it had never occurred to him that the emperor's men would be anything other than invincible. Now he saw them as common soldiers like any others, with tired eyes, torn uniforms and bloodstained faces.

'Perhaps he isn't the all-conquering hero we thought him to be. Maybe even if we'd had a righteous army we'd have lost,' said Plegmond softly.

Ten weeks after leaving Rome, they arrived in Southamwic and stayed the night at its famed abbey, where the papal ring ensured they were treated as princes. They were bathed and massaged with intoxicating oils and slept in beds of the finest down. The following morning they were shown the abbey church, laden with golden crosses and vessels as fine as any in Venice or Pisa.

But they had no time to dawdle. The abbot informed them that the high aethel had arrived in Winchester the previous day. How astounding that Wolf had journeyed from Rome like a plodding tortoise, while they'd made chase like frenzied hares, zigzagging across Europe, barely stopping for rest or to take sustenance, yet he had been first to breast the finishing line. What a prescient philosopher Aesop had been.

They rode to Winchester and found the town engulfed by excitement. Every church bell was ringing, and crowds were streaming towards Winchester Great Hall. Asser and his men climbed onto a roof overlooking it. The doors swung open and Wolf appeared with his eldest son, Bear, and Seneschal François by his side.

'What's that conniving Frankish bastard doing here?' murmured Asser.

'Fellow Westsaxons . . .' Wolf began. He extolled the emperor's hospitality, and lauded the Pope as a saint who had renewed his vigour and given him the strength to govern his realm wisely and well for many years to come. His face softened as he continued. 'As you may know, in his wisdom the Lord Jesus Christ has taken the Lady Osburgh from us and she is now . . . dead. But fellow Saxons, he has not abandoned us. He has bestowed on us the most glorious of gifts, a Bethlehem star who will illuminate our lives and chase the shadows from our darkest moments. My new wife . . .' she appeared in the doorway beside him, her eyes wide, her demeanour modest, 'the great-granddaughter of the mighty Emperor Charlemagne and daughter of Charles the Bald, the Holy Roman Emperor – our Queen Judith.'

A cheer went up from the crowd, albeit one tinged with whispering and derisive laughter. Asser watched bitterly. So this was what his hopes and dreams had come to: a senile old man, a twelve-year-old girl, and the agreement in ruins. He would not accept this, he'd laboured too hard. There must be some way he could save this benighted country from Norland slaughter.

PART FOUR

FIFTY-FIVE

The Saxon Hunting Dog

Asser sat on a wall watching Rollo and Mountjoy kicking a bladder around. On the other side of Wolf's courtyard, Seneschal François and his men were loading up their horses in preparation for their return to Frankia. An eager-eyed dog bounded up to Asser and licked his face. It might have digested a rat or guzzled the innards of a sick pigeon, but Asser didn't care. He was grateful for the affection.

'Do you like him?' called the seneschal. 'I've always been fond of Westsaxon dogs. I call him Asser.'

'Why?'

'He covers long distances without complaining.'

Asser smiled sarcastically.

The seneschal wandered over to him.

'Have a honeyed damson,' he said, proffering a dainty drawstring bag of sweetmeats and sitting on the wall beside him.

Asser took one of the sticky little plums and sucked it meditatively. 'I assume the emperor instructed you to bring Wolf and Judith back here without signing the concord?' he said.

'You understand what a treacherous act that was? It destroyed our plan for Christendom and left my cardinal undermined and humiliated.'

'We are but servants of our masters,' replied the seneschal, ruffling the dog's ears. 'Charles is ruthless. He does only what is best for his Empire.'

Rollo kicked the ball to Asser, who trapped it with one foot and passed it on to the seneschal.

'Ridiculous game,' said the Frank, and let it roll past him.

'In what way is an unsigned concord good for his empire?' said Asser.

'You saw the chaos in Brettony. Our forces in the Lowlands are spent, Prince Louis' army in Burgundy is bogged down, the Bulgars are nibbling at our north-eastern frontier . . .'

'Are you saying he can't afford it?' guffawed Asser. 'The most powerful man in the world is worried about his leaky purse!'

'He's a realist. A righteous army would have been ruinously expensive. He's made a less costly arrangement.'

'So Christendom can go hang.'

'Perhaps. Also he was bored with the old man.'

'Bored?'

'When their journey began, Wolf was strong and playful, I saw it myself. But by the time they got to Modena, he was a miserable curmudgeon. The emperor wanted nothing more to do with him.'

'And that's how our fate has been decided, by Charles the Bald's threshold of boredom?' said Asser.

'Empires rise and fall on such whims,' replied the seneschal, 'and on such slights too. Wolf will never forgive Rome for confronting him with his banished son. Can you blame him?'

Asser shrugged.

'Was it you?' asked François. 'Did you arrange that meeting?'

'If it had been, I'd never forgive myself,' replied Asser.

Noises sounded from above. Doors were slammed; there was the crash of breaking pottery.

'You stupid fools!' Judith was shouting from somewhere inside the hall. 'All of you.'

'When Wolf dies, the emperor will be in a very powerful position because of this marriage,' continued the seneschal. 'In theory, at least, Wolf's children have no precedence. He'll instruct Judith to marry one of his Frankish favourites, the lucky man will become the new high aethel, and Wessex will be part of the Holy Roman Empire.'

Asser laughed scornfully. 'The Westsaxon aldermen would never allow that.'

'Charles bribed all Rome to secure a new Pope. He can afford to purchase a few aldermen.'

'I hate this place,' Judith was yelling. 'It's a pigsty.'

'I'll be happy to leave her behind,' said the seneschal. 'She's very wearing.'

'Is Wolf fucking her?' enquired Mountjoy, a little too loudly.

The courtyard fell silent. Asser suppressed a smile. The twins had been engrossed in their game. He hadn't realised they'd been listening to the conversation.

'Why are you looking at me?' Mountjoy held up his hands in a protest of innocence. 'It's what you all want to know.'

'I'm confident her maidenhead is intact,' said Asser. He wasn't, but her Frisian maids would be examining her sheets every morning, and he could find out the details for the cost of a smile and a silver piece.

One of his men signalled to the seneschal: they were ready to depart. 'Return with me,' François said suddenly to Asser. 'The Norlanders will attack the south coast again within the month. You've nothing to stay for.'

Asser wanted to go back; he was anxious about Balotelli. The collapse of the concord would have damaged the cardinal mightily. His opponents would be only too happy to see him demoted to some bleak province in Afrique or accidentally nudged into the Tiber. He sighed. He couldn't go. He had unfinished business here; it was his duty to stay a while. The righteous army might be no more, but could he somehow pull together its remnants?

'Thank you, but no,' he said. 'Though I'm grateful you asked.'

The two men embraced and the Frankish party moved off.

'Asser!'

He looked up, but it was only the seneschal calling to his new dog.

FIFTY-SIX

The Frankish Whore-Child

Wolf made his way ponderously downstairs from his private quarters.

'Uncle, I wish to share your bed!' Judith, dressed in a modest linen undergarment, was standing in the hall.

'Husband, not uncle,' he replied gruffly, 'and you can't.'

'But I'm being forced to sleep in Hawk's hall, and it's as drear as death.'

Wolf yawned and scratched his head. No, Judith couldn't sleep with him. Never mind issues of propriety, a fresh problem had arisen during the night. At the third bell, Bear had crawled in beside him as drunk as a Rheinish cobbler and had snored for hours. In the morning, he'd refused to leave and declared the room belonged to him. All Wessex was his now, he'd said, and his father could go hang himself. Wolf would whip him for his impudence, of course, but not yet. He was too tired.

'If you deny me your bed, husband, I'll sleep in Lady Swift's hall,' said Judith.

'She needs it,' Wolf replied.

'She doesn't. She's fled.'

'Where?'

'To Mercia. She tried to raise an army to invade your lands while you were in Rome. She was locked up, but escaped.'

'Nonsense.' Wolf was in no mood for this. Judith was becoming ever more irritating.

'It's true. Alderman Godwin told me.'

'My daughter's no traitor!' he shouted. 'Where's Godwin?' He stared furiously at the cluster of servants standing nearby, nervously clutching his morning attire. 'Where's my chief alderman?'

'I believe he's in the counting house, High Aethelwolf,' replied his robing man. 'Would you like the blue cloak or the ochre one?'

Wolf ignored him and strode out of the hall into the courtyard, where he was surrounded by slaves who hadn't seen him since his return home and wanted to welcome him. They kissed his hands and arms with such ardour he couldn't move for fear of falling over.

Stub, his sergeant, came running towards him. 'The Norlanders are on their way, High Aethel. A host of messages are arriving from the east coast. A whole fleet of them are coming. They've plundered Dunwic and set fire to Gipswic.'

'Christ! Have they rounded Dover yet?'

'We don't know,' replied Stub. 'They've vanished.'

'Vanished?' retorted Wolf. 'Fleets of ships don't disappear!'

'No one's seen head nor hide of them for eight days, sire.'

'Bring Bear to me immediately,' yelled Wolf, 'and call my captains.'

He'd have to handle the Norlanders on his own; the emperor wouldn't help him. 'Godwin! Where in hell's name are you?'

Harold Godwin burst out of the counting house. 'What's the matter, High Aethel? Is something vexing you?'

All thoughts of his daughter had vanished from Wolf's mind. The threat of an entire fleet of the bastards filled him with dread.

'The Norlanders are back. Far more than last time, it seems. How quickly can we raise an army?' he said urgently.

'Shall we send word to the emperor? asked Harold.

'No. He'll give us arms, plenty of them, more than you could dream of, but not till next year, or perhaps the year after.'

'How many men? How long will you need them for?'

'I don't know,' Wolf snapped. 'The whole summer, I should think.'

'Were you calling for me, Father?' demanded Bear, striding towards him, tying his shirt threads. 'Be quick, I must return to the south-west in haste. I have problems with Cornish rebels. Pilton's blazing, there are riots in Taunton, and the Welsh have been seen off the north Devon coast.'

'We need you here to fight the Norlanders,' said Wolf.

'You can't have me. I'm leaving for Exeter.'

Wolf gaped at him. 'Have you been seized by madness?' he demanded. 'I tell you when you can come and go. I'm high aethel.'

'No you're not!' replied Bear. 'Not since you married the Frankish whore-child.'

Wolf grabbed him by the shoulder. 'What did you call her?' he demanded.

'What did *you* call her when you were addressing your adoring crowd?' Bear retorted. 'You called her your queen! Did you make my mother your queen? No. Was the Shrew ever queen?'

'I can call her what I like,' bellowed Wolf.

'You're old and incompetent, you've taken a child to your bed, and you've flagrantly broken Wessex law and insulted the aldermen by calling her queen,' said Bear.

They were both panting with anger, but Wolf felt anxious

too. His son had grown in confidence and strength over the last year, whereas he was an old man. He could feel it in the brittleness of his bones, the slowing of his limbs.

They stood face to face. Wolf's cheek was twitching, the veins in Bear's forehead were throbbing.

The cook appeared. 'Would you like venison or hare?' he said.

'Venison!' replied Wolf without taking his eyes off Bear. 'Now fuck off!'

'There can be no Queen of Wessex,' continued Bear. 'Our laws forbid it.'

'I have made a pact with the Holy Roman Emperor,' said Wolf steadily. 'He has promised me arms and Christ knows what else besides to stop the Norlanders. All I have to do is make his sweet little daughter my queen. It's not much to ask.'

'Arms?' retorted Bear. 'I see no arms. There are no arms, and the Norlanders are on our doorstep. Charles is trying to grab our land by marrying off his daughter, you doddering old fool. We'll end up glued to the arse-end of the Holy Roman Empire!'

Wolf leapt at him, but Bear didn't back away as he'd done so many times before. He stood his ground, and Wolf bounced off him like a ball from a wall. Bear punched him and jabbed a crooked elbow into his body, and Wolf dropped to his knees. Bear attempted to kick him, but Wolf grabbed his foot and twisted, and his son slammed onto the ground. They crawled towards each other, grabbed each other's shoulders, both attempting to gain sufficient purchase to throw the other on his back.

Stub strode over to them and prised them apart.

'Please! Please! My lords,' he said. 'The Norlanders could appear any minute. We need to forge a plan.'

There was a lull as the two men pulled themselves to their feet, took deep draughts of air and stared at each other.

'Frankish whore-child,' murmured Bear.

Wolf grabbed his son's head and bit him on the side of the neck. Now they were swinging punches again, heedless of the other's blows.

'Stop! Stop! In the name of Christ the Lord!' Stub yelled.

When they could trade blows no longer, both men dropped to their knees, collapsed backwards on the ground and stared at the sky. Each of Wolf's breaths was like a knife in his ribs. Despair gripped him. He couldn't even give his son a beating. How could he save Wessex from a fleet of Norlanders?

FIFTY-SEVEN

Like a Mantrap

Bear was carried off. Wolf lay on the ground bleeding, surrounded by gawping Westsaxons and anxious nuns mopping his brow. He slowly opened his eyes and saw a face peering down at him.

'Holy St Margaret!' he exclaimed. 'What are you doing here?'

His features were familiar, the cocked head like the birds sailors brought home from foreign climes, but he couldn't put a name to the face.

'You're looking a little peaky,' the man said.

Of course, it was the priest who had tried to inveigle him with strong powders and Roman dancing girls. Father Asser, who drank too much and made him laugh.

'I came to see you,' replied Asser.

'Why?'

'To beg you to reconsider the concord.'

'No. No. Do you not understand the word?' said Wolf. He brushed aside the nun dabbing his temple with lamb's wool. 'I told you a thousand times, but you wouldn't listen. It's over!'

Asser felt a firm hand on his shoulder.

'Leave him be, Father. There's nothing for you here,' said Alderman Godwin. 'I'll arrange a ship.'

Stub gently pulled the high aethel into an upright position.

Asser looked at Wolf again. His large face was contorted with fury and pain, blood dripping from one nostril. There would be no reasoning with him. He was like a child, capable of seeing only what would bring him the most satisfaction that day. I have travelled five hundred leagues to try and save his land from annihilation, he thought. What a fool I was. He began to walk away.

'Wait.'

Asser turned, half expecting to find Wolf talking to someone else, but the high aethel was sitting there staring straight at him, mumbling something.

As Asser leant over him, the old king's arms sprang round him like a mantrap.

'Stay!' he whispered.

'Stay?' repeated Asser, baffled.

'It's an order.'

'You're confused,' said Asser. He knew Wolf was prone to such lapses, but this clutching was more desperate than anything he'd witnessed from him before. 'I must go. The cardinal needs me.'

'I need you more,' insisted Wolf.

He held on so tightly, Asser was in danger of falling on top of him.

'This is madness,' Asser said, trying to ease himself out of the man's iron grip. 'Why do you want me?'

'Keep your voice down,' hissed Wolf, but Asser scarcely heard him. It was terrifying, and a little embarrassing.

'Tell my why, or I'll go!'

'Stop talking, or I'll have you arrested!' Wolf snarled, and now his tone was threatening.

'I'm the Pope's man. You can't have me arrested.'

'Who's nearer, me or the Pope?' There was almost a sneer in the old king's voice. 'Guards!'

'Wait.' Asser squirmed, but Wolf's men were already closing in on him.

'Take him and throw him in jail.'

FIFTY-EIGHT

Collecting Chalk Water

Rhiannon walked in the shadow of Red's wife. There was little she could do to protect her now the Norlanders had occupied the Isle of Wight. If the ghost man wanted to take Winifred for his own, she wouldn't be able to stop him. If his men decided to cook and eat baby Helm, she'd be powerless to prevent it. But she needed to convince her new mistress that her presence was necessary, so she constantly patrolled the grounds, peered into bushes and walked across Winifred's line of view so she'd be noticed. She had no desire to be returned to the slave pen; she wanted to stay in the hall drinking broth all day and sleeping in her mistress's room on a straw palliasse.

Every evening, in order that Winifred could cleanse her face before bed, Rhiannon collected a bucket of chalk water from the small waterfall that trickled onto the far side of the strand. At night the Norlanders sat round their fires on the beach cooking fish and quaffing ale, so she gave it a wide berth.

But one evening she was later than usual filling her bucket because she'd found a rat nesting behind Winifred's bed. The tide was high and the Norlanders were squatting much closer to her path than usual. They called out to her to come and sit with them. She picked up her pace, but the water slopped out of the pail and she had to slow down again. One of them, drunk, with a feathered cap and rotten teeth, lurched over to her and with feigned politeness offered his assistance. She ignored him, but he wouldn't accept her refusal. He put an arm round her shoulder and half walked, half dragged her to his fire, cooing and chattering all the while.

He pushed her down hard on a log and ran his hand up the inside of her legs. Was he trying to put his fingers inside her? If he'd done so and they'd been alone, she would have freed herself from his grip, taken the knife from the back of her belt and stabbed him in the eye. But she stood no chance against his six friends, so she sat quietly, waiting to make her escape, though each time she moved, he pulled her back to him.

'Shush!' he scolded, then bent forward and licked her neck.

She turned her head from him, and the moon appeared from behind a cloud. Standing a little way off was the ghost man, with his thick, straggly hair, his barrel-like chest, his head shaped like a mud brick. He was talking to his comrades, gesturing with his gnarled hand, the one she'd held down while severing his fingers. Terror snaked up her spine. Perhaps this would be the moment he'd recognise her. How would he take his revenge? She tried not to imagine what he might do to her.

The drunk slipped his hand into her shift and squeezed her left breast like a bread maker kneading dough, then rolled her off the back of the log and clambered on top of her. Rhiannon was thinking fast. Should she kill him regardless of the cost? She fumbled behind her for her knife.

Then it was all over. The ghost man had gone, and her attacker was no longer on top of her. The Norland woman who had spoken out loud in Saxon on the day they'd first arrived had pulled him off her by the hair and lifted her to her feet.

'Take the pail of water to your mistress and leave our men alone, little slut,' she said. Her tone was severe, but before going on her way, she gave Rhiannon a sly wink.

FIFTY-NINE

Which of Us is the Christ Child?

Before the prison door slammed shut and Asser was plunged into darkness, he caught sight of a two-wheeled cart in the middle of the floor. He felt his way over to it, clambered in, and lay on the straw in the bottom, trying to make sense of what had happened. How long would he be here? It could be months before Balotelli sent someone to find him. Panic rose in his throat. Would he be tortured again?

Though I walk through the valley of the shadow of death, I shall fear no evil.

Sometimes when he was overwhelmed by pain or loss, he cast his mind back to the priest's house where he'd stayed as a boy and had learnt to decipher the old man's crumpled scribblings. Each letter had been magical, every sentence a discovery. And during the long nights when he felt completely alone, he'd learnt to recite the psalms in his head with alternate lines in Saxon and Latin. It had calmed his mind and given him comfort. He had never spoken to anyone about this trick – in truth he was embarrassed by it – but it had helped him mightily during his long months of imprisonment.

Quoniam tu mecum es, virga tua et baculus tuus, ipsa consolabuntur me.

Fear and confusion finally gave way to exhaustion, and he fell asleep.

He was in the Pope's dungeon. He could hear the familiar sound of feet shuffling towards him, Halfnose relentlessly moving around in the dark ordering beatings and whippings. He was being hung from the prison walls. There was agony in his shoulders.

'I'm sorry,' he cried. 'I'm truly sorry.' He felt a cosy warmth spreading between his legs.

'We're all sorry,' a voice said, and he woke with a start. 'We spend our lives being sorry. What are you so sorry about?'

It took him a moment to understand who was beside him. Aethelwolf was sitting on the edge of the cart, covered in bandages and holding a candle. What in Christ's name was he doing here?

'I don't know,' Asser said wearily. He was wet and cold, his stomach and arms had been bitten by tiny creatures, and he could smell the stink of his own piss.

'I'm the one who should be sorry,' Wolf said. 'I put you in this shithole. But you wouldn't do what I said, would you? You wouldn't stay here, not without me telling you why, which I suppose was understandable. Christ, this place smells! Have some of this!' He produced an egg-shaped cask and a goblet from his pocket and poured Asser a glass of what in the dim light looked to be mead. 'The finest in Wessex,' he said. 'Made by the monks of Bedminster.'

Asser took a mouthful.

'How could I explain why I need you when we were surrounded by all those bastards?' said Wolf, and gestured at the goblet. 'The taste of paradise, isn't it?'

Asser had drunk better for a few copper coins in the streets of Lazio. 'It's Christ's own nectar,' he agreed. 'What bastards?'

'I'm beset by plotters,' said Wolf. 'Twice as many as when I left, aren't there, Stub?'

It hadn't occurred to Asser that there was another man in the room. Wolf's sergeant was hovering by the door. He began lighting candles and propping them up in little dishes. 'It would seem so, High Aethel,' he replied.

'And they were all standing there listening with their heads cocked like hungry falcons,' Wolf continued. 'Godwin, who's been lusting after my throne for nigh on fifteen years. And Bear – do you know what he told me this morning? That he was the new high aethel, the little shit.'

'One of Hawk's spies was there too,' said Stub. 'He thought I didn't notice him!' He was placing the lit candles on the floor now, on the cart, round the two men.

Wolf stared at the sputtering illuminations. 'Very pretty,' he said. 'Like we're in Bethlehem's stable.'

'Which of us is the Christ child?' asked Asser.

Wolf laughed, then winced and held his ribs. 'You see? That's why I need you,' he said. 'You're quick, you're artful . . .'

'. . . and he's got the Pope's ring on his finger,' added Stub.

'Exactly. You've got authority. I need you here, aiding me.'

'Why in the name of St Catherine on her wheel would I want to do that?' said Asser.

'Because you like me,' replied Wolf gruffly. 'We work well together.'

'Like you?' exploded Asser. 'You made a fool of me. You left Rome without a word and brought down our whole vision. I travelled five hundred leagues to persuade you to rekindle it, and you dismissed me with a single word. And you think I like you?'

'He does, doesn't he, Stub?' said Wolf.

'If you say so, High Aethel,' replied his sergeant.

'Asser,' continued Wolf, and his voice was urgent and determined now, 'I may lose my throne within a week and my life the week after. The Norlanders are coming for us and I have no way of stopping them.'

'You can call on the emperor's army; that's why you got married.'

'Not yet, not till next year, when he's finished fighting. Right now I have only forty elderly thanes.'

'Fewer,' said Stub. 'Three died this year past.'

'So what is it you think I can do?' said Asser, shaking his head.

'Find me an army. One that will defeat the Norlanders and keep me on the throne.'

'An . . . army!' Asser said, so frustrated he could hardly speak. 'A fucking army? An army like the one we spent months planning for you until you fucked off, you fucker!'

'Yes. I can't raise one. The Wessex farmers won't fight because they have to get the crops in, Bear's taken all the fighting men he can lay his hands on to Devon, Hawk's thirty leagues away and hates me. I need an army.'

Asser coughed out his mead, wiped his mouth, clambered off the cart and paced round the jail floor several times. 'Fuck!' he said. 'Fuck. All right! I'll try. But if I succeed, you will sit down with me and we'll build a new Wessex, a strong, defendable Christian Wessex like the vision you walked away from. And you'll swear it on Christ's bleeding wounds.'

'See, Stub?' said Wolf. 'I knew he'd say yes.' The high aethel turned back to Asser and stared at him thoughtfully. 'It wasn't you who arranged for me to be harassed by that schoolteacher in Rome, was it?'

'No,' replied Asser. 'It wasn't.'

'Good. Because if I find out it was, I'll kill you.'

SIXTY

Sick Fish

'Lies!' Cardinal Balotelli stormed into the working quarters of his palazzo clutching a bundle of documents. He plucked one out at random and hurled it across the room. 'All lies!' he shouted, and sent another skidding across the floor.

'Calm yourself, Stephen,' said the Doctore, who was sitting at a table quietly conferring with a clerk.

'I will not calm myself,' retorted Balotelli. 'Do you know what this dross is? The Notarii's so-called report on the worth of our activities. This morning, with disdain on their faces and hate in their hearts, they presented it to the Pope. It belittles our work,' he said, and thwacked a pillar with one of the rolls. 'It traduces my character,' he said, hitting the pillar again. 'It sneers at our attempts to come to grips with the Norland threat.' By now the document was becoming decidedly ragged. 'It's a tissue of misinformation! Christ, I wish Asser was here. He'd find some way to shut their troublesome mouths.' He strode through an arch into his adjacent private garden and dumped the manuscripts into the fishpond.

Alfred was in a corner of the room attending to his labours. He spent a good deal of time with the cardinal now. 'Come to the palazzo every day when your school lessons are over,' Balotelli had proposed, and had put his arm round the young man. 'It's far quieter there. Observe the workings of my office away from the hurly-burly of the Undercroft. Educate yourself in Christian governance.'

Alfred had no desire to govern anyone, but he was flattered to be invited into the cardinal's home and happier still to be asked to assist him. His first job had been to reassemble the cardinal's poems from the charred fragments rescued from St Catherine's. It was the ideal task for him. He could immerse himself in Balotelli's writing, so elegantly wrought, so full of intense ideas and emotions that he felt he understood it completely, and after two weeks he'd become confident enough to insert his own words and phrases where the originals had been destroyed.

His next challenge had been to copy and decipher the remnants of Balotelli's allegories. They took him into realms of the mind he'd never known existed. Each one was like tying oneself to a giant eagle and letting it carry you into the sky to who knew where. Not that he could engage with such lofty thoughts while the cardinal was thundering round the room like a bull in a pottery.

'Who gave Benedict the papacy?' Balotelli demanded. 'I did. Who removed every stumbling block from his path, who quelled every modicum of opposition and gained him the support of kings and princes?'

Alfred slipped past him into the garden and rescued the documents from the pond.

'He'd still be tutoring brainless merchants' sons in Padua were it not for me. And now . . .'

'Please sit down, Stephen,' sighed the Doctore.

'... he's humiliated me in front of the entire cardinalate. "The Notarii's report is a legitimate and useful contribution to the debate around church reform and should be considered further." That's what Benedict said. It's nonsense! The only legitimate use for that report is to wipe the fat arses of the rogues who wrote it. And he's now blaming us for the collapse of the concord. Was that our fault?'

Alfred was knee-deep in the pond, mopping water from the documents and laying them out on the little wall to dry.

'It was Charles the Bald who enticed Aethelwolf to scuttle off, Seneschal François who arranged his exit. If the Pope had admonished me in private, I could have borne it and pointed out where he was wrong. Instead, like Salome bearing John the Baptist's head, he's offering me to the Notarii on a platter. How are we to recover from this? ... Alfred, why are you standing in my pond? You're obsessed with those fish!'

'They aren't well, Cardinal,' came Alfred's voice from the garden. 'I've been reading Pliny on the husbandry of animals ...'

Balotelli ignored him. 'And that's not all. There are still seven Antonils to be interrogated. I specifically requested that we perform that task so we could discover whether any senior church figures had been involved in this farrago, but the Pope has handed the job to Ponti, who convinced him that he's highly qualified in such matters and would be the best man for the job. Ponti! A man whose idea of interrogation is to inflict as much pain as he can for his own gratification. Ponti, who licks the arse of any senior churchman who'll accommodate him in order to gain advancement.'

Alfred returned to the room. 'We've been feeding them incorrectly,' he said. 'The crumbled nuts distress their stomachs and they express them undigested, causing the weed to rot and choke them.'

'Sweet Christ, I'm even killing my fish now,' said Balotelli, and slumped into a chair. 'Our vision is fading fast. The Norlanders will overwhelm us and Christendom will crumble.'

'You know that's not true,' said the Doctore calmly. 'This is merely the Notarii whispering in Pope Benedict's ear, trying to undermine his confidence in you. Benedict wants to protect you, but he's fearful of offending them, so he gives them these little titbits. It's a small reverse for us. We must ignore them and carry on with our work, that is all.'

The cardinal sighed. 'I suppose so,' he said, then sprang from his chair. 'Yes, we must!' he said forcefully. 'Thank you. And Alfred, purchase the correct fish-food before I have to read my little darlings the last rites.'

Alfred didn't approve of the bazaar's tawdry temptations; they seduced common folk into wallowing in venality. Nevertheless, he couldn't deny being stimulated by the abundant energy the place exuded and the almost limitless variety of merchandise it had to offer. He headed for a stall where fish were dried, powdered and sold as ingredients for the pungent dishes enjoyed by foreigners, and purchased a large bag of flaked goosefish. He wandered through the crowds and bought a set of spiral spinning tops for his schoolboys, and a lemon with the Lord's Prayer engraved on it in minuscule writing for the cardinal.

He spotted Elswith, the young Westsaxon woman who'd given such compelling evidence against Petr of Macedon. But she was no longer in her novice's robes; instead, she was wearing a shockingly slight dress that exposed the whiteness of her wrists and ankles. Her face was painted in bright colours, but it was definitely her, and a brutish man in an Armenian skirt with vivid pustules on his neck was shaking her violently by the arms.

'Brother! Brother!' Alfred called. 'Please forbear.'

'What's it to you?' demanded the Armenian. 'Do you want a taste of my fist?'

Alfred could have felled him with one blow if he'd been so inclined, but he felt a tinge of pity for the man's suffering and resisted the temptation. 'Forgive me, I see some devil has cursed you with a swelling sickness,' he replied. 'It must trouble you greatly.'

'Mind your business.'

'I am one of Cardinal Balotelli's men,' he said. 'May I bless your cankerous inflammations?'

'What would it cost me?'

'Nothing but a pledge that you will pray for the forgiveness of your sins and henceforth live in peace.'

The Armenian grunted, Alfred touched his blighted neck and murmured an incantation. The man grunted again and left.

Elswith was laughing so much her eyes were watering. 'You charlatan,' she said. 'You're no priest. You can't work miracles; you're only a poor-boys' tutor.'

'I merely offered the man a prayer to save you from injury,' he replied.

'I didn't ask you.'

'Why was the brute attacking you?' enquired Alfred.

'He was a customer who wouldn't pay, 'tis all.'

'Why? What had you sold him?'

She looked at him in disbelief. 'My body.'

Alfred cursed his naivety, and shuffled uncomfortably. 'I wish you wouldn't do that.'

She laughed. 'That's what your little friend Asser said. He promised me money if I'd stop, but it was nothing but fine words. He gave me a few tiny coins and I've not seen him since.'

Alfred was staring at the tawdry shack from which she'd appeared. Over its entrance hung a sign with a pair of breasts painted on it, and women's names and ejaculating penises scrawled on the door.

'Father Asser is not my friend, nor I his,' he said. 'He is

aggressive, undisciplined and has no humility. But his failure to honour his promise would have been unintentional. He was sent to Wessex by the Holy Father many weeks ago and has not yet returned. He is concerned about you, I'm sure.'

Two sailors were walking towards them. One winked at Elswith and waggled his tongue. 'I must go,' she said. 'I have a living to earn.'

'The money Father Asser owes you,' Alfred blurted out. 'I only have five copper coins, but you could clean and cook for us at the Saxon school, and when he returns . . .' He fumbled in his bag for his money, but when he looked up again, she was already walking away arm in arm with the sailor.

Alfred trudged back up the Vatica Hill. Had he committed a sin by telling the Armenian he was one of Balotelli's men when he was merely aiding the cardinal with a little clerking? He shouldn't have lied, but perhaps his prayer would work and the man would be cured. After all, God didn't only answer the prayers of priests. Anyway, he doubted this deception was sufficiently egregious to merit the fiery pit.

On one side of the hill was a row of neatly thatched church properties, where senior functionaries laboured. A finely dressed priest was seated at a window looking at him. 'Hullo!' he called, and beckoned Alfred over. 'You work for Cardinal Balotelli, do you not?'

Alfred didn't recognise the man, who was about thirty years of age, with thin lips and bubbles of spittle in one corner of his mouth. He had nervous eyes and pale, almost translucent skin. 'I am a teacher at the Saxon school,' Alfred said. 'But I perform occasional tasks for him in my capacity as a scribe.'

'I know you do. My people have seen you coming and going from his palazzo. And you work late, I believe, after his other associates have gone home. I applaud your diligence.'

What did the priest mean by *my people?* Was the cardinal being spied upon? 'I do what I can for him,' Alfred said. 'He is a great man.'

'I'm sure he is. And if the cardinal trusts you with his documents, that satisfies me, for he trusts very few of us. You perform other duties for him . . . apart from scribing?'

How much should he be telling the man? He was very unpleasant.

'Sometimes I find information he needs . . . from old manuscripts.'

'Really! Like what?'

'About . . . Petr of Macedon, for instance.' He was happy to offer up this information. Everyone on Vatica Hill now knew of Petr's arrest. 'He's a heretic,' he added.

'Is he?' replied the man. 'You see, you've already told me something I didn't know. A heretic. How clever you are! Perhaps you could assist me in the arrangement of my papers too.'

'I'm not sure . . .' began Alfred.

'I am Father Vincente Ponti, undersecretary to the Notarii. You must come and see me on Thursday after matins,' he added enthusiastically.

The Notarii. The people working against Balotelli, those who had written the report that had so enraged him.

'I—'

'One thing more. My work is of great importance to his Holiness the Pope, and consequently confidential. Please don't repeat any part of this conversation to anyone, not even to your master. It would not be to your advantage, or mine, if you did so, you understand?'

SIXTY-ONE

The Notarii

'Ponti is a devious man in a dangerous organisation,' said Cardinal Balotelli. When Alfred had told him the details of his conversation on the Vatica Hill, it had animated him beyond measure. 'He has invited you to work for him so you can glean information about me. That is good,' he added, pacing the room. 'I want you to take part in a little deception, gain his confidence and discover his plans. He wishes to spy on us, but you'll spy on him, and Christendom will be forever in your debt.' He took Alfred's hands and looked at him intently. 'And I will be too,' he added.

Alfred knew that if Ponti discovered he was double-dealing, he'd be punished. Ungodly men with lowly jobs in high places always found ways to be vicious. But Balotelli wanted him to do this, which meant a great deal. He did not like dissembling, it made him uneasy, but the cardinal had said he would be working in the service of a higher cause, and that was undoubtedly true. He'd do as Balotelli requested.

*

The building that housed the Notarii was unlike any Alfred had ever seen: octagonal, with tall arches at each corner supporting a vast dome with a spike on it like a Chinese hat. It would have been magnificent had it not been for its setting. It was built on an empty waste-strewn plot, as though it had been planned as the first of several similar constructions that had failed to materialise. Balotelli had told him the landowner had fallen on hard times and the Notarii had bought it for a pittance because of the bleakness of its surroundings. Alfred thought this highly plausible.

He was directed through an arch into a paved atrium surrounded by covered walkways. He sat on a bench and waited for Father Ponti to appear.

After a short while, two churchmen came strolling along the walkway deep in conversation.

'Balotelli's notion that the junior clergy should be literate is a nonsense,' said one. 'They can be as stupid as a donkey's head as long as they say mass and conduct the sacrament with dignity.'

They both laughed.

'I concur,' said the other. 'When priests become obsessed with the subtleties of scripture, they find spurious reasons to attack their betters.'

Alfred watched them, appalled to hear Balotelli mocked in this way. But he reordered his expression when Father Ponti came walking towards him with arms outstretched.

'You're here!' he said. Alfred rose to greet him, but Ponti patted the bench. 'Let us sit and talk.' He brushed one side of the seat with the edge of his hand and placed himself on it. 'I'll be direct,' he said. 'You have profound respect for Cardinal Balotelli, do you not?'

'Indeed I do,' replied Alfred. 'He's—'

'A brilliant man, yes,' interrupted Ponti. 'But perhaps sometimes a little too brilliant for his own good, I think.'

'I agree,' said Alfred, and the lie flowed from his mouth like melted butter.

'I knew we'd get on,' said Ponti triumphantly. 'I will tell you a secret. Can I trust you?'

'Indeed you can, Father.'

'Good. Because of the deep respect for your cardinal, which we all share, his Holiness the Pope has asked me to watch over him, discreetly of course, to ensure he doesn't inveigle us into fighting some endless and costly European war. Are we wise to keep an eye on him in this way, do you think?'

'I do, Father. The cardinal does tend to be a little profligate,' agreed Alfred.

'Why do you say that?' said Ponti eagerly. 'Do you have knowledge of such a thing?'

'I do, I've seen it myself.'

'Seen what?'

'I thought you might ask me that, Father, so I've brought you this.' Alfred produced a scroll from his sleeve.

Ponti snatched it, unrolled it, perused it, and looked profoundly disappointed. 'It's merely additions and subtractions,' he said.

'It's the calculations for his proposal to refurbish the Emperor Trajan's ancient aqueduct so the needy can be supplied with clean water – a fine aspiration.'

'I agree,' said Ponti.

'But it would be ruinously expensive,' added Alfred.

'Would it? I suppose it would,' said Ponti. 'Yes, it would,' he repeated, and jumped to his feet. 'This is precisely the kind of information that will assist us. Costly financial proposals could be Stephen's downfall. To protect him we must understand what he's planning. You are in a privileged position. You can make a significant contribution to saving the reputation of the man you care for by sharing such information with us.'

Alfred paused. He knew he shouldn't seem too eager, too trusting. 'And you swear you will not use this information against him? You want to help him?'

'Of course I do, my friend.' Ponti gave him such a warm smile that for a moment Alfred was almost tempted to believe him. 'I have known Balotelli for some time. However mistaken some of his actions, I would hate to see such a high-minded man in difficulty.'

'Then I will do what I can,' said Alfred. 'But I know little of his plans and understand even less.'

'Your knowledge is not important. Bring me everything,' said Ponti. 'Tittle or tattle, I'm happy to browse through it all. And I will compensate you for the extra labour you will have to undertake.'

'There is no need,' replied Alfred. 'I will do so to protect the cardinal from his own excesses.'

'I know you will, Alfred. Nevertheless, a few coins will seal our pledge. I insist. You may know I was once a powerful man but was cast down by those in the devil's pay. Now, though, God has blessed me with this new post serving the Notarii, and if you assist me, your star will rise too. I like you. You're intelligent and loyal.' He squeezed Alfred's bicep playfully. 'And you have the musculature of an Argonaut, which is a pleasure to observe. Soon you'll be able to work for me openly, with a substantial stipend to support you. But for now, secrecy, though cumbersome, is the most prudent policy. I suggest you leave by the back doorway.'

SIXTY-TWO

The Wild Fighters

Asser crossed the border into Mercia with Rollo and Mountjoy at his flanks. Wessex and Mercia were like two sisters, so people said: same blood, same tongue. Wessex in the south, brash, young, contemptuous of its older sister's pretensions; and Mercia, the middle lands, once rich and grandiose, now impoverished. Certainly the differences between the two countries were stark. Mercia was colder, murkier, the drizzle constant, and the people's voices were different too. When Asser stopped to ask the way to Chepstow, he could barely understand the reply; the sounds of the man's words were twisted, his voice nasal, as if he had a bad cold that was causing him distress.

They eventually arrived at Chepstow Great Hall, where half a dozen soldiers were playing dice and drinking pungent infusions from steaming mugs. Asser proffered his ring. 'Good day to you, brothers. I have urgent business and wish to speak to Prince Burgred. I am Father Asser, legate to the Holy Father.'

But before he had finished speaking, a door at the far end of the room had burst open and a woman strode in. She wore the attire of a soldier, her silver-streaked black hair was uncovered and tied at the back, and she sported a sword and scabbard. 'You can talk to me, Father Asser,' she said, pulling off her riding gloves and unbuckling her belt.

'Mistress, we have ridden here from Wessex to address the prince on a matter of state.'

'A matter of state?' she replied. 'How grand.' She untied her hair, which fell around her shoulders, and scratched her scalp vigorously. 'Burgred is away patrolling the dyke. You can sit on your arses for two weeks and wait for him, or attend to your business with me. I am Lady Swift of the house of Wolf. I speak for him.'

'Lady, it is a great honour to address you,' said Asser. 'I have heard tell of your many victories on the Welsh border, and I congratulate you. But I have bad news. Wessex is about to be attacked by a mighty Norland fleet and we require your help.'

'I neither know of this matter nor do I care.' Swift yanked off her boots and began massaging her feet.

Asser considered himself enlightened about matters between men and women, but he was a little shocked by the impropriety of such a gesture, and when he glanced at Rollo and Mountjoy, they had turned their heads away.

'I suppose you've been sent to beg for troops,' Swift continued. 'My father is notoriously unable to hold an army together for more than one battle.'

'We would certainly—' began Asser.

'I will save you the time and trouble. The answer is no.'

'I realise the cost of quartering your men would be—'

'This is not about money,' replied Swift. 'My brothers tried to have me killed. I will not sacrifice my men on their account. As for my father, do you carry with you a letter of apology from him for my incarceration? A pardon? An offer to reinstate me as warden of my lands?'

Of course he didn't. He could offer her nothing but silence.

'Go back to Winchester, Father Asser,' she said. 'If you need an army, you'll have to look elsewhere.' And she practically bundled him out the door.

Rollo and Mountjoy followed, shaking their heads in frustration.

'We've been riding for four days and our interview lasted less time than it takes to have a piss,' said Mountjoy.

'She's an angry vixen,' said Rollo.

'Not angry.'

Rollo turned with a start. Swift was standing at the door with her hands on her hips.

'I speak with brevity, that is all. Call me a vixen again and I'll run you through.'

Rollo began to stutter his apologies, but Swift quieted him with her hand.

'By way of amends, you can perform a task for me,' she said. 'I have a friend in Wessex, Moira, wife of Aethelhawk, to whom I was unable to say goodbye. I have a gift for her. If you agree to deliver it, I'll write an introduction for you to a band of Britons who are encamped over the dyke a few days' ride away. They are skilled in combat and may well take up arms for you if they're happy with the price you offer.'

Asser, Mountjoy and Rollo wound their way over Offa's Dyke towards the Britons' encampment, riding in virtual silence through the pouring rain in the company of two taciturn Welsh guides.

'*Gallem arwain y bygers i gors a dwyn eu pyrsiau*,' murmured one of the Welshmen.

'You'll rob us and throw us in a swamp, will you? You cheeky bastards,' replied Asser. '*Trin ni gyda pharch, frawd.*'

'What in God's name are you saying?' asked Rollo.

'I told them not to piss me about,' said Asser. 'My mother was from Wales. She missed her homeland and often spoke to me in Welsh when we were alone. I was not an easy child; she used such phrases many times.'

The drip-dripping of the rain on the leaves and the sing-song sound of the men's voices brought back memories of the flight from Wales strapped to his father's back, travelling for days through dense forests like this till they finally arrived in Wessex, where they set up home. Wales had soon seemed little more than a dream to him.

After three days, they turned onto a narrow path and were confronted by a large, crudely carved idol of the Mother Goddess, naked, with bulging breasts and fecund thighs, her wide eyes staring straight at them. The Welsh guides would go no further. The Britons' camp was up ahead, they said, before turning their horses and retreating the way they'd come. Twenty paces on was a second carving: Odin, one-eyed, holding a spear and with a wide-brimmed black hat affixed to his head. Beyond him was Christ crucified, his side, hands and feet daubed red. A strange trinity, thought Asser.

The Britons' camp was gloomy. Rivulets of muddy water ran through it, and there was barely any protection from the rain. The inhabitants sheltered in the doorways of their rudimentary huts, staring at the newcomers suspiciously. They had dyed hair, their bodies covered in marks from soot and needle, the men bare-legged to the knee, the women brazenly unbound with their nipples clearly visible under their threadbare tunics.

The largest hut bore the skeleton of an eagle over the door. An elderly man came out of it and strode confidently in their direction, testing the weight of his spear as though eager to use it. Asser addressed him in Welsh and gave him Swift's letter, but received no reply other than a series of clacks and grunts.

Asser said the name 'Fria of the Deep Burns' to him several times as Swift had instructed, and eventually a woman appeared from the hut, skinny, steely, the sleeves of her tunic rolled up, exposing her arms. She took the letter from the man and looked at it for a long time.

'We'll give thee seventy men for seventy days for seventy silver pieces, three sevenths now, four more when summer ends,' she said in a clear Saxon tongue.

She was no Briton. Perhaps she was a refugee from Northumbria or the product of some intertribal coupling. Either way, if any Britons were to survive for much longer, it would surely be those like her of bastard blood.

'A yay or nay is all we need,' she added firmly.

Asser and the twins were ferried back across the River Severn into Wessex accompanied by their new warriors, but trouble broke out as soon as they landed at the old town of Portishead. The inhabitants took one sight of the barbarians and concluded they were under attack. Some barricaded their huts, the rest ran away before Asser could open his mouth to explain.

Word travelled, and in the woods outside Bristowe a gang of a hundred or so local lads attempted an ambush. The Britons, who'd fought off such attacks all their lives, sent the Saxons running, but one of the littlest boys stumbled, cracked his head, fell into a shaking fit and died. News of his death spread fast.

Asser rode on ahead to try to calm matters down. He called on the local reeves and thanes, waved his ring at them and told them the wild men were their friends come to save Wessex from the Norlanders.

But it did no good; by now the mob was beyond all reason. A rabble army of peasants and farmers gathered on the green swards of Frome armed with knives and sickles in abundance.

'I'm going to send the Britons back, or we'll have a hundred dead Wessexmen on our hands,' he said.

'You'll need to pay them in full or they won't go quietly,' said Rollo.

'Nonsense, they've had their due,' said Asser. 'They've only been in our employ for a week. They'll be happy to leave with what they've got.'

But Rollo's fears were justified. The Britons burnt down Radstock, looted the church at Midsomer Norton and went home with twenty Saxon cattle and a dozen slaves.

Asser returned to Winchester with a heavy heart and not one newly recruited soldier.

SIXTY-THREE

The Shield Women

The sound of squealing pigs cut the air. A half-dozen had been confiscated from the surrounding settlements, and Winifred's courtyard had been commandeered by the Norlanders as a suitable place to slit their throats, chop them into pieces and boil them in vats of bubbling water. Trestle tables had been set up across the yard and bare-chested slaves were grinding the meat between big quern-stones, scooping up the mess, mixing it with thyme and cumin and stuffing it into inflated entrails and squares of flour paste.

Rhiannon was standing close to her mistress's hall, well away from the food preparation, partly because she was supposed to be guarding her, but also to avoid the stink and splatter. She had drawn a four-legged figure on the wall and was throwing her knife at it.

'Killing a little piggy, are you?' said a voice behind her. It was the Norland woman who'd rescued her the previous day.

'It's not a pig,' Rhiannon said. 'It's a man.'

'Why's he on all fours?'

'He's trying to crawl away,' she replied.

The woman laughed.

Winifred appeared at the door. 'I greet you, Astrid Haakunson,' she said. Her voice was shaking a little, as it always did when she addressed a Norlander.

'And I you,' Astrid replied. 'One of my girls has caught the plague from the miasma that leaks out of your slave pens. I need a replacement.'

'You will have one by the morrow,' Winifred replied.

'I want her,' said Astrid, pointing at Rhiannon.

'She watches over me,' said Winifred.

'*We* are watching over you. I will take her.'

'But—'

Astrid's eyes narrowed a little. 'Are you denying me?'

'I am not,' replied Winifred hastily.

'Very well,' said Astrid. 'Come, girl!' She turned to go and gave a whistle like a huntress calling her dog. Rhiannon scampered after her down the slope towards the sea. Where was she being taken? She felt a little apprehensive, but excited too. She had a strange compulsion to be close to this woman, and what did it matter as long as she wasn't being taken back to the slave pens.

Seven Norland ships were drawn up on the shore. There were swirling patterns painted along their sides and the faces of monsters carved on their bows. Slaves were wiping down the hulls and greasing the oarlocks; women on ladders were burnishing the heads of the strange creatures. Rhiannon stood awkwardly by, unsure what to do.

The men and one or two boys barely older than her gathered on the strand in a conglomeration of fighting gear: bright waisted-coats and metal helmets, thick leather belts and bindings round their calves and biceps, ribbons in their long hair and swords in their painted scabbards. Some lit fires and cooked the newly made sausages and pies; others painted their faces, or plaited and waxed their beards.

The ghost man lumbered towards them, bare-chested, with leather wrist-guards and strings of black and amber beads round his neck. He stared at the crowd for a long while. Rhiannon shrank from his gaze. At any moment he would spot her, and she'd see the wrath in his eyes as he tore her to pieces. But no, he smiled at a young fighter with red paint round his mouth and down his chin that looked like blood, and ruffled the boy's hair. Then he turned back to the crowd and addressed them in a deep, guttural tone, smacking his fingerless fist into his palm to emphasise each point he made. She had no idea what he was saying, but every time he stopped, his men cheered and roared with laughter. When he finished, they wrapped their arms round each other's shoulders, formed huddles and made a series of loud staccato noises like stallions rutting a mare. Then, so quickly Rhiannon barely had time to register what was happening, they jogged purposefully down to their ships, pushed them into the water and rowed off at speed.

Only the women were left: six including Astrid. They watched the boats depart, then, without a word, they too walked towards the shoreline. Rhiannon followed them, stumbling over the pebbles. One ship had been left behind, bigger and broader than the others, with twenty slaves sitting expectantly on the cross-thwarts, their arms poised at their oars.

Astrid lifted a sack from the ship and tipped the contents onto the sand – short coats, skirts and boots. The women unclipped the shoulder clasps from their dresses and let them drop, then pulled their undersmocks over their heads and discarded those too. They looked like Valkyrie fighters from the old tales, naked, and very beautiful. Each one found herself a padded coat, skirt and pair of boots. Yellow scarves were passed around, and they tied them round their heads and knotted them at the back. Now they resembled coal diggers or butchers, full of purpose and about to embark on an important task.

Astrid flung a jacket at Rhiannon. 'It'll be too big,' she said. 'Roll up the sleeves.'

Rhiannon wriggled out of her shift and put the jacket on, and a skirt too, which was far too long and made the women laugh and chatter in their strange tongue. Astrid tied her headscarf and threw her a small, round shield.

'I'm not a Norlander,' said Rhiannon.

'You are if you think like a Norlander and fight like a Norlander,' replied Astrid. 'Climb aboard *Sea Cat,* and watch and learn.'

Their vessel was so far behind that the other ships were already out of sight. The sun shone fiercely, but there was a gentle wind, the sky was clear blue and there was little for them to do other than pull up the mast and occasionally tweak the sail. The women lay in the bows basking in the warmth, and after a while, Rhiannon fell asleep.

Astrid kicked her awake. She could see the mainland ahead, and a bay with little settlements dotted round it. A pyre of smoke rose lazily from the nearest huts, and one of the fighting ships was moored close by. They could hear cries, shouts of terror and the clang of swords and axes. They sailed past and further along the bay till they came to another hamlet and another of their ships. There were more fires and a bell was ringing. They passed three more villages and from each came the sound of slaughter. At the head of the bay was a larger settlement, where the last fighting ship rested on the little beach. *Sea Cat* pulled in too, and the women slid the leather grips of their shields up to their elbows and strode into the settlement.

Burning torches had been thrust into every hut and house.

Men lay dead with their heads stoved in, women were spread-eagled outside their doors bloody and lifeless, a child had been tossed from a window. The Norland women looked on impassively, as if watching fishermen gutting mackerel. Rhiannon felt no emotion either. The dead were Saxons; she wouldn't weep for them.

Astrid led her through the smoke and screams. She saw three Norlanders jabbing at a Saxon man with their spears while he attempted to defend the woman cowering behind him. He had one hand round her shoulder and the other wielded a club, but he was no match for his assailants. With each spear-thrust his knees buckled a little more, pulling the woman down with him. One of the Norlanders caught her by the arm, snatching her away from the man, who let out a terrible cry. He flung himself after her, but landed on their spears. Rhiannon heard the Saxon woman scream, then the sound came to an abrupt end.

They approached a church. Gold cups, silver-headed staffs and painted books were piled in front of it.

'Take them to the *Cat*,' Astrid yelled over the noise.

They gathered up the loot and made their way back downhill, Rhiannon dragging an enormous leather-bound book, her eyes streaming from the acrid smoke. A Saxon man ran at her wielding an axe. Astrid pushed him away as though he were no bigger than a child and dispatched him with a thrust into his guts.

'Keep your eyes open, girl!' she called, and looked at Rhiannon in a curious way.

They dumped their loads into *Sea Cat*'s belly and jogged back to the settlement. They worked for a long time, collecting loot, fending off attackers and heaving the treasure back to the ship. Occasionally the ghost man loomed out of the smoke bellowing orders, but Rhiannon couldn't comprehend what he was saying, nor did she care. She was part of his army now; that was as good a disguise as she could have wished for.

Eventually, not one building was left standing. The heat was intense, the noise deafening; dogs were barking, a baby cried relentlessly. Rhiannon had never been so elated. She was shouting at the top of her voice, wild, ecstatic cries. The Saxons had beaten her and enslaved her all her life; this was her retribution.

A horse in a pen kicked and bucked. The men threw ropes round its neck and heaved at them, trying to pull the creature down to the shore. Rhiannon grabbed a rope too. The terrified creature flung itself about and jerked her off her feet, but step by step they dragged it down the hill and up a ramp onto the ship. Still it tried to shake itself free, until eventually, exhausted, it slumped against the ship's side and they tied its legs together. Every muscle in Rhiannon's body ached, as though she'd spent the day fighting dragons and had defeated every one.

A long time later, her hands blistered, her face covered in soot and blood, she sat among the Norland women on their way back to the island, staring silently at the horizon. She stood up, her arms pointing to the sky, opened her eyes wide, flung her head back and roared. All the years of being whipped and starved, the lovelessness, the anger and now the joy of so many butchered Saxon bodies were in the jubilation of that cry. It carried on for a long time, and when it finally came to an end, Astrid nodded thoughtfully but didn't say a word.

SIXTY-FOUR

The Dangling Grub

Asser returned from his Mercian journey to find Winchester in the grip of an inexplicable torpor. There were no fighting men going through their paces, no fresh defences being erected, no water-filled buckets lined up round the city walls for dousing fires. The townspeople chattered endlessly, as they always did; they plucked chickens and bartered over the exchange of small tools. It was as if no one had told them the Norlanders were about to burn down their homes and eviscerate their children.

Alderman Godwin was leading a prancing piebald out of its stable.

'Where's Wolf?' Asser enquired.

'Still in bed,' Godwin replied. 'He has a new wife,' he added.

'So you're at the town's helm today?'

Godwin shook his head. 'I'm bound for my wife's mother's house in Putney,' he said, and went blithely on his way.

Asser could find only one person preparing for a potential invasion. Sergeant Stub was on a bench outside a small barred shed that served as the town's armoury and was built up against the great hall. He was surrounded by old swords and shields, and was attempting to fix the hilt back onto what had once been a fine blade.

'Some of this fighting gear is over fifty years old and we still have to use it. I thought Wolf would return from Europe with Toledo steel, but he says we'll receive nothing at all this fighting season,' he said.

'And perhaps not the next either,' said Asser. 'The emperor is notoriously fickle, and he's under no written obligation to arm Wessex now the concord has collapsed.'

'Why in Jesu's name did the old man accept such a promise?' said Stub. 'It gives us nothing.'

Asser sighed. 'Love? Loneliness? I don't think he ever wanted a Frankish army clomping all over his land. Wessex is on its own now, that much is clear, and my hunt in Mercia for new troops has come to nothing.'

'I've done little better,' said Stub. 'The common folk say they'll join us if Winchester is attacked, but they're not prepared to sacrifice a whole summer. They want to get their harvest in, and I can't blame them. If the crops aren't pulled, there'll be no food for the winter.' He split an old shield in two over his knee and threw it on his heap of discarded weapons. 'We defeated the Norlanders last year; our folk think we'll win again by doing what we did then – deploying a few dozen old men on horseback to charge at the enemy.'

'This is intolerable,' said Asser. 'If we don't muster more troops, we'll all be dead by harvest time.'

When Asser was young and worked at the Tribunal of Reconciliation, he borrowed a horse from Carlo the saddler and rode in the Paleo, the race round the streets that brought the city to a halt for an entire day. The narrow alleys were filled to overflowing, the crowds raucous and partisan; children sat on their father's shoulders or peered between their legs. It was the wildest, most exciting event in Rome's year, but that day disaster fell. It was hot, there was a shortage of water; even the most abstemious citizens drank too much ale and wine. Someone's mount tripped on a discarded plank, and the rider fell and was trampled to death by the horses behind. Accusations flew, fighting broke out and the whole town turned on itself. Shops were looted, doors kicked in, young men ran through the streets with stolen sides of pig and sacks of wheat. Asser attempted to ride back through the crowd to ensure the tribunal building was safe. But before he could get to it, a messenger in papal colours grabbed his horse's bridle and ordered him to attend the Church of St Agatha, where he found forty or so of his fellow priests listening to Cardinal Enzo Gilotti, a finely groomed patrician with the bearing of a man who might some day mount the papal throne.

'We have a problem, Fathers,' he said. 'Our few regular troops are twenty leagues away, keeping the peace in Frosinone, and I'm reluctant to turn the city guards on their own fathers and brothers. It would be bloody, and would cast a long shadow over the bond between the Church and its people. We need the Romans themselves to put down the insurrection, and you must help bring this about. Identify trustworthy men from within your congregations, imbue them with Christian zeal, direct them in the policing of their neighbourhoods and pray that together you can save Rome.'

Asser had no church of his own, but he knew the local people well and mustered a small band of dependable citizens. They cleared the streets, cared for the wounded, doused the fires and returned lost children to their desperate parents. Within a few hours Rome was at peace with itself again. No one showered him with praise for his part in saving the city, nor would he have wanted them to, but for him it was memorable. He had discovered within himself a capability for organisation he hadn't realised he possessed. And if he could organise the people of Rome, why would he not be able to do the same among the hamlets and villages of Wessex?

Asser found the bishop in the minster, ensconced in his gloomy private rooms. Plegmond was rubbing a bitter-smelling unguent on the old man's chafed wrists and ankles.

It had been Asser's idea to lend Plegmond's services to the bishop. He knew Humbert had been an able administrator, with a sharp mind and a keen understanding of human frailty. Plegmond, unlike his own priests, treated him with sympathy and respect. He spent many hours each day encouraging him to speak clearly again, walked him painstakingly round the outside of the minster to limber his fat, old legs and instructed the nuns to sew a small pouch into his gown so he could rest his weak arm in it, thus preventing the infirm limb from hanging uselessly by his side. He supervised the bishop's toiletry arrangements, and made decisions on his behalf when he was too tired to make them himself. This had won him Humbert's trust, which gave Asser great satisfaction. It meant he now had one of his own people at the heart of the Westsaxon Church.

'Your Excellency, I need your help,' he said as gently as he could, 'or I fear all Wessex will fall under the Norland sword.'

Humbert rocked back and forth, visibly distressed. 'I am too sick . . . to offer . . . leadership,' he said. 'Wolf is old . . . deluded . . . Bear is a fool . . . and Hawk . . . We have no one.'

'We can throw our pots only with the clay we have,' said Asser.

'If Aethelfraed were here . . .' said the bishop, and sighed.

'You hoped that one day he would take up the Wessex mantle?' asked Asser.

'You know it,' Humbert said.

'I think you sent spies to watch over him when he was banished.'

He nodded.

'And paid for his instruction at the seminarium.'

'I had hoped . . . he would return . . . It should not . . . have been . . . like this.' The bishop's red eye was watering so much, Plegmond had to cleanse it with moistened wool.

'You all say what a fine leader Alfred would have become, but perhaps you're wrong,' said Asser. 'He's clumsy, self-righteous and has little or no ambition.'

Plegmond was washing out the wool in a bowl and tending to the bishop's other eye. 'All that is a mere carapace. Underneath it Alfred is strong and perceptive. He learns quickly and loves the common folk. I'd be happy to be ruled by him,' he said.

Asser laughed. He'd never heard Plegmond talk with such authority. His spiky-haired assistant was acquiring confidence and a maturity beyond his years.

'If he'd not . . . fallen prey . . . to lust,' said the bishop, and his exasperation made him shake a little. 'I curse the devil . . . for making him so.'

Asser and Plegmond exchanged glances at these tantalising words.

Humbert sighed, shook his head and sat up a little straighter. 'What is it you require?' he said.

'I need your priests to travel through the five shires, sending a message to all Christian men,' replied Asser. 'They must join Wolf's army till the autumn harvest, save for one man from each farm who may remain behind to care for the crops and animals. Their mortal souls will be in peril should they refuse.'

Humbert looked pleadingly at Plegmond.

'Let me confer with him alone, Father,' the young priest requested.

Asser left them and wandered to the adjoining chapel, where he walked along its rows of rickety benches. Why were Saxon churches so unbearably dreary, their daub walls stained black from the perpetually leaking thatched roofs? This one was little more than a mouldering haystack. Only one aspect of it gave him pleasure: the preponderance of finely wrought gold and silver crosses. How ironic that the single fine skill the Saxons could offer to the glory of God also put them in the greatest danger from the Norlanders.

Plegmond eventually called for him to return.

'I agree . . . to your request,' the bishop said. 'It will be done . . . Father Plegmond will oversee it.'

'I'm truly grateful,' said Asser. 'One final thing,' he added, emboldened by the news that he'd be able to rely on Plegmond. 'The Norland fleet has vanished. It must be hidden somewhere. Every effort must be made to find it.'

'There's a woman . . . She claims to know,' said the bishop.

'Who?' demanded Asser.

'She's a member of the royal house,' replied Plegmond. 'Moira, the wife of Aethelhawk. She was found wandering near Bath Abbey warning of a Norland attack and assaulting anyone who tried to help her. The nuns are tending to her.'

'I know of her,' said Asser. 'Indeed, I was hoping to find her myself.'

'She'll be . . . no use to you,' said the bishop. 'She's mad . . . quite mad.'

Asser roused Mountjoy and they rode to Bath Abbey, a misshapen cluster of buildings surrounded by a waterlogged garden and gnarled yew trees. Moira's room was neat and tidy with saints painted on the walls, but its gentle simplicity was coarsened by the bolts and locks on the doors and windows.

'I won't speak to you, priest,' she said.

'I have a gift for you,' replied Asser.

She pushed away the proffered package.

'It is from a friend.'

'I have no friends.'

'Lady Swift, the daughter of Aethelwolf?'

Moira stared at him, and her upper lip trembled slightly. She grabbed the little package from his hand, unwrapped it eagerly and held up to the light an exquisite carving of an apple with a bird clinging to its side and a large grub dangling from its beak.

'It's good,' she said, and held it tightly in her lap.

'Tell me about the Norland fleet,' said Asser quietly.

Moira sighed. 'I was staying in the home of Lady Winifred on the Isle of Wight, but I was smuggled off the island—'

'Why smuggled?'

'Do you wish me to talk or not?'

Asser made a gesture of apology.

'Fishermen took me to the mainland to find Lady Swift, but I was assaulted by the nuns here and kept among common madwomen who smelt of shit. Now I am incarcerated in the very room where Swift was kept before she was hanged.'

'She was not hanged.'

'She was.'

'I swear not, m'lady. I have been attending on her in Chepstow to ensure her safety. She is my friend too,' he added, not entirely accurately. 'She told me you came to see her here but you were dragged away before she could tell you she loved you.'

'You are a wheedler,' said Moira. 'You say these things only to make me talk.'

'I'm saying these things because they're true,' said Asser patiently.

She leant into him and whispered, 'My husband doesn't know I'm here. You must help me escape before he discovers where I am.'

'If you tell me where the Norlanders are, I give you my pledge,' said Asser.

'Then listen, this is important,' she said forcefully. 'The Norlanders have occupied the Wight island. No one can get in or out of it. I've tried to tell the sisters here a thousand times, but the bitches say I'm mad. Over two hundred fighters are camped on the beach at Shankalin. Their leader, Guthrum, is as crafty as a hungry fox. He has kidnapped Lady Winifred's child and has her in his power. He is a stump-handed devil. You must kill him, then kill him again. Now go.'

'I will, and I'll raise the alarm,' said Asser.

He bade her adieu, and she vigorously polished her carving as though determined to remove every last speck of dust from it.

He left the room and closed the door behind him. A nun assisted him with his cloak, and he heard Moira sobbing.

Mountjoy was waiting in the abbey garden.

'Take this,' Asser said, sliding the papal ring from his finger. 'Ride to Aethelhawk and tell him we need a hundred men to help drive off the Norlanders. In return we'll tell him where his wife is.'

He didn't want to betray Moira; he doubted she was mad at all, simply a clever woman frustrated by the stupidity that surrounded her. Nevertheless, word of her location would inevitably leak out and she'd be returned to her husband anyway. All Wessex was under threat, and a thousand lives were more important than the incarceration of one woman, mad or not.

SIXTY-FIVE

Tivoli

The success of the new Saxon school was beyond anything Alfred could have wished for, but it brought with it more work than ever. He now had twice as many pupils, each with his own ailments and insecurities. He visited Ponti every day and fed him false information about Balotelli, lacing his lies with enough truth to make his accounts plausible, and of course there were his precious evenings with the cardinal copying his philosophical musings and listening to his poetry. His mind was a whirl and he was constantly tired.

But one night there was a robust knock at the door and Elswith stood there, her face scrubbed, in the attire of a housemaid. 'Father Asser was right. I've decided I'll not waste my life whoring,' she said firmly. 'I will cook and clean for you, tend the children when required and teach them to read. They should have a proper knowledge of Saxon and Latin, and a little Greek as I have. I will work the hours you require and you will pay me a good wage.'

So it was settled, and as the weeks went by Elswith became

ever more valuable to him. She won the trust of the children; even little Cuddie stuttered less and concentrated more when she was in the room. Now with Elswith teaching and John of Old Saxony assisting where he could, Alfred had a lot more free time, which was vital because Ponti had to be brought down as quickly as possible. His vileness was tainting the entire Notarii. Alfred seethed with rage when he sat at the long table alongside the other clerks at the back of the meeting room, watching Ponti fawn and simper around the Notarii. 'Rest assured that despite Balotelli's protestations, you will be showered with God's plenty to reward you for your exemplary work, your Eminences,' he'd say, and they'd giggle and pat him on the back.

At the school entrance, Elswith assisted Alfred in putting on his modest cloak.

'Little Abel's vomiting,' she said. 'He's eaten too many poppy seeds even though I've told him not to. I've rested a cold compress on his head and he's sleeping now.'

'You were not here last evening. Were you visiting old friends?' Alfred enquired.

'Were the boys fed and washed?' she replied sharply. 'Was the school dusted and the courtyard swept? Was your room tidied and your paintbrushes cleaned?'

'They were.'

'Do I enquire where you go of an evening?'

'You do not.'

'Well then,' she said.

Elswith was a good girl, and Alfred shrank from pursuing the matter further.

He was to meet Ponti in the public courtyard of the Dungeon, a well-trodden sanded area where citizens of Rome could, for a small payment, observe the punishment meted out to sinners and the crazed. Along one wall stood a tiered stand for spectators, and around it a few stalls from which vendors sold food during the more popular events. Currently the courtyard was almost empty, the only entertainment provided by the body of Petr of Macedon, which had been strung from a gallow and was swaying in the early-morning breeze. Weights had been applied in order to elicit information, and consequently his corpse had become misshapen, like a dead bat entangled in a bush. Seven exhausted and dispirited men trudged in a circle underneath this hideous sight, encouraged by one of Halfnose's warders, a skinny man with a withered arm and a whipping stick.

'Are those poor souls Petr's accomplices?' enquired Alfred. 'They look so pathetic.'

'Don't let your bleeding heart deceive you,' replied Halfnose, admiring his handiwork. 'They steal our Christian land and fuck our nuns up the arse. But they won't be doing that for much longer. Once they've given us the names of the rest of their kind, they'll share Petr's view over the city. And there's plenty more to come.'

'More? Why? What have they done?' Alfred enquired.

'It's not what they've done that matters, is it?' replied Undersecretary Ponti, who had crept surreptitiously up to them. 'It's what they might do!' He rubbed his hands with glee. 'I take great pleasure in witnessing their punishment,' he said. 'It's our job to keep Rome unsullied by heretics, is it not?' he added, looking contemptuously at Petr's twisting body. 'I could have every one of them dangling like a glut of summer cherries from the walls, were it not for my enemies, the cabal of misguided and mealy-mouthed cardinals who had me dismissed from my previous post simply because I pressed a few idolaters in order to discover their vile ways. I will prove what blind fools these appeasers are. The Antonils are the devil's agents. They use their magic to send their victims into a trance and bend them to their will. You were here when Balotelli's men apprehended this one, Alfred. Did he try to cast a spell on you?'

Until now Alfred had had no idea Ponti knew he'd been at the dungeon participating in Petr's investigation. It would be disastrous were he to realise the depth of his relationship with Cardinal Balotelli's men.

'Indeed I was here,' he replied, 'but I saw no magic. I was called to give testimony against Petr because I knew him. He taught singing at my school and—'

'He was certainly singing when he died,' interjected Halfnose. 'In a very high voice, if I remember correctly.'

'You were right to give evidence against him,' retorted Ponti, and he opened a flask of water and offered it to Alfred. But the spittle from the corners of the priest's mouth still clung to it, and the thought of taking a sip revolted him.

'I thank you, Father Ponti, but I have an abscetic tooth,' he said. 'Water aggravates it.'

'I've been impressed by your labours so far, and I wish you to go on a little journey for me,' said Ponti.

'Of course.' Alfred hoped the trepidation in his voice wasn't obvious. He was being lured ever deeper into the vile man's machinations. Ponti might only be a junior functionary, but his influence was growing by the day. Alfred felt he was wading into a stinking bog, and with each step, the risk of being dragged under by the undersecretary's mischief intensified.

'I have been asked by the Notarii to investigate the circumstances surrounding the arrest of Fabio Gilotti,' said Ponti, 'and in order to do so have exchanged several letters with him. You know he's incarcerated in the family's summer home in Tivoli?'

'I did not.'

'He failed to respond to my last note, which contained information of a delicate nature. His failure to do so is unusual, and I want to ensure the letter has not gone amiss. You shall go in my stead.'

'Of course.'

'But be furtive. If you are asked why you're there . . . ?'

'I will say Cardinal Gilotti employs tutors for Tivoli's celebrated children's choir, and I want to ask him for permission to interview one of them about becoming a teacher at my school,' replied Alfred, a little surprised by the ease with which ever more lies were forthcoming.

'I like you,' crowed Ponti, and planted a salivary kiss on his cheek. 'You share my passion for spiritual purity but are as sly as a weasel in pursuit of it. Ride to Tivoli and ensure Fabio has received my message. It bears an unmistakable seal, the sign of the three crosses of Calvary. One day, when I once again reach lofty heights, I will reward you greatly. But for now, go to the Notarii's stables and find yourself a trusty mount.'

Alfred's first reaction on arriving at the Gilottis' villa was one of awe. His own family had owned a summer house on the Devon coast that his father had confiscated from a disloyal alderman. It was situated on an isolated cliff, its roof was lagged only with moss and leaked when it rained, and the wind blew remorselessly. He visited it every year with his mother when Winchester was airless and the miasma became unbearable, but there was little to occupy them other than staring at the endless waves breaking far below.

By contrast, the Gilottis' villa seemed to offer only joy and excitement. It was freshly painted, large and roomy, with airy windows and a vibrant terracotta-tiled roof. It boasted an ornamental lake where children could play, an abundance of small tables and cushions, and woven mats on which the men could recline. Neat outhouses were set in its verdant gardens, and there was a separate bathing hall fed by a small aqueduct with a furnace attached. Alfred had seen countless bathhouses on his travels comprising scalding caldaria, warm tepidaria and icy frigidaria, but never in a private house. What wealth these people must possess!

He needed to find a means of obtaining entry without drawing attention to himself, but his way was barred. A number of tradespeople were gathered outside the gates with carts bearing oysters, hunks of pig, fresh flowers and the like. They were being prevented from going further by guards wielding stout staves.

'Admission is forbidden,' bellowed their leader. 'Supplies for the Gilottis must be deposited here and will be brought inside later.'

'I must ensure my blooms are properly displayed,' cried an outraged flower seller.

'Go away!' shouted the guard. 'If the Pope himself came knocking he'd be sent off with a flea in his ear.'

Perhaps there was an unlocked door at the back of the house. Alfred dismounted, led his horse to the adjacent stable block and began searching for a bucket of water, but his perusal was interrupted by the sound of approaching horses. He glanced furtively outside. A party eight or nine strong was riding towards the house, led by a man he recognised by his proud demeanour as Cardinal Enzo Gilotti, the primicerius of the Notarii. They came to a halt in a cloud of dust.

'Open up!' Enzo called imperiously to the guards at the gate. 'I must see my brother.' He swung from his mount, his face drawn. His men led their horses to the stable block and Alfred stepped among them. The guards let them enter and the riders strode into the grounds with Alfred in their midst.

A woman rushed out and threw her arms round Enzo. Her hair was greying, her face kind, and she wore the pendulous earrings of a woman of taste. 'Thank God you've come, brother,' she cried.

'Claudia!' the primicerius said tenderly. 'Where is he?'

'In the tepidarium,' she replied. 'We found him lying there this morning and sent for you. We left him as he was until you returned, but I fear you'll find the sight deeply distressing.'

The water in the tepidarium was clear; no clumps of tangled hair or grey, greasy bubbles obscured the pool's extensive mosaic patterning. There was an elaborate fountain at one end of the room, comprising a pyramid of cups down which water poured until it ran into the pool, making a pleasing tinkling sound. But it wasn't this watery concatenation that was attracting the horrified observers' attention.

At the far end of the room, flanked by pots of well-tended ferns, was a rectangular marble table. On it lay Fabio, bound by his hands and ankles, his throat slashed, a knife protruding from his heart, his severed cock lying neatly on his stomach. The pigment he'd used to disguise his grey hair had run down his face like muddy tears. His cheeks were sagging as those of men in their middle age often did. Yet even in death, even despite the humiliation that had been meted out to him, his upper lip twisted upwards as if he were sneering, or perhaps it was simply the terror he felt as his penis was sliced from his body.

'What devil of a man could have committed such an act of savagery?' gasped Enzo.

Claudia leant forward and said softly, 'We do not think it was a man, brother.'

'A boy?' exclaimed Enzo. 'A child? Impossible!'

'We believe it was a woman.'

The primicerius stared at the body, hardly comprehending what Claudia was saying.

'A woman?' he repeated. 'A woman bound him to a table and stabbed him? How could she have done so? He would have resisted violently.'

'We think he acquiesced,' said Claudia. 'We believe he was seeking pleasure . . . in the Spartan fashion.'

'What? The idiot allowed himself to be tied up by a whore?'

'It would seem so. Apparently he brought her in here and sent the attendants away.'

'Some thieving slut marched brazenly into my house, murdered my brother and left again unnoticed?'

'Nothing appears to have been stolen, brother.'

Alfred turned his head away from the butchered body and looked at the anguished yet embarrassed family.

'This is Balotelli's fault,' said Enzo. 'Why did his men not make the house secure? I thought my brother was supposed to be under his supervision.'

Claudia Gilotti took him gently by the arm and spoke softly. 'You told the Holy Father that Fabio's arrest was a family matter, Enzo, and as the nation's primicerius, you insisted on taking charge of his internment yourself.'

'I will not be held responsible for this outrage. Regardless of what I might have said in my distress, he was Balotelli's prisoner. Was there not a single one of his men in the vicinity?'

Alfred felt uneasy. Might someone recognise him from the day of Fabio's arrest? No, he doubted it. Those present were far too occupied by the ghastly sight of Fabio's butchered body. He should take this opportunity to explore unhindered. If Fabio had kept Ponti's message about his person it might be close by. Behind him was a door that bore the image of a Roman centurion. He leant gently backwards; it eased open, he slipped through and closed it behind him.

It was the room where the bathers left their clothing, the walls painted red, with stone benches and rows of pegs on the walls, all empty save one, on which hung a tunic, a light coat and some undergarments, presumably Fabio's. He fumbled through them, then climbed out of a window at the far end of the room into a herb garden and made his way slowly and steadily to the stable block, a message tucked inside his coat bearing a seal with three crosses on it.

Elswith usually slept close to the school doorway to guard against intruders, but she wasn't there now. Alfred called out her name. He searched the entire school, but she was nowhere to be found, and her few possessions had disappeared. She had gone, and if the dreadful suspicion that was nagging at his mind was right, she would not be returning.

SIXTY-SIX

A Deep Egyptian Sleep

At first light on the morning after his journey to Tivoli, Alfred paid a visit to Cardinal Balotelli, who took a silver letter knife from a small chest, warmed it over the fire, wiped it clean and carefully teased the seal open, taking care not to break it. 'It's a long time since I last did this,' he murmured, and passed the letter to Alfred, who read it out loud to him.

'"I have met with those cardinals we identified as potential allies. I told them you are wholly innocent, that you were seized by a band of heretics who magicked you into a deep Egyptian sleep and instructed you to act in ways no good Roman would contemplate but that you were powerless to resist. Some accepted the veracity of my explanation, but it may take time to convince the more sceptical, particularly as Balotelli will doubtless attempt to discredit us. Nevertheless, have no fear. He will not be among us for much longer. Soon it will be as though he and his lackeys never walked the earth. Until then, I counsel patience. Speak to your brother Enzo about interim incentives. Twenty-five gold pieces should be enough. I remain your loyal and trusted friend – VP."'

When he'd finished, Balotelli opened his eyes and smiled.

'So, we will disappear, will we?' he said. 'Are we to be retired, banished, or does Father Ponti have something a little more final in store for us? You must redouble your efforts, Alfred, before we're murdered in our beds.'

When Alfred broke the news of Fabio's death to Ponti, he thought the undersecretary would be horrified, but he was not.

'It's the proof we needed,' he crowed. 'The Antonils did this. They executed him in their ritual way so he wouldn't expose their fanatical network. But they didn't stop there.' He was growing more excited by the moment. 'They butchered his manhood, and doubtless would have eaten it too had they not been disturbed. Oh, they've overreached themselves this time! Now the floodgates will open and we'll be able to purify Rome as thoroughly as Hercules cleansed the Aegean stables. What a great day this is!'

'But Fabio's family?' protested Alfred.

Ponti's face crumpled under the weight of a newly acquired sorrow. 'Of course,' he said, 'you're right. His distinguished brother, Enzo, his delightful sister, Claudia, they must be suffering unimaginable anguish. But in time they too will realise what a God-given moment this is. Fabio's participation in the events at the Undercroft will be forgotten and the blame for his death will fall squarely on Rome's heretics.' He was beaming again now. 'We will make his murder public. I have been nurturing bands of righteous citizens who detest heresy as much as we do. I will now be able to give them the freedom to hunt it out wherever they find it. I'll even slip them a coin or two to assist their endeavours.'

He grabbed the cross from his table and hugged it to him

like a child. 'And with Christ's help, when Rome has been washed clean, we'll turn our attention elsewhere, perhaps even to the whole Roman Empire!' He stared at Alfred passionately. 'I've had dreams of such a purification,' he said, 'dreams that would amaze you,' and he glanced down at his ivory-inlaid table. 'You found my note.' He picked up the letter Alfred had placed there and scrutinised it. 'It is unread, I see. Let it remain so.' He held it over a candle and smiled contentedly as the flame blossomed and the message turned to ashes.

SIXTY-SEVEN

A Fair and Honest Broker

Ten riders skidded to a halt in front of the great hall of King Burrt of Mercia. Burgred swung from his saddle and called to the servants running towards him. 'We need clean water and a change of attire.'

He had been summoned back to the royal court in Tamworth as a matter of urgency. The Welsh border was quieter now, so he'd agreed that Swift should come here with him, along with Brother Hercules and a few of his monks. Something was amiss, and he was eager to know what it was.

'You must follow me,' replied Burrt's chancellor, Gareth, a pompous man far too young for such a weighty role. 'I have orders to bring you into the king's presence as soon as you arrive. Please take your nourishment as you go.'

'Uncle Burgred, welcome back! Come play with us!' Ithael and Maurig, the sons of Rhys of Gwent, came running up behind him and tugged at his legs. They'd adored him since he'd first brought them here after they'd been taken from their father. Whenever he saw them, he played with them constantly.

He swung them round like windcocks and they clambered over his head and shoulders as though their former life in Wales was nothing but a distant memory.

'I'll come to you later, my little chickens,' he said. 'I have work to do.'

Kitchen slaves handed them mugs of ale and pieces of lardy cake as they half walked, half ran into the palace. They brushed the crumbs from their riding attire and entered the great hall, where the king sat sunk in his throne, concern etched on his pale face.

He nodded at them to sit round his antiquated Persian table, and more ale was thrust in front of them.

'Burgred, of all my captains, it is you I trust the most,' he said. 'Your work in the Welsh borderlands has been exemplary, and I thank you for it.'

'I live only to serve,' replied Burgred.

'I know you do, which is why I've brought you back.'

Swift gave King Burrt a charming smile, and a look of friendly recognition appeared on his face.

'Lady Swift, it's good to see you again. My, what a magnificent woman you've become. You have your mother's fine looks about you. I remember you vividly as a child.'

'I too. She was very badly behaved,' said Burgred – and, he thought, as beautiful then as she was now.

'I apologise for my youthful folly, great king,' Swift replied, 'but those days are long past. What can it be that causes you such concern?'

'Wynstan!' replied Chancellor Gareth with a disdainful look on his face.

'Wynstan indeed,' agreed the king. 'Twenty years past, when my predecessor, King Wigmund, died, Wynstan was his heir.'

'A foolish and shy young man,' said Burgred.

'Indeed. He had no interest in taking the mantle of kingship and buried himself in the bowels of the Church. I ascended the throne—'

'To great jubilation. Even though you were not of the previous king's faction,' said the obsequious Gareth.

'That is so. I was deemed the great unifier by all save the rump of Wigmund's supporters, who have made mischief for me ever since.' Burrt stopped, and coughed into a bloodied cloth. 'But I'm too old to deal with such squabbling now,' he continued. 'I desire my son Frith to take my place. He has much to learn and can be a little tiresome. But responsibility will make a man of him, and I have arranged for him to marry the old king's wife.'

'An excellent idea,' said Gareth. 'It will unite the bickering factions and Mercia's future will be secure.'

Burrt threw his bloodied cloth into a silver bucket at his feet and took a fresh one from a little pile by his side.

'It would be,' he agreed, 'but her son has declared the marriage an abomination and refuses to condone it.'

'What could his objection be?' enquired Burgred. He'd always thought Wynstan an insipid man, unconcerned with Mercia's governance.

Swift smirked as though she suspected she knew the answer.

'It is nothing,' said Gareth. 'A foolish prejudice concerning their respective ages. He is nineteen, she is three score years and six. But why should that matter? They truly love each other.'

'How charming,' said Swift. Her gentle mockery could cut though a conversation in a way Burgred could only marvel at.

'Wynstan has charge of the sacred books at Repton Abbey,' continued Burrt, coughing repeatedly as he spoke. 'The old king's supporters are proposing that he leave the Church and seize the throne. They've called their followers to arms and are thronging to the abbey. It's almost impossible for us to gain access to him. My other captains are standing by helpless, so I called for you, Burgred.'

'I am a mere soldier,' Burgred replied. 'What can I do that my fellow captains cannot?'

Swift took his hand. 'You are far too modest, cousin,' she said. 'Your Grace, Burgred and I will resolve the issue.'

Burgred was horrified. The situation was impossible; their intervention would only make things worse. Nevertheless, Swift continued with her usual confidence.

'I was born in Wessex, sire, and have no particular interest in this dispute and no allegiance to either man, though my mother was a friend to both you and Wynstan's father. I believe Wynstan may accept me as a fair and honest broker.'

'He may indeed,' agreed Burrt.

'We'll need fresh horses,' she continued. 'We'll take your son to Repton and seek an accommodation between the two men – won't we, Burgred?'

SIXTY-EIGHT

The Confession

Asser and Wolf sat on St Michael's Slope, half a league up the River Itchen from Southamwic, watching the new recruits on the field below, some wielding freshly cut chestnut sticks and practising thrusts and lunges, others jumping back and forth over rows of barrels, the feeblest running leadenly round the edge of the field being harangued by Stub.

Wolf sighed and blew the air from his cheeks.

'You look sorrowful,' said Asser.

'I am sorrowful,' replied the high aethel.

'This malaise has gripped you for over a week now.'

'Yes,' said Wolf, drawing the word out thoughtfully. 'Are these all the men you could find? If so, we're doomed.'

'Sadly so. We can't press the old, the sick or the lunatics into battle. One man from each farm has to stay behind and manage it, and this is the rest, the flower of the five shires. They'll improve. They're farmers. Most have never fought before.'

'There are barely a hundred!' exclaimed Wolf.

It was a big field, and it made the men look small and insignificant.

'Bear has an army twice as big as this,' said Asser. 'Are you sure you don't want me to ride to Devon and plead for his assistance?'

'No,' replied Wolf. 'Absolutely not. You don't know him like I do. He'd pick fights, attempt to take command, drive me into a week-long rage, then ride to the nearest town for dice and copulation. He's a drunken fool, a dissolute.'

He scratched the back of his neck, then under his armpit.

'I don't suppose you've any of your powder?' he enquired.

Asser shook his head. 'I've attempted to obtain more, but the Wessex apothecaries look at me with blank faces.'

They watched the struggling soldiers for a while. Wolf gave a long groan.

'I might have a few crumbs,' said Asser, taking pity on him. 'Enough for one or two inhalations.'

'I'll have one now and the other before I go into battle,' replied Wolf, staring at him as though daring him to disagree.

They climbed the slope to where they'd left their horses. At the top, Asser unbuckled his saddlebag and searched among clothes and crumpled documents till he found a twist of cloth.

They sat in the shadow of St Michael's Church, under the lychgate, where pall-bearers waited with their dead until the priest was ready to bury them. Asser prepared Wolf's medication, and when the old man had inhaled it, they sat in silence for a while. Wolf rubbed his finger against his itchy nose.

'Feeling better now?' Asser enquired.

'I want to take confession,' Wolf said.

'Now? I'll see if the priest is inside.'

'No!' replied Wolf, shaking his head adamantly. 'You do it.'

'Me? Why me?'

Wolf walked into the church. Asser shrugged and followed him.

It wasn't a welcoming building: tall, dark, narrow and smelling of damp and rotting thatch. To the right of the altar was a stone shriving chair. Wolf sat on the chair, Asser on the wooden stool in front of it.

'Bless me, Father, for I have sinned,' said Wolf. 'I beat a boy for being lazy and kicked his face when he fell. I forced a maid in Wantage to lean over a well and I . . .'

Time passed. Asser wriggled to make himself comfortable. The old man described in lurid detail the beatings he'd ordered, the land he'd confiscated, his blasphemy and adultery. There seemed no end to his sins. Asser's mind drifted; he was imbibing Siena wine in a drinking house in Rome. 'I killed my wife,' Wolf blurted out.

Asser froze. 'Your first wife, Agnes?' he said eventually.

'No, the other one.'

Asser felt sick. Memories of the dreadful night in St Catherine's Abbey came flooding back to him. Her gentle, lifeless face, her white folded hands, the softness of her skin. 'The Lady Osburgh?' he asked steadily.

'Yes. It was me.'

No, that wasn't possible. These were the mumblings of an old man's decayed mind. 'High Aethel,' he replied gently. 'You were travelling to Rome when she died.'

'I gave the order.'

'Again, you're confused. She died a natural death.'

Wolf snapped out of his reverie in the click of a finger. 'No she didn't,' he scoffed. 'She was poisoned. You must have known that. You're not stupid.'

Though I walk through the valley of the shadow of death, I shall fear no evil.

Quoniam tu mecum es, virga tua et baculus tuus, ipsa consolabuntur me.

Somehow he'd always known the old man had been aware of his dalliance with Osburgh.

'I'm sorry,' he said.

'Why? Because you fucked her? Don't shake your head, of course you did. I wouldn't have been stupid enough to let the two of you wander off without someone keeping an eye on you, would I?'

Thou preparest a table before me in the presence of mine enemies.

Inpinguasti oleo caput meum, calix meus inebrians.

'Don't worry, I'm not going to throttle you,' Wolf continued. 'Osburgh probably had half the aldermen in Wessex. You weren't why I killed her. My sin was far worse.'

A pigeon fluttered down from the ceiling and landed on one of the benches.

'I did it so I could marry Judith,' Wolf said eventually.

The bird flew back up to the roof. A tiny yellow shit dropped silently to the floor.

'You look outraged. Why? Judith is a joy and Osburgh was a gorgon. You'd have found that out soon enough.'

What do I do? What do I say? thought Asser. He felt only emptiness, and it was paralysing him. Did he want vengeance? No, he had a war to fight, a nation to protect, a new concord to negotiate. He was a priest, he should occasionally try to act like one.

'Do you wish for Christ's forgiveness?' he said eventually.

'Of course I do,' replied Wolf irritably. 'Why do you think I'm confessing to you? The shame burns inside me like vitriol. It never stops. But I need her company.' He shook his head despondently. 'Being a king is a very lonely calling.' His face crumpled and he began to cry. 'I am so alone,' he said between sobs, then stopped as quickly as he'd started. He was happy again. The clouds had dissipated, his confession was forgotten. 'What were we talking about?' he said.

SIXTY-NINE

Mirandolina

Walking through the city in the early morning, Alfred was usually amidst a jostling throng, but today there was barely a soul about; doors were closed tight, windows shuttered and barred. The news of Fabio Gilotti's murder by a gang of heretics had transformed Rome. The energetic, vibrant city had become listless and fearful.

Two men stepped out of an alleyway and brought him to a halt. They looked like dockers or hauliers, and over their rough garb they wore hessian tabards with red crosses crudely sewn on them, the sign of the so-called Concerned Citizens, who had sprung up out of nowhere over the past few weeks.

'What is your faith?' one demanded.

'My faith is in Christ,' replied Alfred.

'Recite the catechism.'

'I believe in the Lamb of God—'

'Enough! On your way!'

Alfred set off again. When he'd first arrived in Rome, his aspirations had been modest. He'd wanted to teach the young and live as far away from Wessex as possible, nothing more. But lately he'd become ever more drawn into the complex web of church politicking. Of course, Cardinal Balotelli was teaching him well; he already understood the rudiments of church law and finances, and through his unsettling relationship with Ponti he had an inkling of the difference between good and bad governance, but it had come at a price. His hands were dirty. He was a cheat and a liar. He must walk away from here, as he had from Burgheim and Geneva. He'd change his name and start a new life somewhere else. Perhaps he'd make a pilgrimage to Jerusalem.

He was startled out of his reverie by a terrified young woman with blue streaks in her cropped hair who was running towards him and crying out for help. Her shift was torn, exposing her breasts and legs, she was unshod, her nose bloodied, and she was being pursued by three grinning men sporting red crosses.

Alfred looked round for a place where he could stand his ground, and pushed the woman into a tiny alley. The men approached, panting.

'Shame on you!' he cried. 'Why are you pursuing this woman? Do you not have mothers and sisters of your own?'

'She's a heretic, boy. She must come with us,' the oldest man replied, grinning broadly in anticipation of the violence they were about to unleash.

'No woman should be treated this way, regardless of her religion,' replied Alfred. 'You wear the cross of Christ. Show some Christian charity.'

'We are good Christians. She is an Antonil. She taints all Rome with the stink of her cunny. We may do with her as we will.'

'I have done no ill, sir,' said the woman. 'I swear it!'

'Come with us, you lying whore, and we'll give you what you deserve,' said the man, grabbing her shift and attempting to pull her towards him.

A calm descended on Alfred, a familiar sense of quietude he'd learnt from his father. Much to his mother's disapproval, Wolf had sometimes called him from his lessons when he was young and taken him onto the training field, where he'd been taught to thrust, kick and lunge without expending a jot more energy than was absolutely necessary. He had little taste for violence, but he was supple and strong, and took pleasure in engaging with imaginary enemies. For a few hours he could forget the slights and harsh words he constantly received from the rest of his family and become the warrior his father wanted him to be.

He returned to that world now. He grabbed the man's wrist, forcing him to let go of the girl, and twisted it so violently the man tumbled over. He seized the second man's stick and thrust it into his throat, kicked the legs from under the third man and stamped on his hands. He dragged all three up the alley by the scruff of their necks and threw discarded planks and wooden crates on them while they begged him to stop.

He hid the woman in his room, bought her a new shift, new shoes and a bowl of rabbit porridge. She accepted his offerings with a look of curiosity.

'You can't stay here long,' he said. 'More of them will come looking for you. I'll try to smuggle you out of Rome.'

'Who are you?' she asked. 'Why are you risking your life for me?'

'It's the Christian thing to do, is it not?'

'They think I'm an Antonil.'

'Are you?'

'No. I stayed in an Antonil house. I slept with one or two of them, that's all.'

'So you're promiscuous?'

'Ah! There you have me!' she said. 'You must hand me back to them and let them burn me at the stake.'

They laughed, and she gave him a spoonful of her porridge.

'Perhaps you have influential friends among your amours to whom you could flee?'

She shook her head. 'I have no one. Once I lived with a king, but I stole the pretty things he gave me and ran away. I doubt he'd vouch for me. Wait!' She tapped the top of his nose with her spoon in triumph. 'I was briefly employed by a man in Modena who wore the Pope's ring, and he's in Rome now, though I have no idea where. I don't suppose you know a Father Asser?'

SEVENTY

Gaudy Puppets

When Swift was a little girl, her mother, Agnes, had told her stories of Mercia's former magnificence. No other nation in all Britain had outshone its wealth and power. But nations rose and fell, and Mercia's demise had been particularly rapid. Now, as she and her little party rode into Repton, all she could see of its former grandeur were the long-abandoned halls where the kings of Mercia had once been baptised. It was no longer a town, simply a resting place for a few wide-eyed pilgrims to worship at the shrines of tyrants and usurpers. There were no houses or shops, no markets or stockyards, merely churches and pilgrims' lodging houses, dominated by an abbey so ancient it appeared to be about to come crashing down under the weight of its own history.

'See the foolery over there?' said Prince Frith.

King Burrt's son was a sulky young man of middle height with a perpetual frown. After three days on the road together, Swift had concluded he was nothing more than an irritating child in need of a spanking.

Wynstan's followers had pitched their tents outside the front of the abbey. A crowd three or four hundred strong was watching a pair of gaudy puppets as tall as a church roof engaging in a lewd dance. One, dressed as Wynstan's mother, was bouncing up and down, while the other, who appeared to be Frith, had his head buried under her dress and was pleasuring her.

'How stupid they look!' said Frith. 'Who are those puppets meant to be?'

'Keep low!' Hercules warned the young prince. 'We'll find a door round the back.'

'Nonsense,' retorted Frith. 'I am the future king. I will enter through the fine front portal.'

The giant dolls were becoming frenzied. The one bearing Frith's likeness extricated itself from its lover's dress, waved at the crowd, and its head fell off. The spectators roared their appreciation and tossed it in the air like a bladder at a sporting contest. 'Off with his head! Off with his head!' they chanted.

'I think it's your head they're seeking,' said Swift, and yanked Frith's hood over his face.

They found the entrance they were searching for, but discovered that the abbey church wasn't the haven of peace and contemplation they'd expected. A series of trestle tables had been laid out, seated round which were five elderly priests engaged in loud conversation. Standing among them, his arms outstretched like Christ at the Last Supper, was a man with a full white beard, dressed in elaborate regalia, a gold-trimmed mitre on his head and wearing a gold sash and cuffs.

'Who is that man?' whispered Swift.

'The High Bishop of Mercia,' murmured Burgred. 'What's he doing here?'

'You have ridden to Repton on a matter of great importance, so forgive us if we seem a little distracted,' said the high bishop.

'Our meeting has been long in the calling.' He was surprisingly sprightly for such a distinguished man, his shrewd eyes peering from under large, tangled brows. 'Repton needs a cathedral to rival Canterbury. And though this might appear of secondary importance given the baying crowd outside, we are convinced such a project would unite our warring factions.'

'A glorious vision, High Bishop, which I'm sure would inspire your people,' said Swift. 'But it can only be realised once we've resolved the Mercian succession.'

Frith was wandering off towards the winding stone steps of the tower, doubtless to climb to the top in order to see the crowd below.

'And that lad is the house of Burrt's preferred candidate?' the high bishop asked, raising a massive eyebrow. 'He seems a little young to be marrying the old queen. She can barely walk and is overcome by the shaking disease.'

'At least he desires the throne,' said Burgred. 'Wynstan is terrified of it. I suspect it's only the threat of his mother's inappropriate coupling that has made him so exercised.'

'Perhaps if Prince Frith declared that his marriage was to be in name only, separate beds – separate halls even – Wynstan might accept,' suggested Hercules.

'I doubt it. The two men hate each other,' said Burgred.

'Nevertheless, if Frith is to be king, he must mend this rift and swear undying friendship to Wynstan,' replied Swift.

'I'll swear undying friendship to a horse's arse if it'll get me the crown,' said Frith, who had reappeared, flapping the desiccated wings of a dead bat he'd found in the tower. 'I don't want to fuck Wynstan's mother anyway. She smells of piss.'

They led Frith to the door of a side chapel where Wynstan was in prayer. According to one of the old priests, he prayed at length every day for the souls of the five hundred Mercian martyrs so he could avoid talking to anyone. Swift caught a glimpse of him, a feeble specimen, his eyes closed, his hands shaking.

Frith entered and closed the door behind him. They heard raised voices, then nothing but silence. They waited for what seemed an age but was probably little longer than the burning of a small candle. 'This is foolish,' Swift said eventually. She turned the door handle and went in. Burgred followed her. At first the chapel appeared empty, then they saw Frith crouching over a pair of legs protruding from between the benches. He looked up aghast.

'I didn't mean it,' he said. 'He insulted me. He said I wasn't fit to wear the crown, and I grew angry and my dagger . . .'

Wynstan was lying face-down. Burgred rolled him over, revealing a pool of blood. He beat his fist on the floor in frustration. 'Why did you bring us here, Swift?' he said. 'Now we are in collusion with a murderer.'

'Calm yourself,' she said. 'Let me think. Perhaps Wynstan's death offers us an opportunity.'

Hercules dragged the corpse into the body of the church. The high bishop and his priests looked on helplessly.

'Frith killed him,' said Swift.

'God's damnation!' said the high bishop. 'That is the worst of all possible outcomes!'

'Perhaps not. Can we hide the body in the crypt? If the crowd hear their contender for the throne is dead, there'll be a bloodbath, but if we can find a way to pacify them, it might work to our advantage.'

The high bishop looked at her thoughtfully. 'Perhaps if they believed Wynstan had died a natural death . . .'

'. . . and if we were able to find a better candidate than Frith . . .' added Swift.

'Frith must be sent away,' said the high bishop. 'No one must know you were here.'

'Two of my men will take him to Northumbria,' said Hercules. 'I have friends there who'll attend to him.'

Frith glanced at them sourly.

'We need an event to occur that will distract the Mercian people while we find this new contender,' said Swift. 'Archbishop, can you work a miracle?'

Three days later, Swift and Burgred walked into King Burrt's hall. They found the king on his throne, coughing even more vigorously, his chancellor fussing nervously over him and emptying the pile of bloodied linen from the silver bucket.

'Greetings, noble king. You look distressed,' Swift said.

'Why wouldn't I? The marriage plans have collapsed, my son has fled, Wynstan's supporters will declare war on us, Mercia will be torn to shreds—'

'I think not, your Grace. The High Bishop of Mercia and I have come to an arrangement on your behalf. It will involve you in far more expense than you would wish but will guarantee a peaceful kingdom.'

Burrt sat up sharply and flung his stained cloth to one side. 'Were you to arrange such an outcome, you'd earn my undying gratitude, regardless of the sum. What is your plan?'

'Wynstan will become a saint.'

'A what?'

'The high bishop will tell the Mercian people that he was a holy man, so devout that the Lord God Almighty yearned for his company prematurely. Two days past, several senior members of the clergy saw Archangel Michael descend on Repton Abbey and carry Wynstan off to heaven. He will from henceforth be the patron saint of all Mercians, regardless of faction, and tens of thousands will be encouraged to make the journey of pilgrimage to a new cathedral built in his name.'

'Paid for by me?'

'Indeed. You will abdicate and live out the rest of your life in honourable retirement, if that is agreeable?'

'It would be – I'm as sick as a poisoned pigeon – but the problem of an heir remains. My son was feckless, and in some ways I'm glad to see the back of him, but at least he was a viable candidate.'

'Suppose there was someone far more suitable, a man whom all the nation respected, someone brave and heroic . . .'

'That would be perfect,' replied the king. 'But who would that someone be?'

'A candidate springs to mind,' said Chancellor Gareth, who wore the look of a man who knew on which side of the bread he'd find the lard.

'May I have a word with Burgred?' asked Swift. 'We will be brief.' She led her cousin to an anteroom and slammed him against the wall. 'You must make up your mind very quickly,' she said. 'Do you want to be King of Mercia?'

'Me?' replied Burgred. 'But I have no royal blood.'

'Yes you do,' replied Swift firmly.

'I'm merely Burrt's nephew by his brother's second wife. A dozen members of my family are more eligible than I.'

'They are not here. You are,' said Swift. 'Do you wish to be king?'

'Yes, I suppose . . .'

'And would you be content for me to be your queen?'

'Content? I'd always hoped . . . but I've felt so little love from you.'

'The amount of love is less important than the speed of our actions. Would such an arrangement be to your liking?'

'It would.'

'You must be sure.'

'I am.'

'Then I'll make it happen.'

Burgred leant forward and kissed her, but Swift scarcely felt the touch of his lips. She was thinking about what she might do next. She now had the entire Mercian army at her disposal. She'd given Father Asser short shrift when he'd come begging for soldiers, and the Britons she'd suggested had not turned out well. Should she send a detachment from Chepstow to help Wessex in its hour of need? It would cost her little and might smooth the path for her return. It could prove a shrewd move.

SEVENTY-ONE

Constant Titbits

A rider had arrived from Frankia, and Balotelli was scrutinising the scrolls in his copious leather bag. He took one out, glanced at the seal and opened it.

'I wish my carrying pigeons had not proved so sickly,' he said. 'This has taken seven weeks to arrive.'

Alfred was working beside the cardinal at his table in the palazzo, correcting the third draft of his latest work, *The Philistines Rise Once More.*

'It's from your friend Father Asser,' the cardinal continued.

'I have no friends of that name,' replied Alfred. 'There is a self-opinionated and manipulative papal legate called Father Asser, but I barely know him or care to.'

'Read this,' said Balotelli, and passed him the scroll.

Your Eminence, the concord is dead and cannot be resurrected, there is no purpose in believing otherwise. Emperor Charles has lost all interest in it and High Aethelwolf believes his need better served by marrying the emperor's precocious and wilful daughter. This may appear foolish, but perhaps his native instincts will stand him in good stead. He'll no longer have cause to host Charles's army on his soil, and won't be obliged to come to the emperor's aid in some faraway part of Europe if summoned to do so. If Charles does eventually furnish him with the weapons he requires, he may well find the means to keep the Norlanders at bay for a few more fighting seasons and be able to rule a pacified Wessex unfettered by European interests.

However, though the concord is no more, I am attempting to keep its spirit alive. Aethelwolf has asked me to raise an army for him from among his neighbours, and this I intend to do on the proviso that he enters into discussions with me about creating a more equitable Wessex. I will shortly be proposing to him the introduction into his country of a team of Roman priests to reform the Westsaxon church and begin alleviating sickness and poverty among the common people, a vision you have advocated for so long.

Despite recent setbacks, we should not be disheartened. I am ably supported by Father Plegmond, who is doing commendable work at Winchester Minster and seems destined for advancement. He sends his greetings, as do I.

'Asser appears to have done well,' the cardinal said. 'What do you think?'

'I'm flattered you should ask my opinion,' replied Alfred.

'That's not an answer.'

'I think he should return,' said Alfred. 'Plegmond seems well suited to continuing Asser's work in Wessex.'

'But you don't like him,' said the cardinal. 'You think him wily and devious.'

'Is that important? Aren't his talents what we need? Ponti's thugs patrol the streets, and he is exerting ever more influence among the Notarii. The Holy Father is rudderless, Ponti is playing on his fears, and you are weighed down by the Pope's constant vacillation.'

The cardinal nodded thoughtfully. 'Yes. Asser's acumen and energy, my experience, and your ability to glean information from Ponti . . . We'd be quite formidable together. I'll call him back.'

That evening, Alfred and Kennet walked down to the Tiber, as they did every Friday, to eat fresh grayling. Alfred had grown fond of the rotund, red-faced priest in the few months he'd been working for Balotelli. He knew that Kennet had been Father Asser's closest friend when they were boys at the Emmaus, but he possessed a kindness that Asser couldn't match. They both wanted a better world, but Kennet had a special way of understanding people's problems and uplifting them with kind words and deeds. Alfred thought if Kennet found a man lying unconscious in the road, he'd take him home and tend to him as the heretical Good Samaritan had done in the Bible. Whereas Asser would raise his hands in horror, march to the authorities and demand better security on the streets.

Kennet was good company as always. They chose the fish they wanted, and were given long, thin sticks to cook them on an open brazier. They shared a pot of red wine and toasted Asser's potential return.

'Mirandolina,' said Alfred as he sucked the meat from his fish bone. 'Do you remember her? She was in Modena when you went there to bring Wolf to Rome.'

'That's a name I never thought I'd hear again,' replied Kennet. 'A lovely girl. When Asser returned with Lady Osburgh and left me in charge, Mirandolina fed me constant titbits of information she'd procured from Wolf and his advisers.'

'How in the name of Christ's charity did she obtain such intelligence? She was a puppeteer.'

'How do you garner your information about Ponti, Alfred? You have freedom to roam, and so did she. She was Wolf's paramour and wandered from one room to the next as free as a bird searching for Christmas berries. Asser paid her, of course, but she was a great help.'

Alfred tossed the bone into the fire. 'They're accusing her of being an Antonil,' he said.

Kennet laughed. 'That's absurd. She's a good Christian girl with a wicked smile, that is all. But what if she *was* an Antonil? Would that concern us overmuch? They're not all dissolutes like Petr.'

'They have shocking views on the nature of Christ's body,' said Alfred a little primly.

Kennet's laughter redoubled. 'Shocking? Did the disciples concern themselves about the nature of his body? I'm sure Mary of Magdala didn't. Christ came to earth, he saved our souls, and he'll reward the faithful at the Second Coming. Until then, our Christian duty is to feed the poor and tend the sick. Amen!' He tossed a copper coin to a little boy, who ran off and refilled their mugs.

'Mirandolina is in grave trouble,' said Alfred. 'Ponti's brutes are hunting for her, and their number grows by the day.'

'Tell me where she is and I'll find a solution. She's a fine woman and we had many a tipple together. I know a hiding hole that not even a truffling hound could find. Leave it to me and keep out of harm's way,' said Father Kennet.

'I can't ask you to protect her. Why should you take the risk?'

Kennet, always so light-hearted and affable, put his hands on Alfred's shoulders and stared at him long and hard. 'My life is a grain of sand,' he said, 'but you are chosen. God has a task for you, the cardinal has made that very clear to us, even if you can't yet see it. Leave thugs, heretics and beautiful women well alone. Not only for your own sake, but for the sake of Wessex and Christ's church on earth.'

SEVENTY-TWO

How Strange

When the first refugees arrived on St Michael's Slope, they stared straight ahead and said nothing. No one knew where they'd come from. They had few possessions; some had hideous burns, others bore deep wounds from swords and axes. There were lone children blank and sallow; a few were dead but still being carried by their distraught mothers.

Gradually their story emerged. They were seeking shelter with Wolf's army because the Norlanders were wreaking havoc along the coast. They'd sailed into Langstone Harbour, set fire to Havant, Cosham, Farlington and Portsea. The Little Ham was in ruins, the East Bourne deserted. No one had seen where they'd come from or where they went, but they'd doubtless return.

Wolf's training field was soon full to overflowing, not only with folk who'd been attacked, but also with those terrified they'd be the next to be put to the sword. He rode off to see the ruined towns and villages for himself, while Asser stayed and attended to the newcomers. Everyone now knew he was the

Pope's representative and treated him with respect and a little awe. When he instructed the soldiers to dig a line of privies, they did so; when he asked the local farmers for straw to make bedding, they obliged. The nearby churches gave him money to buy food; he called for monks and they came, for nuns, who arrived with bandages and nostrums. Since he'd started working for Balotelli, he'd attended countless meetings and made endless journeys. Today a few people felt a little safer because of him. If it hadn't been for Wolf's confession playing on his mind, he would have been content.

At nightfall, the high aethel returned, his face as bitter as gall. 'Our people were raped, pillaged and murdered three leagues from here while we were playing soldiers,' he said. 'We should have deployed scouts to watch out for the bastards. Why didn't we? We should have completed the line of warning beacons long ago, but we didn't.'

'You have scouts out now.'

'Indeed I do. And when the Norland ships appear, we'll tear them apart.'

'Have patience,' said Asser. 'Wait till Aethelhawk's men arrive.'

Wolf shot him a bitter look. 'If they do,' he mumbled.

Asser heard Mountjoy before he saw him. Since first light he'd been listening out for approaching horses.

'Hawk's men are on their way,' Mountjoy shouted triumphantly as he rode through the camp.

'How many?' Asser demanded, climbing out of his little tent. 'And how soon?'

'Five-and-seventy foot soldiers and ten horsemen,' replied Mountjoy.

'Five-and-seventy, the cheapskate!' replied Asser. 'Still, it's better than nothing.'

'It practically doubles our forces,' said Mountjoy. He swung off his horse and began loosening her saddle. 'When I left them, they were a league out of Horsham. They'll be here in three or four days.'

'Let's pray we can wait that long,' said Asser.

Wolf was demonstrating various thrusts and parries on the training field. His men were repeating them to the beat of a drum, and Rollo and Mountjoy walked up and down the lines correcting arm movements and body posture. It was two days later, and his little army was fast improving. Word had spread through the shires that the high aethel was building a serious fighting force, and more men were coming to join them.

'Why weren't you here earlier, you feckless scum?' Wolf yelled.

'Been sorting out the pigs, High Aethel.'

'I've had a bad leg, High Aethel.'

'Only just heard about it, High Aethel.'

And Wolf would shout, 'Sharpen a stick and prepare to sweat.'

He was showing off his legendary downward cut when Stub approached and whispered in his ear. It was the news Wolf had both dreaded and welcomed.

'Jesus Christ! Take over, Stub,' he said. 'I will talk to Father Asser.'

Stub drew his sword and demonstrated the cut once more. 'Again, lads,' he shouted to the men. 'This time faster,' and the drumbeat quickened.

Wolf found Asser tending to the leg of a young child.

'Our scouts have spotted Norland ships off the Solent. They're a few hours away, sailing along the coast towards Southamwic,' he said, his eyes shining with excitement. 'Only two and a storage vessel, sixty maybe seventy men. We can handle seventy without Hawk's men; we've a hundred here. We can't let them take Southamwic.'

'I doubt it's the port they're interested in,' said Asser. 'How far upstream is Southamwic Abbey?'

'Half a league or so, perhaps a little more.'

'That'll be their destination.'

'Christ, they'll find rich pickings there. The local merchants pour gold into it to save their grubby little souls from hell. It's the richest abbey in South Hamwicshire. It would be a disaster if the Norlanders got their hands on it.'

'Indeed,' said Asser. 'A second Lindisfarne, a sign to all Christendom that we can't defend ourselves even when our finest treasures are at stake. We must stop them for sure. We can be at Southamwic by noon. We must requisition all the boats in the port and anchor them across the River Itchen where it begins to narrow. It's what the Franks did to protect Paris when the Norlanders rowed up the Seine. Our archers can fire on them from the banks and from the boats, and if necessary we can torch them.'

Wolf waved at him dismissively, as though brushing aside a troublesome moth. 'You have no understanding of warfare, priest,' he said. 'I won't indulge in Frankish tactics. We're not going to keep them out, we'll lure them in.'

'I care not whose tactics you adopt, High Aethel,' replied Asser. 'You are the general, not I. But we must move fast.'

'Your job is to pray for bold hearts and good weather,' said Wolf. 'The Pope blessed me and told me I'd be a legendary leader of my people, and I'm about to make that a reality.'

The Pope mistook you for the King of Sardinia, thought Asser. Let's hope the blessing is transferable.

The path that led from the river beach to the abbey was a mere two hundred paces through a wooded dene that offered perfect cover for an ambush. Wolf's men were hidden in the trees. Asser slid down the slope to where Wolf was tucked away.

'What are you doing here?' the high aethel demanded. 'You're supposed to be praying.'

'I've come to offer you God's forgiveness,' Asser said softly, 'and to give you the rest of the powder.'

He rummaged in his habit, produced the piece of cloth and tipped the contents onto the palm of his hand. It was damp, and the powder clung together like a small red slug. He teased it apart and chopped it with his fingernail.

'This is the last. It's a little moist and lumpy,' he said. 'Are you sure you want it?'

'Of course I do,' replied Wolf irritably, and snatched the proffered stem.

'Hush,' hissed Asser. The Norlanders could be upon them any moment.

'Yes, all right,' replied Wolf. He inhaled the elixir and shook his head vigorously. 'Not very pleasant,' he murmured.

'I've written to Rome for more,' said Asser.

'So I'm forgiven, am I?'

However deep Asser's fury, this was not the time for retribution.

'If you truly confess, Christ will forgive you,' he whispered. 'But you must tell me who did the deed.'

'What deed?'

'Who poisoned Osburgh?'

Stub crawled up to them. 'The fighting ships are pulling in. The big one's anchored offshore,' he said softly. 'They'll be here any moment.'

Wolf looked over his shoulder and signalled his men to be at the ready, then turned back to Asser. 'I'll tell you tonight,' he said.

*

The Norlanders made their way up the path, casting their eyes about for signs of movement.

Wolf relished such moments. He didn't shake or twitch. He breathed slowly and deeply, without apprehension. He and the stillness were one.

He felt a tickling sensation in his left nostril, and sneezed; only a tiny sneeze, but in the silence of the dene, it echoed and re-echoed like the note a choirmaster sang before his boys began a psalm. He sneezed again, and a third time.

The Norlanders' hands moved to their sword hilts.

Wolf knew he'd revealed their position, but it didn't matter. His opponents were trapped, he had more men than they did and he was holding the high ground. It would be a bloody battle, but he would be victorious. He gave the peewit call, and there was the sound of a hundred Saxon swords being drawn from their scabbards. Now the fight would begin.

Except the Norlanders didn't stay their ground. A giant of a man bawled an order, and they ran. All of them. Wolf could hardly believe it, a whole army fleeing like foxes before the hunt, tripping, stumbling, bumping into one another. He put his fingers between his lips once more and gave the call to charge. Then he set off down the hill, and with a roar, his soldiers followed him.

Wolf arrived at the beach first, his men racing behind him. The enemy were pushing their ships into the river and clambering onboard. What cowards, he thought, slipping away like children stealing from an orchard. How had such faint-hearts terrorised the whole of Europe?

Only one Norlander, the giant, was still on the strand. He was strangely familiar, and he smiled warmly, as though he'd been waiting for Wolf for a long time.

Wolf stopped. He knew he wasn't the man he had been in

his heyday, but the courage and energy of old coursed through him. Was it the powder that made him feel fearless? No, it was the Pope's blessing, his love for his country and the confidence he had in his own skill. He'd faced foes with drawn swords a hundred times and had never once been beaten. In the two steps before they came together, he swung his weapon as he always did and made his long-famous sweeping cut.

He heard a gasp, and waited for the man to fall to the ground. But he didn't. The giant stepped back and grinned. The gasp had been his own.

He was aware of an odd sensation: a warmth, not unpleasant, deep in his gut, and a heaviness as in the moments before sleep. He looked down. The giant's sword was buried in his stomach, so deep only its hilt was visible.

How strange, Wolf thought, as he fell to his knees. There was someone he wished was by his side, a young man, but he couldn't remember who it was.

SEVENTY-THREE

Sea Cat

Rhiannon peered into the choppy water, watching the shoals of tiny fish. She dipped her hand in and tried to catch one, but it swam off. She wondered what it would be like to be able to swim. Maybe one day Astrid would teach her.

She and the shield women had been left on *Sea Cat* while the men went off raiding. There was so much loot on board from the forays of the last few days that they had to stack it up to make room for the next load. She hated the gold crosses – their edges cut her arms and legs – and the carvings of the saints were heavy and hard to lift. She liked the holy books best; they were easy to hold and fitted snugly on top of each other. The slaves were dozing, lashed tight to their oars. She woke them and tried to talk to them, but they spoke in tongues she couldn't understand. She found some dried meat in a hatch, tore it up and put the pieces in their mouths. They wolfed them down so fiercely they almost bit off her fingers, and the other women laughed. She ruffled the hair of one of them, and wiggled his nose, and there was nothing he could do about it because his hands were bound.

There was a roar from somewhere among the trees. The men were running back, but they had no booty. Something was amiss. They pushed their ships out into the river, and an army of Saxons waded into the water behind them in wild pursuit. The women began heaving up *Cat*'s anchor, and she joined them, her heart pounding.

Only the giant remained on the beach, a Saxon standing in front of him, his sword raised. Rhiannon shouted out. The fear and loathing she'd felt for the Norlander had evaporated. He was Guthrum, their leader. If he was killed, what would they do? But he ran the man through like a stuffed doll. Guthrum was Odin's servant, and the Saxon had been nothing but an old fool in a wolf's hat.

More Saxons surrounded him, but Guthrum wrested an axe from one of them and whirled it round his head, hacking his way down to the shore and through the fighting crowd into the water. He tried to pull himself aboard *Cat* with his sound hand, but the current was too strong and it dragged him down. The women attempted to help him up, but he was slippery and wet. A Saxon leapt on his back and wrapped his fingers round his throat. Guthrum tried to shrug him off, but he couldn't use his fighting hand for fear of tumbling back into the water. The man drew a seax from his belt and raised it high. With a cry, Rhiannon took her knife, jumped on him and stabbed him again and again in the neck and shoulders. He let go of Guthrum and fell backwards, pulling her in with him. The water was so cold, she thought her heart would stop beating, but she kept plunging her knife into the Saxon's thrashing body until he was still and began to sink.

She was swept out into the river, surrounded by bobbing bodies. She tried to grab hold of one of them, but it sank under her weight. The current caught her, smacked her into the side of *Sea Cat*, and she was dragged under. She cried out to the

White Goddess, but the water choked her cry. She was going to die. She'd see her mother again, her sisters, the great lake, the dark green forests.

A hand grabbed her, lifted her into the air and dumped her on board, coughing and vomiting water. When she could breathe again, she opened her eyes to see who had come to her rescue. The giant Guthrum nodded, then turned away.

On the way back, there was bitterness. Men cursed and kicked the sides of the boat in frustration. It was many years since they'd left a raiding site empty-handed, and they'd lost five men. Guthrum stepped to the bucking prow, steadied himself with his strong hand and berated them. 'Are your minds askew?' he said. 'Have you been seized by a fever? Look around at our riches. Two full shiploads of gold are already on their way back north, and there's more than double that amount packed away on the island. This is our most successful campaign for twenty years. Yes, we lost men today, and I grieve for that, but far more would have died had you not conducted your retreat with such skill. And what was the outcome? Was it all for nothing? Should we be whining like babies? No, we killed the high aethel of the Westsaxons. You will be remembered for that for ever. I salute you! Now drink deep, sleep well and thank Odin for our triumph.'

The Norlanders said nothing, but later, when they landed at Shankalin beach, they leapt ashore with whoops and victory shouts and threw a pig on the fire.

The celebrations had almost come to an end. The sun would rise soon. Only a few fighters were left on the beach, sitting round softly singing 'The Song of the Seal Islands'. Astrid took Rhiannon's hand. 'You did well,' she said. 'You fought fearlessly; it will not go unnoticed.' She raised the girl's arm in triumph with one hand and tickled her ribs with the other. 'You're a proper Norlander now,' she said, and Rhiannon felt her cheeks glow with pride.

She led Rhiannon to her tent, laid her down, and kissed her mouth softly. Rhiannon lay back as though she was on summer grass.

'I was like you, when I was young,' Astrid said. 'Perhaps that's why you stir me. I was a slave too.' She pulled the fur cover over them and Rhiannon nestled into the curve of her neck. 'I was strong, and men called me pretty and wanted my body, even Guthrum. He was handsome then. I gave myself to him, but Haakun Haakunson would not let me be and fled with me to the mainland. For many years I worked hard as I had to, and played with his cock as I had to, and when I came to womanhood, he told me he loved me and would set me free.'

'What is free like?' asked Rhiannon. She thought of being free often, but it was hard to comprehend it.

Astrid roared with laughter. 'It was like nothing. He married me. I was his slave still.'

'Is he here?' Rhiannon asked. 'Shall I stab him like I stabbed the Saxon man?'

Astrid laughed again. 'No, he's dead already. But his killer is here. He saved your life today.'

SEVENTY-FOUR

Locked Down

Asser stumbled into the refectory at Southamwic Abbey calling for help. The monks had been so busy devouring their eel and bean stew that they'd heard nothing of the skirmish taking place little more than a hundred paces away, but when they were told their high aethel was dead, they tolled the doleful bell and a few of them cried.

Wolf's men carried his battered body into the room. They swept the platters and beakers from the refectory table and laid him gently down. The monks sang hymns for the dead, and three hospitallers cut the fighting gear from his body, washed him with rosemary-scented oils, combed his tangled grey beard and trimmed his hair.

His fierce frown had vanished in death, the lines around his eyes had softened. He was a tyrant and a murderer, thought Asser, but now his face revealed a tenderness he'd seldom shown in life. This was the man Osburgh had fallen in love with, and he could see why.

The battle had been fought in the time it took to milk a cow.

Apart from Wolf, the Westsaxons had lost only four men out of a hundred; it would have been a triumph had it not been such a tragedy. They collected the discarded weapons from the sand, burnt the Norland bodies and camped by the river in case of further attacks. Rollo requisitioned a donkey cart, and Asser and a small party of guards loaded up Wolf's body and accompanied it on the twelve-mile journey to Winchester.

When they arrived, the city gate was locked and bolted.

'We can't stand shivering outside the walls all night with the high aethel's body in a cart,' said Mountjoy.

'I've knocked twenty times,' said Rollo.

'For Jesu's sake,' exclaimed Mountjoy. He drew his sword and hammered on the metal hinges with its hilt like a frenzied blacksmith.

Eventually the gate opened a crack. 'No one's allowed in or out of the city,' a voice said firmly.

'You might want to make an exception,' said Asser. 'We've got the high aethel here, and he needs burying!'

The squeaky cart was escorted through the streets. There were no burning candles in the windows; all was quiet save for the occasional barking dog or crying baby. There was a burst of shouting on the far side of town that made them start, but it lasted only a few moments before silence fell again.

They were accompanied by a town guardsman Asser vaguely knew, a curly-haired ginger youth with a face pitted with pocks. He didn't know the man's name, but they'd drunk together a few times.

'What's going on?' asked Asser. 'The place is as empty as a plague town.'

'All hell broke loose when news of Wolf's death reached us. Everybody and his uncle wants to be the next high aethel. The aldermen began yelling at each other, fights broke out and an order was issued to lock the town down.'

'That was a bold move. Who gave the command? Godwin?'

The soldier laughed. 'Not he. Godwin was the worst offender. He hectored the drinkers in the alehouses and marched round the town with a bunch of stick-wielding cattlemen claiming the rule of the House of Wolf was over and he was the candidate of unity. It was the bishop who gave the order, or at least his Roman priest, Plegmond, announced it.'

They turned a corner. A line of town guards was walking slowly up the street with swords drawn. A small crowd was shouting at them, throwing stones while backing away at the same time. One foolhardy soul raced forward and flung a torch before attempting to run back to the shelter of his comrades. He was sought out, grabbed and beaten to the ground.

'We'll get you off the streets as quickly as possible,' said the ginger-haired guard. 'We only have a limited number of men, and mayhem could break out at any moment.'

Asser called to Mountjoy, who was following a few paces behind.

'Ride back to the beach,' he said. 'Tell the captains the legate needs every horseman back here before morning.'

No one had granted Asser the authority to give orders to Wolf's forces, but nor was anyone likely to challenge him. He'd once ridden in a hunt and had been caught up among the other horsemen at breakneck speed. He'd managed to get to the front and stayed there because it seemed safer that way. That was how he felt now.

They arrived at the minster church. The cart was wheeled into a chapel and Asser was ushered into the presence of Bishop Humbert, who was sitting at a great table with Plegmond by his side. Town guards and priests were leaning against the walls, drinking broth and talking in low voices.

The bishop glanced up. He was still a wreck of a man, but looked considerably better than he had done. 'Father Asser!' he said. 'I'm glad you're here.'

Plegmond clapped his hands. 'Out, please!' he ordered. 'All out.'

In moments the minster was empty. The bishop, Plegmond and Asser were left alone in the vast nave.

Humbert gestured to Asser to sit.

'The high aethel is dead, the town's locked down, what do we do now?' said Asser.

'Keep the peace and pray . . . It's all we can do,' replied the bishop.

He was less slurred than Asser remembered, but spoke slowly, choosing every word with care.

'The rioting is bound to continue till the question of the accession is resolved,' said Plegmond, scratching his head as he so often did.

'It's worse than that,' said Asser. 'If the Norlanders discover we're divided, they'll pounce on us like wolves in a famine.'

He sprang to his feet. He always thought best when he was pacing about. 'When a high aethel dies, a consensus is arrived at and a new one is installed, which is fair but takes an age. Aldermen come from far and wide, they make tedious speeches, interminable votes are conducted. We can't afford such a rigmarole, can we?'

'We cannot,' agreed Bishop Humbert.

'Particularly as so many aldermen, not least the odious Harold Godwin, are positioning themselves to take the throne,' added Plegmond.

'Very well,' said Asser. 'The bishop will announce that this is an emergency and dangerous times require strong action. Only aldermen currently in Winchester will be allowed to cast their vote, only one candidate will be nominated, and any alderman who has shown interest in being high aethel will be put into protective custody until the voting is over. In addition, if there are any noisy expressions of disapproval on the streets, the army will be back before dawn and will put a stop to them. Are you both happy with this?'

Humbert thought for a moment.

'Who will be our candidate?' he said finally.

'Who indeed?' said Asser. 'If he were here, I suspect we'd all cry out the name Alfred.'

'But he is not,' replied Plegmond, 'and he doesn't want to come. And even if we bound and gagged him, it would take months to get him here.'

'If the succession is to be implemented without fuss . . . the new high aethel must be . . . a son of the house of Wolf,' said the bishop. 'So which one should it be?'

The men looked at each other. The choice was as inspiring as a scrawl on a wall. Eventually Asser spoke. 'Bear,' he said reluctantly.

'Bear,' said the bishop, his frustration evident. 'He's a . . . brainless . . . braggard.' He coughed and gasped for air, and they ceased their deliberations while Plegmond gave him a little water.

When he had recovered, Asser continued. 'Bear has an army that can either fight for us because he's high aethel or against us because he isn't. Who else, in your wisdom, would you choose? The deranged Hawk, sailor-boy Red, Swift the traitor?'

Plegmond and Humbert said nothing.

'Very well,' continued Asser. 'We'll send our fastest riders to Devon with a message of congratulations to High Aethelbear. Meanwhile, I will bury the old man.'

'We have nothing to put him in,' Asser said. 'Wolf was one of the great figures of his age. He can't go to his maker in a plain wooden box.'

It was late the same night. He was standing in front of the high altar at the minster with Rollo and Mountjoy. There was the sound of rhythmic chipping as a young mason repaired a damaged stone angel on the altarpiece by candlelight. Apart from him, they were alone save for two bodies: the high aethel and, lying next to him, Hilderic the merchant, who was to be buried on the morrow in a fine carved stone sarcophagus that he'd commissioned the previous year when his stomach pangs had become intense.

Mountjoy looked at Hilderic thoughtfully.

'We could set him aside and put Wolf in instead,' he suggested.

'Don't be absurd. Look at the carving on the lid,' replied Asser. 'Its head is round and beardless, with two chins. He's nothing like the high aethel.' His gaze fell on the young mason. 'You there,' he called.

The man turned, surprised.

'Can you leave what you're doing and reshape this face for me?'

The mason approached and surveyed the coffin. 'What do you want him to look like?'

Asser nodded towards Wolf's body, surrounded by candles. 'Like him,' he replied.

The lad stared at the high aethel. 'When do you need it done?'

'By the morning.'

'The beard and long hair won't be easy,' he said, 'and I'll have to work through the night. It'll cost you.'

'Of course,' said Asser.

The lad shrugged, and without further fuss began cutting into Hilderic's stone face with his mallet and chisel.

At some point Rollo and Mountjoy slipped away to bed. Asser had a thousand tasks to perform, but he was enthralled by the chopping and chivvying and the way the mason constantly changed the tools in his belt to make the different cuts. By the early hours, he had finished. Asser handed over the money willingly.

'You're a true craftsman, my lad,' he said. 'The first I've seen since I landed in Wessex.'

Asser oversaw the service. It was brief – there'd be a grand memorial at some future time to which nobles from far and wide would be invited. Judith and her maids were there, a handful of Wolf's senior officers, the keeper of his wardrobe, the trainer of his horses.

When the ceremony was over, Asser took Judith and her new puppy for a walk round the minster green. She'd been overlooked in the chaos of the last few days, so he'd bought her a dog for company. He didn't know if she wanted one, but both girl and puppy seemed happy enough. The little pet trotted along by her side; her Frisian maids walked in a line behind her like well-fed ducklings.

'I'm calling him Wolfie in memory of my late husband,' she said, and bent down and kissed the dog loudly and profusely.

'You must prepare to return to your father so he can decide on your future,' Asser said.

'I cannot become his child again,' she replied firmly. 'That part of my life came to an end when I was crowned queen.' They walked in silence, watching a pair of seagulls mobbing a buzzard. 'Now my husband has died, what will happen to the promise my father made to give him weapons?' she asked eventually.

'I imagine it will come to an end,' said Asser.

'That wouldn't be in Wessex's best interests,' she said. 'Perhaps I should continue to be queen.'

'That could only happen if . . .' he began. Did she understand what she was saying?

'Yes! I would like that,' she said firmly, as though choosing a pudding. 'I believe it is common practice among women in my position to assume a similar role with the new king to the one they occupied with the previous one.'

The dog had stopped to sniff a discoloured patch of grass. 'Stop dawdling, Wolfie,' she snapped, and yanked its lead.

'Sweet girl! You have only recently celebrated your thirteenth birthday,' Asser exclaimed. 'You'd have to marry Bear. Are you sure you have weighed the consequences?'

She stopped for a moment and stared at him haughtily. 'I am the great-granddaughter of the Emperor Charlemagne,' she said. 'I always weigh the consequences.'

Seven days later, Bear entered Winchester drunk and triumphant. He rode his horse through the doors of the hastily refurbished moot house and was greeted with a thunderous ovation. He pushed his way through the benches, hugging and kissing the aldermen, lingering on those who'd been forced to sacrifice their ambitions.

Hawk, who'd ridden down from Dagen's Ham far too late to attempt to seize the throne for himself, remained silent. The bishop had given him the shire of Dorset and the entire coastal lands of Sussex in return for his acquiescence, and Asser had presented him with a formal scroll signed by every alderman stating that he would be the next high aethel on Bear's demise. He was hopeful it would be enough to appease him, at least for now.

Godwin was the most fulsome in his greeting, and seemed resigned to the fact that he'd never be high aethel. To punish him for his hubris Humbert had taken the Wardenship of the Sussex Coast from him and demanded he make a large donation to the minster roof fund, but he'd let him keep his old title of chief alderman. Godwin had reluctantly accepted this demotion and returned to his fawning ways. He stood on the little dais and formally addressed his fellow aldermen.

'Do you acknowledge Bear of Wessex as your new high aethel?' he said.

'We do!' they responded.

The crown was set firmly on Bear's head and the entire assembly followed him to the great hall. Musicians from all over Wessex sang of his greatness, a clown told riddles about his prowess in bed, and Judith, still dressed in mourning, sat next to him holding his hand and giggling. At midnight he was carried round the room on the shoulders of his soldiers with his crown askew, and when he leant down to plant wet kisses on the mouth of an alderman's wife, it fell off and rolled round on the ground like a dropped penny.

Asser assisted the bishop on a quiet walk round the garden, the sound of flutes and drums ringing in their ears.

'I cannot ever remember feeling . . . so weary,' Humbert said.

'You did excellently,' Asser told him. 'Even in your sickness I believe you enjoyed the frenzy of the last few days.'

The bishop gave a modest lopsided smile. 'Such manoeuvrings . . . are new to me.'

'I doubt that,' replied Asser. It was sad. Humbert had done his best to hold the country together. Wessex was as much his creation as Aethelwolf's, but now his light was fading.

A rowdy rendition of 'The Cock and the Baker's Daughter' echoed round the garden.

'Let's slip away and sleep for a week,' said Asser.

The bishop nodded, and they began to leave, but an excited voice brought them to a halt. Stub strode towards them.

'Fresh soldiers have crossed the border from Mercia. Lady Swift has sent them,' he cried.

'What an extraordinary and unpredictable woman she is,' said Asser. 'So our journey was worthwhile after all. How many men has she given us?'

'A hundred.'

'Excellent! That makes us nigh on three hundred strong. Time to resharpen our swords, I think.'

SEVENTY-FIVE

The Wrath of Christ

Stub, shirtless and purposeful, pushed a wheeled barrow full of clay up a crude ramp into Winchester Great Hall and tipped it on the floor. He beat the knee-high pile with the flat of his shovel till it was as flat as a giant pancake, knelt down, picked up a handful of the stuff and rubbed it between his fingers.

'Too dry,' he said.

Two of his men were standing round the flattened pile, one with a bucket in his hand. Stub made a hole and the man dribbled water into it.

'Enough!' said Stub. He gave the mixture a stir, squatted by its side and began to mould the clay.

'What's that mess?' demanded Bear, who was on the hall steps watching two of his soldiers playing leapfrog.

'It will soon be a representation of the Isle of Wight, High Aethel,' replied Asser. He was sitting on the edge of the great table swinging his legs. 'See the undulations Stub's making? They're the hills and valleys.'

Stub stood up for a moment and wiped his hands on a rag. The clay was now in the rough shape of the island, with the long attenuation of Alum Bay running towards the Needles in the west, and St Catherine's Point to the south.

'I need to put in all the salient features. What should we include?' he asked.

'Headon Hill,' replied one of his men.

'Chombley Great Wood,' said the other.

They pressed twigs and stones into the clay to represent the woodlands and settlements, and Stub produced a pot of paint and painted the rivers and shoreline blue. Asser jumped off the table and inserted a small flag into a little mound. 'This is where we think the Norlanders are holding Red's son,' he said. 'And we're almost certain Lady Winifred is in her hall above Shankalin Bay,' he added, and put in another flag.

A voice interrupted their deliberations.

'I'm here! I've come! What may I do?'

Red was standing in the open doorway looking deeply anxious, with an unkempt beard, his clothes tattered, his face rimed with salt. 'I'm sorry I've been away for so long. I've had such an adventure,' he said. 'I've left *The Wrath of Christ* in Southamwic. I met Godwin on the road and he told me the sad news about Father and what the Norlanders have done to my Winni.'

'I am the new high aethel,' said Bear.

'Hoorah, brother,' replied Red. 'I congratulate you, but I'm very anxious about my wife and son and can think of little else.'

Stub wrapped his clay-daubed arms round the bedraggled sailor. 'Where have you been?' he asked. 'We were worried for you.'

'To Frankia,' replied Red. 'It was nothing, but we were caught in a storm off Brettony and foundered on the rocks. It's taken us two months to put *The Wrath* back together. She leaks like an old pipe, and we're constantly bailing her out, but we'll find a use for her. Please tell me how we're going to get Winni back.'

'Welcome home, Aethelred,' said Asser. 'I am Father Asser, the Pope's legate, and I am deeply sorry for your distress. We are planning to attack the island as soon as your sister's troops arrive from Mercia. We are mightily glad to have you with us. You've been away too long.'

News came that Swift's Mercians had reached Abbots Worthy, and Asser rode out with Plegmond at his side to join them for the last few leagues of their march.

'It's a fine day. I'm glad of your company,' said Asser.

'Father, I must confess I wanted to speak to you alone,' said Plegmond. 'I am the bearer of distressing news. Aethelhawk has taken his wife back to Dagen's Ham. She fought like one possessed, but her captors bound her hands and bundled her into a carriage.'

Asser winced. His betrayal of Moira weighed heavy on him. He could only pray that one day he could earn her forgiveness.

They pulled up at a wayside cottage, watered their horses and purchased mint cordial and a handful of sliced apple from an old woman who lived there. The smell of the apple rekindled memories of his Westsaxon childhood. For all its barbarity he was still fond of Wessex.

'I hardly see you now, Plegmond, you're so immersed in your work for Bishop Humbert,' he said. 'I'm sorry I saddled you with the tedium of a sick bishop, but it is in Rome's interest.'

'There is no need for apologies,' replied Plegmond. 'He's a shrewd old man. Even though he's been very sick, I've learnt a great deal from him.'

'And he admires you, I think.'

'Perhaps. But I'm frustrated that I can't do more for him.

The priests who surround him are jealous men and thwart me at every turn.'

'I can ease your burden,' said Asser. 'I've spoken to Humbert, and we've agreed you should be appointed Dean of Winchester.'

Plegmond looked astounded. 'But I'm far too young, Father,' he said. 'I've no experience. Surely there are others . . .'

'Since we first met, I've watched you closely,' said Asser. 'You are diligent, kind and loyal, you have a subtle understanding . . . and I like you.'

'You have said nothing like that to me before, ever,' replied Plegmond softly. 'I always thought you found me foolish!'

'Not at all,' replied Asser. 'Perhaps you should wipe your eyes. You don't want to appear distressed when we meet the Mercians.'

The captains of Asser's forces gathered round the newly completed model of the Isle of Wight. The Mercian captain stood a little way apart from the others, looking at it intently.

'This is a fine piece of work,' he said in his thick middle-land accent. 'It tells me all I need to know about the terrain. It's as though I'd walked the island myself.'

Stub remained silent, but Asser could see he was inordinately pleased with the compliment. Asser picked up a long, thin stick and addressed the assembled officers.

'If High Aethelbear will forgive me, I'll explain the plan,' he said.

'Explain what you like. It's all one to me,' said Bear, who was rummaging through a bowl of fruit on a side table.

'Thank you, High Aethel,' said Asser. 'Our intelligence tells us the Norlanders keep themselves to the south side of the island and don't occupy the interior at all. We will land here, here and here on the landward side,' he said, pointing at various rocks and inlets. 'We'll cross the heart of the island at night and hopefully will remain undetected till we arrive at Shankalin. Two smaller units will attack here and here.' Once more he pointed with his stick. 'They'll effect the rescue of Lady Winifred and her child and will be led by two of my men, Rollo and Mountjoy. When they were younger, they undertook many night-time missions against Rome's enemies. I trust them implicitly.'

'So you should,' said Rollo.

Asser gave him a nod of gratitude. This strategy had been entirely of the twins' making, but Asser, who'd never fought a battle in his life, was unveiling it with all the empty confidence of a cockalorum.

Bear stepped forward. 'This is all humbuggery,' he said. 'We're not going to waste our time stomping across the island in the dead of night. We will sail to Shankalin and I will challenge their leader to single combat. If I win, the Norlanders will leave; if I lose, you will hack them to pieces.'

Asser cringed at the dim-wittedness of this proposal, and by the looks on their faces, the various captains were similarly unimpressed. But how could they contradict a high aethel who only a few days earlier had been lauded as the greatest fighter in Wessex?

The following day, Bear received an urgent message informing him that his Exeter estates had been occupied by Cornish Britons. He set off without delay for the south-west with half his troops, leaving instructions that the attack should be delayed till his return.

'I congratulate you on your penmanship,' Rollo said to Asser. 'We may have lost some fighting men, but it will be well worth it to be rid of him. Our only problem now is persuading our disparate forces to act in concert.'

Rollo was right. Hawk's men and Bear's didn't speak a word

to each other, the Saxons struggled to understand the strangled vowels of the Mercians, and the men who had fought at Southamwic were contemptuous of everyone else because they'd only recently won a great victory. The only man among them who everyone accepted ungrudgingly was the Pope's legate. Asser seemed to have become the accidental figurehead of this fractious and uncoordinated fighting force.

Three nights later, two boats lay tucked into the shallows of Moorland Bay, five off Copley Head, four at the Great Shingle and thirteen in Southamwic water. They were not big craft – crabbers, dabbers, mussel pickers and river ferries – but each was full of armed men.

The sun sank over the horizon and they quietly set off. When they reached the Isle of Wight, Asser's men rowed up the Middle River past the West Cowe sandbank and moored at the Old Port quay, where they disembarked.

It wasn't easy in the darkness – there were bogs, and the grass was long and tangled – but they followed the route that Stub's model had shown them and eventually came to the woods above Shankalin Bay where the Norlanders were camped.

All was quiet, but Asser could see the shadows of many men already hiding among the trees, and more creeping up behind. Had all his troops arrived yet? He had no idea, but there were enough. He nodded to the Mercian captain, who gave a soft call, and his soldiers moved out onto the ridge overlooking the bay. The other forces did likewise, and stood waiting. But Bear's men had been drinking along the way, and three of them drew their swords and began running down the slope at full tilt. The moon appeared from behind a cloud and revealed to the drunk men that the rest of the army weren't with them. They turned back and emitted a series of mighty roars to encourage the others to charge. Asser gave a soundless scream of frustration.

The moonlight illuminated the scene in the Norland camp. Fighters were blundering out of their tents half-naked, pointing to the top of the hill and grabbing their apparel. A giant – was it the one who'd killed Wolf? Asser wondered – strode among them gesticulating and bellowing instructions. Some of them seized their weapons ready to fend off the attack, the rest ran to crude shanties that had been thrown up on the far side of the camp, pulled out basketfuls of loot and began dragging them through the sand to the boats.

There was no time for further delay. Asser's captains gave the order, and their men charged down the hill. Asser had no weapon; he was foolish to be among them, but the shouting of the soldiers was exhilarating. He ran along with them shouting too, his excitement growing to fever pitch as the first Saxons reached the camp.

Twenty or so Norland warriors had stayed forward to defend it and were fighting fiercely, but they were outnumbered by the charge and were forced ever closer to the shoreline. There were Norland fighting women too – how strange that was – and slaves, running to the sheds, forming a line, rescuing loot and passing it down to the ships.

Asser could see *The Wrath of Christ* out in the bay bearing down on them like an avenging angel. Halfway to the shore, her rowers dived into the water and swam to the safety of the nearby rocks. The few remaining crew ran from bow to stern dousing the decks with buckets of pitch. They lit torches from a brazier on the prow, threw them into the thick black liquid, then followed their crewmates overboard.

The vessel, now engulfed in flames, sped towards the beach. Only Red remained aboard, standing at the prow, his sword at the ready. His ship was sinking – she was half underwater by the time she reached the shallows – but she'd done what was required of her. A Norland vessel was trapped between her and the shore. Red leapt onto the Norland boat and set about the occupants with unrestrained fury, hacking his foes down like a woodsman chopping saplings.

The burning pitch spread across the water until the whole bay appeared to be alight. The sheer weight of Saxon and Mercian numbers had overwhelmed the camp's defenders; the tents were trampled underfoot, and almost all the survivors were in the sea, wading out to the remaining ships. Three of them began pulling away from the shore, but one sank under the weight of its load and the number of desperate men attempting to climb aboard.

Asser stumbled over a Norland fighter who was lying on the strand whimpering, a sword buried in his chest. When he saw the priest, he gestured frantically as though pleading with him to pull the weapon out. Asser put his foot on the man's body to gain purchase and heaved. The sword came free, the Norlander gave a terrible scream, then all was quiet.

Still clutching the weapon, Asser walked across the beach towards the uproar he'd set in motion, men fighting for their lives, grunting, shouting, bellowing in agony.

Two Norland women were lugging a large golden cross down towards the final boat. One was scarcely more than Judith's age, but it was the other who commanded his attention. She was a few years older than him, strong, determined, and oh! so familiar, even after all these years. He wasn't mistaken, was he? No, it was her.

'Anna?' he called.

She looked up.

'It is I, your brother Asser!'

She stared at him for a long time.

'Sister,' he cried, and held out his arms.

The younger girl ran at him, screeching like a harpy. He wished he could bring the fighting to a halt, to tell the warriors he'd found his sister and only wanted a few quiet moments with her, but he crashed to the ground, felled by the girl's flying kick, losing the sword in the process. He tried to curl into a ball to protect himself, but she pinned him down with one hand on his neck and her thumb in his throat. She raised the other arm in the air, and he saw the glint of a knife. He resigned himself to the inevitability of death.

'Leave him!' barked the woman he knew to be his sister. 'It's time to go.'

The harpy stood up reluctantly, kicked him in the face and ran off.

The two women waded to their ship, leaving the cross on the sand, and leapt on board. With blood cascading from his nose, Asser watched as it sailed after the other two vessels out of the bay.

Had Anna recognised him? He had no idea.

He looked about him, coughing violently. They had won. For a few moments his disparate armies had miraculously become one. His soldiers wandered through the camp eating discarded Norland victuals, breaking open flasks of Norland mead, slaughtering the Norland injured.

Two horsemen galloped across the beach towards him, yelling in triumph, their swords held high above their heads. Was it Rollo and Mountjoy? He couldn't be certain. His eyes were too full of tears.

SEVENTY-SIX

The Fresco

'We'd have got nowhere without the Mercians,' said Rollo.

'They fought bravely,' agreed Mountjoy.

It was true, thought Asser. He'd sent a letter to Lady Swift. *I thank you from the depths of my heart. Your men tipped the balance of the battle. Whatever you ask of me in future I will do my utmost to fulfil.* It was not a letter he would have felt able to send to any of the Westsaxon captains. Their men had been uncoordinated, unfit, and in the case of Bear's men had actively hindered the mission.

The three men were sitting outside a drinking shop in the middle of Winchester, celebrating their victory with innumerable beakers of dandelion mead. They'd driven the Norlanders out of Wessex, wrecked their boats and rescued Winifred and her child, but the faces of the local people were blank and lethargic.

'Wessex has been saved!' Rollo shouted to a passer-by who was walking along wheeling a quern stone, but the man shrugged his shoulders and went on his way.

'Wessex women can sleep safe in their beds tonight,' Mountjoy called to a nun pushing a vegetable cart, and she glared at him as though he'd made an indecent suggestion.

'The problem is no one cares about Wessex,' said Rollo. 'Saxons love their little piece of God's earth – Dover, Dartmoor, Sussex, Wiltonshire, they'll fight to the death for them – but Wessex is too big; it's a thousand places bolted together by Aethelwolf's insatiable hunger for more territory. No one wants to die for it. There'll be more Norlanders arriving in the spring and they'll have learnt lessons from this campaign. Next time, the Westsaxons will be undone.'

They sat around gloomily supping their mead for a while, then Asser lurched to his feet and said, 'Come with me. We'll imbue these people with such a sense of the wonder of Wessex that they'll soon love it like their own mothers.'

They strode up the street a little unsteadily, Asser waving his arms around as though defending his head from hornets.

'Wolf is dead and buried, but we'll hold a grand memorial service for him. It'll be the biggest, most ostentatious celebration Wessex has ever seen. Wessex! Wessex! Wessex! The name will be on everyone's lips. I'll even engage the Mendip Bard to write a new "Song of Wessex" for their children.'

The twins loved an excuse for jollity and were only too happy to assist Asser in the pursuit of his dream. They tottered along weaving fantasies of barrel-lifting competitions, pig racing, tables groaning with food set up on the streets, until Asser came to a halt in front of the minster – grey, soulless, as cheerful as the Angel of Death about to smite the firstborn of Egypt.

He sagged. 'My plan has crumbled to dust already,' he said, his voice a little slurred. 'The service will have to take place here, in the gloomiest shithole in Christendom. It lays the curse of misery on any who enter its portals. Let's go home!'

'Use your imagination, Father,' said Rollo. 'We'll transform it into another St Peter's. We'll burnish its pillars, polish its tiles and paint it as bright as a meadow full of flowers.'

'It's not a whorehouse,' said Asser. 'It'll have to look sanctified.'

'We can do that,' replied Rollo. 'Follow me.'

A little while later, they came to a nondescript little church squashed between a brickyard and a metal smith.

'Feast your eyes,' Rollo said, and they went in.

On a shadowy wall in a side chapel was a six-panelled fresco illustrating the story of Christ's birth: the ox, the ass, the shepherds and magi all gathered round a tiny, happy Christ child. The colours were vibrant and the characters so convincing they practically leapt from the wall.

'If I'd seen such a thing in Italia, I'd have thought it the work of a master,' whispered Asser. 'But here . . .'

'It's a fucking miracle,' agreed Rollo.

Word had gone round Harestock that the papal legate was due to arrive, and the entire village turned out, though they had to wait till noon for the three men, as they'd lain too long in bed.

They were there to see a family of masons. 'Though they also turn their hands to carving, carpentry, painting and the like,' explained Rollo. 'You know Chad, he's the one who remade Wolf's sarcophagus, but it's his brother Leof we're after.'

The local reeve gave a rambling speech of welcome, the local landowner an even longer one, and finally they were introduced to Leof and his mother. The lad was no more than twenty and mumbled so incoherently it was difficult to understand what he was saying, but he took them to a large cattle shed, followed by the entire village and its dignitaries.

The shed's interior walls had been roughly plastered and were covered in frescos and seccos: Moses crossing the Red Sea, the stoning of St Stephen, flowers entwined round the baby

Jesus. Broken eggshells, buckets of soot and ground stone lay on the floor, forcing them to tread carefully among the debris.

'Do you like his work?' said Rollo softly.

'None of it is bad,' replied Asser. 'Some is masterly. How much does he charge?'

Leof's mother consulted the mumbling boy. 'He only does them 'cos he's minded, not for coin. He's a stone cutter by trade.'

'God has given you a rare talent, Leof,' Asser said. 'I want you to create a fresco for High Aethelwolf's memorial. A large one, as big as this barn. I will pay you for your time, and I will pay you well.'

A shiver of excitement ran through the villagers.

'At the top of it will be God the Father looking down on his children, but with a face like Aethelwolf's; below it will be Noah in his Ark resembling Aethelred; Aethelhawk will be St Matthew the tax collector, and the Holy Virgin will look like Lady Swift. You will also leave an empty stool, very small, to subtly remind people of Aethelfraed. In the centre of all this will be our new High Aethelbear, like King Nebuchadnezzar, with the twisted bodies and severed limbs of a thousand Philistines at his feet, but in Norland garb of course. The entire fresco will be a song of praise to Wessex and the house of Wolf. Can you create such a thing?'

Leof mused for a while; a frown crossed his face and he mumbled again.

'Is there a problem?' Asser asked.

'He says the minster stonework is a mess. It will distract from his work. Will you pay his brothers to tidy up the stone?' asked Leof's mother.

'I'll pay your uncles and cousins too if they're as skilled as you. I want the minster as shining bright as the stairway to heaven,' said Asser. 'How much do you want?'

*

'I must look my best for Father's memorial,' said Hawk. 'Am I a little resentful that my brother is high aethel? Surprisingly not! I'm happier living with you here in Dagen's Ham, my love. I'm powerful and wealthy thanks to my financial acumen, and one day Bear will die and I'll succeed him – I have that in writing. I will attend as his equal, looking like a king and with a beautiful wife by my side. You will come, won't you?'

'No thank you,' replied Moira, who was sitting hunched in a chair on the far side of her hut in the grounds of the hall, dressed in the night attire she seldom took off these days and playing with her greasy, uncombed hair.

'Are you sure?' her husband said. 'Who knows, perhaps your friend Swift will be there . . . although I doubt it,' he added with a snigger.

'No thank you,' repeated Moira.

'You're disobeying your husband, aren't you, my love?'

'Probably,' said Moira.

'Very well,' said Hawk. 'It's your decision.' He stood up abruptly, locked the door behind him and crossed the compound to his hall.

'She's being contrary again,' he said to her chambermaid. 'Make her diet a little more austere. She may walk the lower field every other day for exercise, but if she tries to break free, tell Kretch to castigate her with a willow branch. I'll return within the month.'

Red rode to the memorial alone. He enjoyed his own company – it gave him time to think about his ships. He was still having trouble with the ingress of water, but he'd salvaged the wrecked Norland vessels and that had been useful. They were better made than his; he could copy their carpentry and the shape of their hulls.

He was glad he and his family were back in South

Hamwicshire, working Swift's estates. Winni thought the whole of Sussex should be theirs, but the bishop had given it to Hawk. Red didn't mind, as long as it was kept in the family, but it made Winni angry. Sometimes she kicked tables over and slapped the servants. 'It's your fault I've become like this,' she said to him. 'You left me alone with the Norlanders while you sailed off in your stupid boat, and now I'm in a rage.'

She was always in a rage nowadays. He kept out of her way as much as possible.

Bear was in Bath, discussing how much the town should give him towards the pacification of south Devon. Its aldermen had offered him an insulting amount; they were more concerned about the threat from the Norlanders. But when he and his men broke into the chief alderman's house and threw his furniture around, they'd come to their senses and given him what he'd wanted and a little more besides.

He and his companions celebrated by riding to an all-night dice game in Keynsham. Bear had thrown a one and a two and lost Stern, the samphire island he'd only recently had returned to him in his father's will. But what did it matter? He was high aethel, there were plenty more islands where Stern came from, and he didn't like samphire anyway.

He'd fallen asleep on the floor of the Dean of Keynsham's house with two pretty young servants. He'd intended to borrow the dean's boat that day so he could take them up the Avon, but the Dean had politely reminded him about his father's memorial, and that Bishop Humbert had threatened to excommunicate him if he wasn't there on time.

The service was a long time coming because they had to wait two days for Bear's arrival, but Asser was proud of how it unfolded.

For the entire morning, all the church bells in Wessex rang. Every monastery refectory gave slices of goose to the local people and peg-doll saints to the children. The rich distributed small coins to the poor, fishermen gave half their catch, brewers a few barrels of beer, all in memory of Aethelwolf and in celebration of Wessex.

In the minster, two hundred young throats sang the new 'Song of Wessex' while dancers with garlands passed among the congregation. If the bishop disapproved of the gaiety, he didn't show it. He officiated alongside Asser and looked confident and dignified, even though he needed assistance from Plegmond and struggled to stay upright. High Aethelbear looked regal if a little grey; Aethelhawk gave an oration in honour of his father, which was eloquent but included several disparaging riddles that some said were disrespectful.

The minster had been repainted and Leof's fresco towered over the congregation, vivid and inspiring: a great king surrounded by his siblings, standing triumphant with his legs apart on top of a pile of his enemies. This was the message Asser had wanted to convey: the Norlanders were not invincible; under Bear's leadership they had been defeated and would be again. He knew that on its own the fresco would have little effect – it would be forgotten tomorrow, subsumed under the trials and tribulations of the new day – but if the message was repeated often enough in every church, the Westsaxons' loyalty to Wessex and Aethelbear would blossom. Next year Bear would lead his confident and unified people to total victory.

Ten days later, Asser received a letter from Exeter. Bear was dead.

PART FIVE

SEVENTY-SEVEN

The Two Boys

King Burrt of Mercia relinquished his throne as promised. Burgred was crowned king, and he and Swift became husband and wife, but their wedding wasn't a grand affair; neither of them had the time nor taste for overblown demonstrations of royal power and instead devoted themselves to the task of governing their fractious domain, although they quickly discovered that bringing Mercia back to its former glory would not be easy. Ancient resentments lingered, decades-old disputes remained unresolved, the new cathedral was proving three times as costly as the high bishop had originally estimated, and simmering resentments along the Welsh border required Swift to patrol the dyke constantly while her husband shuttled between Tamworth and Repton mollifying angry courtiers and unpaid creditors. But however hard they tried to calm their subjects, the protests and incursions grew worse.

Swift heard rumours of trouble in eastern Mercia and rode there accompanied by Hercules to establish what they needed to do in order to stamp it out. They found nothing to concern them until they arrived at Henbery Abbey. As darkness fell, there was angry shouting in the town and the abbot told them in the firmest terms to stay in their rooms. Throughout the night the sky was illuminated by flames from burning huts and hayricks.

The following morning, they were asked to leave quickly and surreptitiously.

'Who are these disorderly people? Why are they so angry?' Swift asked, but the abbot mumbled a reply that told them nothing.

That night they lodged with a landowner in Shipston. Once again they were urged to stay hidden. Even so, Hercules slipped into the town under cover of darkness and reported back to her.

'Frith has resurfaced. There's a crowd a hundred strong chanting his name and demanding that he be their ruler.'

'What simpletons,' Swift replied. 'We'll go to Tamworth and return with a force large enough to silence them.'

As they rode cross-country, it began to rain and they sought shelter in a remote soldiers' watchtower, where they discovered Captain Derwin, one of Burgred's officers who had fought with them the previous year on Offa's Dyke. He was a good man, young and capable, and Swift embraced him warmly.

'Why are so many of our people calling for Frith?' she asked. 'He's an incapable crackbrain.'

'He has royal lineage,' replied Derwin. 'He tells the people lies and they believe him.'

'Can you not give them a sound thrashing and send them back to their homes?'

'Would we could, but our forces are thin on the ground. Let me show you something.'

They wrapped themselves against the elements and he led them to a grassy slope overlooking a familiar Mercian landscape: fine grazing dotted with well-fed sheep, neatly trimmed hedges and copses of pollarded beech. But a strange object was disturbing the scene: the two halves of a Norland longship were lying in the grass as if they'd fallen from the sky.

'Frith has bought the support of gangs of Norland mercenaries. They appear out of nowhere,' said Derwin. 'They're as much of a threat to us as the malcontented townsfolk. We're stretched to the limit.'

'But how could one of their ships be lying in the middle of a field?' said Swift. 'The nearest water is a league away.'

'They are not like the Norlanders who harass Wessex,' he replied. 'They have light boats, which they sail up the smallest of rivers, and when the water is too shallow to navigate, they lift the craft out and push them on rollers till they come to the next waterway.' He poked a pair of long greased logs with his foot in a disparaging fashion. 'Unless one slips from its rollers and smashes in two like this, then they run away.'

'Is Queen Swift safe to travel onwards? These devils could still be close by,' said Hercules.

'She is not,' replied Derwin, and shivered. 'We'll escort you home, your Grace, and keep you safe.'

Tamworth had become an army town, with tents pitched everywhere, patrols constantly leaving and returning and victuallers standing behind great vats doling out food to long lines of exhausted troops.

Burgred met Swift at the entrance of their compound. 'I am happy to see you again, my dear,' he said, embracing her warmly, 'but you cannot stay long. The entire north is in Frith's hands.'

She was stunned. She had assumed their problem was a few unruly malcontents, not an invading army. 'Why is this happening?' she demanded. 'Despite our setbacks the people love us. Mercia is beginning to grow rich again under our stewardship. What reason could they have for their outrage?'

Burgred sighed. 'Perhaps it's simply the Mercian way. If our people stayed loyal to their leaders, we'd be the mightiest nation in Britain, but no, they denigrate us and squabble among themselves like greedy children over the last piece of pudding.'

'We can put a stop to it,' said Swift, and kissed him on both cheeks. 'With your leadership and my cunning, we are invincible.'

Swift made her way to the boys' room but was disappointed to find them fast asleep. She'd wanted to tell them tales of her adventures. She'd never been interested in children until she'd met these two, but they were loving and curious and she found their Welsh lilt charming. They drew a warmness from her that she'd seldom felt before; she barely thought of them as hostages now. Not that she played with them in the spirited fashion that Burgred did, but she enjoyed their times together immersed in the stories of King David and Daniel in his den of lions. She stroked their cheeks and went to bed.

'Ithael! Maurig!' The following morning she returned to their room, but the boys weren't there. They must have risen already; perhaps they were playing in the next room. But that too was empty. She hurried along the corridor and into the forecourt; there was no sign of them there either. She called to the servants, but to no avail. Within an hour, every guard and slave was looking for them, and Swift was consumed by anxiety. She stormed into the council room, where her husband was deep in conversation with his officers. He looked up at her irritably.

'They've gone,' she gasped. 'The boys have been taken.'

*

It wasn't simply the loss of the boys that distressed Burgred; the vulnerability of the compound threw him into a state of wild agitation.

'Do we have enemies in our own house?' he demanded. He sent fifty scouts to find the kidnappers, Derwin at their head, and at Swift's request Hercules accompanied them.

For two days and nights she paced the courtyard, feeling an odd sense of hostility in the air. Two soldiers were washing their faces in a tub, and when she bade them good morrow, they ignored her. She asked an officer a casual question about his horse, and his reply was curt. Servants glanced at her and whispered conspiratorially. Were they laughing at her? Not that it mattered. All that concerned her was getting the boys back.

Time and again she went to the front gate and stared out, eager for the scouts to return. At night she couldn't sleep for the thoughts spinning through her head. She would head north dressed as a merchant woman, or perhaps as a nun. She would find Frith. She would offer to leave Burgred and become his queen. She would lure him to Tamworth. She would . . .

Three days later, there was the sound of boots in the corridors. The scouts had returned.

She slipped on her shawl and followed them through the palace, calling Hercules' name, but he didn't stop to answer her. He gave her only the briefest of glances as he and Derwin disappeared into the council room. Burgred and his officers came running to join them, and before Swift could launch herself after them, the door slammed shut and the bolt was drawn.

She was outraged. Why was she not in there too? She was the queen, it was her right. If the news was dreadful, she was strong enough to bear it. Should she hammer on the door? No, that would make her appear a foolish woman. She paced about, trying to make out what was being said, but could hear only murmurs.

Eventually the door opened and Derwin gestured for her to enter. Now was not the time to show how affronted she felt about her exclusion. 'Where are the boys? Are they safe?' she demanded.

Her husband was seated at the far end of the table, his face drawn. 'They are alive,' he replied.

'Blessed Christ!' she gasped.

'They were stolen on Rhys of Gwent's orders by a band of Norlanders practised in the art of kidnapping the children of the wealthy.'

'Thank God and all his angels they're unharmed,' she said. 'But now they're gone, we have no means of restraining Rhys.'

'We do not,' agreed Derwin. 'He has sent messages to all the tribe chiefs of west Wales summoning an army to cross the Dyke and march towards us.'

'Frith in the north and Rhys in the west; we are in double peril,' said Swift. 'At noon I will address our people. I will tell them that this is their darkest hour and that their freedom is at stake unless they hold firm.'

Burgred shook his head.

'Have no fear,' she continued. 'I have spoken such words before in South Hamwicshire to great effect. Then I will ride north—'

'Stop, Swift,' said Burgred sharply. 'You cannot do this.'

'I can and I will. The people will respond to my urging.'

'This is not South Hamwicshire, your Grace,' said Derwin. 'They will not listen.'

'They will,' she replied desperately. 'Won't they, Hercules?'

He shook his head and looked at her tenderly. 'I have not been entirely truthful with you,' he said.

'In what way?' she demanded.

'It is you against whom the people are protesting,' he continued sadly. 'I have known this since we arrived in Henbery. You are the reason Frith has been able to advance at such speed.'

She turned to Burgred. 'I don't understand. Husband, tell me what I've done.'

All eyes were on the king. He said nothing for a while, then reluctantly he spoke. 'They say you came to Mercia because you had been disgraced in Wessex, and married me only for the sake of your ambition. They say you murdered Wynstan and banished Frith so you could seize the throne, and that you are the cause of their misery.'

'That's all nonsense!' she protested, and looked round the table for support.

'It is a vile calumny,' agreed Burgred. 'Of course it is. But now word is being put about that you ordered the family of King Rhys to be murdered and stole his boys, so it was you who provoked this potential invasion. And that is an accusation that is harder to deny.'

Swift felt her knees tremble. She wanted to sit down, but she would not show weakness. 'Vicious rumours inevitably emerge in times of crisis,' she said. 'We will ignore them and prepare to fight. I will ride at the head of our forces. One victory and this foolishness will be forgotten.'

'You must go, Swift,' said Burgred.

'Go?'

'You must leave Mercia. It breaks my heart, but there is no alternative.'

'Shame on you, husband. We are not cowards. You cannot ask me to do such a thing.'

'For the sake of the country, you must,' Burgred replied.

Swift couldn't believe what she was hearing. 'I cannot return home, you know this. My brother Hawk has taken the throne. His hatred for me knows no bounds. The moment I cross the border, I will be seized and executed. I cannot go south, or west to Wales, nor to the north or east because of Frith. I must stay!'

'You will be smuggled to Southamwic, where you'll take a ship to Rome,' said Burgred softly.

'No!'

'That is my command. I have sent a fast rider with a message to the Pope's legate, Father Asser. Hercules will accompany you to Wessex, where you will meet him. He is beholden to us, and will ensure your escape.'

'Our country is being torn apart,' said Swift, her mind desperately trying to gain some purchase. 'I cannot agree to such a ridiculous request. Where would I live in Rome?'

It wouldn't break her heart to leave. Burgred's inability to stem the tide of support for Frith had demonstrated how ineffectual he was, and though Mercia was her mother's country, she had always found it a little gloomy. But she had no desire to live among the crumbling ruins of Italia. Could she return to Hamblesea and live there in secret? No, that was fanciful.

Burgred took her hand.

'My late mother was from one of the finest Roman families. Her sister will take care of you. You will have a life far finer than I could ever have offered you in Mercia. You will be happy, my dear, I know it. The Gilottis are good people.'

SEVENTY-EIGHT

Going Home

High Aethelhawk, newly crowned, was wriggling around in his throne, seeking out the most comfortable site for his gaunt bottom. When he finally succeeded, he sighed like a swain in love.

'Mine at last,' he said. 'It fits me like a courtesan's glove!'

'Congratulations!' replied Asser. 'All Wessex is celebrating your accession.'

'The plans you recently concocted with my father are now dead, of course,' said Hawk. 'I have no interest in your continental reforms. I'm not going to lick the Holy Roman arse of Charles the Bald, and thank God I already have a wife; I certainly wouldn't want to marry his dreadful daughter as my father and brother did. You can take her with you.'

Asser wasn't distressed by Hawk's dismissal of him, nor indeed by his command that Judith should return to Frankia. The young queen had been nothing but trouble since Bear's death. She'd insisted on remaining on the throne until Asser had shown her the document that guaranteed Hawk's accession.

She'd proposed that Moira be executed and that she marry Hawk in her stead, and when that plan was politely rejected, she demanded to go home immediately. It suited Asser to take her. He'd received a concerning letter from Balotelli indicating that he needed help in Rome and wanted Asser to return. The cardinal wouldn't have made such a request unless serious trouble had arisen.

Hawk held a spread-eagled hand in front of his face and scrutinised it. 'Pass me that blade,' he demanded, nodding at a hunting knife that lay on a nearby table. 'I have something unpleasant under my fingernails.'

Asser handed it to him. It bore the image of a hawk on its hilt. 'A keen weapon,' he said.

'Indeed,' replied Hawk. 'At one time I considered burying it between my brother's shoulder blades, but there was no need. He died, and with God's blessing I took his place.'

'You did,' replied Asser. 'Humbert and I arranged your accession well, I think, particularly given how unexpected it was. We fall into the trap of assuming our rulers will be stabbed, poisoned or killed in battle.' He silently prayed that one of those outcomes would befall Hawk. 'But the truth is, most of us fall victim to sour teeth, the ague or, as in the case of your brother, some internal rupture. We should congratulate ourselves if we reach two-score years. Most men don't.'

Hawk busied himself extricating the filth from his fingers, while Asser sipped a final goblet of the excruciating Bedminster wine.

'Tell me something,' said the high aethel eventually. 'Not as a priest, but as a man. Now that Moira's been returned to me, what should I do with her? I've tried everything. I'm kind, I impose discipline, I shower her with gifts, I show her the whip, but whatever approach I take, she sulks like a child. I'm not a passionate man, but I occasionally attempt to assert my husband's right, and when I do, she becomes so unpleasant I'm in a bad mood for days. How am I to make her . . .' He waved his hand in the air, searching for the appropriate word, but couldn't find it.

'Happy?' suggested Asser. 'Perhaps a wife is not dissimilar to a horse. Whiteflash was wild when you bought her, was she not? But you managed to tame her and she's a fine mount now.'

'She is!' replied Hawk, with a tinge of pride.

'If you wanted to lead her forward, did you pull her violently towards you?'

'Of course not. I stood by her side, talked gently to her, and we walked together as one.'

'On a loose rein?'

'Exactly.'

'So perhaps you should offer Lady Moira a similar consideration.'

'She's not a horse!' scoffed Hawk. 'She's my wife! My possession! The fount Christ has given me for my pleasure!' He shook his head disparagingly. 'Loose rein? You've been reading too much Greek philosophy. Be off with you! Go back to Rome. And don't return till you've learnt some sense.'

Asser rode to the minster to bid farewell to Rollo and Mountjoy. Plegmond's first job as its new dean had been to order the long-delayed repairs to the ceiling to prevent it from crashing down onto the worshippers below. Leof and four of his brothers had erected a network of scaffolding, and the twins were supervising them.

Rollo, in his yellow workman's smock, his arm wrapped round a stone statue, yelled down to Asser. 'The timberwork up here's shit. They'll need a new minster soon.'

'You're not coming home with me?' Asser shouted back.

'This is home now, it's the new frontier,' replied Rollo. 'Half of

Wessex is in a state of ruin because of the Norlanders. We could renovate the lot with these boys. And you know what we're like.'

'Anything for the right price,' agreed Mountjoy, moving nimbly around the scaffolding.

A memory flashed through Asser's mind; the Doctore looking up, observing the work at St Peter's; the yellow coat, the toppling statue.

There were moments when the whole world turned about-face and revealed another side, grimy and ugly, thought Asser. 'You were there, weren't you?' he said. 'At St Peter's. When I first joined Balotelli's men.'

'Dunno,' said Mountjoy. 'I shouldn't think so. When would that have been?' He was looking down at Asser, his arm still wrapped jauntily round the ancient carved figure.

'It was you two bastards!' Asser exclaimed.

'What was?'

'You dropped that statue on me and Doctore Guido!'

'Us? No!' protested Mountjoy. 'Never.'

'It was a warning, that was all,' said Rollo.

'From whom?' demanded Asser.

'Can't remember. Probably one of the Notarii. When you left the dungeon, they all wanted you kept in check. Why do you think we trotted around after you for so long? It's what we did for a living in those days.'

'But you could have killed us!'

The two men roared with laughter.

'With St Andrew? He landed ten paces away from you!' shouted Rollo.

'He didn't!'

'He certainly did. If we'd wanted to kill you, we would have,' added Mountjoy. 'It's what we're good at. But we love you, little man. Always have, always will.'

*

Asser rode down to Southamwic with Judith and her Frisian maids. He was so consumed by sadness and anger, he could barely hear her chatter. He'd revelled in the twins' company; they'd seemed so straightforward, brave, competent and open-hearted, untrammelled by the demands of the cloth. But he'd been duped. They'd been frauds, lackeys of Ponti or the Gilottis or whoever. How lonely the world could be!

And how else might they have betrayed him? They'd accompanied him and Lady Osburgh from Modena. Had they told Wolf of their trysting? The more he thought about the strange sequence of events since he'd left the Pope's dungeon, the more suspicious he became. The twins would not go unpunished.

He and Judith arrived at Southamwic water and boarded Red's new ship, *The Winifred*, which was waiting for the evening tide. Judith wailed that her berth was too small. She was right; she and her maids were squashed in like kittens in a basket, and her dog, Wolfie, was barking in a frenzied fashion, jumping up and licking their faces. But it was the only cabin on board.

Asser told her he'd be back at dusk, then retraced his journey, taking the ferry at the Itchen crossing point and heading for Hamblesea. The hall was now in Red's possession, and Asser found him playing in the orchard with baby Helm. Red waved cheerily as the priest approached. 'Well met,' he said.

'Well met indeed,' replied Asser. 'Have you been able to do as I requested? Is Queen Swift safely here?'

Red smiled broadly. 'She is. It was a great game. I met her and Brother Hercules at Portishead; the abbess there is one of Swift's oldest friends. It wasn't difficult to persuade her to let Swift don a habit for a few days and join her party of nuns taking orphaned children to be sold to the South Hamwicshire farmers. It took us barely three days to get here. Not a single person noticed us, and she'll be able to board the ship tonight and travel with you and Judith, an innocent nun on pilgrimage to Rome.'

'You have the guile of Odysseus,' said Asser.

'I think I do,' replied Red, looking very pleased with himself.

They wandered into the hall and found Swift sitting by the fire in the home she'd occupied for so many years, still dressed in her nun's garb.

'Father Asser!' she said. 'I thank you for responding to my husband's request. Come and sit with me.'

She conducted herself with such common grace that he quickly forgot her plight, particularly as she seemed interested in talking only about the future.

'Do you know the Gilottis?' she enquired.

'I do,' he replied.

'There is something in your voice that tells me I should be wary of them.'

'As a member of their family I'm sure you'll be treated with the utmost affection and respect,' Asser said carefully, 'but I would advise you not to fall foul of them.'

'I don't see why I would. I have no power, no authority. I intend to be nothing other than the perfect guest,' she replied a little bitterly.

'Of course you will. But there is the question of your brother, Alfred.'

'Alfred?'

'Indeed, it is what Aethelfraed now calls himself. He is in Rome and perhaps you should meet him, though I believe he wishes to hide his parentage.'

'That I understand,' replied Swift. 'His mother worked him to the bone, his father banished him, his elder brothers bullied him, and I confess that I, though fond enough of him, was far too engaged in a young girl's fancies to take much notice of him. It was clear from the beginning that he was the best of us;

his intellect was sharper, he had a natural authority and he was as strong as an ox. But every one of us felt threatened by him in some way. We failed him . . . so he turned his back on us and that is very sad. Perhaps this is something we should address.'

Winifred entered the room with a plate of mulberry fancies. She looked a little ill and was wearing a sour expression. Asser suspected she was with child again.

'I don't want you two drawing my husband into your plots and getting my house into trouble,' she said. 'Have a cake, it'll stop your mouths for a few moments.'

'We cannot take my sister aboard till dark, Winni,' said Red.

'She, Judith and Father Asser will be more trouble to you than three ferrets in a hen coop,' said Winifred.

They all laughed, though they knew she was serious.

'*The Winifred*! A fine name for your new ship, Red,' Swift said.

'*The Winifred*!' his wife repeated in a voice that indicated she found the name jarring. 'I'd rather he stayed home more. We had fun before we married. Don't have children, Swift, they're a constant trial.'

Swift said nothing.

The fire crackled. Somewhere an owl hooted.

'It is in all our interests that Alfred should return to Wessex, is it not?' said Asser.

'He is the only one of my kin who would dare overrule Hawk and make it possible for me to come back here,' said Swift.

'I always wished he could be my friend,' said Red. 'I'm glad he's safe now, but I'd dearly love him to be by my side at the helm of *The Winifred*.'

'Once you are in Rome, Lady Swift, we will prise him away from the city's clutches,' said Asser. 'My cardinal wishes him to return too. As do I.'

And it was partly true, he did. Even if Alfred was the most infuriating young man he'd ever met.

SEVENTY-NINE

The Shape Shifter

On the day of the Battle of Shankalin, Guthrum's young cousin, Sigurd, had escaped from Winifred's hall, scrambled down the slope and arrived on the beach just before the last Norland boat had set sail. Now he was back in the north again, and once the booty had been divided up, he was exceedingly wealthy thanks to Guthrum's leadership. He was not usually of generous spirit, but his gratitude to his cousin was boundless. On Astrid's prompting, he summoned the finest bards in the north-east to the Shields.

'All shall know of Guthrum's deeds,' he announced. 'To whoever can tell the finest tale of his triumphs I will give a pig, a plot of land, five farm-slaves and a purse of silver.'

Why would anyone be given such riches for telling stories? thought Rhiannon. Not that she cared about Norland foolishness. She was content with her lot. Guthrum had become clan chief of the entire north-east coastline. No matter that he'd lost nigh on forty men, he'd brought back more gold than the islanders had seen for years. He was a hero. He and Astrid moved from the Farnes to the mainland, and he built a grand house overlooking Whitley Bay. Rhiannon tended Astrid's children. She had her own pair of leather shoes, which had been taken from a dead girl, and a spoonful of giblets to eat whenever she was hungry. She slept in Astrid's bed when Guthrum was away, and on the floor when he wasn't. She had no need to fight and curse any more. She was warm, safe and was never bound or beaten. The other slaves envied her, and sometimes she gave them tripe and chitterlings from the stewpot.

Occasionally she'd remember the moment on Shankalin beach when the little priest had called her mistress by another name. *Anna! Sister!* he'd shouted, and Astrid had told her not to kill him. Why had she done that? Was he really her brother? She'd wanted to ask, but there had been something in Astrid's eyes that had warned her not to.

On the day of the tale-telling, the crowds climbed Cleadon Hill to watch the bards below. The first to perform was dressed in green scales like a snake. He had two drummers alongside him and five dancers, and he told the story of Guthrum defeating the Great Worm of the Isle of Wight. Next, a chanter and ten singers from north Sunderland acted out a tale in which Guthrum was led into the Underworld through a magic portal and slew a triple-headed monster. The saga-maker of Rothbury made Rhiannon smile. He recited an ode about six Valkyries who joined Guthrum's expedition, led by their goddess, Astrid. They stole his eyes and wouldn't return them till he'd sworn to lie with each of them twenty times. Astrid called out that it must have been the Valkyries who'd had their eyes stolen, and everyone laughed, even Guthrum. There were songs, poems, dances and recitations throughout the day, and the next day too. Rhiannon watched spellbound, every story reminding her of the exhilaration and terror of those weeks, although throughout all the time she'd lived in Wessex she'd never seen a portal into hell, and not a single giant worm.

Thorvik of Whitley spoke simply, without need of song or gaudy show. His story was of Guthrum Stumphand, son of Thor, who killed the Seven Sons of Aethelwolf and brought the kingdom of Wessex to its knees. Rhiannon could see the characters before her eyes: craven and cowardly Wolf, the slut-queen Winifred, Sigurd fierce as a shark, the demigod Guthrum. During the other tellings, some of those listening had discussed the weather, chomped on strips of dried fish or pushed their way through the crowd for a piss. But when Thorvik told his tale, no one stirred. He was crowned a worthy champion.

Guthrum stepped forward and said he'd been moved by all the storytellers, and he called for those watching to cast lots for four additional winners, who would henceforth be known as his saga men. He would give them each a strip of land and a purse, and all five bards would spend a whole year travelling through Britain and beyond telling the tale of Guthrum's triumph in Wessex.

Time passed, the season changed, it became even colder. Rhiannon had been given one of Astrid's old undershirts, and the scent of her body lingered on it. A longship arrived from far away manned by weather-beaten Norland adventurers seeking out new lands. They brought with them a message for Guthrum.

He strode into his house, his head high. 'Fill your travelling bags, wife,' he said. He called Astrid wife now, though Rhiannon never heard them coupling. 'We're to set sail for Ireland. The great Norland leader Ivar the Boneless has heard my story and wishes me to attend him.'

Ivar the Boneless, the Norland warrior who had conquered the Irish coast and transformed Dunnblinn into the Rome of the Northern seas, even Rhiannon had heard tell of his shape-shifting and his forked tongue. On the day Guthrum's ship was due to depart, she went down to the quay while the servants and soldiers clambered aboard. She'd packed Astrid's bags with a heavy heart. She'd wanted to see the shape-shifter – perhaps he had wings and breathed fire; instead she was to stay here tending Astrid's children. But as the ship was about to pull away, Guthrum looked around and said, 'Where's the slave Rhiannon?' Astrid nodded to where she stood on the quay. 'Climb on board, you little fool,' he called brusquely. 'My mother's sister will care for the children. Astrid needs you.'

Rhiannon now knew Norse well enough to understand what he was saying. It was almost impossible for her to remember that she'd once loathed him, that she'd hacked off his fingers, that she'd thought he'd eat her if he recognised her. He was her master, the finest man in the north, and he wanted her with them. She boarded the ship for Ireland, her face expressionless but with triumph in her heart.

Rhiannon had never seen so many slaves, most crowded into pens, others being brought ashore in boats or shuffling along in lines waiting to be auctioned. Some of the women were naked, a few of the men wore ragged monks' habits; many looked like her, white-skinned and wiry-haired, others had the dusky faces of folk from five thousand leagues away.

Dunnblinn was ten times the size of Winchester. They were led through row after row of dingy huts till they came to the longest hall she'd ever seen, with devil's masks, horse skulls and the bones of ancient monsters protruding from its thatch. They ducked through the open entranceway. It was crowded with sweet-smelling Norlanders, the women draped in fine jewellery, the men wearing strings of looted crosses round their necks.

One end sloped upwards to a platform that overlooked the

crowd. The press of people was tight, but when Rhiannon stood on the tips of her toes, she could make out the strangest man she'd ever seen, with a gaunt, aged face and a head completely bald save for thin strands of white hair that dangled down to his waist. His arms were hunched and bent, his hands were shaking, and he was sitting on a burnished bronze dish with his withered legs tucked under him. At any moment she thought he might fly into the air and disappear out of the doorway.

A brute-faced Norlander stood next to him dressed in a Frankish jacket with shining buttons. He hammered his staff on the packed earth and the crowd fell silent.

'Show me Guthrum Stumphand,' croaked the strange old man.

''Tis I,' said her master. He held his gloveless, fingerless arm in the air and the crowd drew back in horror.

'I hear tell you killed the Seven Sons of Aethelwolf,' croaked the old man.

'So the storytellers say, your Mightiness,' replied Guthrum.

'But it is true you brought great wealth back from Wessex, more than we've seen for years, all in a single fleet?'

'It is, your Mightiness.'

'They say you think we Norlanders are a little stupid.'

'They say wrong.'

'But you believe we're without ambition?'

Guthrum spoke carefully now as though he was walking on the ice of early spring. 'Not so, your Mightiness. I have always been as eager as any Norlander to seize as much loot as I can and destroy any Saxon who gets in my way. But I know now what a fine land Wessex is; its warm sun, its lush grass, the countless bays and harbours. We care only for the Westsaxons' gold. We fail to see the far greater wealth we could make by trading with these people, and the fat livestock we could breed on their downs and meadows.'

'I see only their gold and I've become the richest man in the world by taking it from them,' said the strange creature. 'Am I stupid?'

'Any man who said so would die on the spot, your Mightiness,' replied Guthrum.

'You think so? I can barely lift a page of parchment!'

'But if you wrote on that parchment that the man should die, he would do so.'

Ivar made a squeaking sound like a tomb lid opening.

'They said you were clever,' he said finally, 'and brave too, I hear.' He turned to the man with the shiny buttons. 'I will talk to Stumphand alone. Send the crowd away.'

Astrid took Rhiannon to the market. Every fine thing she could imagine was on sale there, and thousands of things she couldn't imagine. She walked through the crowds keeping a wary eye out, certain that some artful slave-dealer would try to snatch her away.

'Look at this!' said Astrid. She was holding up a tiny carving of a shiny green monster on a chain. It had sharp teeth and little legs.

Rhiannon examined it closely and gave it back to her.

'It's a gift,' said Astrid, and dropped it in her palm.

Rhiannon didn't know what a gift was, but she took it anyway.

Later, they found Guthrum. He was very drunk, and they sat him down carefully on a log to make sure he didn't topple over.

'Listen to me!' he said. 'There are rumours that the Romans are building a great army. They think they will defeat us. But under Ivar's leadership, we will build three armies. Three, Astrid! Ivar's brothers are fine men indeed. They will lead two of them, and I, General Guthrum, for I am a general now, will lead the other . . . and we will overwhelm Britain, every single handspan of it!' He kissed his wife on the lips, put his arm round her, put the other round Rhiannon and held onto them, swaying, for a long time. 'And when we do, Wessex will be mine.'

Rhiannon held her tiny monster tight. She felt a strange and unfamiliar warmth spreading through her belly and her chest; it was something like she imagined contentment might be.

EIGHTY

The Hiding Hole

Alfred stood by the small platform in the school courtyard to ensure none of his boys tripped over as they trooped onto it. They sang 'The Ox and the Ass' and 'Samson was a Strong Man'. Wealthy merchants and their wives sat on a semicircle of benches in front of them, wearing the smiles they employed only for the singing of the young.

'Learn! Learn! Learn!' Balotelli had said. He had been deeply impressed by the new school and how little it cost to transform the lives of the boys who attended it. 'You have led the way, Alfred; you must persuade our supporters to fund the building of more schools for the poor throughout the city.'

When the singing was finished, Alfred addressed his listeners. 'Friends, what did Christ command his disciples in the gospel of St Matthew? "Suffer the little children to come unto me." And do we do so? We do not. We suffer them to pull weeds, drive off crows and beg in the streets.'

He was well aware that some of those present believed that teaching the poor would lead to curiosity, that curiosity led to dissent and ultimately to armed rebellion, but he also knew that whenever little Cuddie recited the Beatitudes and forgot his words, as he invariably did, the audience was charmed by his innocence and considerable money flowed forth. They had already built a second school; they'd soon have enough for a third.

For a moment, he felt a pang of yearning. Places of learning like this should flourish in Wessex, a hundred of them from Truro to Winchester. But who would support such a notion? No, he'd made the right decision. The boys needed him as did Balotelli. He would stay in Rome, however hard he was pressed to do otherwise.

At the end of his speech, Carlo the saddler, one of the cardinal's longest-serving and most ardent supporters, whispered in his ear. 'We have a problem. The rich are becoming anxious. They see thugs patrolling the streets, doors and windows being smashed, and worse, rumours abound that the Pope will increase their taxes. They'll not open their purses today.'

Alfred went to the Undercroft to report Carlo's concerns.

'Higher taxes!' exploded Balotelli, prowling up and down between the rows of scribbling priests and banging his fist into the palm of his hand. 'Of course we need higher taxes; how else will we pay for Christ's work? But it would be a grave miscalculation to attempt to implement such a thing now. It would be vigorously resisted by the rich. The collapse of the concord has severely diminished our support. We cannot afford another such defeat.'

Eventually the priests went back to their work, but they were interrupted by the sound of men outside shouting, then the dusty curtain at the bottom of the stairs was flung back and Ponti appeared, pushing his way towards them between the tables.

'Good morning, your Eminence,' he called. 'Christ has blessed us with a lovely day. Excuse my interrupting your secret labours.' He laughed heartily, embraced Balotelli and gestured towards Alfred. 'Who is this?' he asked. 'Another of your handsome young men? Where do you find them?'

'Have you not met Alfred, our newest acquisition?' enquired the cardinal.

Ponti turned towards him. 'I have not,' he said smoothly.

'I teach at the Saxon school,' said Alfred, joining in the tawdry subterfuge.

'Do you? Do you indeed?' replied Ponti. 'Yet already you are at the heart of the cardinal's coterie. How impressed he must be with you! Make sure you serve him well.' He took Alfred's hand and patted it.

The sounds outside were growing louder. Ponti turned back to Balotelli. 'I came here to relay to you a most shocking event, your Eminence,' he said. 'You will know that his Holiness Pope Benedict has instructed me to seek out heretics wherever they may be hiding. Well, I received information from my informant at the papal dungeon that certain priests had plied the prisoners there with strong drink, joined in their heretical songs and promised them their sentences would be shortened. I was shocked, of course, who would not be, but I was particularly horrified to discover that the priests who were alleged to have done this terrible thing were among your number. I didn't want to distress you – the story could have been a wicked calumny – but what could I do?'

'What did you do?' replied Balotelli softly.

'When you came to office last year, you sequestered several houses in the town for your priests, did you not? I therefore asked some good Christians of my acquaintance to observe the comings and goings in these properties to ensure there was no sign of heresy there, although I was confident I wouldn't find any, of course. But they reported – and this is the disturbing part – that one of your men had surreptitiously taken food, wine, flowers and women's clothing into his room on several occasions.'

A wave of coldness ran through Alfred like a winter stream. What madness had possessed Kennet to take Mirandolina to his own room?

'Why would this priest do such a thing, your Eminence?' continued Ponti. 'Women are forbidden in such residences; even the man's sick mother would not be allowed shelter there, would she? So to satisfy myself that nothing untoward was taking place, I visited his room during this morning's matins. When I found it empty, I was mightily relieved, I truly was. All was as it should be. But as I was leaving, I heard noises from above the ceiling. Fortunately I had brought a small drill with me, and on investigating further, I discovered an attic accessible only through a cunningly hidden trapdoor, and in this hiding hole was a young woman, an Antonil, a heretic, who had been provided with washing facilities, a table and chair and – I blush to say it – a bed. And most horrible is the fact that the room belonged to one of your priests. Can you guess which one? Have you any idea? Who among your number would be so libidinous, so profoundly sinful?' He cast his eyes round the Undercroft; everyone was transfixed by what he was saying while feigning a profound lack of interest.

Alfred looked anywhere but at Kennet, but he heard him rise slowly. 'It was I,' he said.

'Indeed it was, wasn't it?' exclaimed Ponti, a look of sorrow mingled with intense pleasure coursing across his face. 'Father Kennet! I would never have thought it. Who would believe such a fine priest capable of such a terrible thing?'

Kennet shrugged. 'Mirandolina is not a heretic. She worked

for us in Modena. She gave us useful information, and now her life is under threat.'

'Information!' repeated Ponti. 'And did she receive money for this information?'

'She did.'

'So it was a financial arrangement for which she was suitably compensated?'

'It was.'

'And thus irrelevant to the matter in hand, which is that she is a heretic – of this I have proof – and you were hiding her in order that she should avoid retribution.' He turned to Balotelli. 'You'll be pleased to know, your Eminence, that in order to confirm her guilt, I've had her arrested. I'm sure her confession will be forthcoming.'

Mirandolina. Poor sweet, funny Mirandolina, thought Alfred. Hatred was not a Christian virtue, but at this moment he loathed Ponti with all his soul.

'Thank you,' said Balotelli. 'You need concern yourself with this matter no more. I will attend to it.'

'I wish you could. I really do,' replied Ponti. 'Unfortunately, it is more significant than the mere coupling of a young whore and a licentious priest. I suspect the woman who Father Kennet has been sheltering also murdered Fabio Gilotti. She certainly has the same heretical faith and wanton instincts. If so, it makes Kennet's position profoundly disturbing, doesn't it? You live among a nest of vipers, your Eminence, who must be stamped out before they infest us with their venom.'

He and Balotelli stared at each other like dogs in a fighting pit. The noise outside had reached fever pitch. The curtain opened again. Asser stood there in his travelling clothes, bleary-eyed.

'I have returned!' he announced. There was no reaction. 'My, how miserable you all look.'

*

When Asser had approached the Undercroft, he'd been shocked to find club-wielding ruffians outside denouncing Cardinal Balotelli and his men as lechers and heretics. Some of them he recognised. What in God's name were the Illyrian soldiers doing among them?

He'd demanded entry and walked slowly and carefully down the Undercroft stairs. Pausing at the bottom, he listened for some time to Ponti's story. In order to throw him off his stride and drive him and his zealots away from the building, he'd have to act swiftly and decisively.

'Undersecretary Ponti, how good of you to be here to welcome me back,' Asser continued as he walked into the room. 'But I fear you've made a horrible mistake.'

'Me? How? What do you mean?' demanded Ponti.

'You have brought a band of thugs here to undermine the work of Holy Mother Church.'

'That is not true. The men outside are devoted fellow countrymen who are outraged by those who enable heretics to go about their lecherous and murderous ways. They call themselves the Concerned Citizens, and that is indeed what they are.'

'Concerned citizens with knives and staves? They are brigands who you have whipped into a fury. You must send them away. You have made certain allegations, and Cardinal Balotelli and I will deal with them. Please leave immediately.'

'I will not!'

'As the Pope's legate, I insist you do.'

'I am acting on the Pope's authority,' said the outraged Ponti.

'I am senior to you in every aspect of our lives,' said Asser. 'I order you to leave our building and take your myrmidons with you. If not, I will call the papal guard and have you dragged out!'

*

After much rowdiness and expressions of outrage, Ponti and his mob had departed, threatening retribution at some later time. Now Balotelli and Asser were making their way in haste to the papal palace.

'Thank the sweet Christ you're back,' said the cardinal. 'I've missed you. We all have, even Alfred.'

'I knew some of the rabble outside the Undercroft,' Asser said.

'Indeed? Old acquaintances?'

'Not really. They were your soldiers.'

'My soldiers?'

'The ones who wrote to you from Illyria, the first advocates of a righteous army.'

'Holy Jesu! What strange bedfellows.'

'Do you think so?' said Asser. 'Both they and the so-called Concerned Citizens believe the Church has betrayed them and that only they have the answer to the world's woes. All fanatics do. The fact that they are becoming indistinguishable doesn't surprise me.'

'Thank God I'm not a fanatic,' said Balotelli.

'Nor I,' replied Asser. 'We yearn for the good, but we're sceptics too. Doubtless it's all that saves us from madness.'

Asser felt comfortable in Balotelli's company. The experiences of the last year or so had brought them closer together. He felt less of an acolyte, more like the cardinal's companion.

'There's something at play here we do not understand,' he continued. 'The arrests at the market square, the destruction of the map, the tumbling statue, Wolf's flight from Rome, now this. We're constantly being undermined. Ponti is causing us considerable damage, but could there also be an enemy among us?'

Balotelli shook his head. 'Each incident has its own cause; they're not interconnected. Ponti is attempting to turn the entire Church against us. We cannot afford the luxury of turning against each other.'

They arrived at the Pope's palace, but were told the Holy Father had left for the papal treasury on urgent business.

They set off again, anxious and frustrated.

'Who would have guessed that such a shallow, vainglorious man as Ponti could attract so many devoted followers,' said Balotelli. 'He must be stopped before he tears Rome to pieces.'

The treasury was a squat building made of large blocks of black stone and guarded by silent Serbians with cold eyes. Once inside, Asser and the cardinal were quizzed and searched, then led through a pair of metal doors protected by robust locks and bolts and into a windowless basement in which stood the diminutive figure of Pope Benedict.

'We need to talk to you urgently, your Holiness,' said Balotelli.

'And I to you,' replied the Pope. 'I have something deeply concerning to show you.'

In one corner of the room thousands of golden coins were piled up to a height three times that of a man. It was an impressive sight, but there was sufficient space for at least thirty more such piles and the rest of the floor was empty. It reminded Asser of the last corn in a farmer's barn at the end of winter.

'This is all the gold we have left,' said Pope Benedict, and he began pacing round the room, gesticulating wildly. 'Each and every aspect of our vision requires resources, and we have barely any. It is the Notarii's duty to supply me with money, yet they give me nothing. The rents from their lands, the donations from the living and the dead, they keep it all to themselves. I'll tolerate it no more. I will do as the Holy Book instructs us and levy a tax of one tenth on all the rich possess. It will strike the high churchmen hardest, but our wealthy families, the landowners and the merchants will pay their part too, as Christ would have wished. Only then will we be able to deliver what we have pledged.'

'Excellent, your Holiness!' said Balotelli. 'But it will take time to implement.'

'You will draft the order today!' said the Pope.

'Today! Is this the best time?' replied the cardinal. 'We are not popular. There are armed mobs in the streets. The city may soon be engulfed in discord.'

'They are not mobs. They are committed citizens patrolling Rome in order to ensure its safety,' said the Pope, still striding about. 'We're surrounded by dangerous heretics. They've already killed Fabio Gilotti. They must be stopped or they'll weave their vile magic on every one of us!'

Ponti has been whispering in his ear, thought Asser. The Antonils have become the scapegoat for all our ills.

'The heretics are a minor irritation,' said Balotelli in the soothing voice of one trying to calm a frightened child. 'They've lived among us for many years, kept themselves to themselves and have never been a threat. One of them committed a grave sin and has been put to death for it, but now they are all being treated as the devil's spawn. Please don't be swayed by those who wish to conduct such a purge. That way insanity lies. Even my priests are being accused of heresy. This fanaticism must stop before serious harm is done.'

'You are wrong, Stephen,' replied the Pope, and there was fear in his eyes. 'The devil is worming his way into our Church. That is why I've given Undersecretary Ponti authority to act against the heretics on my behalf.'

'Ponti is a man obsessed, your Holiness.'

'He may be headstrong, but he's popular with the masses, and Enzo Gilotti will keep watch over him to ensure he doesn't overreach himself,' said the Pope and dismissed the conversation with a wave of his hand. 'That is not your concern. Attend to what you do best: write me a speech I can use in my address tomorrow about my proposed new tax.'

He turned to Asser. 'And you, Father Asser. It has been suggested to me that as the concord has failed, we no longer need your services as legate to Wessex. I agree. It would be a waste of the papal purse. Return your ring to me, please.' And he held out his hand.

EIGHTY-ONE

Thank You a Thousand Times

Alfred pushed his way through the crowded bazaar. Had Elswith returned? If not, would someone be able to tell him where she was?

He arrived at the house of pleasure. It was quieter here, seedy and decrepit. Fresh graffiti graced its walls; there was a rotting rat under the window and a pool of vomit in the doorway.

'Elswith!' he called, and when no one answered, he called her name again.

An old man stumbled out of the adjacent House of Illusion, yawning and with a flask of steaming mead in his hand. 'What's all this noise? There's no one here of that appellation,' he said, and sat down hard on a stump.

'Please tell me where I can find her,' Alfred pleaded. 'My friends are in great danger, one is to be tortured, another arrested, and only she can help them.'

'How? Why her?' asked the old man, dropping a pinch of cinnamon in his mead and stirring it with his finger. 'I'm her uncle. You can tell me.'

Alfred was sceptical about this alleged relationship but could see no alternative other than to seek his help. 'I believe she may know something about the death of a man,' he said urgently. 'Someone I—'

'Shush!' the man said. 'Talk quietly or fuck off.'

'I'm sorry. But I am at a loss,' said Alfred, and sat down beside him. 'Cardinal Balotelli's priests are under threat too. And they are good people: Father Philip, Father Asser—'

'Asser!' guffawed the old man. 'Little Cuckoo's back, is he? I might have known he'd be involved.' He blew on his mead and took a sip. 'Well now . . .' he said. 'I'm sure my little Elswith's as innocent as the day is long, but . . . How much did you say you'd pay to find her?'

'Whatever is required, sir. Money is not an issue.'

'Is it not? That's unusual. Let's see if she'll let the cat out the closet.' Slowly he clambered to his feet. 'It'll take me a while to find her. I'm rather short of assistance. The bully boys of the Concerned Citizens are playing havoc with my business, my servant, Clovis, has left me and run off with my dog cart, and . . .'

His voice faded as he disappeared round the back of the brothel. Alfred waited, then Elswith was standing at the door, tired and wan but still wearing the look of aggression and innocence that had so charmed him.

'I'm sorry I had to leave your employ,' she said.

'The boys miss you,' replied Alfred.

She had dark circles under her eyes, blemishes on her cheeks, and her hands were shaking a little.

'It was you, wasn't it?' he said.

'What was me?' Her lip was upturned in challenge, and when Alfred didn't answer, she continued: 'You want me to confess to some terrible thing you've dreamed up? A murder, perhaps?'

'Yes.'

'And then what? Am I to repeat my confession to some high-ranking grandee?'

Alfred sighed. All he'd thought about was finding her; he hadn't considered what he might expect of her once he had. 'I don't know,' he replied lamely.

'And will this grandee tell me I'm a brave, honest woman and I'm forgiven?'

'I merely thought—'

'You thought nothing, Alfred! You came here shouting my name like a drunkard, making accusations against me to my brothel keeper—'

'I didn't know he was . . .'

Elswith sighed heavily. 'This is what I propose to do, though I doubt it'll be of use. You want to know who killed Fabio Gilotti?'

'I do.'

'Despite everything, I am a Christian and I will not let innocent people die for something they didn't do. You have been kind to me and you need me to do this thing, so I will tell you.'

'Thank you. Thank you so much!'

'But not to your face, nor to that of any other man. I will make a written confession to Abbess Clothilde, and once it's done, you may have it. I'll vanish from sight and you will never see me again.'

'Thank you a thousand times. I will pray for your soul every day for the rest of my life,' said Alfred.

For a moment, Elswith stared at him pensively. Perhaps she doesn't know what to say, he thought, perhaps nobody has ever shown her such care before, and she is grateful.

'My soul is not your concern, Alfred,' she said quietly. 'Go back to your school.'

*

Alfred found Asser hastily sorting through piles of documents.

'Where's the cardinal?' he asked. 'He's not at his palazzo.'

Asser ignored his question. 'We're not safe here at the Undercroft. Ponti and his men could be back at any moment. We need to ensure our most important papers are well hidden.'

'I must see Balotelli,' Alfred persisted.

'You can't. He's returned to the Pope with fresh proposals to stave off this damnable new tax, but Benedict is proving intransigent. Our troubles grow deeper by the hour.'

'Perhaps I can ease them with regards to the events at Tivoli,' said Alfred, and he told Asser of Elswith's proposed confession. 'Would it be possible to arrange a meeting between Balotelli and Enzo Gilotti? The cardinal could present him with sworn evidence proving that neither Father Kennet nor the heretics were involved in the murder. Enzo would realise that Ponti's frenzied attacks on us are unjustified and might well be persuaded to call him off.'

Asser grabbed a fresh piece of parchment. 'I know who could broker such a meeting,' he said. 'Someone at the very heart of Enzo's household.'

'Who among his people would be prepared to help us?' asked Alfred.

'How long is it since you last saw your sister?' said Asser.

'Why?'

'Because you're going to be seeing her again very soon.'

Alfred watched him scrawl a note.

'Where's your legate's ring?' he said. 'You're never without it.'

'It was ugly, and constantly chafed my fingers,' Asser said. 'I gave it back willingly.'

EIGHTY-TWO

A Door She Hadn't Noticed

'We would be intrigued to hear your observations on our city, Queen Swift,' said Enzo.

Swift smiled at her host. He's tantalised by me, she thought. Not only am I a foreign dignitary, but I'm also a woman, yet I am not intimidated by him.

Enzo Gilotti was entertaining a few friends: a Polish merchant, two portly Bavarian counts and his sister Claudia's three nieces. Swift was only too happy to perform for them. She enjoyed being here. Enzo was witty and erudite, her life wasn't under threat, and she was feted wherever she went. There was little for her to do, and though life was a touch boring, this ennui was something of a relief after so many years of intrigue.

'I've been here barely a week,' she replied, 'so forgive my naivety, but as a newcomer it strikes me that there are three Romes in one. Every day I'm confronted by the imperial city of half a millennium ago, although sadly its architecture is a little battered now, as if a giant's petulant child had wandered through it lashing out at random.'

There was much laughter.

'There is also the new Rome that has sprung from its loins,' she continued. 'A luxuriance of thatch and wattle dedicated to the pursuit of wealth. And there's the city of the poor and transient crammed into its empty spaces, which is currently causing you such a problem. I've never seen so many angry men assaulting their fellow citizens in the streets. I do hope I'm not marked down for such punishment, for I too am a penniless wanderer seeking refuge here.'

She was exaggerating her plight, of course. Her elegant clothes and demeanour spoke of wealth and confidence, but a little modesty was appreciated by her audience. There was applause when she finished speaking, and one of the Bavarian counts gave her that wry look that offered intimacy, although she doubted whether she could summon up the effort. Would she take a lover? Might she bear children? It was probably too late for that. She'd been told Prince Louis was in Rome, but she wouldn't seek him out. His broken promise had lost her South Hamwicshire and almost her life. He'd know she was here. If he wanted to meet, he could approach her.

'Your description of our city was hilarious, my dear.'

It was the end of the evening, and Swift and her new friend, Claudia, were lying side by side on cushioned couches in a freshly decorated ladies' retiring room, while slave girls cleansed their faces of paint and powder. Claudia was a charming widow of middle age whom Swift had taken to from the moment she'd arrived.

'Your taste is exquisite, dear aunt,' she said.

'Thank you, but I pray don't call me aunt. I feel we are more like sisters.'

'Of course, dear sister.'

'This part of the house has been furnished anew,' said

Claudia. 'The Grecian hangings, the Anglian lyre, the bright Illyrian cushions are all freshly purchased. These rooms belonged to our brother Fabio, who died recently in tragic circumstances. It was so gloomy here that Enzo gave me the wherewithal to make it cheery again, and here is the result: this room, two for our most cherished guests and a separate bathing area.'

'What's through there?' Swift said, her eyes falling on a door she hadn't previously noticed. It was freshly painted like the rest of the room, but bore a sturdy lock, and a large bushy plant in a gaily decorated pot had been placed in front of it.

'It's where we're storing all Fabio's things until Enzo has had a chance to go through them,' Claudia replied. 'Very tedious, but Enzo is particular that they aren't disturbed in the meantime. And perhaps he's right. Fabio was, well . . .' Shaking her head as though dispelling her gloom, she jumped up and clapped her hands. 'I am so glad you are among us,' she said. 'Enzo has been very agitated recently, and your presence has calmed him a little.'

They took each other's hands and looked fondly at one another.

'We shall visit my dressmaker,' Claudia continued. 'Some musicians from Constantinople are in the city and I have purchased their first performance as a gift for Enzo. It will be held here in three nights' time. I will serve Byzantine food and wine, and a host of Eastern delicacies. We shall dress in alluring and exotic costumes like two ruthless empresses in the old stories. You will come with me, won't you?'

The next day, the two women were taken by carriage through the streets of Rome. Swift revelled in the bustle and thrum. She had never seen so many people of different hues and in such varied attire. Shoppers shopped, beggars begged, hawkers bawled their wares, but the city's bustling spirit was tempered by prowling thugs staring at all and sundry. Nevertheless, the two women were well protected by Enzo's unsmiling guards, and they spent a giddy morning in the dressmaker's little house, trying on exotic costumes. For the past year Swift had hardly stepped out of her sweat-stained riding gear, and she rejoiced in the ornate tunics, long, with multiple layers and embroidered with bands of satin stitching. While they were waiting for their purchases to be wrapped in muslin, they were given tiny cups of a bitter Ethiopian beverage that made their heads spin, and they left the house laughing and giggling about nothing in particular. They were stopped by two priests in well-tailored habits.

'I pray you forgive us, ladies, we are collecting money to build new schools for the poor children of Lazio. Might you make a donation?' enquired one.

'Of course, Father!' replied Claudia. 'Anything for the children.'

A guard took the parcels from her hands and she searched her pouch for coins. The other priest, who had the build and demeanour of a soldier, approached Swift.

'This will be our third school,' he said. 'They're the work of a talented young Wessex man of our acquaintance.'

'A Wessex man!' repeated Claudia. 'How splendid. Swift, do you need some coins?'

'His birth name is Aethelfraed,' the priest said softly.

Swift started, but Claudia didn't seem to notice. She accepted the proffered coins and gave them to the priest, who put them in a small purse tied to his waist. Before she could draw back, he took both her hands gently and firmly and held them for a moment. 'You are welcome here,' he said, and his gaze was so intense she couldn't look away. Then he released her and the two men walked off.

'How strange that priest was,' Claudia muttered as they climbed back into their carriage. Swift said nothing; she was distracted by the tiny piece of parchment now in her hand. She rolled it between her fingers and shivered with excitement.

Early the following morning, Swift took a carriage to the outer skirts of Rome and made her way up the Janiculum Hill as the note had instructed. She'd already climbed the Palatine Hill a few days previously, to admire the view of the Forum. Its paths were well trodden, lined with stalls selling wine, ale and roasted nuts, and she'd been pestered by garrulous young men who'd offered to show her the enchanting view in exchange for a few coins. But the Janiculum offered no such seeing of sights. For centuries its network of aqueducts had provided water for Rome's citizens, but now the once mighty stone structures were in an advanced state of decay. Its paths were littered with piles of sand and building detritus, the pipework was leaking and muddy pools abounded. As she approached the summit, she could hear the pitter-patter of dripping water. The runnels and gullies were cracked and broken, as much water was escaping onto the ground as was trickling down the pipes to the city, and swarms of insects hovered over her head. This was not a place where the casual visitor was likely to be disturbed.

At the very top of the hill was a plateau dotted with ruined watermills. Two men were sitting on a tumbledown wall.

'You came,' said Asser.

'Of course,' replied Swift.

'We're deeply grateful,' said Alfred.

She looked closely at her brother. The face she'd known previously had been that of a boy, insular and a little fearful, but he was a man now, taller than she remembered, with the broad shoulders of a rowing slave.

'Sister,' he said, stepping forward a little awkwardly and

embracing her, but his hug was too tight and his elbows pressed hard into her ribs. Her family had never found displays of affection easy.

'Aethelfraed,' she replied, pulled back from him a little, smiled, then put her arms round him again. 'Forgive my discourtesy. You are Alfred now, I hear. *Wise counsellor* in the old tongue. It's a good name, you'll wear it well.'

The three of them sat a little below the ridge of the hill to avoid the flies. Father Asser had a sack with him containing a flask of wine and three beakers. Swift hung her arm round Alfred's shoulder and they drank for a while. She told him about her expulsion from Wessex and her accession to the throne of Mercia, but though he made polite noises, she felt he was waiting for her to finish.

Eventually he could contain his agitation no longer. 'We need your help, sister,' he said. 'A young woman I promised to protect has been charged with heresy and murder and is in danger of being tortured. Our friend Father Kennet has been accused of complicity in this, all our companions are under threat . . .'

He was growing more and more exercised. The confident Alfred she thought he'd become had been replaced by the angry, ardent younger brother of yore. She remembered him a decade previously talking to himself because he had no one else to speak with, arguing intently with some imaginary philosopher, defending the flag tower from invisible assailants, climbing to the top of the highest oak to avoid a whipping from the Shrew.

'Calm yourself, my dear,' she said. 'I know you seek my aid; why else would you have wanted to meet me in secret. What is it you would have me do?'

'You are staying with the Gilottis,' replied Alfred. 'Enzo Gilotti's brother was a foul libertine who indulged in the darkest sins but was murdered before he could be punished for them. It is his murder of which our friends are being accused . . . and all sorts of heresy besides.'

'We need you to contrive a meeting between Enzo and Cardinal Balotelli, in order to persuade Enzo they are innocent,' added Asser. 'They took no part in the murder; we have written evidence from a woman involved in the deed . . .'

However distressed the two men might be, Swift was revelling in their company and their passion for the problems they wished to see resolved. They were driven by a cause, unlike most men of her acquaintance, who were driven only by their cocks and their purses. She wanted to share their commitment, and for their enemies to be hers too.

Eventually Asser ground to a halt.

'I am appalled by what you've said,' she replied steadily, her mind spinning at the complexity of it all and the intensity of its telling. 'I will consider your words carefully and do my utmost to arrange the meeting you desire. Now I must go. I fear Claudia Gilotti will be growing concerned. I will send word to you soon.' She bade them farewell and made her way back down the hill, her heart pounding.

Swift returned to the Gilotti household and mumbled her apologies to Claudia. She was tired after her long morning walk, she said, and wished to lie down for a while. She went straight to the refurbished retiring room and turned her attention to the door bearing the stout lock. She searched the painted pot and the branches of the bushy plant, looking for a key, but found nothing. Eventually, though, she discovered one hidden on a hook behind a shutter. She tried it in the lock and it fitted. She opened the door and was confronted by the sour smell of a dirty bed and unwashed clothes.

She ran her fingers over every item in the room – mounds of coins, knives, a string of beads, some wooden plugs. She looked behind and under everything, searching for evidence of Gilotti's dark side. On a high shelf behind two folded sheep's-wool coats, she discovered a wooden box and a pile of parchments covered in drawings. She lifted them down, spread the parchments out on the bed and began looking through them.

Swift knew that men gazed upon pictures of naked women for their arousal and pleasure, but the ones in front of her now were beyond titillation – vivid drawings, many with depraved descriptions scrawled alongside: tales of bestiality, violent acts of gratification on slaves and children, necrophilia, pictures of bound men and women with objects of all shapes and sizes inserted into their various orifices. If Enzo's brother was so obsessed by images of cruelty and domination, would he not also desire to re-create them in his own life? The box was locked, but she prised it open in a fury and tipped the contents onto the bed: bound snippets of pubic hair, women's dirtied loincloths, weird metal objects stained with what appeared to be blood, whose purpose she could only begin to guess at. She had seen enough. If this man was dead, she was glad of it. She'd been cocooned and protected for weeks, but her brother's passionate words had brought back to her the world she knew best, one populated by dangerous, obsessive enemies and constant threats of betrayal.

She had forgotten how much she'd loved Alfred. For her whole life she'd acted only on her own behalf, but she was her brother's ally now, and was glad to be so.

EIGHTY-THREE

The Sanest Man in the Room

When Alfred and Asser returned to the Undercroft, they found the courtyard in chaos. Twenty or more Concerned Citizens were setting fire to bundles of documents, smashing benches and tables and dragging Balotelli's priests out of the building.

Father Philip came running towards them. 'Ponti's men have returned with a vengeance,' he said. 'They had a papal order stating the Undercroft is to be renovated for the storage of church documents and that we must leave it for good. They said they had proof positive you were no longer a papal legate and that Ponti could not be countermanded. Worse still, Balotelli's guard have been stood down, and Father Kennet has been arrested and taken Christ knows where.'

Alfred grabbed one of the Citizens and shook him violently. 'What have you done with Kennet?' he demanded.

Asser pulled him away. 'Remember you are one of them,' he hissed. 'If they think you are on our side, you'll be useless to us. Yes, we need to know where Kennet is, but we also have to find out whether the Notarii are behind the attacks on us. If it's simply vindictiveness on Ponti's part, we can ensure the edict is quickly rescinded, but only you can find that out.'

He broke away from Alfred and ran towards an older priest, who was clutching a large rolled manuscript that he wouldn't release until Asser prised it from him.

'We've already removed the most important papers, Father,' he whispered. 'There's no purpose attempting to stand up to these bastards. Our most important task is to leave unharmed and find somewhere to hide.'

'Where is Balotelli?' asked Alfred urgently.

'He and the Doctore arranged a meeting at the Notarii to protest against our treatment,' replied Philip. 'That must be why Ponti sent the Citizens here now. He knew Balotelli would be elsewhere.'

'I'll go to the Notarii, find the cardinal and apprise him of what's happening,' said Alfred.

'And I'll take a horse and ask Carlo the saddle-maker to find somewhere for us to stay,' said Asser.

Alfred ran across Hadrian's Bridge into the city and through the bleak wasteland surrounding the Notarii building. By the time he arrived at the entrance, his breath was like a spear in his throat, but still he didn't stop. An angry voice was coming from the council chamber; he crept in and joined the other clerks at the back of the packed room. Balotelli was haranguing two cardinals Alfred knew well. Zuppi and Barberini had been members of the Notarii for decades. Perhaps at one time they'd had the interests of the Holy See at heart, but now they were concerned only with gleaning as much wealth as possible for themselves and their families. Alfred suspected they had no real awareness of what Ponti was doing but were happy to remain in ignorance.

'His Holiness the Pope has stated categorically that he will not tolerate arbitrary arrests of my people on unsubstantiated charges,' said Balotelli.

'Has he?' replied Cardinal Zuppi, his voice brimful of reasonableness. 'Well of course! That's absolutely fair.'

'But arrests are still being threatened,' argued Balotelli, his face flushed, his frustration palpable.

'They are, Stephen,' replied Cardinal Barberini. 'But the threats come from Father Ponti, not from us. Ponti may be our Undersecretary, but his task of freeing Rome from heretics is a direct papal instruction and is not under our auspices.'

'That is correct,' agreed Zuppi. 'And to ensure he behaves appropriately, the Pope has appointed Primicerius Gilotti to countersign all arrests and executions authorised by him.'

'A man in whose fairness and impartiality we have every confidence,' added Barberini. 'As I'm sure you do.'

Eventually the meeting was declared at an end and Balotelli and the Doctore left, Balotelli threatening to bring down God's wrath upon the lot of them.

The room cleared, the clerks packed up and departed; only a few Notarii remained. Alfred slowly arranged his papers and kept his head down as the cardinals stretched and relaxed. Cardinal Barberini called for a flask of cherry wine, and a young priest with his hair tied back in a neat bow served it with cherry biscuits.

'I think that went well,' said Cardinal Zuppi. 'We were right to draw the distinction between what we do as the Notarii and what individual employees may do. Yes, we wish to see an end to Stephen's absurd obsessions, we yearn for him and his men to be brought low, we may even believe his Holiness has become worryingly senile and should be replaced as soon as possible, but all that is for private discussion.'

'I agree,' said Barberini, picking the cherries from a biscuit and popping them into his mouth one by one. 'The Pope has given Ponti a free hand. He is an eccentric, and the activities he's currently indulging in at the Colosseum may be dubious, but they are nothing to do with us. Enzo will ensure all is done with propriety. There are far more important issues for us to worry about than a few impoverished heretics. A tax on wealth would deliver a mortal blow to us all. Addressing that threat must be our first priority.'

Alfred left the building and found Balotelli and the Doctore crossing the bridge.

'Ponti's men ejected us from the Undercroft and they've arrested Father Kennet,' he said breathlessly. 'They were waving a papal order saying they could do so.'

'A papal order? That can't be genuine, can it?' said Balotelli. 'I'll find out. Benedict is becoming more of a problem by the hour. Call my guards and have our people reinstated.'

'Your guards have been stood down,' said Alfred.

Balotelli gave a bitter laugh. 'Of course they have,' he said. 'Our enemies grow ever more impudent.'

'I'll speak to the few friends we have left among the cardinals and ask them to protest at the way we're being treated,' said the Doctore.

'Good,' said Balotelli. 'Do you know where they've taken Kennet?'

'I'm not sure, Cardinal,' replied Alfred. 'The Notarii said Ponti is in the Colosseum, but God only knows what he's doing there.'

A mass of struggling people were being coerced towards the Colosseum's entrance by Ponti's club-wielding men.

Alfred nodded at one, who let him through a small side gate. Inside, the crowd were being cajoled into queues, which culminated in stony-faced interrogators writing down their details. *When did you last attend mass? Where do you live? What are the names of your children? Who are your friends and accomplices?* Each bewildered victim was then sent to one of ten or so pens arranged at intervals around the rubble-strewn arena.

Ponti came bustling up to him. 'Isn't this impressive?' he crowed, taking Alfred by the arm and leading him round as though showing him the wonders of Lake Garda. 'These first three pens are for those who've confessed to heresy. The next two are for suspects who need a little more prodding, the ones to the left contain troublemakers who became aggressive or blasphemous during interrogation, the one on the right is for those whose neighbours we wish to interview, and so on. For months I've argued that the real threat facing us isn't the Norlanders, it's the radical priests and heretics who've infested Christendom. I was right, but who would listen? No one. They said I was mad. But I'm not, I'm the sanest man in the room.'

Alfred spotted Father Kennet huddled in the corner of a pen, looking cold and defeated. He turned his head away and resumed his feigned interest in Ponti's ramblings.

'Then one day, one Christ-blessed day, manna from heaven dropped into my outstretched hands. Gilotti's murder, the girl heretic, that idiot Kennet, the outrage against the new tax ... Now I no longer have to lift a finger. Everyone wants stern measures implemented. I can hardly keep up with all that's asked of me. Tomorrow we'll finish bringing in the heretics, and once I have Enzo Gilotti's permission, we'll sweep up Balotelli's men and the other radicals; there must be at least two hundred of them spreading his poison round the city. But we've got plenty of room for them here, thank the Lord! We've already started the hangings, and I'm organising a grand event for Kennet's execution the day after tomorrow. There'll even be a trumpet band. And I mustn't forget that bitch Clothilde. My head is in such a spin. So much to do. Sometimes I think the weight of my responsibilities is driving me demented.'

'Would you like me to make a list of all those to be tortured or executed, so you don't forget?' said Alfred.

'I would indeed!' said Ponti. 'I knew I could rely on you.'

When Asser had asked Carlo for help, the saddler had immediately offered shelter to all Balotelli's priests in his store by the river. It was a new wooden building that exuded the sweet, nutty smell of fresh leather. All thirty priests were propped up inside it among piles of saddles, eating fruit and nuts and passing around Carlo's skins of wine.

'We're living the life of princes,' said Philip.

'Perhaps, but we should get all of you out of the city as soon as possible,' replied Asser. 'We thought the attack on the market square was bad, but only a handful of us suffered. I suspect this will be a thousand times worse.'

He left Philip to prepare for the exodus and rode round the city warning Balotelli's supporters of the unfolding threat. Then he galloped out of the city gates leaving Rome behind him, and found a dozen or so sympathisers prepared to give shelter to the most vulnerable of his priests. By evening he still had one more call to make, and he was not looking forward to it.

When Asser was young and still at the Emmaus, he and his fellow students Philip and Kennet had climbed out of their dormitory window one night and, on the Doctore's recommendation, had taken a long, furtive walk to a church on the outskirts of the city to hear the words of the infamous Dean Stephen Balotelli. It was a secret event with guards at the door, and the boys were transformed by it. The dean talked about the holy battles ahead, a vital necessity if they were to create a new world in which common folk's suffering would be relieved. Asser knew straight away that he wanted to become one of the chosen men who would bring this vision about. Not that there were only men in that little church; there were a number of nuns standing modestly at the back, as well as merchants, clergymen, farmers, soldiers, an earl even – people of all walks of life and social ranking. It was exciting and terrifying. Balotelli was proposing that the entire church hierarchy should be brought to its knees; even to say such a thing could lead to imprisonment and death.

His words stayed with Asser ever after. And though he was careful to disguise his admiration for Balotelli behind brusqueness and irony, it had never faded, even when he'd suspected the cardinal of perfidy. He knew Balotelli was arrogant and snobbish, that he poured all his energy into his latest obsession and discarded it the moment he hit on a new one, but he was a visionary, the only truly perceptive man he had ever known, and he would happily serve him till the day he died . . . which might well be tomorrow.

It occurred to him that almost every one of those who'd attended the little church that night had stayed loyal to Balotelli, and when he finally had the means to do so he'd rewarded them for their loyalty. Some had been given jobs in his service, others had supervised his projects, drafted new laws, become deans or bishops or, in the case of Clothilde, an abbess. But now these brave and remarkable people were under attack once more, and it was Asser's duty to find sanctuary for them, even if it meant re-entering the portals of his old seminarium.

Asser rode to the chapel at the Emmaus and sat on the bench at the back where he'd chattered, giggled and prayed so many times when he was young. Master Spinoza was conducting the afternoon service, and an inordinate number of psalms were being sung, as though he was deliberately dragging it out as long as possible to punish the rows of boys and young men stifling their yawns, praying only to be allowed to go and eat. The master finally gave the benediction and disappeared through a little curtain into his disrobing room. Asser followed, and found him sitting on a stool while a very young student attempted to pull off the sweaty black hose from under Spinoza's bell-shaped chasuble.

The master looked up. 'I have nothing to say to you,' he said. 'I hear that fool of a Pope is attempting to impose a new tax. Go back and help him, then Father Ponti can hang you both.'

'I fear Ponti is being a little overzealous,' said Asser.

'I pray he is,' replied Spinoza. 'The Church has been lacking such zeal for too long.'

'It will go badly for some of your former students should he be successful.'

'Yes. The threatened mass arrests,' mused Spinoza. 'Good. That's what the city needs.'

'You nurtured so many fine young men, Master. The years you spent instructing them in the intricacies of Christian law. All those you awarded with the St Matthew's chalice for their deliberations on the Book of Revelations. They may suffer terrible and arbitrary punishment over the next few days. Might you not offer them a little support? Speak the right words to the right prelate? Perhaps give some of them shelter.'

'You expect me to risk my reputation and that of my establishment for your gang of troublemakers?' Spinoza replied icily. 'I warned you things would go badly for you, but in your arrogance you treated me like a fool. If they die, it will stain your soul, not mine!'

Asser returned to Rome, where Alfred was waiting for him at the Saxon school.

'I found Father Kennet. He's imprisoned in the Colosseum,' Alfred said anxiously. 'He's alive, but appears to be in poor spirits. He's surrounded by guards and I don't know how we'll release him.'

'Which is why we must obtain that meeting between Balotelli and Enzo Gilotti as quickly as possible,' said Asser. 'Let's hope we hear some good news from your sister soon. In the meantime, come with me and we'll take counsel with Balotelli.'

But their journey back to the palazzo wasn't easy. The crowd had grown denser, and there was manic dancing and singing. Stave-wielding Citizens beat a path through the mass of people, followed by a solitary drummer. Behind him were more Citizens pulling a cart on which a tree trunk was mounted. Nailed to it was a naked body, every part of which was so mutilated Asser had to look away.

'Heretic! Filthy heretic!' people cried, and they threw stones and spat at it.

Another drummer appeared, and a cart containing a second brutalised body. But it was the third that shook them to the core. The body would have been impossible to identify had it not been for its blue hair. It was Mirandolina.

Alfred gave a wail so profound Asser had to seize him and put a hand to his mouth for fear they would attract the suspicion of the mob.

'We must go,' he said, but Alfred stood his ground, weeping like a child.

'Now!' Asser insisted. 'We are putting ourselves in danger. Come, give me your arm.'

Alfred buried his face in his hands and turned away.

'Compose yourself. This is the world against which the cardinal is fighting,' Asser said. 'It is brutal, cruel and stupid, and we shut our eyes to it at our peril.'

Alfred shook his head, and Asser was suddenly consumed by the frustration and rage that had been bubbling up inside of him since he first met Wolf's son.

'In the name of Christ the Redeemer! If you want to avenge

Mirandolina, if you want to punish those who maim and torture and murder, stand up to them. You are a Westsaxon aethel, so act like one. I saw you bold and resolute when you rescued Balotelli at the Gilottis' house, but now you hide your manhood like a child behind its mother's skirt. Enough of playing the children's friend and the secret spy. Come out into the open, take matters into your own hands, or what has your life been for?'

Alfred didn't move. Asser shrugged, turned, and pushed his way through the throng. But when he glanced back, Alfred was following him.

EIGHTY-FOUR

A Byzantine Dream

The Concerned Citizens were on the streets and there were bodies hanging from the trees, but tonight the Gilottis' home was a Byzantine dream.

'We chose well,' said Claudia. She and Swift paraded among the guests in their newly acquired regalia, their hair piled high and topped with gold-plated crowns, their necks bejewelled, their ears and fingers laden with brightly enamelled rings. It had been four hundred years since the Roman Empire had split asunder, but the wealthier sort of Romans still tried to ape the luxury flaunted by the women of the city of Constantinople.

Drinks were served. Enzo clapped his hands and made a brief speech of welcome, and ten musicians dressed in white and wearing little skullcaps sang to the glory of the Most High. The music was mellifluous and multi-layered, echoes of Greece, Syria and Persia reverberating round the room, but Swift kept her attention firmly on Enzo. Not only had he acceded to her entreaty; he had seemed grateful she'd made it. 'I think you know how eager I am to give you anything you might ask of me, and besides, I need to see Stephen,' he'd said benignly.

Swift had suspected his affection for her might be more than simply familial. At any other time, such attentions might have proved an annoyance, but now she was grateful for them. She had achieved what she'd set out to do. Enzo had sent Balotelli an invitation to the recital.

The cardinal arrived a little later than the other guests. Enzo greeted him courteously, if a little distantly. Swift was introduced to him, and he bestowed on her the subtle but knowing look of a co-conspirator. He seemed pleasant enough: well mannered, dressed impressively in his formal white robes, scented appropriately with saffron, the ubiquitous Byzantine perfume. But Alfred had described him as one of the great minds of the Empire, whereas to her he appeared only another powerful man seeking advantage.

The audience immersed themselves in the musicians' chants, canons and counterpoint. An interval was announced and a feast was served: cheese and black caviar, red mullet, baby deer, a special delicacy of spiced rice pudding, and wine infused with caraway and nutmeg.

Enzo glanced at Swift and left the room. She approached a small group of guests clustered round Balotelli, talking enthusiastically about his poetry and less enthusiastically about the Pope's proposed new taxes. She took his arm, apologised for taking him from them, and they followed Enzo into the garden, at the far end of which was a small wooden house where he conducted his business. As they entered, a solitary monk looked up from his work and scrutinised them. He held a pen, but from the size of his hands and the breadth of his shoulders, Swift suspected he offered Enzo a secure workplace rather than finely crafted documents.

They walked past him into a second room. On the far wall

was a fresco of a bear at bay surrounded by agitated dogs and spear-wielding huntsmen; long, dark brown leather drapes hung from the walls, and a stuffed hawk was suspended from the ceiling. Enzo was drumming his fingers on the arm of his leather chair. He didn't stand to greet Balotelli, but smiled and nodded as Swift placed herself discreetly on an upright seat by the door. Balotelli sat opposite him, the two men gazing at each other like gladiators.

Enzo broke the silence. 'Her Grace Queen Swift, for whom I have the greatest respect and admiration, has asked me to speak with you on behalf of her brother, who I understand is an acquaintance of yours.'

'I appreciate your invitation, Enzo,' replied Balotelli. 'It cannot have been an easy decision to make.'

'It was not. Not only did you order my brother to be detained, but you attended his arrest in person.'

'I did, Enzo, to try to ensure it was conducted with propriety. I failed, and for that I profoundly apologise, but I had no alternative other than to apprehend him. A novice nun had been savagely despoiled, and the evidence against your brother was overwhelming. You know the kind of man he was. I had helped him out of compromising situations at your request on many occasions. Had events run smoothly, I have no doubt the Pope would have exiled him for a while, and I suspect your family would not have been unhappy with such an outcome.'

'We could have resolved this problem discreetly if you'd been so minded. But your actions led to his death,' said Enzo.

'That is not so,' replied Balotelli. 'He was complicit with his killer. He invited her into his house. He paid her to bind him.'

The discussion was going nowhere. Swift needed to coax the two men towards the matter of Father Kennet's innocence before acrimony descended.

'Forgive my presence here,' she said. 'My brother was deeply concerned about a woman who was falsely accused of your brother's murder, but she was recently put to death before he could prove her innocence. However, her protector, one of Cardinal Balotelli's priests named Father Kennet, is still under arrest and is shortly to be executed. A witness to the murder has been found who has sworn on the Holy Bible that Father Kennet is innocent. She is a young God-fearing girl called Elswith, who has given a written confession to Abbess Clothilde of St Catherine's. I believe you know the abbess well.'

'Indeed I do,' replied Enzo. 'Before I entered the Church, her father and I bought and sold slaves and timber together. It was a fine business. She was a bright girl destined for great things, though sadly her head has been turned in recent years by the man sitting opposite me.'

'But she is honest and trustworthy?' asked Swift.

'She is indeed.'

'Good. Our witness has revealed intimate details of the events on the night in question, which the abbess has incorporated into a confession. May I have your permission to read it?'

Enzo nodded. Swift unrolled the document. 'There is a brief formal introduction,' she said, 'followed by this statement. "I, Elswith of Yeovil, do hereby swear that neither Father Kennet nor the woman known as Mirandolina were involved in the killing of Fabio Gilotti. While I was serving as a novice at St Catherine's Abbey, I was attacked by him and he took my honour forcibly. I became possessed of a righteous anger and sought revenge. I learnt where Signor Gilotti was being held from Clovis of Sicily, who had provided him with women for his gratification on many occasions. Clovis escorted me to Tivoli, where Signor Gilotti was residing. Having been told of his predilection for intimacies of the Spartan kind, I adopted the role of a sinful woman prepared to provide him with such pleasures, and on his instruction I bound him to a table in his tepidarium. I had planned to take his life, but he pleaded with me to be allowed to live, and I became overcome by remorse. I chose instead to leave him bound and helpless, to be exposed to shame and humiliation when his family returned. However, I was unaware that some weeks previously he had refused to pay Clovis a sum of money due for the provision of similar activities, and when I told Clovis I'd spared his life, he took my knife and entered the tepidarium. Though I did my best to prevent him from so doing, he attacked Signor Gilotti, killed him and mutilated him. He then brought me back to Rome. I resolved to flee, and—"'

'That's enough,' said Enzo. He had wandered over to the window and was gazing across the garden to the illuminated hall, from where a single voice and the tinkling of a dulcimer were emanating.

'Where is the girl now?' he said eventually.

'She has gone,' answered Balotelli.

'Of course she has. How convenient. We will catch her and interrogate her.'

Swift's heart sank. 'Clothilde swears she's telling the truth.'

'Clothilde has a kind heart,' Enzo replied, 'but the girl behaved like a whore and is an accomplice to the murder of my brother. She admits it.' He sat down again and stretched his legs. 'I'll give you Kennet. He clearly had nothing to do with the affair. Elswith and her associate Clovis will be tracked down, interrogated and punished. That is my final offer.'

'And I thank you for it,' replied Balotelli.

They listened as the music swelled and faded.

'My guards have been taken away from me,' he said.

'I know nothing of that,' replied Enzo.

The singing came to an end and there were cries for more.

'And there is another matter,' the cardinal said after a while. 'You understand that the allegations of heresy being made against my men are baseless? Ponti has been seized by a certain wildness, which has provoked uproar. We both know he is capable of gross irresponsibility. It was you and I who ensured he was expelled from his role at the Office of Christian Orthodoxy on my return to Rome. He has no temperance. Please instruct him to persecute my people no longer.'

'That is not the reason I agreed to this meeting,' replied Enzo. 'The Pope has asked Ponti to address the matter of heresy. I merely help keep him in check. We have a more important matter to discuss, do we not?'

Balotelli smiled ruefully. 'Benedict's new tax?'

Enzo spoke slowly, pausing between each phrase as though talking to a child. 'It is unacceptable, Stephen, and must be withdrawn. If you persuade the Pope to do so, I will exert my power and ensure Ponti leaves you and your men be, though I'm sceptical about your desire to do so. Taxation is a subject you and I have debated long and hard since we were students. You advocated a tithe on the rich then, and I have no reason to think you've changed your view in the intervening years.'

'You are correct,' replied Balotelli. 'I believe paying a levy on wealth is a fair requirement for those who have been given the gift of it. But I also believe now is not the moment to implement such a thing. It would cause too much disturbance at a time when I wish to persuade the cardinals to support other radical reforms, many of which you were in favour of in your younger days. I have attempted to have the tax reduced or delayed. I have proposed numerous circumstances in which it should not apply, but the Pope is wedded to it and insists it should remain unamended.'

'You must try again,' said Enzo. 'This is not one of your Persian board games, Stephen. Lives are at stake. *Your* life is at stake. While we have been listening to this enchanting music, my men have been installing checking points at the gates of the city. No one will be allowed through them until the issue is resolved. The people of Rome will of course be deeply discomforted by this action, and you and the Pope will be blamed for it. If you have still failed to change Benedict's mind by noon tomorrow, I will give Ponti full rein to do as he wishes and unleash his dogs, and your tiresome experiment in church governance will be replaced by judicious men more suited to the job of ruling Christendom in a dignified and proper manner.'

There was a long silence.

Lo, though I walk through the valley of the shadow of death, sang the Byzantine choir.

'So be it,' said Balotelli eventually.

Enzo sprang to his feet. 'Good! Our business has come to an end. I will prepare and seal the papers for Father Kennet's happy release and will call on a messenger to send them to Ponti. Then we'll return to the house, my friend, and listen to more of these delightful songs.'

EIGHTY-FIVE

The Farewell

The recital came to an end; the guests tossed a few small coins into a dish to assist the victims of an earthquake in an impoverished part of the eastern Byzantine Empire, those who lived outside Rome were given a pressed metal disc which would allow them to pass through the city gates, and everyone went home to their beds. The musicians wrapped soft cloths round their pipes and horns, dismantled their dulcimer and put the pieces back carefully in its ivory box. The servants swept the hall and rearranged the furniture. Soon the only sounds were from the kitchen on the far side of the building, where the slaves were scraping and sanding the last cooking vessels.

Swift returned to her room and reluctantly hung her exquisite dress in the closet. She donned her riding gear, packed her saddlebag and lay on the bed waiting for the noise to stop. She was going to betray her hosts, but so be it, there were lives to be saved. She left her room, took a metal disc from a bowl by the front door, and went cautiously outside. Alfred was waiting in the shadow of the garden house. 'Father Kennet will live,' she whispered. 'Enzo has sent Ponti an official order demanding his release.'

'You saved a good man's life tonight, sister,' said Alfred.

'Perhaps,' replied Swift, 'but Elswith is to be arrested – Enzo's guards are tracking her down – and the attack on Balotelli's men will begin in earnest if he is unable to persuade the Pope to rescind his threatened tax. Enzo has already barred the city gates to prevent your men from leaving. Balotelli has until midday to resolve the issue. If he fails, Enzo will give Ponti a free hand to initiate a slaughter.'

'I had hoped we could put a stop to this madness,' said Alfred. 'Cardinal Balotelli said Enzo is a rational man. It seems he is wrong.'

'He *is* rational. He cares little about the heretics and even less about Ponti; he will simply use them to his advantage. But he is determined to protect his wealth and that of the ancient families by whatever means necessary, regardless of the cost.'

Alfred sighed and stared at the ground.

'Don't look so defeated,' she added briskly. 'We have twelve hours to resolve matters. Where will I find you?'

'At Carlo's saddlery in the southern quarter.'

'I will see what help I can give you. In the meantime, take this disc. It is stamped with Enzo's authority and will allow you to escape through the city gates if the time comes.'

Alfred shook his head.

'I won't leave without my comrades, but your concern touches me deeply,' he replied.

'Hold onto it anyway, and use it as you think best,' she said.

'Sister, when I was a child, I was a little afraid of you and we seldom spoke. But I will tell you now that my love and gratitude for you know no bounds.'

*

Swift took a horse from Enzo's stable and rode to Caesar's Haven. The door was opened by an old woman with a gaping mouth and a blanket wrapped round her shoulders. Swift demanded that Prince Louis be brought to her forthwith.

The woman scuttled away, and moments later, Louis appeared in his sleeping attire, yawning, tousled, like one of her Welsh boys when they'd been woken from a bad dream. It had been seven years since she'd last seen him. She'd been on a visit to Amiens to buy jewellery and purchase sheep, and Louis had been staying in the same city with his entourage. They'd become friends again, as they'd been as children, and little by little they'd been drawn into something more intimate.

Might I see you t-tomorrow? he'd asked. *Will you s-stay till Thursday? If I carry you over this stile, will you give me a k-kiss? Will you allow me to visit you this evening?* And when she finally agreed to his requests and he'd stayed the night, all the next day and the next night too he'd said, *One day will you m-marry me?* and she'd replied, *Yes, if you give me an army.*

Years later, when she became Warden of South Hamwicshire, she wrote to him offering her hand in exchange for a troop of Frankish soldiers. Tedious negotiations followed involving Louis' father, the emperor, but eventually it was agreed: they would marry and take possession of the entire South Coast of Wessex. The plan had turned to dust, of course, as most plans did, and in the course of its collapse, he broke the promises he'd made to her. This had made her deeply unhappy, but his guilt was now a currency she could use to her advantage.

'How w-wonderful you look,' he said. 'I'd thought you'd not want to see m-me.'

'I always want to see you, Louis,' she replied.

They talked a while of foolish things until a young woman bustled in and Louis introduced her as Gretta, his new wife.

She was Flemish, spoke little Saxon or Latin, and had two large front teeth. It occurred to Swift that kissing her would not be a particularly enjoyable experience. They had a desultory conversation about cloth prices and the architecture of Amiens, and eventually Gretta brushed her husband's cheek with her lips and left.

'She l-loves me very much,' he said.

'She is an only child?' enquired Swift.

'She is,' replied Louis.

'So she'll inherit . . .'

'Alsace and Lorraine,' said Louis. 'Although I would be lying if I didn't admit how d-distressed I was to have to m-marry her for the sake of . . .'

'Alsace,' said Swift.

'And Lorraine,' added Louis regretfully, and they both smiled.

'We could have ruled the south coast, Louis. Perhaps even Wessex itself. Everything augured so well.'

'It did,' agreed Louis. 'I'm b-bitterly sorry. Ours would have b-been a marriage of the heart. How cruel it is that we cannot find love as common folk do. I b-broke my vow to you only on my father's insistence; he said our marriage would p-prejudice a concord he'd negotiated. You'll never know the agony that cost me, and the irony was that my sacrifice was all for nothing. Shortly afterwards he repudiated the concord. B-but if there is ever anything I can do to repay the d-debt I owe you . . .'

'Why do you think I came to you in the middle of the night?' said Swift. 'You can repay it now.'

Louis blinked. 'Whatever you ask of me, I will do my b-best to fulfil.'

'I know you will, though we will need to move in haste. Our task must be accomplished by noon.'

*

Half a dozen candles were burning in Balotelli's palazzo. Shafts of light played across the wooden crates and piles of documents were stacked up next to them in the middle of the floor. Alfred called out the cardinal's name.

'Wait a moment,' a voice replied from another room.

'You're packing up?' Alfred shouted back.

Balotelli came in with his hands full of scrolls and dropped them in a crate. 'I was with the Pope long into the night. I told him repeatedly of Enzo's threats, but he was adamant. He said Enzo would back down in the face of our resolve. I said I doubted it, and that the whole city was in turmoil, but he insisted that in such difficult times, firm leadership is required. Then he went back to bed.'

'Enzo's locked the city gates. They won't let you through,' said Alfred.

The cardinal put a lid on the crate and began binding it with hemp string. 'My brother Salvatore will smuggle me out along with my effects, and we'll head to Puglia. Will Ponti send his men for me soon?'

'At midday. You are the first on his list.'

Balotelli burst out laughing. 'You've learnt how to discover his every move. I was right to persuade you to work for him. You possessed a sweet but unhelpful naivety when we first met; now you know how evil works and it will be of great use to you.'

Alfred watched him trying to tie a knot. He was overwhelmed by sadness.

'You must take care,' he said. 'Have this,' and he held out the disc Swift had given him. 'It will let you out of the city.'

'Thank you, but no,' replied Balotelli. 'I have no need of it. You keep it.' He began filling another crate. 'You'll go back to Wessex, of course,' he said.

'I don't think so,' replied Alfred.

Balotelli stopped, stood up and faced him. 'You must,' he

said firmly. 'Why do you think Christ put you on this earth? Why did he bring you to me? We're alike, you and I. God has given us talents we must use to protect the world from harm. We may not wish to, we might rather stay in our beds revelling in the words of Socrates and Seneca, but we have no choice. Ultimately, I failed. Not merely with little projects like my birds and my inability to finish St Peter's. I was arrogant and underestimated my enemies, I became obsessed by my vision of a great war, I chose a weak Pope and gave him insufficient counsel. I regret all that deeply. But I have taught you well and you will do better.'

'I have no desire to—'

'You do!' Balotelli was almost shouting. 'You have possibilities without limit. You are strong, brave and thoughtful, you have the potential for wisdom. Your mother knew it, your father too, which was why he feared you so. Your siblings knew it. *You* know it. You act the fool because the life of those who have power is onerous and sometimes unbearable. You babble like a mountain stream, your ambitions are the size of a thimble, but you are one of God's chosen. Go back to Wessex. The skills I've taught you will help you, as will Asser, who has far more understanding than you believe. Do what I failed to do and transform your land into God's bulwark against the Norlanders.' He bent down and began packing again.

'Do so,' he added, and his voice was so soft it was barely audible, 'or my life will have been for nothing.'

Alfred looked at him packing his documents for a long time. Was he right? Was it ordained that he should have some great future? He had no idea. Occasionally he was overwhelmed by the belief that he was capable of great things, but everyone had those thoughts sometimes, and weren't they mere arrogance?

Balotelli's thumb was tangled in the string. Alfred felt a deep and abiding love for him.

'It was not your fault the vision failed,' he said.

'You're right,' replied Balotelli. 'Had life run its usual course, we would have triumphed, but sometimes a devil like Ponti is thrown into this world, a man so wicked and unpredictable that he breaks every rule and undoes all our best endeavours. Why God allows this to happen is beyond our understanding, but at such times the best that good men can do is prepare for a better future. It is sad. Ponti will deploy all his energy against our finest people. Many will die before his wickedness ends, and there is little we can do to stop it.'

He put his crate to one side and picked up another.

'Shall we share a bed tonight?' Alfred asked.

'No, my dear boy, not tonight,' said Balotelli. 'I must wait for Salvatore to collect my possessions, then I have other business to attend to. We'll see each other again ere long.'

Alfred left. The disc still lay on the cardinal's table.

EIGHTY-SIX

Fide Nemini

Close by the Colosseum's main entrance, the Concerned Citizens had erected a shanty in which Ponti could deliberate and store his documents. Alfred pushed the door open and peered inside. There was no sign of life.

The shelves were piled high with scrolls, and on a rough table at one end was a scatter of slates and discarded pieces of parchment, on top of which were a few unopened messages including one bearing Enzo Gilotti's seal. Alfred tore it open, extracted Kennet's release document and put it in the purse on his belt. He browsed through the slates and parchment, then sat down at the table, picked up a pen and began to write. He knew he must rescue Kennet, but these notes bore the names of other men and women who were also under grave threat. He wouldn't let their lives be wasted. As he completed the list, a shadow fell across him. Ponti was standing in the doorway.

'What are you doing, Alfred?' he said sharply.

Alfred turned and bestowed on him a look of intense relief. 'Thank the dear Lord you're here,' he said. 'While I was waiting for you, I began putting your documents in order as you requested. I'm making a list of all those who are not heretics or radicals but who nevertheless you deem worthy of execution: Jews, Musselmen, bands of travelling horse dealers and pot menders. It will make life much easier for you.'

Ponti pulled Alfred to him and gave him a long hug. 'You are the finest of men,' he said. 'Why do you wish to see me so urgently?'

'Please sit for a moment, Father, I have exciting news. Cardinal Balotelli is in communication with the last remaining Antonils. They're hidden in the ruined Chapel of St Marco on the road to the Alban Hills, twenty of them. They're sick, desperate and have no food. May I have your permission to take some of your horsemen to St Marco's and put them to the sword?'

'No,' Ponti replied sharply. 'Thank you, but no,' he added a little more calmly. 'It is only proper that I should lead such an attack. This will be a moment of great significance.'

'You cannot do so, sir,' persisted Alfred. 'You must be here at midday. You have to discover if you have Enzo Gilotti's authority to arrest Balotelli's men.'

'It is early morning, Alfred,' replied Ponti. 'St Marco's is only a league and a half away. I'll marshal some of my Citizens and go straight away.'

'You cannot leave the Colosseum unguarded, sir,' Alfred said, but Ponti was already halfway out the door.

'Half a dozen men will stay here,' he said. 'Let nobody enter without your authority. *Fide nemini.*'

'Trust no one,' replied Alfred. 'An apposite maxim.'

Within no time, Ponti had called together his horsemen. They were rough and rowdy, jostling and lackadaisical, like a band of thieves on the highway.

'Farewell,' he said as he swung into the saddle. '*Fide nemini.*'

Alfred watched the Concerned Citizens canter off and smiled. He was taking control of the situation.

Alfred had known Ponti wouldn't be able to resist being present at such a slaughter. Of course there was nothing at St Marco's but rubble and dog shit, but it would take the Undersecretary half the morning to discover this.

He went to a small store at the back of the hut and dragged out a barrel of lamp oil. He swept the scrolls from the shelves, and as they tumbled to the floor, he kicked over the barrel and oil cascaded over the documents. He picked up the lone candle flickering in the corner and tossed it on the pile, then took a bunch of keys from the table and left, shutting the door casually behind him. Sauntering over to Kennet's pen, he showed Enzo's release document to the guards and picked his way through the dozing prisoners till he came to Kennet, lying on his side, his eyes closed.

'We're going home, my friend,' he said and pulled him to his feet.

'Ponti told me what he did to Mirandolina. It was my fault she died,' Kennet said. 'I am not worthy.'

'None of us are,' replied Alfred. 'Come on!'

There was smoke billowing out of the hut now, and shouts of 'Fire!' The guards had left their posts and were heading towards the conflagration.

Alfred assisted his friend out of his confinement, then turned to the other prisoners. 'Take these,' he said, and threw them the keys.

The hut roof was blazing, the Concerned Citizens ran back and forth. Prisoners began cautiously appearing from their pens.

'Where's Ponti?' said Kennet.

'Chasing wild geese,' replied Alfred.

EIGHTY-SEVEN

Once in a Hundred Years

Philip returned to the saddlery accompanied by three young priests.

'Bad news,' he said. 'We were turned back. The city gates have been closed and won't be opened again till the new tax has been rescinded. The people are irate, commerce has ground to a halt and Balotelli is being blamed. We're trapped.'

Most of the priests had escaped, there were only eight people left now: Asser, Philip, the Doctore, the three young priests and Carlo and his wife, all hoping the Pope would relent at the last moment. He wouldn't, of course. The same stubbornness that had stood him in such good stead under torture would now result in Asser's death and that of his friends. A miracle might occur, although probably not.

Asser sat astride a saddle beating a tattoo on the leather with his fingers. There was nothing else to do. The young priests were whiling their time away repeatedly spinning an old shoe to see which of them it would point to when it came to a halt.

They were resolute and amusing and had insisted they should be the last to leave. They reminded Asser of himself and his friends a dozen years previously. Apart from at church services, he seldom prayed, but he did now. 'Sweet Christ, don't let them die,' he murmured, then stood up and shook off his melancholy. 'Where's Balotelli?' he asked. 'I thought he'd be here by now.'

'I believe he's packing his belongings before the Citizens come knocking,' said the Doctore, who was lying on the beaten-earth floor with his eyes shut, resting his head on a pile of sacks. 'He wants to ensure his life's work isn't destroyed.'

'What about you, Carlo?' Asser asked. 'Do you want to try to slip away before they arrive? You can't be found here with us.'

'No. We're staying. My family's home is here,' replied the saddle-maker. 'So is my livelihood. We've survived before; people need saddles. Maybe we can keep our enemies at arm's length. If not . . .' He shrugged.

He was a good man, brave and true, the kind that made Asser's heart sing.

Carlo's wife crept in through the door and whispered in Asser's ear. 'There's a slave outside. He's asking for you.'

Asser peered out, and Carlo's wife nodded to the far side of the alley. Trug the Emmaus gardener was leaning against the wall.

'You're a hard man to find,' Trug said. 'I have a message from Spinoza.'

'Why did he send you?' asked Asser.

'Because I know you and I can keep my mouth shut.'

'So what does the old bastard want?'

'He says he'll take three.'

'Three what?'

'Three of your priests. He has a secure house in the city where they can lie low till the gates reopen.'

Asser looked bemused. 'So he's got a peck of goodness in him after all,' he said.

'I wouldn't go that far,' Trug replied.

Time passed slowly. The room seemed empty now Trug had taken the three priests away. Carlo found a skin of Albanum wine and they all took a swig. Philip tried to start a conversation, but no one wanted to join in. The Doctore's eyes were still shut and he was softly singing the song of Jude: 'Mercy, peace and love be yours in abundance.'

There was a flurry of noise and a gasp from Carlo's wife. Alfred was standing in the doorway carrying the exhausted Father Kennet in his arms like a baby.

'We've come to join you,' he said, and kicked the door shut behind him. 'Any news from the Pope?'

'None,' said Asser. 'Thank our Lord and Christ you found Kennet. Leave him with us. You should go back to Ponti as quickly as you can; you'll be safe with him.'

Alfred laughed. 'I doubt it. I sent him into the hills on a fool's errand and burnt down his hut and all his documents. That should slow him for a while.'

'You should have killed him,' said Asser.

'If I'd killed him, he'd have become a saint,' Alfred replied, 'but I made him look a fool and now he'll be a laughing stock.'

'Is that strong drink?' said Kennet, pointing to Carlo's half-finished skin of wine.

'We were saving it for you,' said Carlo.

Kennet put it to his mouth and drank furiously till it was empty.

'I thought my sister might be here,' said Alfred. 'She said she'd try to help us.'

'I've not heard from her,' said Asser, 'but I fear there's nothing more she can do for us.'

Carlo and his wife tended to Father Kennet, Alfred occasionally peered out the door looking for Swift, and Philip attempted to strike up yet another conversation.

'Suppose we were to escape. Where would we go?' he asked. 'I see myself on Homer's Ithaca with a twenty-strong congregation, tending a vineyard sloping down to the sea.'

'We'll give you a nunnery too, and you can be the sisters' attentive priest,' said Asser.

'I will serve them as best I can,' said Philip. 'How about you, Guido? Are you awake? Where will you go?'

The Doctore opened an eye. 'I'm waiting for you to leave, then I'll go to Enzo,' he said.

'Why?' asked Philip, wryly amused.

'I'm staying here,' the Doctore replied.

'You're not serious.'

'Somebody has to,' he continued. 'We may have won Benedict the papal crown, but he'll topple from a window like his predecessor if he isn't protected. He's a vacillator, an obsessive, and he has no sense of strategy, but he shares our passion for a reformed Church. You and I are expendable, but only a visionary Pope can transform Christendom. How often does such a man mount the papal throne? Once in a hundred years? Enzo has offered me a post if I require one; he needs me to prevent mayhem, and it will allow me to protect Benedict.'

'How could you be such a Judas?' exclaimed Philip, hardly believing what he was hearing.

'Don't be absurd. One of us must hold fast to what we've built,' the Doctore retorted. 'The refuges for the poor, the feeding of the hungry, the beds for the sick, your school, Alfred. My first loyalty is to the Church, Enzo knows that, it's why he trusts me. With careful handling, and support from the Pope, I can introduce some good men into the Notarii, gradually gain control of its procedures and implement the changes we want.

That's all that matters to me. It's more important even than the love I bear for all of you.'

'Ponti will be promoted and he'll put an end to you,' said Philip.

'Ponti won't be promoted. The Notarii don't want him, they simply needed someone to quash the threat you posed to them. I don't think they realised how unstable he is, how far he would go. Once the Pope learns what has happened to you all, Ponti will disappear.'

'Maybe one day you'll be primicerius,' said Philip bitterly.

'It has been suggested,' replied the Doctore.

Asser thought about the last few months. How the Doctore had constantly been among them, always listening, always counselling a soft hand towards their enemies. A revelation dawned on him, so painful it almost made him cry.

'You betrayed us from the start,' he said. 'You warned the Notarii we were going to the market square. You survived unscathed in Rome while the rest of us suffered. You knew the Notarii well enough to persuade them to vote for Benedict even though they mistrusted him. You were the conduit between them and Charles the Bald and filled their pockets with gold.'

'And land,' added the Doctore. 'And advancement.'

'You prevented us from bringing them down when they destroyed the mappa mundi. You betrayed us a thousand times!'

'It wasn't betrayal. I merely passed them the occasional morsel of information, just as Alfred did,' replied the Doctore. 'The mappa mundi wasn't important. It was an obscure allegory that would have changed the mind of no one. And as for you, did I not try to dissuade you from going to the market square that day? I told you we needed to hold back until we had sufficient supporters in high places. And I was right. A year later, we had the support of the emperor, and Balotelli took power peacefully.'

'But at what cost?' cried Asser.

His old teacher gave him a sorrowful look. 'I'm truly sorry for your pain. I didn't know how brutally you'd be treated, and that will weigh on my conscience for the rest of my life.'

'But they tried to kill you in St Peter's with the statue of St Andrew,' said Philip.

'I don't think they did,' said Asser. 'You arranged that too, didn't you, you treacherous bastard, with Rollo and Mountjoy?'

'A little charade,' admitted the Doctore, 'to show you how serious the situation was, and so none of you would guess I was close to Enzo. I knew you wouldn't understand.'

'But the attack at the Undercroft was no charade. Fabio practically battered you to death,' said Philip.

'That wasn't supposed to happen,' said the Doctore. 'Enzo instructed his brother merely to scare you all. He told Fabio to go to the Undercroft and break a few things, nothing more. But Fabio was a fool. He hired heretics from the taverns, and in his drunken state thought he could bring us down with one cruel blow. Why did he attack me? Because he was a bigot who thought the colour of my face should preclude me from high office. Why did he attack St Catherine's? Because he was venal and cruel, and believed he had a God-given right to do so. But I couldn't let his actions prevent us from bringing the vision to fruition. Enzo apologised fulsomely, and I accepted his apology. Such unpleasant accidents occur in church governance, but we must not let them deflect us from our path. All would have been well had it not been for Fabio's death.'

'Did Balotelli know all this?' asked the bewildered Philip.

'A little, but he chose not to enquire too deeply.'

There was silence. Asser felt numb. When he was a homesick child, the Doctore had shown him such kindness. He had stroked his hair as tenderly as a father, had nurtured and nourished his mind. Another thought struck him, and it was as though the whole world keeled on its side.

'Holy Mary! Holy sweet Jesus! It was you who pushed Pope Leo out of the window, wasn't it?'

'Why would I do that?' replied the Doctore.

'It was the only way you could achieve a reforming papacy.'

'He fell,' said the Doctore. 'He was pushed by the hand of God, that is all. I'll say no more.'

For a moment Asser wondered whether he might attack the Doctore, strangle him in front of his former friends and students, but he was too tired, and in a strange way he'd found what the Doctore had said compelling. Everything he'd done, even if he'd murdered Pope Leo, had been because he'd wanted the fulfilment of their vision. No, he wouldn't harm him. Despite all the killings and betrayals with which he'd been beset over the last few months, he'd not once responded violently. Wolf, Mountjoy, Rollo and now his beloved Doctore Guido; he'd listened to their justifications, had suffered pain and disappointment for a while, then returned to the tasks Christ had set him. Doubtless there was a profound rage smouldering somewhere inside him, and one day, if he survived, it would ignite like a forest fire and he'd have blood on his hands, but he prayed that when that day came, it would be in defence of some higher cause rather than out of blind rage.

There was a thunderous hammering at the door. Philip threw up his hands in agonised frustration.

'In the name of Christ's bloodied thorns, it's not midday yet. For a few precious moments leave us be!'

Asser flung the door open, but it wasn't Ponti. Queen Swift was mounted on a fine horse at the head of a band of soldiers wearing the uniform of the Holy Roman Empire.

Alfred peered over his shoulder. 'Sister! You've brought us an army!' he said.

'They're your escort out of the city. Prince Louis has lent them to me,' replied Swift. 'He promised me an army long ago. How many are you? We have horses enough.'

Philip and Kennet dropped to their knees and shed tears of joy. Even Asser, who detested ostentatious demonstrations of emotion, joined them on the floor for a brief moment.

'Hurry!' called Swift.

Asser picked himself up and went outside. There were twenty soldiers, with ten spare horses, and Abbess Clothilde was among them. 'Praise be to St Catherine!' he exclaimed. 'You're safe.'

'I am, and all my sisters are too.'

'But why should you have had to endure such maltreatment? You were merely copyists, you committed no crime,' said Alfred.

'We were guilty of making ourselves heard, which has been a sin for centuries, since Pope Gelasius forbade us women from preaching in the pulpit,' replied Clothilde. 'Like you, my sisters are happy to suffer for their convictions.'

'But where are they?' said Asser.

'All women understand the need for places away from the cruel predations of men,' said Clothilde. 'My fellow abbesses were only too happy to give them sanctuary.'

'Yet you kept one novice with you,' Alfred said, 'and a troublesome one, I think.'

'I'm no trouble, as you well know,' replied Elswith, who was sitting astride the horse next to Clothilde. 'The abbess and I were under particular threat. She knew Abdulalah had hidden me in his harbourside warehouse, so she came for me and invited me to join her.'

'We're heartily glad to see you,' said Alfred.

'Heartily indeed,' agreed Asser.

*

The saddler and his wife waved them goodbye, but no one bade the Doctore farewell until Alfred returned. 'You are not the man we believed you to be, but you have goodness in you, of that I'm sure. Even if you cannot reassemble the fragments of our vision, will you seek out those of our calling who are left?'

'I will,' said the Doctore.

'Here is a list of all the innocents upon whom Ponti wishes to wreak his revenge. They are not heretics, simply those whose lives and conduct offend him in some way. Will you swear on Christ's bleeding side to protect them?'

'I will,' said the Doctore again, and smiled. 'Ponti will be sorry you betrayed him. He is consumed by demons, but I suspect he believed you to be his best and only friend.'

'*Fide nemini*,' replied Alfred.

The priests and nuns rode through the city rejoicing in their new-found fortune. They were not stopped. The streets were as empty as on the day of some great man's funeral.

At the bottom of Vatica Hill, Asser pulled up his horse.

'We'll collect Balotelli and escort him out of the city with honour.'

'There is no need. His brother is taking him,' said Alfred.

'His what?' replied Asser.

'His brother, Salvatore. He's being smuggled to Puglia.'

Asser stared at Alfred, then said quietly: 'Salvatore died ten years ago.'

They looked at each other for a moment. Asser turned to Swift. 'Please wait a brief while,' he said. 'We need to ensure the cardinal is safe.'

'Make haste!' she cried as the two men cantered up the hill.

Balotelli's palazzo had been the beating heart of their glorious vision; now it was enveloped in silence and emptiness. Asser and Alfred strode from room to room calling his name, each time more urgently than the last. The crates of manuscripts had disappeared. Alfred glanced at the desk; the disc still lay there untouched.

The two men stood at the entrance to the bathing quarters. The cardinal was lying in his bath white-faced; his arms hung over the sides, marred by two deep red gashes. Pools of congealed blood lay on the floor. Below his right hand was a long, bloodied knife.

'How could he have done this?' said Alfred, appalled beyond measure. 'Such a thing is an offence in the sight of God.'

'He loved Christ, but he loved the ancients more,' replied Asser. 'Socrates and Seneca took their lives once their ability to do the right thing had been taken from them. This is what our cardinal has done.' He kissed the tip of his finger and laid it gently on Balotelli's forehead. 'You met your end with honour, my friend,' he said.

At the city wall, there were interminable queues of frustrated Romans waiting for the gates to be opened. But when the gatekeepers were confronted by a phalanx of grim-faced soldiers wearing the uniform of the Holy Roman Empire, their papers went unchallenged and they were let through.

They all knew where they were heading, but seldom spoke of it. They crossed into Frankia and bade farewell to Louis' soldiers.

At Harfleur, the local abbot found a boat to ferry them across the Narrow Sea. They climbed aboard and rested for a while, then one by one wandered to the prow. Alfred stood with his arm round Swift, Asser at his side. Elswith was squatting on the deck in front of them; standing behind were Phillip and Kennet. Clothilde was a little way off, unveiled and staring at the horizon. Wessex came slowly into view. Perhaps Balotelli's vision was not dead, and this was where it would flourish and blossom. Perhaps here they would feed the poor, shelter the homeless, teach the ignorant and, as the cardinal had so desperately desired, build God's bulwark against the Norlanders.

Swift and Alfred were outcasts and would be in constant danger from their brother Hawk, who would doubtless resist them. Asser had neither money nor authority, but Plegmond would be waiting for him and would help him start again and become the kind of priest he'd always wanted to be. He had a new task now, and a new leader with a vision to uphold. Alfred was raw and unskilled; he would find it hard to make the compromises required, harder still to be ruthless. But Balotelli had taught him well. The cardinal's shrewdness, his commitment, perhaps even his wisdom would live on in the young man. And they had time on their hands; it would be a while before they could remove Hawk from the throne.

'Wessex, the new Rome?' proposed Asser wistfully.

'Indeed. Perhaps even Britain, the new empire,' retorted Swift, and they all laughed at the ridiculousness of such a conceit.

But Asser looked at Alfred – tall, muscular, a little confused perhaps, yet with a hint of nobility about his face – and saw a man heading towards his destiny.

Epilogue

Life is good, Hawk thought. He'd buried two more gold hoards for safe keeping, instructed the building of new halls in Wantage and Reading, and had paid the monks of Beechenfield to pray for his soul each day. Moira had finally left her exile in Dagen's Ham and joined him here in Winchester. Only the previous evening she'd taken a turn with him round her new flowered garden.

His door creaked open and she stood there in the silken chemise he'd bought her. It was patterned with daisies and she looked very fetching. She was holding an elegant goblet and a plate with two currant biscuits on it. Her hair was loose and there was promise in her smile.

'Good morning, husband. A sip of Frankish wine?' she said.

'I will. How kind, my dear,' he replied.

He took a long draught and looked at her longingly. It had taken a great deal of patience and some brute force, but she had come back to him.

'My dear,' he said, 'today they begin the construction of the new halls. Our power and wealth will be undeniable. I will make this the best day of your life.'

She smiled at him, but it was not the smile of gratitude or desire that he had expected.

'You already have,' she replied.

Then the pain began, like a thrust in the guts from a Norland sword.

Author's Note

The story of Alfred and his cakes has never made much sense to me. The Great King is hiding from the Vikings in an old woman's hovel, she asks him to watch over the cakes on her griddle while she goes off in search of firewood, but he's rapt in thought, and when she returns, the cakes have been burnt to cinders. It's a story of incompetence and arrogance. The man is so bound up in his own affairs that he ignores the basic needs of an old woman who has given him one simple task. What's the point of it? Why has it echoed down the ages? Is it supposed to make Alfred appear great? If so, how? Because it makes him sound humble? Thoughtful? A man of the people? I've been given various explanations over the years, but none of them convince.

There's another Alfred conundrum. He was the youngest of five princes, received no training in kingship, and was wracked by a mysterious illness that left him profoundly debilitated. He was certainly not expected to rule Wessex, but his brothers died, he took the throne . . . and his kingdom was rapidly reduced to twenty-five square miles of Somerset bog surrounded by bloodthirsty Vikings. Yet somehow he managed to pull together a raggle-taggle army, comprehensively defeat the invaders and convert them to Christianity.

And this was only the beginning of his extraordinary reign. He instituted military, legal, economic, religious and educational reform, redesigned the Saxon townships and translated great theological tomes from Latin into the common tongue. By annexing neighbouring Mercia, he created the Kingdom of the Anglo-Saxons, which under his son and grandson became what we now call England.

How did he do all this? Where did he get his ideas from? Was he really the superhero we're led to believe, or were there other factors at play?

Nothing I've read has given me satisfactory answers to these questions. What we know about him comes from a handful of contemporary books, which are inevitably partisan. They assert the rights of powerful families, justify ecclesiastic land grabs, exaggerate victories and minimise defeats. It is hard to ascertain the bare bones of his story from among their obfuscations, fabrications and the narratives they borrowed from other documents. It even appears that the tale of the cakes was a fiction inserted into his life-story long after his death, and one that was – ironically – originally told about a Viking leader known as Ragnar Hairybreeks.

So how might I write about this man who impressed me so much but about whom I knew so little? It's my belief that novelists should occupy the shadows of history without fear or trepidation. As Joseph O'Connor firmly asserts of his glorious novel *Shadowplay*, '[it] is based on real events but is a work of fiction. Many liberties have been taken with facts, characterisations and chronologies . . . All sequences presenting themselves as authentic documents are fictitious.' That's certainly the approach I've taken in my book.

The House of Wolf is a fictional account inspired by *The Life of Alfred*, a brilliant piece of ninth-century propaganda written by Alfred's friend and mentor, Bishop Asser of Sherbourne, in order to celebrate the king and justify and bolster the position of the Westsaxon royal family.

Many of the incidents in my book are taken directly from it, but I have invented characters like Cardinal Balotelli and Seneschal François, and have changed the names of others primarily because their original names create unnecessary confusion. This is particularly the case with family members of the House of Wolf; there are dozens of Aethelreds and Aethelstans in the historical record – aethel merely means 'noble', and I have used it sparingly. In the spirit of the Saxons I have called Wolf's children by the names of attributes their parents might have wished them to possess: thus Aethelbald becomes Bear, Aethelberht is Hawk, and Aethelswyth, Swift.

As for place names, some like Winchester I've kept as we now know them, while others such as Gipswic and Southamwic I've given their Saxon names because they're easy to identify. A few are fictitious: Hamblesea is situated in the location of modern-day Hamble-le-Rice and I've set my Nutley Monastery on the site of the later Netley Abbey. I've also altered chronologies and distances where my narrative demands it.

The Roman Church was in continual crisis during the ninth century and I've tried to reflect that. But there was no contemporary organisation called the Notarii, although there must have been groups of senior clerics performing a similar function; there certainly were in later centuries. Likewise, the Antonil heretics are an invention, but are based on the contemporary Paulicians and the tenth-century Bogomils. I know of no Roman proto-amphetamine like the one Abdulalah sells Asser, although I'm convinced an entrepreneurial alchemist like him would have been able to concoct one, even if its effect was only that of a Vicks inhaler. Some of the more bizarre-sounding characters and their lives are from the record: for instance, the Holy Roman Emperor really was called Charles the Bald, his son was Louis the Stammerer and his daughter Judith married Aethelwulf when she was twelve, then married his son Aethelbald a couple of years later. However, in the year AD 843 the Empire was divided into three parts, all ruled by Charlemagne's progeny including Charles. I have not reflected this, nor have I delved into the relationship between Wessex and surrounding Kent, Canterbury and East Anglia, a subject that will be addressed in the next part of my trilogy.

I spent two decades working with some of our nation's finest and most scrupulous historians and archaeologists while making the television series *Time Team*. For a further decade I was employed alongside a coterie of highly talented, well-educated young men who loved history but were happy to bend it to their creative need when necessary, and from their endeavours *Blackadder* was created. I respect the work of all these people, and their influence is evident in my book, as is that of Ken Follett, Anthony Powell, J. R. R. Tolkien, George R. R. Martin, Jesse Armstrong, Iain Pears, Seamus Heaney (in particular his magnificent reworking of *Beowulf*), Robert Graves, Mary Renault, Shonda Rhimes and the late, lamented Terry Pratchett, whose entire oeuvre I recorded for Transworld and who I grew to know well. His humour and mine were very similar, but I was particularly affected by the vividness of his writing and the Technicolor quality of his descriptions, a style that I've tried to incorporate into my own work. I thank these fine writers and am in awe of their attempts to wrestle with the vagaries of history. If there are any mistakes or unintentional anachronisms in this book, don't blame me – blame them for setting such a bad example.

Acknowledgements

My literary agent, Antony Topping, has been my guide, mentor and *The House of Wolf*'s most enthusiastic champion since he saw the first few tentative chapters in 2023. In Little, Brown we chose the ideal publisher. Editor Ed Wood cared passionately about the book and gave me superb structural guidance during its initial stages, and latterly Rosanna Forte has employed her awesome creative acumen and sensitivity to help me craft it. The support I've been given by my assistant Heledd Mathias has also been incalculable. She is a stalwart advocate of the project with a keen eye and a sharp mind. Her rigour has made it a far better book than it would have been without her input. Occasionally the cards of life fall kindly, and in Antony, Ed, Rosanna and Heli I was dealt straight aces.

There are others to be thanked, too. I am deeply proud of my daughter Laura Shepherd-Robinson, an exquisitely accomplished and successful novelist. Her wisdom and discernment have proved invaluable. Justin Pollard has also been an important part of the team. We worked together on the archaeological TV series *Time Team* many years ago, and he has gone on to become one of the country's most sought-after experts on ninth-century England. He has been a constant source of inspiration and I heartily recommend his book *Alfred The Great: The Man Who Made England* if you want to explore the subject a little further. My team at Sphere Books, particularly Tilda Key, Stephanie Melrose, Celeste Ward-Best and Nithya Rae, and all those at Greene & Heaton couldn't have been more efficient and supportive.

Sarah Dalkin at Jeremy Hicks Associates has been by my side since the book's inception and I treasure her shrewdness and friendship. Sinead Jordan has given me perceptive advice and encouragement, and a special mention must go to Professors Martin Carver and Katy Cubitt for insights that opened my eyes to so much of ninth-century culture. Thanks, too, to Paul Hobbs for sharing his knowledge of pigeons, and to Gregg Jenner and the Twitterstorians for their kind assistance.

As always, my family has been my constant support: Laura, of course, and her husband, Adrian; my son Luke, my daughter-in-law Gemma, and the two best granddaughters ever, Holly and Lyla.

But most important has been the love and unswerving loyalty to this project I've received from my wife, Louise, particularly during the dark time when five hand-written chapters and all my research notes were stolen from the back of my car which I'd foolishly left unlocked outside a motorway service station. Thanks Lou, you raised me up! She is my partner in all things, and I would wish for no other.